BABY
IS THREE

Theodore Sturgeon, Congers, New York,
1952.

BABY
IS THREE

Volume VI:
The Complete Stories of
Theodore Sturgeon

Edited by
Paul Williams

Foreword by
David Crosby

North Atlantic Books
Berkeley, California

Published by
North Atlantic Books
P.O. Box 12327
Berkeley, California 94712

Cover art by Richard M. Powers
Cover design by Catherine Campaigne
Book design by Paula Morrison
Printed in the United States of America

Baby Is Three is sponsored by the Society for the Study of Native Arts and Sciences, a nonprofit educational corporation whose goals are to develop an educational and cross-cultural perspective linking various scientific, social, and artistic fields; to nurture a holistic view of arts, sciences, humanities, and healing; and to publish and distribute literature on the relationship of mind, body, and nature.

North Atlantic Books' publications are available through most bookstores. For further information, visit our website at www.northatlanticbooks.com or call 800-733-3000.

ISBN-13: 978-1-55643-319-1

Library of Congress Cataloging-in-Publication Data

Sturgeon, Theodore
    Baby is three / Theodore Sturgeon : edited by Paul Williams.
        p.   cm. — (The complete stories of Theodore Sturgeon : v. 6)
        Contents: The stars are the Styx—Rule of three—Shadow, shadow on the wall—Special aptitude—Make room for me—The traveling crag—Excalibur and the atom—The incubi of parallel X—Never underestimate—The sex opposite—Baby is three.
        ISBN 1-55643-319-0 (alk. paper)
        1. Science fiction, American.   2. Fantasy fiction, American.   I. Williams, Paul, 1948–   .   II. Title.   III. Series: Sturgeon, Theodore.   Short stories : v. 6.
PS3569.T875   A6   1999 vol. 6
813'.54—dc21   99-31975
                                                                                CIP

3 4 5 6 7 8 9 SHERIDAN 14 13 12 11 10

EDITOR'S NOTE

THEODORE HAMILTON STURGEON was born February 26, 1918, and died May 8, 1985. This is the sixth of a series of volumes that will collect all of his short fiction of all types and all lengths shorter than a novel. The volumes and the stories within the volumes are organized chronologically by order of composition (insofar as it can be determined). This sixth volume contains stories written between 1950 and 1952. Two have never before appeared in a Sturgeon collection. The title story, "Baby Is Three," is the original text of one of Sturgeon's most-loved stories, as it appeared in a magazine before he significantly reworked its ending for the purposes of *More Than Human,* the novel he wrote by adding extensive material about what happened to Homo Gestalt before and after the events described in "Baby Is Three."

Preparation of each of these volumes would not be possible without the hard work and invaluable participation of Noël Sturgeon, Debbie Notkin, and our publishers, Lindy Hough and Richard Grossinger. I would also like to thank, for their significant assistance with this volume, David Crosby, the Theodore Sturgeon Literary Trust, Emily Weinert, Marion Sturgeon, Jayne Williams, Ralph Vicinanza, Ron Colone, David Hartwell, Tair Powers, Eric Weeks, Bill Glass, Dixon Chandler, Gordon Benson, Jr. and Phil Stephensen-Payne, Paula Morrison, Catherine Campaigne, T. V. Reed, Cindy Lee Berryhill, The Other Change of Hobbit Bookstore, and all of you who have expressed your interest and support.

BOOKS BY THEODORE STURGEON

Without Sorcery (1948)

The Dreaming Jewels [aka *The Synthetic Man*] (1950)

More Than Human (1953)

E Pluribus Unicorn (1953)

Caviar (1955)

A Way Home (1955)

The King and Four Queens (1956)

I, Libertine (1956)

A Touch of Strange (1958)

The Cosmic Rape [aka *To Marry Medusa*] (1958)

Aliens 4 (1959)

Venus Plus X (1960)

Beyond (1960)

Some of Your Blood (1961)

Voyage to the Bottom of the Sea (1961)

The Player on the Other Side (1963)

Sturgeon in Orbit (1964)

Starshine (1966)

The Rare Breed (1966)

Sturgeon Is Alive and Well... (1971)

The Worlds of Theodore Sturgeon (1972)

Sturgeon's West (with Don Ward) (1973)

Case and the Dreamer (1974)

Visions and Venturers (1978)

Maturity (1979)

The Stars Are the Styx (1979)

The Golden Helix (1979)

Alien Cargo (1984)

Godbody (1986)

A Touch of Sturgeon (1987)

The [Widget], the [Wadget], and Boff (1989)

Argyll (1993)

Star Trek, The Joy Machine (with James Gunn) (1996)

THE COMPLETE STORIES SERIES

1. *The Ultimate Egoist* (1994)
2. *Microcosmic God* (1995)
3. *Killdozer!* (1996)
4. *Thunder and Roses* (1997)
5. *The Perfect Host* (1998)
6. *Baby Is Three* (1999)
7. *A Saucer of Loneliness* (2000)
8. *Bright Segment* (2002)
9. *And Now the News...* (2003)
10. *The Man Who Lost the Sea* (2005)
11. *The Nail and the Oracle* (2007)
12. *Slow Sculpture* (2009)
13. *Case and the Dreamer* (2010)

CONTENTS

Foreword

by David Crosby

I'M AN INVETERATE LOVER of science fiction. I always have been and still am. I read it constantly. I started as an early teenager—long before the Byrds, or Crosby, Stills & Nash, even before I became a musician—back in the mid-1950s. I started with Robert Heinlein's juvenile novels, *Rocket Ship Galileo* then *Red Planet, Farmer in the Sky, Between Planets, Space Cadet...* I read them all. They were my escape. I was a little chubby kid in a high school, not at all popular, and lonely, and this was a world where I could ... I could *really* dig it. Then it just progressed, the natural steps you would expect, Clarke and Van Vogt, Campbell, *Analog ...* and I just went right into it from there.

Then somebody passed Theodore Sturgeon's *More Than Human* to me. And that novel—which of course is built around the title story of this collection, "Baby Is Three"—was the standout for me. The relationship described in that story, people transcending the lacks in themselves and making a whole that's greater than anybody else could be because of it... There was a perceived lack in me and I felt sort of like a person that wasn't gonna... So there was a strong emotional resonance for me—and for every other little lonely kid—with those people, because they were different too. They didn't fit in either. But when they *linked*, they were this awesome being...

Paul Williams tells me my friend Phil Lesh of the Grateful Dead has described "Baby Is Three"/*More Than Human* as the only model he and his bandmates had to understand what was happening to them when they began playing together. He might have been more conscious about that than I was, but it affected me in the same place.

There is a thing that happens in a band, where these diverse human beings link up, through this language that they're speaking together, this music.

They create a thing where the whole is greater than the sum of the parts. And there springs into existence over them another being. So if there's four of them, there's a fifth being, or if there's five there's a sixth being, that is a composite of them, and that is bigger than all of them. And if they understand what they're doing, they submit to this personality, they give up their individuality for this unity. And they create this new being that can make the art of the instant, that can make the magic happen when you're playing live.

That's how it feels. And it requires a—if it isn't telepathic, it's certainly *em*pathic—link-up and union. And the relationship described first by Theodore Sturgeon in "Baby Is Three" really hit all of us that wanted that kind of "above the family," taking the idea of a family to a new place, to a new level.

It really rang *my* bell. When I was a child my favorite comic book was one about a whole group of very different orphans who got together and somebody let them live together on a ranch, and they ran this ranch together. And when I read *More Than Human*, I—and all the other kids who were loners and didn't really fit in—said, "I could fit in *there*. I would love to be part of that kind of incredible link-up where people really understand each other and love each other and have a unity of purpose." It was a high thing to do. And bands emotionally so closely resembled that, that it was inevitable that we musicians would love that story.

Although I loved the story *before* I became a band member. But once I became a band member I had this whole resonant blueprint in the back of my head about what that was. And so I understood what it was and I submitted to it, and I have always loved being a part of that, more than being a solo . . . I like union so much more than autonomy that there must have been some basic tilt in me towards it. I think "Baby Is Three" was a large part of me having that tilt. It just rang my bell. Big time.

That *homo gestalt* experience of creating a fifth entity by forming a four-person unit is such a startling thing, it's very hard to explain it to people who haven't played music with other people or done some kind of unity-forming for a purpose. I'm sure a group of Amish farmers getting together for a barn-raising have some of the same thing. But with a band, the thing that you're trying to create is so ethereal, and so hard to put salt on its tail, that it's very difficult to explain to people when it's there and when it's not there. Too many people think that it's just about turning up and striking a pose. Trying to do the other thing is intricate, and requires people with enough ego to go on stage who are also over here to dissociate from the ego and disassemble it, in order to create this other thing. It's a rare deal. Anybody, any really good band, particularly a band that improvises together—the Grateful Dead for absolute sure, they were built on it, it was their lifeblood—any band that improvises together and tries to push the envelope (which of course is where the best shit is), they know this thing. Anybody from a band like that would read "Baby Is Three" and say, "Oh yeah! Yeah!!" and recognize it right away.

I met Ted Sturgeon in 1970. He was an unusual guy. He wasn't all cosmic and airy-fairy in how he thought about things. He was actually sort of acerbic and funny and had a great kind of wry wit about stuff. But he could conceive idealism on a level that most other people couldn't get to. He was a great cat. We put him through a really unbearable experience, Crosby, Stills, Nash & Young did, when we hired him to write a screenplay for *Wooden Ships,* a proposed CSNY film based on one of our songs.

It was a nightmare for him, because each guy would get him alone and tell him how *he* wanted the script to be. And of course in each guy's view, *he* was the hero. The other guys were sort of posed around the edges, like a Greek chorus. Mine was populated with young girls—and had all this sex in it. Stephen's was populated by this lonely military hero out there. Neil took one look at the whole film idea and said, "No ... No, man, I don't think so, man..." It was hysterical. We were all such complete egotists by that time, and living so much in our own universes, and everything was so contrary to the vision I just told you about...

It was a complete hopeless tar-baby of a project. And Ted tried to do it in all good faith. He kept trying to be positive about it. He would write and write and write and say, "What about this?" And we'd say, "Well, no, that's too much of *them* and not enough of me." It was a terrible thing, and I'm mostly responsible for having done it to him. He had a good sense of humor about it. I'm sure he must have laughed a lot privately

He was a *delightful* man, very very very bright, great sense of humor, witty, had a good skeptical and skewed take on things. I regret that I didn't get to hang out with him more. I should have stayed friends with him and stayed close to him, but at a certain point there the drugs took over, and friendships got less important...

Shadow, Shadow on the Wall

IT WAS WELL after bedtime and Bobby was asleep, dreaming of a place with black butterflies that stayed, and a dog with a wuffly nose and blunt, friendly rubber teeth. It was a dark place, and comfy with all the edges blurred and soft, and he could make them all jump if he wanted to.

But then there was a sharp scythe of light that swept everything away (except in the shaded smoothness of the blank wall beside the door: someone *always* lived there) and Mommy Gwen was coming into the room with a blaze of hallway behind her. She clicked the high-up switch, the one he couldn't reach, and room light came cruelly. Mommy Gwen changed from a flat, black, light-rimmed set of cardboard triangles to a night-lit, daytime sort of Mommy Gwen.

Her hair was wide and her chin was narrow. Her shoulders were wide and her waist was narrow. Her hips were wide and her skirt was narrow, and under it all were her two hard silky sticks of legs. Her arms hung down from the wide tips of her shoulders, straight and elbowless when she walked. She never moved her arms when she walked. She never moved them at all unless she wanted to do something with them.

"You're awake." Her voice was hard, wide, flat, pointy too.

"I was asleep," said Bobby.

"Don't contradict. Get up."

Bobby sat up and fisted his eyes. "Is Daddy—"

"Your father is not in the house. He went away. He won't be back for a whole day—maybe two. So there's no use in yelling for him."

"Wasn't going to yell for him, Mommy Gwen."

"Very well, then. Get up."

I

Wondering, Bobby got up. His flannel sleeper pulled at his shoulders and at the soles of his snug-covered feet. He felt tousled.

"Get your toys, Bobby."

"What toys, Mommy Gwen?"

Her voice snapped like wet clothes on the line in a big wind. "Your toys—all of them!"

He went to the playbox and lifted the lid. He stopped, turned, stared at her. Her arms hung straight at her sides, as straight as her two level eyes under the straight shelf of brow. He bent to the playbox. Gollywick, Humptydoodle and the blocks came out; the starry-wormy piece of the old phonograph, the cracked sugar egg with the peephole girl in it, the cardboard kaleidoscope and the magic set with the seven silvery rings that made a trick he couldn't do but Daddy could. He took them all out and put them on the floor.

"Here," said Mommy Gwen. She moved one straight-line arm to point to her feet with one straight-line finger. He picked up the toys and brought them to her, one at a time, two at a time, until they were all there. "Neatly, neatly," she muttered. She bent in the middle like a garage door and did brisk things with the toys, so that the scattered pile of them became a square stack. "Get the rest," she said.

He looked into the playbox and took out the old wood-framed slate and the mixed-up box of crayons; the English annual story book and an old candle, and that was all for the playbox. In the closet were some little boxing-gloves and a tennis racket with broken strings, and an old ukulele with no strings at all. And that was all for the closet. He brought them to her, and she stacked them with the others.

"Those things, too," she said, and at last bent her elbow to point around. From the dresser came the two squirrels and a monkey that Daddy had made from pipe cleaners, a small square of plate-glass he had found on Henry Street; a clockwork top that sounded like a church talking, and the broken clock Jerry had left on the porch last week. Bobby brought them all to Mommy Gwen, every one. "Are you going to put me in another room?"

"No indeed." Mommy Gwen took up the neat stack of toys. It was tall in her arms. The top fell off and thunked on the floor, bounced, chased around in a tilted circle. "Get it," said Mommy Gwen.

Bobby picked it up and reached it toward her. She stooped until he could put it on the stack, snug between the tennis racket and the box of crayons. Mommy Gwen didn't say thank you, but went away through the door, leaving Bobby standing, staring after her. He heard her hard feet go down the hall, heard the bump as she pressed open the guest-room door with her knee. There was a rattle and click as she set his toys down on the spare bed, the one without a spread, the one with dusty blue ticking on the mattress. Then she came back again.

"Why aren't you in bed?" She clapped her hands. They sounded dry, like sticks breaking. Startled, he popped back into bed and drew the covers up to his chin. There used to be someone who had a warm cheek and a soft word for him when he did that, but that was a long time ago. He lay with eyes round in the light, looking at Mommy Gwen.

"You've been bad," she said. "You broke a window in the shed and you tracked mud into my kitchen and you've been noisy and rude. So you'll stay right here in this room without your toys until I say you can come out. Do you understand me?"

"Yes," he said. He said quickly, because he remembered in time, "Yes ma'am."

She struck the switch swiftly, without warning, so that the darkness dazzled him, made him blink. But right away it was the room again, with the scythe of light and the shaded something hiding in the top corner of the wall by the door. There was always something shifting about there.

She went away then, thumping the door closed, leaving the darkness and taking away the light, all but a rug-fuzzed yellow streak under the door. Bobby looked away from that, and for a moment, for just a moment, he was inside his shadow-pictures where the rubber-fanged dog and the fleshy black butterflies stayed. Sometimes they stayed . . . but mostly they were gone as soon as he moved. Or maybe they changed into something else. Anyway, he liked it there, where they all lived, and he wished he could be with them, in the shadow country.

Just before he fell asleep, he saw them moving and shifting in the blank wall by the door. He smiled at them and went to sleep.

When he awoke, it was early. He couldn't smell the coffee from downstairs yet, even. There was a ruddy-yellow sunswatch on the blank wall, a crooked square, just waiting for him. He jumped out of bed and ran to it. He washed his hands in it, squatted down on the floor with his arms out. "Now!" he said.

He locked his thumbs together and slowly flapped his hands. And there on the wall was a black butterfly, flapping its wings right along with him. "Hello, butterfly," said Bobby.

He made it jump. He made it turn and settle to the bottom of the light patch, and fold its wings up and up until they were together. Suddenly he whipped one hand away, peeled back the sleeve of his sleeper, and presto! There was a long-necked duck. "Quack-ack!" said Bobby, and the duck obligingly opened its bill, threw up its head to quack. Bobby made it curl up its bill until it was an eagle. He didn't know what kind of noise an eagle made, so he said, "Eagle-eagle-eagle-eagle-eagle," and that sounded fine. He laughed.

When he laughed Mommy Gwen slammed the door open and stood there in a straight-lined white bathrobe and straight flat slippers. "What are you playing with?"

Bobby held up his empty hands.

"I was just—"

She took two steps into the room. "Get up," she said. Her lips were pale. Bobby got up, wondering why she was so angry. "I heard you laugh," she said in a hissy kind of a whisper. She looked him up and down, looked at the door around him. "What were you playing with?"

"A eagle," said Bobby.

"A what? Tell me the truth!"

Bobby waved his empty hands vaguely and looked away from her. She had such an angry face.

She stepped, reached, put a hard hand around his wrist. She lifted his arm so high he went on tiptoes, and with her other hand she felt his body, this side, that side. "You're hiding something. What is it? Where is it? What were you playing with?"

"Nothing. Reely, reely truly nothing," gasped Bobby as she shook and patted. She wasn't spanking. She never spanked. She did other things.

"You're being punished," she said in her shrill angry whisper. "Stupid, stupid, stupid . . . too stupid to know you're being punished." She set him down with a thump and went to the door. "Don't let me hear you laugh again. You've been bad, and you're not being kept in this room to enjoy yourself. Now you stay here and think about how bad you are breaking windows. Tracking mud. Lying."

She went out and closed the door with a steadiness that was like slamming, but quiet. Bobby looked at the door and wondered for a moment about that broken window. He'd been terribly sorry; it was just that the golf ball bounced so hard. Daddy had told him he should be more careful, and he had watched sorrowfully while Daddy put in a new pane. Then Daddy had given him a little piece of putty to play with and asked him never to do it again and he'd promised not to. And the whole time Mommy Gwen hadn't said a thing to him about it. She'd just looked at him every once in a while with her eyes and her mouth straight and thin, and she'd waited. She'd waited until Daddy went away.

He went back to his sunbeam and forgot all about Mommy Gwen.

After he'd made another butterfly and a dog's head and an alligator on the wall, the sunbeam got so thin that he couldn't make anything more, except, for a while, little black finger shadows that ran up and down the strip of light like ants on a matchstick. Soon there was no sunbeam at all, so he sat on the edge of his bed and watched the vague flickering of the something that lived in the end wall. It was a *different* kind of something. It wasn't a good something and it

5

wasn't bad. It just lived there, and the difference between it and the other things, the butterflies and dogs and swans and eagles who lived there, was that the something didn't need his hands to make it be alive. The something—stayed. Some day he was going to make a butterfly or a dog or a horse that would stay after he moved his hands away. Meanwhile, the only one who stayed, the only one who lived all the time in the shadow country, was this something that flickered up there where the two walls met the ceiling. "I'm going right in there and play with you," Bobby told it. "You'll see."

There was a red wagon with three wheels in the yard, and a gnarly tree to be climbed. Jerry came and called for a while, but Mommy Gwen sent him away. *"He's been bad."* So Jerry went away.

Bad bad bad. Funny how the things he did didn't used to be bad before Daddy married Mommy Gwen.

Mommy Gwen didn't want Bobby. That was all right—Bobby didn't want Mommy Gwen either. Daddy sometimes said to grown-up people that Bobby was much better off with someone to care for him. Bobby could remember 'way back when he used to say that with his arm around Mommy Gwen's shoulders and his voice ringing. He could remember when Daddy said it quietly from the other side of the room, with a voice like an angry "I'm sorry." And now, Daddy hadn't said it at all for a long time.

Bobby sat on the edge of his bed and hummed to himself, thinking these thoughts, and he hummed to himself and didn't think of anything at all. He found a ladybug crawling up the dresser and caught it the careful way, circling it with his thumb and forefinger so that it crawled up on his hand by itself. Sometimes when you pinched them up they got busted. He stood on the windowsill and hunted until he found the little hole in the screen that the ladybug must have used to come in. He let the bug walk on the screen and guided it to the hole. It flew away, happy.

The room was flooded with warm dull light reflected from the sparkly black shed roof, and he couldn't make any shadow country people at all, so he made them in his head until he felt sleepy. He lay down then and hummed softly to himself until he fell asleep. And through the long afternoon the thing in the wall flickered and shifted and lived.

At dusk Mommy Gwen came back. Bobby may have heard her on the stairs; anyway, when the door opened on the dim room he was sitting up in bed, thumbing his eyes.

The ceiling blazed. "What have you been doing?"

"Was asleep, I guess. Is it night time?"

"Very nearly. I suppose you're hungry." She had a covered dish.

"Mmm."

"What kind of an answer is that?" she snapped.

"Yes ma'am I'm hungry Mommy Gwen," he said rapidly.

"That's a little better. Here." She thrust the dish at him. He took it, removed the top plate and put it under the bowl. Oatmeal. He looked at it, at her.

"Well?"

"Thank you, Mommy Gwen." He began to eat with the teaspoon he had found hilt-deep in the grey-brown mess. There was no sugar on it.

"I suppose you expect me to fetch you some sugar," she said after a time.

"No'm," he said truthfully, and then wondered why her face went all angry and disappointed.

"What have you been doing all day?"

"Nothing. Playin'. Then I was asleep."

"Little sluggard." Suddenly she shouted at him, "What's the matter with you? Are you too stupid to be afraid? Are you too stupid to ask me to let you come downstairs? Are you too stupid to cry? Why don't you cry?"

He stared at her, round-eyed. "You wouldn't let me come down if I ast you," he said wonderingly. "So I didn't ast." He scooped up some oatmeal. "I don't feel like cryin', Mommy Gwen, I don't hurt."

"You're bad and you're being punished and it should hurt," she said furiously. She turned off the light with a vicious swipe of her hard straight hand, and went out, slamming the door.

Bobby sat still in the dark and wished he could go into the shadow country, the way he always dreamed he could. He'd go there and play with the butterflies and the fuzz-edged, blunt-toothed dogs and giraffes, and they'd stay and he'd stay and Mommy Gwen would never be able to get in, ever. Except that Daddy wouldn't be able to come with him, or Jerry either, and that would be a shame.

He scrambled quietly out of bed and stood for a moment looking at the wall by the door. He could almost for-sure see the flickering thing that lived there, even in the dark. When there was light on the wall, it flickered a shade darker than the light. At night it flickered a shade lighter than the black. It was always there, and Bobby knew it was alive. He knew it without question, like "my name is Bobby" and "Mommy Gwen doesn't want me."

Quietly, quietly, he tiptoed to the other side of the room where there was a small table lamp. He took it down and laid it carefully on the floor. He pulled the plug out and brought it down under the lower rung of the table so it led straight across the floor to the wall-receptacle, and plugged it in again. Now he could move the lamp quite far out into the room, almost to the middle.

The lamp had a round shade that was open at the top. Lying on its side, the shade pointed its open top at the blank wall by the door. Bobby, with the sureness of long practice, moved in the darkness to his closet and got his dark-red flannel bathrobe from a low hook. He folded it once and draped it over the large lower end of the lamp shade. He pushed the button.

On the shadow country wall appeared a brilliant disk of light, crossed by just the hints of the four wires that held the shade in place. There was a dark spot in the middle where they met.

Bobby looked at it critically. Then, squatting between the lamp and the wall, he put out his hand.

A duck. "Quackle-ackle," he whispered.

An eagle. "Eagle—eagle—eagle—eagle," he said softly.

An alligator. "Bap bap," the alligator went as it opened and closed its long snout.

He withdrew his hands and studied the round, cross-scarred light on the wall. The blurred center shadow and its radiating lines looked

8

a little like a waterbug, the kind that can run on the surface of a brook. It soon dissatisfied him; it just sat there without doing anything. He put his thumb in his mouth and bit it gently until an idea came to him. Then he scrambled to the bed, underneath which he found his slippers. He put one on the floor in front of the lamp, and propped the other toe-upward against it. He regarded the wall gravely for a time, and then lay flat on his stomach on the floor. Watching the shadow carefully, he put his elbows together on the carpet, twined his forearms together and merged the shadow of his hands with the shadow of the slipper.

The result enchanted him. It was something like a spider, something like a gorilla. It was a brand-new something that no one had ever seen before. He writhed his fingers and then held them still, and now the thing's knobby head had triangular luminous eyes and a jaw that swung, gaping. It had long arms for reaching and a delicate whorl of tentacles. He moved the least little bit, and it wagged its great head and blinked at him. Watching it, he felt suddenly that the flickering thing that lived in the high corner had crept out and down toward the beast he had made, closer and closer to it until—whoosh!—it noiselessly merged with the beast, an act as quick and complete as the marriage of raindrops on a windowpane.

Bobby crowed with delight. "Stay, stay," he begged. "Oh, stay there! I'll pet you! I'll give you good things to eat! Please stay, *please!*"

The thing glowered at him. He thought it would stay, but he didn't chance moving his hands away just yet.

The door crashed open, the switch clicked, the room filled with an explosion of light.

"What are you doing?"

Bobby lay frozen, his elbows on the carpet in front of him, his forearms together, his hands twisted oddly. He put his chin on his shoulder so he could look at her standing there stiff and menacing. "I was—was just—"

She swooped down on him. She snatched him up off the floor and plumped him down on the bed. She kicked and scattered his slippers. She snatched up the lamp, pulling the cord out of the wall with the motion. "You were not to have any toys," she said in the

9

hissing voice. "That means you were not to make any toys. For this you'll stay in here for—what are you staring at?"

Bobby spread his hands and brought them together ecstatically, holding tight. His eyes sparkled, and his small white teeth peeped out so that they could see what he was smiling at. "He stayed, he did," said Bobby. "He stayed!"

"I don't know what you're talking about and I will not stay here to find out," snapped Mommy Gwen. "I think you're a mental case." She marched to the door, striking the high switch.

The room went dark—except for that blank wall by the door. Mommy Gwen screamed.

Bobby covered his eyes.

Mommy Gwen screamed again, hoarsely this time. It was a sound like a dog's bark, but drawn out and out.

There was a long silence. Bobby peeped through his fingers at the dimly glowing wall. He took his hands down, sat up straight, drew his knees up to his chest and put his arms around them. "Well!" he said.

Feet pounded up the stairs. "Gwen! Gwen!"

"Hello, Daddy."

Daddy ran in, turning on the light. "Where's Mommy Gwen, Bob boy? What happened? I heard a—"

Bobby pointed at the wall. "She's in there," he said.

Daddy couldn't have understood him, for he turned and ran out the door calling "Gwen! Gwen!"

Bobby sat still and watched the fading shadow on the wall, quite visible even in the blaze of the overhead light. The shadow was moving, moving. It was a point-down triangle thrust into another point-down triangle which was mounted on a third, and underneath were the two hard sticks of legs. It had its arms up, its shadow-fists clenched, and it pounded and pounded silently on the wall.

"Now I'm never going into the shadow country," said Bobby complacently. "*She's* there."

So he never did.

The Stars Are the Styx

EVERY FEW YEARS *someone thinks to call me Charon. It never lasts. I guess I don't look the part. Charon, you'll remember, was the somber ferryman who steered the boat across the River Styx, taking the departed souls over to the Other Side. He's usually pictured as a grim, taciturn character, tall and gaunt.*

I get called Charon, but that's not what I look like. I'm not exactly taciturn, and I don't go around in a flapping black cloak. I'm too fat. Maybe too old, too.

It's a shrewd gag, though, calling me Charon. I do pass human souls Out, and for nearly half of them, the stars are indeed the Styx— they will never return.

I have two things I know Charon had. One is that bitter difference from the souls I deal with. They have lost only one world; the other is before them. But I'm rejected by both.

The other thing has to do with a little-known fragment of the Charon legend. And that, I think, is worth a yarn.

It's Judson's yarn, and I wish he was here to tell it himself—which is foolish; the yarn's about why he isn't here. "Here" is Curbstone, by the way—the stepping-off place to the Other Side. It's Earth's other slow satellite, bumbling along out past the Moon. It was built 7800 years ago for heavy interplanetary transfer, though of course there's not much of that left any more. It's so easy to synthesize anything nowadays that there's just no call for imports. We make what we need from energy, and there's plenty of that around. There's plenty of everything. Even insecurity, though you have to come to Curbstone for that, and be someone like Judson to boot.

It's no secret—now—that insecurity is vital to the Curbstone project. In a cushioned existence on a stable Earth, volunteers for

Curbstone are rare. But they come in—the adventurous, the dissatisfied, the yearning ones, to man the tiny ships that will, in due time, give mankind a segment of space so huge that even mankind's voracious appetite for expansion will be glutted for millennia. There is a vision that haunts all humans today—that of a network of force-beams in the form of a tremendous sphere, encompassing much of the known universe and a great deal of the unknown—through which, like thought impulses through the synaptic paths of a giant brain, matter will be transmitted instantly, and a man may step from here to the depths of space while his heart beats once. The vision frightens most and lures a few, and of those few, some are chosen to go out. Judson was chosen.

I knew he'd come to Curbstone. I'd known it for years, ever since I was on Earth and met him. He was just a youngster then, thirty or so, and boiling around under that soft-spoken, shockproof surface of his was something that had to drive him to Curbstone. It showed when he raised his eyes. They got hungry. Any kind of hunger is rare on Earth. That's what Curbstone's for. The ultimate social balance—an escape for the unbalanced.

Don't wince like that when I say 'unbalanced.' Plain talk is plain talk. You can afford to be mighty plain about social imbalance these days. It's rare and it's slight. Thing is, when a man goes through fifteen years of primary social—childhood, I'm talking about—with all the subtle tinkering that involves, and still has an imbalance, it's a thing that sticks with him no matter how slight it is. Even then, the very existence of Curbstone is enough to make most of 'em quite happy to stay where they are. The handful that do head for Curbstone do it because they have to. Once here, only about half make the final plunge. The rest go back—or live here permanently. Whatever they do, Curbstone takes care of the imbalance.

When you come right down to it, misfits are that way either because they lack something or because they have something *extra*. On Earth there's a place for everything and everything's in its place. On Curbstone you find someone who has what you lack, or who has the same extra something you have—or you leave. You go back feeling that

Earth's a pretty nice safe place after all, or you go Out, and it doesn't matter to anyone else, ever, whether you're happy or not.

I was waiting in the entry bell when Judson arrived on Curbstone. Judson had nothing to do with that. Didn't even know he was on that particular shuttle. It's just that, aside from the fact that I happen to be Senior Release Officer on Curbstone, I like to meet the shuttles. All sorts of people come here, for all sorts of reasons. They stay here or they don't for all sorts of other reasons. I like to look at the faces that come down that ramp and guess which ones will go which way. I'm pretty good at it. As soon as I saw Judson's face I knew that this boy was bound Out. I recognized that about him even before I realized who it was.

There was a knot of us there to watch the newcomers come in. Most were there just because it's worth watching them all, the hesitant ones, the damn-it-alls, the grim ones. But two Curbstoners I noticed particularly. Hunters both. One was a lean, slick-haired boy named Wold. It was pretty obvious what he was hunting. The other was Flower. It was just as obvious what she had her long, wide-spaced eyes out for, but it was hard to tell why. Last I had heard, she had been solidly wrapped up in an Outbounder called Clinton.

I forgot about the wolf and the vixen when I recognized Judson and bellowed at him. He dropped his kit where he stood and came bounding over to me. He grabbed both my biceps and squeezed while I thumped his ribs. "I was waiting up for you, Judson," I grinned at him.

"Man, I'm glad you're still here," he said. He was a sandy-haired fellow, all Adam's apple and guarded eyes.

"I'm here for the duration," I told him. "Didn't you know?"

"No, I—I mean . . ."

"Don't be tactful, Jud," I said. "I belong here by virtue of the fact that there's nowhere else for me to go. Earth isn't happy about men as fat and funny-looking as I am in the era of beautiful people. And I can't go Out. I have a left axis deviation. I know that sounds political; actually it's cardiac."

"I'm sorry." He looked at my brassard. "Well, you're Mr. Big around here, anyway."

"I'm just big around *here*," I said, swatting my belt-line. "There's Coordination Office and a half-squad of Guardians who ice this particular cake. I'm just the final check on Outbounders."

"Yeah," he said. "You don't rate. Much. The whole function of this space station waits on whether you say yes to a departure."

"Shecks now," I said, exaggerating my embarrassment to cover up my exaggerated embarrassment. "Whatever, I wouldn't worry too much if I were you. I could be wrong—we'll have to run some more tests on you—but if ever I saw an Outbounder, it's you."

"Hi," said a silken voice. "You already know each other. How nice."

Flower.

There was something vaguely reptilian about Flower, which didn't take a thing from her brand of magnetism. Bit by bit, piece by piece, she was a so-so looking girl. Her eyes were too long, and so dark they seemed to be all pupil and the whites too white. Her nose was a bit too large and her chin a bit too small, but so help me, there never was a more perfect mouth. Her voice was like a cello bowed up near the bridge. She was tall, with a fragile-in-the-middle slenderness and spring-steel flanks. The overall effect was breathtaking. I didn't like her. She didn't like me either. She never spoke to me except on business, and I had practically no business with her. She'd been here a long time. I hadn't figured out why, then. But she wouldn't go Out and she wouldn't go back to Earth—which in itself was all right; we had lots of room.

Let me tell you something about modern women and therefore something about Flower—something you might not reason out unless you get as old and objective as I've somehow lived to become.

Used to be, according to what I've read, that clothes ran a lot to what I might call indicative concealment. As long as clothes had the slightest excuse of functionalism, people in general and women in particular made a large fuss over something called innate modesty—which never did exist; it had to be learned. But as long as there was weather around to blame clothes on, the myth was accepted. People exposed what the world was indifferent to in order to whip up interest in the rest. "Modesty is not so simple a virtue as honesty," one of the old books says. Clothes as weatherproofing got themselves all mixed up with clothes as ornament; fashions came and went and people followed them.

But for the past three hundred years or so there hasn't been any "weather" as such, for anyone, here or on Earth. Clothes for only aesthetic purposes became more and more the rule, until today it's up to the individual to choose what he's going to wear, if anything. An earring and a tattoo are quite as acceptable in public as forty meters of iridescent plastiweb and a two-meter coiffure.

Now, most people today are healthy, well-selected, and good to look at. Women are still as vain as ever. A woman with a bodily defect, real or imagined, has one of two choices: She can cover the defect with something artfully placed to look as if that was just the best place for it, or she can leave the defect in the open, knowing that no one today is going to judge her completely in terms of the defect. Folks nowadays generally wait until they can find out what kind of human being you are.

But a woman who has no particular defect generally changes her clothes with her mood. It might be a sash only this morning, but a trailing drape this afternoon. Tomorrow it might be a one-sided blouse and clinging trousers. You can take it as a very significant thing when such a woman *always* covers up. She's keeping her natural warmth, as it were, under forced draft.

I didn't go into all this ancient history to impress you with my scholastics. I'm using it to illustrate a very important facet of Flower's complex character. Because Flower was one of those forced-draft jobs. Except on the sun-field and in the swimming pools, where no one ever wears clothes, Flower always affected a tunic of some kind.

The day Judson arrived, she wore a definitive example of what I mean. It was a single loose black garment with straight shoulders and no sleeves. On both sides, from a point a hand's-breadth below the armpit, down to the hipbone, it was slit open. It fastened snugly under her throat with one magne-clasp, but was also slit from there to the navel. It did not quite reach to mid-thigh, and the soft material carried a light biostatic electrical charge, so that it clung to and fell away from her body as she moved. So help me, she was a walking demand for the revival of the extinct profession of peeping Tom.

This, then, was what horned in on my first few words with Judson. I should have known from the way she looked that she was planning something—something definitely for herself. I should have been doubly warned by the fact that she took the trouble to speak up just when she did—just when I told Jud he was a certifiable Outbounder if I ever saw one.

So then and there I made my big mistake. "Flower," I said, "this is Judson."

She used the second it took me to speak to suck in her lower lip, so that when she smiled slowly at Jud, the lip swelled visibly as if by blood pressure. "I *am* glad," she all but whispered.

And then she had the craft to turn the smile on me and walk away without another word.

"... Gah!" said Judson through a tight glottis.

"That," I told him, "was beautifully phrased. Gah, indeed. Reel your eyeballs back in, Jud. We'll drop your duffel off at the Outbound quarters and—*Judson!*"

Flower had disappeared down the inner ramp. I was aware that Judson had just started to breathe again.

"What?" he asked me.

I waddled over and picked up his gear. "Come on," I said, and steered him by the arm.

Judson had nothing to say until after we found him a room and started for my sector. "Who is she?"

"A hardy perennial," I said. "Came up to Curbstone two years ago. She's never been certified. She'll get around to it soon—or never. Are you going right ahead?"

"Just how do you handle the certification?"

"Give you some stuff to read. Pound some more knowledge into you for six, seven nights while you sleep. Look over your reflexes, physical and mental. An examination. If everything's all right, you're certified."

"Then—Out?"

I shrugged. "If you like. You come to Curbstone strictly on your own. You take your course if and when you like. And after you've been certified, you leave when you want to, with someone or not, and without telling anyone unless you care to."

"Man, when you people say 'voluntary' you're not just talking!"

"There's no other way to handle a thing like this. And you can bet that we get more people Out this way than we ever would on a compulsory basis. In the long run, I mean, and this is a long-term project ... six thousand years long."

He walked silently for a time, and I was pretty sure I knew his thoughts. For Outbounders there is no return, and the best possible chance they have of survival is something like fifty-four per cent, a figure which was arrived at after calculations so complex that it might as well be called a guess. You don't force people Out against those odds. They go by themselves, driven by their own reasoning, or they don't go at all.

After a time Judson said, "I always thought Outbounders were assigned a ship and a departure time. With certified people leaving whenever they feel like it, what's to prevent uncertified ones from doing it?"

"That I'm about to show you."

We passed the Coordination offices and headed out to the launching racks. They were shut off from Top Central Corridor by a massive gate. Over the gate floated three words in glowing letters:

SPECIES
GROUP
SELF

Seeing Jud's eyes on it, I explained, "The three levels of survival. They're in all of us. You can judge a man by the way he lines them up. The ones who have them in that order are the best. It's a good thought for Outbounders to take away with them." I watched his face. "Particularly since it's always the third item that brings 'em this far."

Jud smiled slowly. "Along with all that bumbling you carry a sting, don't you?"

"Mine is a peculiar job," I grinned back. "Come on in."

I put my palm on the key-plate. It tingled for a brief moment and then the shining doors slid back. I rolled through, stopping just inside the launching court at Judson's startled yelp.

"Well, come on," I said.

He stood just inside the doors, straining mightily against nothing at all. "Wh—wh—?" His arms were spread and his feet slipped as if he were trying to force his way through a steel wall.

Actually he was working on something a good deal stronger than that. "That's the answer to why uncertified people don't go Out," I told him. "The plate outside scanned the whorls and lines of my hand. The door opened and that Gillis-Menton field you're muscling passed me through. It'll pass anyone who's certified, too, but no one else. Now stop pushing or you'll suddenly fall on your face."

I stepped to the left bulkhead and palmed the plate there, then beckoned to Judson. He approached the invisible barrier timidly. It wasn't there. He came all the way through, and I took my hand off the scanner.

"That second plate," I explained, "works for me and certified people only. There's no way for an uncertified person to get into the launching court unless I bring him in personally. It's as simple as that. When the certified are good and ready, they go. If they want to go Out with a banquet and a parade beforehand, they can. If they want to roll out of bed some night and slip Out quietly, they can. Most of 'em do it quietly. Come on and have a look at the ships."

We crossed the court to the row of low doorways along the far wall. I opened one at random and we stepped into the ship.

"It's just a room!"

"They all say that," I chuckled. "I suppose you expected a planet-type space job, only more elaborate."

"I thought they'd at least *look* like ships. This is a double room out of some luxury hotel."

"It's that, and then some." I showed him around—the capacious food lockers, the automatic air recirculators, and, most comforting of all, the synthesizer, which meant food, fuel, tools and materials converted directly from energy to matter.

"Curbstone's more than a space station, Jud. It's a factory, for one thing. When you decide to go on your way, you'll flip that lever by the door. (You'll be catapulted out—you won't feel it, because of the stasis generator and artificial gravity.) As soon as you're gone, another ship will come up from below into this slot. By the time you're clear of Curbstone's gravitic field and slip into hyperdrive, the new ship'll be waiting for passengers."

"And that will be going on for six thousand years?"

"More or less."

"That's a powerful lot of ships."

"As long as Outbounders keep the quota, it is indeed. Nine hundred thousand—including forty-six per cent failure."

"Failure," said Jud. He looked at me and I held his gaze.

"Yes," I said. "The forty-six per cent who are not expected to get where they are going. The ones who materialize inside solid matter. The ones who go into the space-time nexus and never come out. The ones who reach their assigned synaptic junction and wait, and wait, and wait until they die of old age because no one gets to them soon enough. The ones who go mad and kill themselves or their shipmates." I spread my hands. "The forty-six per cent."

"You can convince a man of danger," said Judson evenly, "but nobody ever believed he was really and truly going to die. Death is something that happens to other people. I won't be one of the forty-six per cent."

That was Judson. I wish he was still here.

I let the remark lie there on the thick carpet and went on with my guided tour. I showed him the casing of the intricate beam-power apparatus that contained the whole reason for the project, and gave him a preliminary look at the astrogational and manual maneuvering equipment and controls. "But don't bother your pretty little head about it just now, I added. "It'll all be crammed into you before you get certified."

We went back to the court, closing the door of the ship behind us.

"There's a lot of stuff piled into those ships," I observed, "but the one thing that can't be packed in sardine-size is the hyper-drive. I suppose you know that."

"I've heard something about it. The initial kick into second-order space comes from the station here, doesn't it? But how is the ship returned to normal space on arrival?"

"That's technology so refined it sounds like mysticism," I answered. "I don't begin to understand it. I can give you an analogy, though. It takes a power source, a compression device, and valving to fill a pneumatic tire. It takes a plain nail to let the air out again. See what I mean?"

"Vaguely. Anyway, the important thing is that Outbound is strictly one way. Those ships never come back. Right?"

"So right."

One of the doors behind us opened, and a girl stepped out of a ship. "Oh . . . I didn't know there was anyone here!" she said, and came toward us with a long, easy stride. "Am I in the way?"

"You—in the way, Tween?" I answered. "Not a chance."

I was very fond of Tween. To these jaded old eyes she was one of the loveliest things that ever happened. Two centuries ago, before variation limits were as rigidly set as they are now, Eugenics dreamed up her kind—olive-skinned true-breeds with the silver hair and deep ruby eyes of an albino. It was an experiment they should never have stopped. Albinoism wasn't dominant, but in Tween it had come out strongly. She wore her hair long—really long; she could tuck the ends of it under her toes and stand up straight when it was loose. Now it was braided in two ingenious halves of a coronet that looked like real silver. Around her throat and streaming behind her as she walked was a single length of flame-colored material.

"This is Judson, Tween," I said. "We were friends back on Earth. What are you up to?"

She laughed, a captivating, self-conscious laugh. "I was sitting in a ship pretending that it was Outside. We'd looked at each other one day and suddenly said, 'Let's!' and off we'd gone." Her face was luminous. "It was lovely. And that's just what we're going to do one of these days. You'll see."

" 'We'? Oh—you mean Wold."

"Wold," she breathed, and I wished, briefly and sharply, that someone, somewhere, someday would speak my name like that. And on the heels of that reaction came the mental picture of Wold as I had seen him an hour before, slick and smooth, watching the shuttle passengers with his dark hunting eyes. There was nothing I could say though. My duties have their limits. If Wold didn't know a good thing when he saw it, that was his hard luck.

But looking at that shining face, I knew it would be her hard luck.

"You're certified?" Judson asked, awed.

"Oh, yes," she smiled, and I said, "Sure is, Jud. But she had her troubles, didn't you, Tween?"

We started for the gate. "I did indeed," said Tween. (I loved hearing her talk. There was a comfortable, restful quality to her speech like silence when an unnoticed, irritating noise disappears.) "I just didn't have the logical aptitudes when I first came. Some things just wouldn't stick in my head, even in hypnopedia. All the facts in the universe won't help if you don't know how to put them together." She grinned. "I used to hate you."

"Don't blame you a bit." I nudged Judson. "I turned down her certification eight times. She used to come to my office to get the bad news, and she'd stand there after I'd told her and shuffle her feet and gulp a little bit. And the first thing she said then was always, 'Well, when can I start retraining?'"

She flushed, laughing. "You're telling secrets!"

Judson touched her. "It's all right. I don't think less of you for any of his maunderings ... You must have wanted that certificate very much."

"Yes," she said. "Very much."

"Could—could I ask why?"

She looked at him, in him, through him, past him. "All our lives," she said quietly, "are safe and sure and small. This—" she waved back towards the ships—"is the only thing in our experience that's none of those things. I could give you fifty reasons for going Out. But I think they all come down to that one."

We were silent for a moment, and then I said, "I'll put that in my notebook, Tween. You couldn't be more right. Modern life gives us infinite variety in everything except the magnitude of the things we do. And that stays pretty tiny." And, I thought, big, fat, superannuated station officials, rejected by one world and unqualified for the next. A small chore for a small mind.

"The only reason most of us do puny things and think puny thoughts," Judson was saying, "is that Earth has too few jobs like his in these efficient times."

"Too few men like him for jobs like his," Tween corrected.

I blinked at them both. It was me they were talking about. I don't think I changed expression much, but I felt as warm as the color of Tween's eyes.

We passed through the gates, Tween first with never a thought for the barrier which did not exist for her, then Judson, waiting cautiously for my go-ahead after the inside scanning plate had examined the whorls and lines of my hand. I followed, and the great gates closed behind us.

"Want to come up to the office?" I asked Tween when we reached Central Corridor.

"Thanks, no," she said. "I'm going to find Wold." She turned to Judson. "You'll be certified quickly," she told him. "I just know. But, Judson—"

"Say it, whatever it is," said Jud, sensing her hesitation.

"I was going to say get certified first. Don't try to decide anything else before that. You'll have to take my word for it, but nothing that ever happened to you is quite like the knowledge that you're free to go through those gates any time you feel like it."

Judson's face assumed a slightly puzzled, slightly stubborn expression. It disappeared, and I knew it was a conscious effort for him to do it. Then he put out his hand and touched her heavy silver hair. "Thanks," he said.

She strode off, the carriage of her head telling us that her face was eager as she went to Wold. At the turn of the corridor she waved and was gone.

"I'm going to miss that girl," I said, and turned back to Judson. The puzzled, stubborn look was back, full force. "What's the matter?"

"What did she mean by that sisterly advice about getting certified first? What else would I have to decide about right now?"

I swatted his shoulder. "Don't let it bother you, Jud. She sees something in you that you can't see yourself, yet."

That didn't satisfy him at all. "Like what?" When I didn't answer, he asked, "You see it, too, don't you?"

We started up the ramp to my office. "I like you," I said. "I liked you the minute I laid eyes on you, years ago, when you were just a sprout."

"You've changed the subject."

"Hell, I have. Now let me save my wind for the ramp." This was only slightly a stall. As the years went by, that ramp seemed to get steeper and steeper. Twice Coordination had offered to power it for me and I'd refused haughtily. I could see the time coming when I was going to be too heavy for my high-horse. All the same, I was glad for the chance to stall my answer to Judson's question. The answer lay in my liking him; I knew that instinctively. But it needed thinking through. We've conditioned ourselves too much to analyze our dislikes and to take our likes for granted.

The outer door opened as we approached. There was a man waiting in the appointment foyer, a big fellow with a gray cape and a golden circlet around his blue-black hair. "Clinton!" I said. "How are you, son? Waiting for me?"

The inner door opened for me and I went into my office, Clinton behind me. I fell down in my specially molded chair and waved him to a relaxer. At the door Judson cleared his throat. "Shall I— uh . . ."

Clinton looked up swiftly, an annoyed, tense motion. He raked a blazing blue gaze across Jud, and his expression changed. "Come in, for God's sake. Newcomer, hm? Sit down. Listen. You can't learn enough about this project. Or these people. Or the kind of flat spin an Outbounder can get himself into."

"Clint, this's Judson," I said. "Jud, Clint's about the itchy-footedest Outbounder of them all. What is on your mind, son?"

Clinton wet his lips. "How's about me heading Out—*alone?*"

I said, "Your privilege, if you think you'll enjoy it."

He smacked a heavy fist into his palm. "Good then."

"Of course," I said, looking at the overhead, "the ships are built for two. I'd personally be a bit troubled about the prospect of spending—uh—however long it might be, staring at that empty bunk across the way. Specially," I added loudly, to interrupt what he was going to say, "if I had to spend some hours or weeks or maybe a decade with the knowledge that I was alone because I took off with a mad on."

"This isn't what you might call a fit of pique," snapped Clinton. "It's been years building—first because I had a need and recognized it; second because the need got greater when I started to work toward filling it; third because I found who and what would satisfy it; fourth because I was so wrong on point three."

"You *are* wrong? Or you're *afraid* you're wrong?"

He looked at me blankly. "I don't know," he said, all the snap gone out of his voice. "Not for sure."

"Well, then you've no real problem. All you do is ask yourself whether it's worthwhile to take off alone because of a problem you haven't solved. If it is, go ahead."

He rose and went to the door. "Clinton!" My voice must have crackled; he stopped without turning, and from the corner of my eye I saw Judson sit up abruptly. I said, more quietly, "When Judson here suggested that he go away and leave us alone, why did you tell him to come in? What did you see in him that made you do it?"

Clinton's thoughtfully slitted eyes hardly masked their blazing blue as he turned them on Judson, who squirmed like a schoolboy. Clinton said, "I think it's because he looks as if he can be reached. And trusted. That answer you?"

"It does." I waved him out cheerfully. Judson said, "You have an awesome way of operating."

"On him?"

"On both of us. How do you know what you did by turning his problem back on himself? He's likely to go straight to the launching court."

"He won't."

"You're sure."

"Of course I'm sure," I said flatly. "If Clinton hadn't already

24

decided *not* to take off alone—not today, anyhow—he wouldn't have come to see me and get argued out of it."

"What's really bothering him?"

"I can't say." I wouldn't say. Not to Judson. Not now, at least. Clinton was ripe to leave, and he was the kind to act when ready. He had found what he thought was the perfect human being for him to go with. She wasn't ready to go. She never in all time and eternity would be ready to go.

"All right," said Jud. "What about me? That was very embarrassing."

I laughed at him. "Sometimes when you don't know exactly how to phrase something for yourself, you can shock a stranger into doing it for you. Why did I like you on sight, years ago, and now, too? Why did Clinton feel you were trustworthy? Why did Tween feel free to pass you some advice—and what prompted the advice? Why did—" No. Don't mention the most significant one of all. Leave her out of it. "—Well, there's no point in itemizing all afternoon. Clinton said it. *You can be reached.* Practically anyone meeting you knows—feels, anyhow—that you can be reached . . . touched . . . affected. We like feeling that we have an effect on someone."

Judson closed his eyes, screwed up his brow. I knew he was digging around in his memory, thinking of close and casual acquaintances . . . how many of them . . . how much they had meant to him and he to them. He looked at me. "Should I change?"

"God, no! Only—don't let it be *too* true. I think that's what Tween was driving at when she said not to jump at any decisions until you've reached the comparative serenity of certification."

"Serenity . . . I could use some of that," he murmured.

"Jud."

"Mm?"

"Did you ever try to put into one simple statement just why you came to Curbstone?"

He looked startled. Like most people, he had been living, and living ardently, without ever wondering particularly what for. And like most people, he had sooner or later had to answer the jackpot question: "What am I doing here?"

"I came because—because ... no, that wouldn't be a simple statement."

"All right. Run it off, anyway. A simple statement will come out of it if there's anything really important there. Any basic is simple, Jud. Every basic is important. Complicated matters may be fascinating, frightening, funny, intriguing, worrisome, educational, or what have you; but if they're complicated, they are, by definition, not important."

He leaned forward and put his elbows on his knees. His hands wound tightly around one another, and his head went down.

"I came here ... looking for something. Not because I thought it was here. There was just nowhere else left to look. Earth is under such strict discipline ... discipline by comfort; discipline by constructive luxury. Every need is taken care of that you can name, and no one seems to understand that the needs you *can't* name are the important ones. And all Earth is in a state of arrested development because of Curbstone. Everything is held in check. The *status quo* rules because for six thousand years it must and will. Six thousand years of physical and social evolution will be sacrificed for the single tremendous step that Curbstone makes possible. And I couldn't find a place for myself in the static part of the plan, so the only place for me to go was to the active part."

He was quiet so long after that, I felt I had to nudge him along. "Could it be that there *is* a way to make you happy on Earth, and you just haven't been able to find it?"

"Oh, no," he said positively. Then he raised his head and stared at me. "Wait a minute. You're very close to the mark there. That— that simple statement is trying to crawl out." He frowned. This time I kept my mouth shut and watched him.

"The something I'm looking for," he said finally, in the surest tones he'd used yet, "is something I lack, or something I have that I haven't been able to name yet. If there's anything on Earth or here that can fill that hollow place, and if I find it, I won't want to go Out. I won't need to go—I *shouldn't* go. But if it doesn't exist for me here, then Out I go, as part of a big something, rather than as a something missing a part. Wait!" He chewed his lower lip. His knuckle-joints crackled as he twisted his hands together. "I'll rephrase that and you'll have your simple statement."

He took a deep breath and said, "I came to Curbstone to find out ... whether there's something I haven't had yet that belongs to me, or whether I ... belong to something that hasn't had me yet."

"Fine," I said. "Very damned fine. You keep looking, Jud. The answer's here, somewhere, in some form. I've never heard it put better: Do you owe, or are you owed? There are three possible courses open to you no matter which way you decide."

"There are? Three?"

I put up fingers one at a time. "Earth. Here. Out."

"I—see."

"And you can take the course of any one of the words you saw floating over the gate to the launching court."

He stood up. "I've got a lot to think about."

"You have."

"But I've got me one hell of a blueprint."

I just grinned at him.

"You through with me?" he asked.

"For now."

"When do I start work for my certificate?"

"At the moment, you're just about four-ninths through."

"You dog!" All this has been—"

"I'm a working man, Jud. I work all the time. Now beat it. You'll hear from me."

"You dog," he said again. "You old *hound*-dog!" But he left.

I sat back to think. I thought about Judson, of course. And Clinton and his worrisome solo ideas. The trip can be done solo, but it isn't a good idea. The human mind's communications equipment isn't a convenience—it's a vital necessity. Tween. How beautiful can a girl get? And the way she lights up when she thinks about going Out. She's certified now. Guess she and Wold will be taking off any time now.

Then my mind spun back to Flower. Put those pieces together ... something should fit. Turn it this way, back—Ah! Clinton wants Out. He's been waiting and waiting for his girl to get certified. She hasn't even tried. He's not going to wait much longer. Who's his girl now ...?

Flower.

Flower, who turned all that heat on Judson.

Why Judson? There were bigger men, smarter, better-looking ones. What was special about Judson?

I filed the whole item away in my mind—with a red priority tab on it.

The days went by. A gong chimed and the number-board over my desk glowed. I didn't have to look up the numbers to know who it was. Fort and Mariellen. Nice kids. Slipped Out during a sleep period. I thought about them, watched the chain of checking lights flicker on, one after another. Palm-patterns removed from the Gate scanner; they'd never be used there again. Ship replaced. Quarters cleared and readied. Launching time reported to Coordination. Marriage recorded. Automatic machinery calculated, filed, punched cards, activated more automatic machinery until Fort and Mariellen were only axial alignments on the molecules of a magnetic tape ... names ... memories ... dead, perhaps; gone, certainly, for the next six thousand years.

Hold tight, Earth! Wait for them, the fifty-four per cent (I hope, I ardently hope) who will come back. Their relatives, their Earth-bound friends will be long dead, and all their children and theirs; so let the Outbounders come home at least to the same Earth, the same language, the same traditions. They will be the millennial traditions of a more-than-Earth, the source of the unthinkable spatial sphere made fingertip-available to humankind through the efforts of the Outbounders. Earth is prepaying six thousand years of progress in exchange for the ability to use stars for stepping-stones, to be able to make Mars in a minute, Antares and Betelgeuse afternoon stops in a delivery run. Six thousand years of sacred stasis buys all but a universe, conquers Time, eliminates the fractionation of humanity into ship-riding, minute-shackled fragments of diverging evolution among the stars. All the stars will be in the next room when the Outbounders return.

Six thousand times around Sol, with Sol moving in a moving

galaxy, and that galaxy in flight through a fluxing universe. That all amounts to a resultant movement of Earth through nine Möllner degrees around the Universal Curve. For six thousand years Curbstone flings off its tiny ships, its monstrous power plant kicking them into space-time and the automatics holding them there until all—or until enough—are positioned. Some will materialize in the known universe and some in faintly suspected nebulae; some will appear in the empty nothingnesses beyond the galactic clusters, and some will burst into normal space inside molten suns.

But when the time comes, and the little ships are positioned in a great spherical pattern out around space, and together they become real again, they will send to each other a blaze of tight-beam energy. Like the wiring of a great switchboard, like the synapses of a brain, each beam will find its neighbors, and through them Earth.

And then, within and all through that sphere, humanity will spread, stepping from rim to rim of the universe in seconds, instantaneously transmitting men and materials from and to the stars. Here a ship can be sent piecemeal and assembled, there a space station. Yonder, on some unheard-of planet of an unknown star, men light years away from Earth can assemble matter transceivers and hook them up to the great sphere, and add yet another world to those already visited.

And what of the Outbounders?

Real time, six thousand years.

Ship's time, from second-order spatial entry to materialization— *zero.*

Fort and Mariellen. Nice kids. Memories now; lights on a board, one after another, until they're all accounted for. At Curbstone, the quiet machinery says, "Next!"

Fort and Mariellen. Clinging together, they press down the launching lever. Effortlessly in their launching, they whirl away from Curbstone. In minutes there is a flicker of gray, or perhaps not even that. Strange stars surround them. They stare at one another. They are elsewhere ... else*when*. Lights glow. This one says the tight-beam has gone on, pouring out toward the neighbors and, through them, to all the others. That one cries *"emergency"* and Fort whips to the manual controls and does what he can to avoid a dust-cloud, a planet ... perhaps an alien ship.

Fort and Mariellen (or George and Viki, or Bruce, who went Out by himself, Eleanor and Grace, or Sam and Rod—they were brothers) may materialize and die in an intolerable matter-displacement explosion so quickly that there is no time for pain. They may be holed by a meteor and watch, with glazing freezing eyes, the froth bubbling up from each other's bursting lungs. They may survive for minutes or weeks, and then fall captive to some giant planet or unsuspected sun. They may be hunted down and killed or captured by beings undreamed of.

And some of them will survive all this and wait for the blessed contact; the strident heralding of the matter transceiver with which each ship is equipped—and the abrupt appearance of a man, sixty centuries unborn when they left Curbstone, instantly transmitted from Earth to their vessel. Back with him they'll go, to an unchanged and ecstatic Earth, teeming with billions of trained, mature humans ready to fill the universe with human ways—the new humans who have left war and greed behind them, who have acquired a universe so huge that they need exploit no creature's properties, so rich and available is everything they require.

And some will survive, and wait, and die waiting because of some remotely extrapolated miscalculation. The beams never reach them; their beams contact nothing. And perhaps a few of these will not die, but will find refuge on some planet to leave a marker that will shock whatever is alive and intelligent a million years hence. Perhaps they will leave more than that. Perhaps there will be a slower, more hazardous planting of humanity in the gulfs.

But fifty-four per cent, the calculations insist, will establish the star-conquering sphere and return.

The weeks went by. A chime: Bark and Barbara. Damn it all, no more of Barbara's banana cream pie. The filing, the sweeping, the recording, the lights. Marriage recorded.

When a man and woman go Out together, that is marriage. There is another way to be married on Curbstone. There is a touch less speed involved in it than in joined hands pressing down a launching lever. There is not one whit less solemnity. It means what it means because it is not stamped with necessity. Children derive their names from their mothers, wed or not, and there is no distinction. Men and women, as responsible adults, do as they please within limits which are extremely wide. *Except. . . .*

By arduous trial and tragic error, humanity has evolved modern marriage. With social pressure removed from the pursuit of a mate, with the end of the ribald persecution of spinsterhood, a marriage ceases to be a rubber stamp upon what people are sure to do, with or without ceremonies. Where men and women are free to seek their own company, as and when they choose, without social penalties, they will not be trapped into hypocrisies with marriage vows. Under such conditions a marriage is entered gravely and with sincerity, and it constitutes a public statement of choice and—with the full implementation of a mature society—of inviolability. The lovely, ancient words "forsaking all others" spell out the nature of modern marriage, with the universally respected adjunct that fidelity is not a command or a restriction, but a chosen path. Divorce is swift and simple, and—almost unheard of. Married people live this way, single people live that way; the lines are drawn and deeply respected. People marry because they intend to live within the limits of marriage. The fact that a marriage exists is complete proof that it is working.

I had a word about marriage with Tween. Ran into her in the Gate corridor. I think she'd been in one of the ships again. If she was pale, her olive skin hid it. If her eyes were bloodshot, the lustrous ruby of her eyes covered it up. Maybe I saw her dragging her feet as she walked, or some such. I took her chin in my hand and tilted her head back. "Any dragons I can kill?"

She gave me a brilliant smile, which lived only on her lips. "I'm wonderful," she said bravely.

"You are," I agreed. "Which doesn't necessarily have anything to do with the way you feel. I won't pry, child; but tell me—if you ever ate too many green apples, or stubbed your toe on a cactus, do you know a nice safe something you could hang on to while you cried it out?"

"I do," she said breathlessly, making the smile just as hard as she could. "Oh, I do." She patted my cheek. "You're ... listen. Would you tell me something if I asked you?"

"About certificates? No, Tween. Not about anyone else's certificate. But—all he has to do is complete his final hypnopediae, and he just hasn't showed up."

She hated to hear it, but I'd made her laugh, too, a little. "Do you read minds, the way they all say?"

"I do not. And if I could, I wouldn't. And if I couldn't help reading 'em, I'd sure never act as if I could. In other words, no. It's just that I've been alive long enough to know what pushes people around. So's I don't care much about a person, I can judge pretty well what's bothering him.

"'Course," I added, "if I do give a damn, I can tell even better. Tween, you'll be getting married pretty soon, right?"

Perhaps I shouldn't have said that. She gasped, and for a moment she just stopped making that smile. Then, "Oh, yes," she said brightly. "Well, not exactly. What I mean is, when we go Out, you see, so we might as well not, and I imagine as soon as Wold gets his certificate, we'll ... we kind of feel going Out is the best ... I seem to have gotten something in my eye. I'm s-sor...."

I let her go. But when I saw Wold next—it was down in the Euphoria Sector—I went up to him very cheerfully. There are ways I feel sometimes that make me real jovial.

I laid my hand on his shoulder. His back bowed a bit and it seemed to me I felt vertebrae grinding together. "Wold, old boy," I said heartily. "Good to see you. You haven't been around much recently. Mad?"

He pulled away from me. "A little," he said sullenly. His hair was too shiny and he had perfect teeth that always reminded me of a keyboard instrument.

"Well, drop around," I said. "I like to see young folks get ahead. You," I added with a certain amount of emphasis, "have gone pretty damn far."

"So have you," he said with even more emphasis.

"Well, then." I slapped him on the back. His eyeballs stayed in, which surprised me. "You can top me. You can go farther than I ever can. See you soon, old fellow."

I walked off, feeling the cold brown points of his gaze.

And as it happened, not ten minutes later I saw that *kakumba* dance. I don't see much dancing usually, but there was an animal roar from the dance-chamber that stopped me, and I ducked in to see what had the public so charmed.

The dance had gone through most of its figures, with the caller already worked up into a froth and only three couples left. As I shouldered my way to a vantage point, one of the three couples was bounced, leaving the two best. One was a tall blonde with periwigged hair and subvoltaic bracelets that passed and repassed a clatter of pastel arcs; she was dancing with one of the armor-monkeys from the Curbstone Hull Division, and they were good.

The other couple featured a slender, fluid dark girl in an open tunic of deep brown. She moved so beautifully that I caught my breath, and watched so avidly that it was seconds before I realized it was Flower. The reaction to that made me lose more seconds in realizing that her partner was Judson. Good as the other couple were, they were better. I'd tested Jud's reflexes, and they were phenomenal, but I'd had no idea he could respond like this to anything.

The caller threw the solo light to the first couple. There was a wild burst of music and the arc-wielding blonde and her arc-wielding boy friend cut loose in an intricate frenzy of disjointed limbs and half-beat stamping. So much happened between those two people so fast that I thought they'd never get separated when the music stopped. But they untangled right with the closing bars, and a roar went up from the people watching them. And then the same blare of music was thrown at Jud and Flower.

Judson simply stood back and folded his arms, walking out a simple figure to indicate that, honest, he was dancing, too. But he gave it all to Flower.

Now I'll tell you what she did in a single sentence: she knelt before him and slowly stood up with her arms over her head. But words will never describe the process completely. It took her about twelve minutes to get all the way up. At the fourth minute the crowd began to realize that her body was trembling. It wasn't a wriggle or a shimmy, or anything as crude as that. It was a steady, apparently uncontrollable shiver. At about the eighth minute the audience began to realize it was controlled, and just how completely controlled it was. It was hypnotic, incredible. At the final crescendo she was on her tiptoes with her arms stretched high, and when the music stopped she made no flourish; she simply relaxed and stood still, smiling at Jud. Even from where I stood I could see the moisture on Jud's face.

A big man standing beside me grunted, a tight, painful sound. I turned to him; it was Clinton. Tension crawled through his jaw-muscles like a rat under a rug. I put my hand on his arm. It was rocky. "Clint."

"Wh—oh. Hi."

"Thirsty?"

"No," he said. He turned back to the dance floor, searched it with his eyes, found Flower.

"Yes, you are, son." I said. "Come on."

"Why don't you go and—" He got hold of himself. "You're right. I am thirsty."

We went to the almost deserted Card Room and dispensed ourselves some methyl-caffeine. I didn't say anything until we'd found a table. He sat stiffly looking at his drink without seeing it. Then he said, "Thanks."

"For what?"

"I was about to be real uncivilized in there."

I just waited.

He said truculently, "Well, damn it, she's free to do what she wants, isn't she? She likes to dance—good. Why shouldn't she? Damn it, what is there to get excited about?"

"Who's excited?"

"It's that Judson. What's he have to be crawling around her all the time for? She hasn't done a damn thing about getting her certificate since he got here." He drank his liquor down at a gulp. It had no apparent effect, which meant something.

"What had she done before he got here?" I asked quietly. When he didn't answer I said, "Jud's Outbound, Clint. I wouldn't worry. I can guarantee Flower won't be with him when he goes, and that will be real soon. Hold on and wait."

"Wait?" His lip curled. "I've been ready to go for weeks. I used to think of ... of Flower and me working together, helping each other. I used to make plans for a celebration the day we got certified. I used to look at the stars and think about the net we'd help throw around them, pull 'em down, pack 'em in a basket. Flower and me, back on Earth after six thousand years, watching humanity come into its own, knowing we'd done something to help. I've been waiting, and you say wait some more."

"This," I said, "is what you call an unstable situation. It can't stay the way it is and it won't. Wait, I tell you: wait. There's got to be a blow-off."

There was.

In my office the chime sounded. Moira and Bill. Certificates denied to Hester, Elizabeth, Jenks, Mella. Hester back to Earth. Hallowell and Letitia, marriage recorded. Certificates granted to Aaron, Musette, n'Guchi, Mancinelli, Judson.

Judson took the news quietly, glowing. I hadn't seen much of him recently. Flower took up a lot of his time, and training the rest. After he was certified and I'd gone with him to test the hand-scanner by the gate and give him his final briefing, he cut out on the double, I guess to give Flower the great news. I remember wondering how he'd like her reaction.

When I got back to my office Tween was there. She rose from the foyer couch as I wheezed in off the ramp. I took one look at her and said, "Come inside." She followed me through the inner door. I waved my hand over the infra-red plate and it closed. Then I put out my arms.

She bleated like a new-born lamb and flew to me. Her tears were scalding, and I don't think human muscles are built for the wrenching those agonized sobs gave her. People should cry more. They ought to learn how to do it easily, like laughing or sweating. Crying piles up. In people like Tween, who do nothing if they can't smile and make a habit-pattern of it, it really piles up. With a reservoir like that, and no developed outlet, things get torn when the pressure builds too high.

I just held her tight so she wouldn't explode. The only thing I said to her was "sh-h-h" once when she tried to talk while she wept. One thing at a time.

It took a while, but when she was finished she was finished. She didn't taper off. She was weak from all that punishment, but calm. She talked.

"He isn't a real thing at all," she said bleakly. "He's something I made up out of starshine, out of wanting so much to be a part of something as big as this project. I never felt I had anything big about me except that. I wanted to join it with something bigger than I was, and, together, we'd build something so big it would be worthy of Curbstone.

"I thought it was Wold. I *made* it be Wold. Oh, none of this is his fault. I could have seen what he was, and I just wouldn't. What I did with him, what I felt for him, was just as crazy as if I'd convinced myself he had wings and then hated him because he wouldn't fly. He isn't anything but a h-hero. He struts to the newcomers and the rejected ones pretending he's a man who will one day give himself to humanity and the stars. He ... probably believes that about himself. But he won't complete his training, and he ... now I know, now I can see it—he tried everything he could think of to stop me from being certified. I was no use to him with a certificate. He couldn't treat me as his pretty slightly stupid little girl, once I was certified. And he couldn't get his own certificate because if he did he'd have to go Out, one of these days, and that's something he can't face.

"He—*wants* me to leave him. If I will, if it's my decision, he can wear my memory like a black band on his arm, and delude himself for the rest of his life that his succession of women is just a search for something to replace me. Then he'll always have an excuse; he'll never, never have to risk his neck. He'll be the shattered hero, and women as stupid as I will try to heal the wounds he's arranged for me to give him."

"You don't hate him?" I asked her quietly.

"No. Oh, no, *no!* I told you, it wasn't his fault. I—loved *something*. A man lived in my heart, lived there for years. He had no name and no face. I gave him Wold's name and Wold's face and just wouldn't believe it wasn't Wold. I did it. Wold didn't. I don't hate him. I don't like him. I just don't ... *anything!*"

I patted her shoulder. "Good. You're cured. If you hated him, he'd still be important. What are you going to do?"

"What shall I do?"

"I'd never tell you what to do about a thing like this, Tween. You know that. You've got to figure out your own answers. I can advise you to use those new-opened eyes of yours carefully, though. And don't think that that man who lives in your heart doesn't exist anywhere else. He does. Right here on this station, maybe. You just haven't been able to see him before."

"Who?"

"God, girl, don't ask me that! Ask Tween next time you see her; no one will know for sure but Tween."

"You're so wise...."

"Nah. I'm old enough to have made more mistakes than most people, that's all, and I have a good memory."

She rose shakily. I put out a hand and helped her. "You're played out, Tween. Look—don't go back yet. Hide out for a few days and get some rest and do some thinking. There's a suite on this level. No one will bother you, and you'll find everything there you need, including silence and privacy."

"That would be good," she said softly. "Thank you."

"All right ... listen. Mind if I send someone in to talk to you?"

"Talk? Who?"

"Let me play it as it comes."

The ruby eyes sent a warm wave to me, and she smiled. I thought, I wish I was as confident of myself as she is of me. "It's 412," I said, "the third door to your left. Stay there as long as you want to. Come back when you feel like it."

She came close to me and tried to say something. I thought for a second she was going to kiss me on the mouth. She didn't; she kissed my hand. "I'll swat your bottom!" I roared, flustered. "Git, now,

37

dammit!" She laughed . . . she always had a bit of laughter tucked away in her, no matter what, bless her cotton head. . . .

As soon as she was gone, I turned to the annunciator and sent out a call for Judson. *Hell,* I thought, *you can try, can't you?* Waiting, I thought about Judson's hungry upward look, and that hole in his head . . . that quality of reachableness, and what happened when he was reached by the wrong thing. Lord, responsive people certainly make the worst damn fools of all!

He was there in minutes, looking flushed, excited, happy, and worried all at once. "Was on my way here when your call went out," he said.

"Sit down, Jud. I have a small project in mind. Maybe you could help."

He sat. I looked for just the right words to use. I couldn't say anything about Flower. She had her hooks into him; if I said anything about her, he'd defend her. And one of the oldest phenomena in human relations is that we come to be very fond of the thing we find ourselves defending, even if we didn't like it before. I thought again of the hunger that lived in Jud, and what Tween might see of it with her newly opened eyes.

"Jud—"

"I'm married," he blurted.

I sat very still. I don't think my face did anything at all.

"It was the right thing for me to do," he said, almost angrily. "Don't you see? You know what my problem is—it was you who found it for me. I was looking for something that should belong to me . . . or something to belong to."

"Flower," I said.

"Of course. Who else? Listen, that girl's got trouble, too. What do you suppose blocks her from taking her certificate? She doesn't think she's *worthy* of it."

My, I said. Fortunately, I said it to myself.

Jud said, "No matter what happens, I've done the right thing. If I can help her get her certificate, we'll go Out together, and that's what we're here for. If I can't help her do that, but find that she fills

that place in me that's been so empty for so long, well and good—
that's what *I'm* here for. We can go back to Earth and be happy."

"You're quite sure of all this."

"Sure I'm sure! Do you think I'd have gone ahead with the marriage if I weren't sure?"

Sure you would, I thought. I said, "Congratulations, then. You
know I wish you the best."

He stood up uncertainly, started to say something, and apparently couldn't find it. He went to the door, turned back. "Will you
come for dinner tonight?" I hesitated. He said, "Please. I'd appreciate it."

I cocked an eyebrow. "Answer me straight, Jud. Is dinner your
idea or Flower's?"

He laughed embarrassedly. "Damn it, you always see too much.
Mine ... sort of ... I mean, it isn't that she dislikes you, but ... well,
hell, I want the two of you to be friends, and I think you'd understand her, and me too, a lot better if you made the effort."

I could think of things I'd much rather do than have dinner with
Flower. A short swim in boiling oil, for example. I looked up at his
anxious face. Oh, hell. "I'd love to," I said. "Around eight?"

"Fine! Gee," he said, like a school kid. "Gee, thanks." He shuf-
fled, not knowing whether to go right away or not. "Hey," he said
suddenly. "You sent out a call for me. What's this project you wanted
me for?"

"Nothing, Jud," I said tiredly. "I've ... changed my mind. See
you later, son."

The dinner was something special. Steaks. Jud had broiled them
himself. I got the idea that he'd selected them, too, and set the table. It
was Flower, though, who got me something to sit on. She looked me
over, slowly and without concealing it, went to the table, pulled the
light formed-aluminum chair away, and dragged over a massive relaxer.
She then smiled straight at me. A little unnecessary, I thought; I'm bulky,
but those aluminum chairs have always held up under me so far.

I won't give it to you round by round. The meal passed with
Flower either in a sullen silence or manufacturing small brittle whips

of conversation. When she was quiet, Jud tried to goad her into talking. When she talked, he tried to turn the conversation away from me. The occasion, I think, was a complete success—for Flower. For Jud it must have been hell. For me—well, it was interesting.

Item: Flower poked and prodded at her steak, and when she got a lull in the labored talk Jud and I were squeezing out, she began to cut meticulously around the edges of the steak. "If there is anything I can't stand the sight or the smell of," she said clearly, "it's fat."

Item: She said, "Oh, Lord" this and "Lord sakes" that in a drawl that made it come out "Lard" every time.

Item: I sneezed once. She whipped a tissue over to me swiftly and politely enough, and then said "Render unto sneezers ..." which stood as a cute quip until she nudged her husband and said, "*Render!*" at which point things got real hushed.

Item: When she had finished, she leaned back and sighed. "If I ate like that all the time, I'd be a big as—" She looked straight at me and stopped. Jud, flushing miserably, tried to kick her under the table; I know, because it was me he kicked. Flower finished, "—as big as a lifeboat." But she kept looking at me, easily and insultingly.

Item—You get the idea. All I can say for myself is that I got through it all. I wouldn't give her the satisfaction of driving me out until I'd had all she could give me. I wouldn't be overtly angry, because if I did, she'd present me to Jud ever after as the man who hated her. If Jud ever had wit enough, this evening could be remembered as the time she was insufferably insulting, and that was all I wanted.

It was over at last, and I made my excuses as late as I possibly could without staying overnight. As I left, she took Jud's arm and held it tight until I was out of sight, thereby removing the one chance he had to come along a little way and apologize to me.

He didn't get close enough to speak to me for four days, and when he did, I had the impression that he had lied to be there, that Flower thought he was somewhere else. He said rapidly, "About the other night, you mustn't think that—"

And I cut him off as gently and firmly as I could: "I understand it perfectly, Jud. Think a minute and you'll know that."

40

"Look, Flower was just out of sorts. I'll work on her. Next time you come there'll be a real difference. You'll see."

"I'm sure I will, Jud. But drop it, will you? There's no harm done." And I thought, next time I come will be six months after the Outbounders get back. That gives me sixty centuries or so to get case-hardened.

About a week after Jud's wedding, I was in the Upper Central corridor where it ramps into the Gate passageway. Now whether it was some sixth sense, or whether I actually did smell something, I don't know. I got a powerful, sourceless impression of methyl-caffeine in the air, and at the same time I looked down the passage and saw the Gate just closing.

I got down there altogether too fast to do my leaky valves any good. I palmed the doors open and sprinted across the court. When anything my size and shape gets to sprinting, it's harder to stop it than let it keep going. One of the ship ports was open and I was heading for it. It started to swing closed. I lost all thought of trying to slow down and put what little energy I could find into pumping my old legs faster.

With a horrible slow-motion feeling of disaster, I felt one toe tip my other heel, and my center of gravity began to move forward faster than I was traveling. I was in mid-air for an age—long enough to chew and swallow a tongue—and then I hit on my stomach, rocked forward on my receding chest and two of my chins, and slid. I had my hands out in front of me. My left hit the bulkhead and buckled. My right shot through what was left of the opening of the door, which crunched shut on my forearm. Then my forehead hit the sill and I blacked out.

When the lights dimmed on again, I was spread out on a ship's bunk, apparently alone. My left arm hurt more than I could bear, and my right arm hurt worse, and both of them together couldn't match what was going on in my head.

A man appeared from the service cubicle when I let out a groan. He had a bowl of warm water and the ship's B first-aid kit in his hands. He crossed quickly to me, and began to stanch the blood from between some of my chins. It wasn't until then that my blurring sight made out who he was.

"Clinton, you hub-forted son of a bastich!" I roared at him. "Leave the chin alone and get some plexicaine into these arms!"

He had the gall to laugh at me. "One thing at a time, old man. You are bleeding. Let's try to be a patient, not an impatient."

"Impatient, out-patient," I yelped, "get that plex into me! I am just not the strong, silent type!"

"Okay, okay." He got the needle out of the kit, squirted it upward, and plunged it deftly into my arms. A good boy. He hit the biceps on one, the forearm on the other, and got just the right ganglia. The pain vanished. That left my head, but he fed me an analgesic and that cataclysmic ache began to recede.

"I'm afraid the left is broken," he said. "As for the right—well, if I hadn't seen that hand come crawling in over the sill like a pet puppy, and reversed the door control, I'd have cut your fingernails clear up to the elbow. What in time did you think you were doing?"

"I can't remember; maybe I've got a concussion. For some reason or other it seemed I had to look inside the ship. Can you splint this arm?"

"Let's call the medic."

"You can do just as well."

He went for the C kit and got a traction splint out. He whipped the prepared cushioning around the swelling arm, clamped the ends of the splint at the wrist and elbow, and played an infra-red lamp on it. In a few seconds the splint began to lengthen. When the broken forearm was a few millimeters longer than the other, he shut off the heat and the thermoplastic splint automatically set and snugged into the cushioning. Clinton threw off the clamps. "That's good enough for now. All right, are you ready to tell me what made you get in my way?"

"No."

"Stop trying to look like an innocent babe! Your stubble gives you away. You knew I was going to solo, didn't you?"

"No one said anything to me."

"No one ever has to," he said in irritation, and then chuckled. "Man, I wish I could stay mad at you. All right—what next?"

"You're not going to take off?"

"With you in here? Don't be foolish. The station'd lose too much and I wouldn't be gaining a thing. Damn you! I'd worked up the most glamorous drunk on methyl-caffeine, and you had to get me all anxious and drive away the fumes . . . Well, go ahead. I'll play it your way. What do we do?"

"Stop trying to make a Machiavelli out of me," I growled. "Give me a hand back to my quarters and I'll let you go do whatever you want."

"It's never that simple with you," he half-grinned. "Okay. Let's go."

When I got to my feet—with more of his help than I like to admit—my heart began to pound. He must have felt it, because he said nothing while we stood there and waited for it to behave itself. Clinton was a good lad.

We negotiated the court and the Gate all right, but slowly. When we got to the foot of my ramp, I shook my head. "Not that," I wheezed. "Couldn't make it. Down this way."

We went down the lateral corridor to 412. The door slid back for me.

"Hi!" I called. "Company."

"What? Who is it?" came the crystal voice. Tween appeared. "Oh—oh! I didn't want to see anyone just—why, what's happened?"

My eyelids flickered. I moaned. Clinton said, "I think we better get him spread out. He's not doing so well."

Tween ran to us and took my arm gently above the splint. They got me to a couch and I collapsed on it.

"Damn him," said Clinton good-humoredly. "He seems to be working full time to keep me from going Out."

There was such a long silence that I opened one eye to look at them. Tween was staring at him as if she had never seen him before—as, actually, she hadn't, with her eyes so full of Wold.

"Do you really want to go Out?" she asked softly.

"More than . . ." He looked at her hair, her lovely face. "I don't think I've seen you around much. You're—Tween, aren't you?"

She nodded and they stopped talking. I snapped my eyes shut because they were sure to look at me just for something to do.

"Is he all right?" she asked.

"I think he's—yes, he's asleep. Don't wonder. He's been through a lot."

"Let's go in the other room where we can talk together without disturbing him."

They closed the door. I could barely hear them. It went on for a long time, with occasional silences. Finally I heard what I'd been listening for: "If it hadn't been for him, I'd be gone now. I was just about to solo."

"No! Oh, I'm glad . . . I'm glad you didn't."

One of those silences. Then, "So am I, Tween. Tween . . ." in a whisper of astonishment.

I got up off the couch and silently let myself out. I went back to my quarters, even managing to climb the ramp. I felt real fine.

I heard an ugly rumor.

I'd seen a lot and I'd done a lot, and I regarded myself as pretty shockproof, but this one jolted me to the core. I took refuge in the old ointment, "It can't be, it just can't be," but in my heart I knew it could.

I got hold of Judson. He was hollow-eyed and much quieter than usual. I asked him what he was going these days, though I knew.

"Boning up on the fine points of astrogation," he told me. "I've never hit anything so fascinating. It's one thing to have the stuff shoveled into your head when you're asleep, and something else again to experience it all, note by note, like music."

"But you're spending an awful lot of time in the archives, son."

"It takes a lot of time."

"Can't you study at home?"

I think he only just then realized what I was driving at. "Look," he said quietly, "I have my troubles. I have things wrong with me. But I'm not blind. I'm not stupid. You wouldn't tell me to my face that I couldn't handle problems that are strictly my own, would you?"

"I would if I were sure," I said. "Damn it, I'm not. And I'm not going to pry for details."

"I'm glad of that," he said soberly. "Now we don't have to talk about it at all, do we?"

In spite of myself, I laughed aloud.

"What's funny?"

"I am, Jud, boy. I been—handled."

He saw the point, and smiled a little with me. "Hell, I know what you've been hinting at. But you're not close enough to the situation to know all the angles. I am. When the time comes, I'll take care of it. Until then, it's no one's problem but my own."

He picked up his star-chart reels and I knew that one single word more would be one too many. I squeezed his arm and let him go.

Five people, I thought: Wold, Judson, Tween, Clinton, Flower. Take away two and that leaves three. Three's a crowd—in this case, a very explosive kind of crowd.

Nothing, *nothing* justifies infidelity in a modern marriage. But the ugly rumors kept trickling in.

"I want my certificate," Wold said.

I looked up at him and a bushel of conjecture flipped through my mind. So you want your certificate? Why? And why just now, of all times? What can a man do with a certificate that he can't do without one—aside from going Out? Because, damn you, you'll never go Out. Not of your own accord, you won't.

All this, but none of it slipped out. I said, "All right. That's what I'm here for, Wold." And we got to work.

He worked hard, and smoothly and easily, the way he talked, the way he moved. I am constantly astonished at how small accomplished people can make themselves at times.

He was certified easy as breathing. And can you believe it, I worked with him, saw how hard he was working, helped him through, and never realized what it was he was after?

After going through the routines of certification for him, I wasn't happy. There was something wrong somewhere . . . something missing. This was a puzzle that ought to fall together easily, and it wouldn't. I wish—Lord, how I wish I could have thought a little faster.

I let a day go by after Wold was certified. I couldn't sleep, and I couldn't eat, and I couldn't analyze what it was that was bothering me. So I began to cruise, to see if I could find out.

I went to the archives. "Where's Judson?"

The girl told me he hadn't been there for forty-eight hours.

I looked in the Recreation Sector, in the libraries, in the stereo and observation rooms. Some kind of rock-bottom good sense kept me from sending out a general call for him. But it began to be obvious that he just wasn't around. Of course, there were hundreds of rooms and corridors in Curbstone that were unused—they wouldn't be used until the interplanetary project was completed and the matter transmitters started working. But Jud wasn't the kind to hide from anything.

I squared my shoulders and realized that I was doing a lot of speculation to delay looking in the obvious place. I think, more than anything else, I was afraid that he would *not* be there. . . .

I passed my hand over the door announcer. In a moment she answered; she had apparently come in from the sun-field and hadn't bothered to see who it was. She was warm brown from head to toe, all spring-steel and velvet. Her long eyes were sleepy and her mouth was pouty. But when she recognized me, she stood squarely in the doorway.

I think that in the back of every human mind is a machine that works out all the answers and never makes mistakes. I think mine had had enough data to figure out what was happening, what was going to happen, for a long while now. Only I hadn't been able to read the answer until now. Seeing Flower, in that split second, opened more than one door for me . . .

"*You* want something?" she asked. The emphasis was hard and very insulting.

I went in. It was completely up to her whether she moved aside or was walked down. She moved aside. The door swung shut.

"Where's Jud?"

"I don't know."

I looked into those long secret eyes and raised my hand. I think I was going to hit her. Instead I put my hand on her chest and shoved.

46

She fell, unhurt but terrified, across a relaxer. "What do you th—"

"You won't see him again," I said, and my voice bounced harshly off the acoust-absorbing walls. "He's gone. *They're* gone."

"They?" Her face went pasty under the deep tan.

"You ought to be killed," I said. "But I think it's better if you live with it. You couldn't hold either of them, or anyone else."

I went out.

My head was buzzing and my knitting arm throbbed. I moved with utter certainty; never once did it occur to me to ask myself: "Why did I say that?" All the ugly pieces made sense.

I found Wold in the Recreation Sector. He was tanked. I decided against speaking to him, went straight to the launching court and tried the row of ship ports. There was no one there, no one in any of them. My eye must have photographed something in the third ship, because I felt compelled to go back there and look again.

I stared hard at the deep-flocked floor. The soft pile of it looked right and yet not-right. I went to the control panel and untracked an emergency torch, turned it to needle-focus and put it, lit, on the floor. A horizontal beam will tell you things no other light knows about.

I turned the light on the door and slowly swung the sharp streak across the carpet. The monotone, amorphous surface took on streaks and ridges, shadows and shadings. A curved scuff inside. Two parallel ones, long, where something had been dragged. A blurred sector where something heavy had lain long enough to press the springy fibers down for a while, over by the left-hand bunk.

I looked at the bunk. It was unruffled, which meant nothing; the resilient surface was meant to leave no impressions. But at the edge was a single rubbed spot, as if something had spilled there and been wiped hard.

I went to the service cubicle. Everything seemed in order, except one of the cabinet doors, which wouldn't quite close. I looked inside.

It was a food locker. The food was there all right, each container socketed in place in the prepared shelves. But on, between, and among them were micro-reels for the book projector.

I frowned and looked further. Reels were packed into the disposal lock, the towel dispenser, the spare-parts chest for the air exchanger.

Something was where the book-reels belonged, and the reels had been hidden by someone who could not leave them in sight or carry them off.

And where did the reels belong?

I went back to the central chamber and the left-hand bunk. I touched the stud that should have rolled the bunk outward, opening the top, so that the storage space under it could be reached. The bunk didn't move.

I examined the stud. It was coated over with quick-setting leak-sealer. The stuff was tough but resilient. I got a steel rod and a hammer from the tool-rack and, placing the rod against the stud, hit it once. The leak-sealer cracked off. The bed rolled forward and opened.

It was useless to move him or touch him, or, for that matter, to say anything. Judson was dead, his head twisted almost all the way around. His face was bluish and his eyes stared. He was pushed, jammed, wedged into the small space.

I hit the stud again and the bunk rolled back. Moving without any volition that I could analyze, feeling nothing but a great angry numbness, I cleaned up. I put the rod and the hammer away and fluffed up the piling of the carpeting by the bunk. Then I went and stood in the service cubicle and began to wait.

Wait. Not just stay—wait. I knew he'd be back, just as I suddenly and belatedly understood what it was that every factor in five people had made inevitable. I was coldly hating myself for not having known it sooner.

The great, the admirable, the adventurous in modern civilizaton were Outbounders. To one who wanted and needed personal power, there would be an ultimate goal, greater even than being an Outbounder. And that would be to stand between an Outbounder and his destiny.

For months Flower had blocked Clinton. When she saw she must ultimately lose him to the stars, she went hunting. She saw Judson— reachable, restless Jud—and she heard my assurance that he would soon go Out. Then and there Judson was doomed.

Wold needed admiration the way Flower needed power. To be an Outbounder and wait for poor struggling Tween suited him perfectly. Tween's certification gave him no alternative but to get rid of her; he couldn't bring himself to go Out.

Once I had taken care of Tween for him, there remained one person on the entire project who could keep him from going Out—and she was married to Jud. Having married, Jud would stay married. Wold did what he could to smash that marriage. When Jud still hung on, wanting to help Flower, wanting to show me that he had made the right choice, there remained one alternative for Wold. Evidence of that lay cramped and staring under the bunk.

But Wold wasn't finished. He wouldn't be finished while Jud's body remained on Curbstone. In Wold's emotional state, he would have to go somewhere and drink to figure out the next step. There was no way of sending a ship Out without riding it. So—I waited.

He came back all right. I was cramped, then, and one foot was asleep. I curled and uncurled the toes frantically when I saw the door begin to move, and tried to flatten my big bulk back down out of sight.

He was breathing hard. He put his lips together and blew like a winded horse, wiped his lips on his forearm. He seemed to have difficulty in focusing his eyes. I wondered how much liquor he had poured into that empty place where most men keep their courage.

He took a fine coil of single-strand plastic cord out of his belt-pouch. Fumbling for the end, he found it and dropped the coil. With the exaggerated care of a drunk, he threw a bowline and drew the loop tight, pulled the bight through the loop so he had a running noose. He made this fast to a triangular bracket over the control panel, let it along the edge of the chart-rack and down to the launching control lever. He bent two half-hitches in the cord, slipped it over the end of the lever and drew it tight. The cord now bound the lever in the up—"off"—position.

From the bulkhead he unfastened the clamps which held the heavy-duty fire extinguisher and lifted it down. It weighed half as much as he did. He set it on the floor in front of the control panel, brought the dangling end of the cord through the U-shaped clamp gudgeons on the extinguisher, took a loose half-hitch around the bight, and, lifting the extinguisher between his free arm and his body, pulled the knot tight. Another half-hitch secured it.

Now the heavy extinguisher dangled in mid-air under the control panel. The cord which supported it ran up to the handle of the launching lever and from there, bending over the edge of the chart-rack, to the bracket.

Panting, Wold took out a cigarette and shook it alight. He drew on it hungrily, and then put it on the chart-rack, resting it against the plastic cord.

When the cigarette burned down to the cord, the thermoplastic would melt through with great enthusiasm. The cord would break, the extinguisher would fall, dragging the lever down. And Out would go all the evidence, to be hidden forever, as far as Wold was concerned, and six thousand years from anyone else.

Wold stepped back to survey his work just as I stepped forward out of the service cubicle. I brought up my broken arm and swung it with all my weight—and that is really weight—against the side of his head. The cast, though not heavy, was hard, and it must have hit him like a crowbar.

He went down like an elevator, hitched to his knees, and for a second seemed about to topple. His head sagged. He shook it, slowly looked up and saw me.

"I could use one of those needle-guns," I said. "Or I could kick you cold and let Coordination handle you. There are regulations for things like you. But I'd rather do it this way. Get up."

"I never ..."

"Get up!" I bellowed, and kicked at him.

He threw his arms around my leg and rolled. As I started down, I pulled the leg in close and whipped it out again. We both hit with a crash on opposite sides of the room. The bunk broke my fall; he was not so lucky. He rose groggily, sliding his back up the door. I lumbered across, deliberately crashed into him and heard ribs crack as the wind gushed out of his lungs.

I stood back a little as he began to sag. I hit him savagely in the face, and his face came back and hit my hand again as his head bounced off the door. I let him fall, then knelt beside him.

There are things you can do to a human body if you know enough physiology—pressures on this and that nerve center which paralyze and cramp and immobilize whole motor-trunk systems. I did these things, and got up, finally, leaving him twisted, sweating in agony. I wheezed over to the control bank and looked critically at the smoldering cigarette. Less than a minute.

"I know you can hear me," I whispered with what breath I could find. "I'd ... like you to know ... that you'll be a hero. Your name will ... be on the Great Roll of the ... Outbounders. You always ... wanted that without any ... effort on your part ... now you've got it."

I went out. I stopped and leaned back against the wall beside the door. In a few seconds it swung silently shut. I forced back the waves of gray that wanted to engulf me, turned and peered into the port. It showed only blackness.

Jud ... Jud, boy ... you always wanted it, too. You almost got cheated out of it. You'll be all right now, son. ...

I tottered across the court and out the gate. There was someone standing there. She flew to me, pounded my chest with small hard hands. "Did he go? Did he really go?"

I brushed her off as if she had been a midge, and closed one eye so I could get a single image. It was Flower, without her come-on tunic. Her hair was disarrayed and her eyes were bloodshot.

"*They* left," I croaked. "I told you they would. Jud and Wold ... you couldn't stop them."

"Together? They left *together?*"

"That's what Wold got certified for." I looked bluntly up and down her supple body. "Like everybody else who goes Out together, they had *some*thing in common."

I pushed past her and went back to my office. Lights were blazing over the desk. Judson and Wold. Ship replaced. Quarters cleared. Palm-key removed and filed. I sat and looked blindly until they were all lit and the board blanked out.

I thought, this pump of mine won't last much longer under this kind of treatment.

I thought, I keep convincing myself that I handle things impartially and fairly, without getting involved.

I felt bad. Bad.

I thought, this is a job without authority, without any real power. I certify 'em, send 'em along, check 'em out. A clerk's job. And because of that I have to be God. I have to make up my own justice, and execute it myself. Wold was no threat to me or Curbstone, yet it was in me to give oblivion to him and purgatory to Flower.

I felt frightened and disgusted and puny.

Someone came in, and I looked up blindly. For a moment I could make out nothing but a silver-haloed figure and a muted, wordless murmuring. I forced my eyes to focus, and I had to close them again, as if I had looked into the sun.

Her hair was unbound beneath a diamond ring that circled her brows. The silver silk cascaded about her, brushing the floor behind her, mantling her warm-toned shoulders, capturing small threads of light and weaving them in and about the gleaming light that was her hair. Her deep pigeon's-blood eyes shone and her lips trembled.

"Tween. . . ."

The soft murmuring became words, laughter that wept with happiness, small shaking syllables of rapture. "He's waiting. He wanted to say good-by to you, too . . . but he asked me to do it for him. He said you'd like that better."

I could only nod.

She came close to the desk. "I love him. I love him more than I thought anyone could. Somehow, loving him that much, I can . . . love you, too."

She bent over the desk and kissed my mouth. Her lips were cool. She—blurred then. Or maybe it was my eyes. When I could see again, she was gone.

The chime, and the lights, one after another.

Marriage recorded. . . .

Suddenly I relaxed and I knew I could live with the viciousness of what I had done to Wold and to Flower. It had been my will that Judson go Out, and that Tween be happy, and I had been crossed, and I had taken vengeance. And that was small, and decidedly human—not godlike at all.

So, I thought, every day I find something out about people. And, today, I'm people. I felt the pudgy lips that Tween had kissed. I'm old and I'm fat, I thought, and by the Lord, I'm people.

When they call me Charon, they forget what it must be like to be denied both worlds instead of only one.

And they forget the other thing—the little-known fragment of the Charon legend. To the Etruscans, he was more than a ferryman.

He was an executioner.

Rule of Three

THEY WERE A decontamination squad—three energy-entities (each triple)—on a routine check of a known matter-entity culture. What they traveled in was undoubtedly a ship, since it moved through space, except that it was not a physical structure of metal. It slowed down like a light wave that had suddenly grown tired.

"There it is," said RilRylRul.

The two other triads merged their light-perceptions and observed it. "Out at the edge," said KadKedKud, in satisfaction. "It should not be too difficult to handle out there. When infection spreads near the heart of a Galaxy, it can be troublesome."

MakMykMok cautioned, "Don't underestimate the job until it's surveyed."

"It's a very small sun," said Ril. "Which one of the planets is it? The fourth?"

"No, the greenish-blue one, the third."

"Very well."

In due time the ship—a bubble of binding energy and collapsed, rarefied gas molecules—entered the atmosphere. It reshaped itself gradually into a round-nosed, tapered transparency and dropped sharply, heading due west over the planet's equator.

"Busy little things, aren't they?"

As the world turned under them, they watched. They saw the ships, the cities. In the microscopic, intangible fluxes of force which were nerve and sinew and psyche to their triple structure, they stored their observations. They recorded the temperature of steel converters and ships' power plants, calculated the strength of materials of buildings and bridges by their flexure in a simply computed wind velocity, judged and compared the flow-shapes of air and ground vehicles.

"We could return right now," said Kad. "Any race which has

54

progressed this far in such a brief time must be a healthy one. Otherwise, how could—"

"Look!" Ril flashed.

They watched, appalled. "They are *killing* one another!"

"It must be a ritual," said Kad, "or perhaps a hunt. But we'd better investigate closer."

They dropped down, swiftly overtook a low-flying open-cockpit biplane with a black cross on the fuselage, and settled on the cowling behind the pilot's head. Mak interpenetrated the ship's wall and, treading and passing the air molecules which fled past, reached the pilot's leather helmet at the nape of the neck. Contact was made and broken almost in the same moment of time, and Mak hurtled back in horror to the skin of their ship.

"*Get clear!*" he ordered.

In three microseconds the invisible ship was in the upper atmosphere, with Mak still clinging to the outer skin.

"What was it?"

"Pa'ak, the most vicious, most contagious energy-virus known. That creature is crawling with them! Never have I *seen* such an infestation! Examine me. Irradiate me. Be careful, now—be sure."

It was strong medicine, but effective. Mak weakly permeated through the ship's wall and came inside. "Disgusting. Utterly demoralizing. How can the creature live in that condition?"

"Worse than Murktur III?"

"Infinitely worse. On Murktur I never saw a concentration higher than 14, and that was enough to reduce the natives to permanent bickering. These bipeds can apparently stand a concentration of over 120 on the same scale. Incredible."

"Perhaps that individual is quarantined."

"I doubt it. It was flying its own machine; it can apparently land at will anywhere. But we will check further. Mak, you were quite right," said Ril. "Don't underestimate the job indeed. Why, with an infestation like that, and a drive like that . . . what couldn't they accomplish if they were clean?"

They swooped close to the land, barely touched the hair of a child on a hilltop, and soared again, shaken and frightened.

"From what we've seen, that one was no more than 15% of maximum size. How do you read the Pa'ak concentration?"

"Over 70. This place is a pesthole. These creatures must be stopped—and soon. You know how soon such a technology reaches for the stars."

"Shall we send for reinforcements?"

"Before investigating? Certainly not. And after all, there are three of us."

"We shall have to protect ourselves," Ril pointed out.

"You mean—dissociate? Divide our triple selves?"

"You know that's the only way we can remain undetected by the Pa'ak. Of course, once we know exactly how they have developed here, and have analyzed the psychic components of the natives, we can re-synthesize."

"I hate the thought of dividing myself. So weak, so impotent . . ."

"So safe. Don't forget that. Once we've encased ourselves in the minds of these creatures and analyzed them, we'll have to join ourselves again to fight the Pa'ak."

"Yes, indeed. And we'll be together again soon. Take care," added Mak, the cautious one. "The Pa'ak are mindless, but exceedingly dangerous."

"Hungry," Kad supplemented.

"Especially for our kind. Shall we begin?"

The ship disappeared, bursting like a bubble. The three dropped, sharing a wordless thought that was like a handclasp. Then each of them separated into three, and the nine particles drifted down through the atmosphere.

The news is apples for the unemployed . . . disarmament . . . the Model A Ford.

A young girl lay on her stomach under a tree, reading. She yawned widely, choked a little, swallowed, and went back to her book.

Two friends shook hands. Later, one absentmindedly palmed the back of his neck. Something was rubbed into his skin. The other young man scratched his wrist as he walked away.

Something was in the drinking water, though neither the nurse, as she filled the glass, nor the little girl, as she drank, knew of it.

Some dust settled on a toothbrush.

A small boy sank his teeth into his bread-and-jam. The rich, red preserve drooled to the table. The boy put his finger in it, thrust the finger into his mouth.

Another youngster ran through the dewy morning grass in his bare feet.

Somewhere, two dust motes were waiting their turn.

And a number of years went by.

> *The news is Korea and Tibet ... protein synthesis ... Aureomycin ... leaf and grain hormone poisons ... the McCarran Act.*

There was a character at the party named Irving, and Jonathan Prince, Consulting Psychologist, didn't like him. This Irving played guitar and sang folk songs in a resonant baritone, which was fine; but after that he would put a lampshade on his head and be the "March of the Wooden Soldiers" or some such, and that was as funny, after the fourth viewing, as a rubber crutch. So Jonathan let his eyes wander.

When his gaze came to the dark girl sitting by the door, his breath hissed in suddenly.

Priscilla was sitting next to him. She said "Ouch," and he realized he had squeezed her hand painfully.

"What's the matter, Jon?"

"I just—nothing, Pris." He knew it was tactless, because he knew the sharpness of Priscilla's tilted eyes, but he couldn't help it; he stared back at the dark girl.

The girl's hair was blue-black and gleamed like metal, yet he knew how soft it would be. Her eyes were brown, wide apart, deep. He knew how they would crinkle on the outside ends when she smiled. He knew, as a matter of fact, that she had a small brown mole on the inside of her left thigh.

Irving was still singing. Of course it had to be "Black Is the Color of My True Love's Hair." Priscilla pressed Jon's hand, gently. He leaned toward her.

She whispered, "Who's the charmer? Someone you know?"

He hesitated. Then he nodded and said, without smiling, "My ex-wife."

Priscilla let his hand go.

Jonathan waited until Irving finished his song and, in the applause, rose. " 'Scuse . . ." he muttered. Priscilla didn't seem to be listening.

He crossed the room and stood in front of the dark girl until she looked up at him. He saw the little crinkle by her eyes before he saw the smile.

"Edie."

"Jon! How *are* you?" Then she said, in unison with him, "Can't complain." And she laughed at him.

He flushed, but it was not anger. He sat on the ottoman by her feet. "How've you been, Edie? You haven't changed."

"I haven't," she nodded seriously. There was an echo in his mind. *"We'll always be friends, Jon. Nothing can change that."* Was that what she meant? She said, "Still trying to find out how the human mind works?"

"Yes, on the occasions when I find one that does. Are you in town for long?"

"I've come back. They closed the Great Falls office. Jon . . ."

"Yes?"

"Who's the redhead?"

"Priscilla. Priscilla Berg. My assistant."

"She's lovely, Jon. Really lovely. Is she . . . are you. . ."

At last he could smile. "You can ask, Edie," he said gently. "Here, I'll ask you first. Are you married?"

"No."

"I didn't think so. I don't know why, but I didn't think so. Neither am I."

He looked down at his hands because he knew she was smiling, and somehow he didn't want to look into her eyes and smile too. "I'll get us a drink."

She waited until he was on his feet and a pace away before she said what she used to say: "Come back quickly."

Someone jostled him at the bar.

"What's up, Doc?" said Irving, and nickered. "Hey, that assistant of yours, she drinks scotch, doesn't she?"

"Rye on the rocks," he said absently, and then realized that the scotch suggestion was Irving's shot in the dark, and that he'd given the idiot an opening gambit with Priscilla. He was mildly annoyed as he ordered two Irish-and-waters and went back to Edie.

Communication was dim and labored.

"We're trapped . . ."

"Don't give up. Ked is very close to me now."

"Yes, you and Ked can achieve proximity. But these creatures won't combine emotionally in threes!"

"They can—they must!"

"Do not force them. Remain encysted and work carefully. Did you know the Pa'ak got Mak?"

"*No!* How horrible! What about Myk and Mok, then?"

"They will be guardians, watchers, communicators. What else can they do?"

"Nothing . . . nothing. How terrible to be one-third dead! What happened to Mak?"

"The creature Mak occupied killed itself, walked in front of a speeding vehicle as Mak tried to synthesize. Mak could not get clear in time from the dead thing."

"We must hurry or these beasts will leap off into space before we join our strength again."

The club wouldn't be open for hours yet, but Derek knew which of the long row of herculite doors would be unlocked. He shouldered it open and sidled in, being careful not to let it swing shut on his bass viol.

Someone was playing the piano out back. Piano . . . hadn't Janie been knocking herself out looking for a piano man before he went away? He mumbled, "Hope she—" and then Jane was on, over, and all around him.

"Derek, you tall, short underdone yuk, you!" she crooned. She hugged him, and put a scarlet print of her full mouth on his cheek. "Why didn't you wire? God, man, I missed you. Here, put down that Steinway and smooch me once. Am I glad to see your ugly head ... Look at the man," she demanded of the empty club as he leaned the big bass against the wall and stroked its rounded flank with the tips of his fingers. "Hey, this is me over here."

"How are you, Janie?" He delivered a hug. "What's been giving around here?"

"Me," she said. "Giving, but out. Ma-an ... a hassle. For ten days I had a sore throat clear from neck to tonsil, carrying that piano man. Damn it, I got a way I sing, and a piano's got to walk around me when I do it. Chopsticks this square makes—*eggs—ack—ly—on—the—beat,*" she stressed flatly. "And then a bass player I had, a doghouse complete with dog, and tone-deaf to boot. I booted him. I worked the last three nights without a bass, and am I glad you're back!"

"Me too." He touched her hair. "We'll get you a piano player and everything'll riff like Miff."

"A piano I *got,*" she said, and her voice was awed. "Little cat I heard in a joint after hours. Gives his left hand a push and forgets about it. Right hand is *crazy.* Real sad little character, Derek. Gets the by-himself blues and plays boogie about it. Worse he feels, the better he plays. Sing with him? Man! All his chords are vocal cords for little Janie. He's back there now. Listen at him!"

Derek listened. The piano back there was talking to itself about something rich and beautiful and lost. "That just one man?" he asked after a moment.

"Come on back and meet him," she said. "Oh, Derek, he's a sweetheart."

"Sweetheart?"

She thumped his chest and chuckled. "Wait till you see him. You don't need to lie awake nights over him. Come on."

He was a man with a hawk face and peaceful eyes. He huddled on the bench watching what his hands did on the keyboard as if he hadn't seen them before but didn't much care. His hands were extraordinarily eloquent. He didn't look up.

Derek said, "I'm going to go get my fiddle."

He did, and picked up the beat so quietly that the pianist didn't hear him for three bars. Then he looked up and smiled shyly at Derek and went on playing. It was very, very good. They volleyed an intro back and forth for a while and then, before Derek fully realized what they were playing, Janie was singing "Thunder and Roses":

> *"When you gave me your heart*
> *You gave me the world ... "*

And, after, there was a chord with a tremendous emphasis on an added sixth, and then it was augmented—a hungry, hungry leading tone, which led, with a shocked sort of satisfaction, into silence.

Derek put by his bass, carefully, so it wouldn't make any sound.

Jane said, in a mouselike voice, "I can breathe now?"

The pianist got up. He was not tall. He said, "You're Derek Jax. Thanks for letting me play along with you. I always wanted to."

"Thanks, he says." Derek gestured. "You play a whole mess of piano. What's your name?"

"Henry. Henry Faulkner."

"I never heard of you."

"He was head of the Orchestration Department at the Institute for twelve years," said Jane.

"Hey? That's all right," said Derek. "Symphony stuff. What'd you leave for?"

"Squares," said Henry. To Derek, it was a complete explanation. "I'd like to work here."

Jane closed her eyes and clasped her hands. "Yummy."

Derek said, from a granite face, "No."

Jane stood frozen. Henry came out from behind the piano. He walked—he all but trotted up to Derek. "No? Oh, please! A—joke?"

"No joke. Just no."

Jane breathed, "Derek, what are you on? Goofballs?"

Derek threw up his hands. "No. It's a good word. Ain't 'no' better than a whole lot of yak? No, that's all."

"Derek—"

"Mr. Jax," said Derek.

"Mr. Jax, please think it over," Henry said. "I've been wanting to work with you ever since you recorded 'Slide Down.'" You know how long ago that was. I don't just want to play piano someplace. I want to play here—with you. I don't care about the pay. Just let me back up that bass."

"He never talked like that to me," said Jane with a small smile. "You've made yourself a conquest, puddin'head. Now—"

"I don't want to hear that kind of talk," exploded Derek. "I don't want to hear any kind of talk. I said no!"

Jane came to him. She squeezed Henry's forearm and gave him a long look. "Walk around some," she said kindly. "Come back and see me later."

Derek stood looking at the piano. Jane watched Henry go. He walked slowly, holding himself in, his head forward. At the other side of the dance floor he turned and opened his mouth to speak, but Jane waved him on. He went out.

Jane whirled on Derek. "Now what the God—"

Derek interrupted her, rasping, "If you got any more to say about this, you can look for a new bass man too."

Pallas McCormick was fifty-three years old and knew what she was about. She strode briskly down Eleventh Street, a swift, narrow figure with pointed shoulders and sharp wattles at the turn of her thin jaw. It was late and the tea room would be closed before long.

Verna was there before her, her bright white hair and bright blue eyes standing out like beacons in the softly lit room.

"Good evening, Pallas." Verna's voice was soft and pillowy, like her pudgy face and figure.

"Evening," said Pallas. Without preliminaries she demanded, "How are yours?"

Verna sighed. "Not so well. Two are willing, one isn't. The little fool."

"They're all fools," said Pallas. "Two billion stupid fools. Never heard of such a place."

"They want to do everything by twos," said Verna. "They're all afraid they'll lose something if they don't pair off, pair off. They've been schooled and pushed and ordered and taught that that's the way it must be, so—" she sighed again—"that's the way it is."

"We haven't much more time. I wish we hadn't lost—" There followed a dim attempt to project "Mak," a mental designation for which there was no audible equivalent.

"Oh, dear, *stop* saying that! You're always saying that. Our first third is gone, all eaten up, and that's the way it is."

"We're two," said Pallas caustically, "and we don't want to be. Are you all right?"

"Thoroughly encysted, thank you. Pa'ak can't get to me. I'm so well encased I can barely get through to control this—" she lifted her arms and dropped them heavily on the table—"this bag of bones. And I can't telepath. I wish I could communicate with you and the others directly, instead of through this primitive creature and its endless idioms. I've even got to use that clumsy terrestrial name of yours—there's no vocalization for our real ones." Again there was an effort to identify the speaker as "Myk" and the other as "Mok," which failed.

"*I* wish I could get through to the others. Goodness! A weak signal once in a while—a mere 'come close' or 'go away'—and in between, nothing, for weeks on end."

"Oh, but they've got to stay closed up so tight! You know how the Pa'ak infection works—increasing the neurotic potential so that the virus can feed on the released nervous energy. There are two groups of three people who must come together by their own free emotional merging, or Ril's three parts and Kad's three parts can never become one again. To allow them that emotional freedom is to allow the Pa'ak virus which infests them to remain active, since they tend to be attracted to one another for neurotic reasons. At least we don't have *that* much trouble. There was so little neurosis or anything else left in these minds when we took them over that they were poor feeding grounds for Pa'ak. And that's the—"

"Verna, can you spare me that everlasting—"

"—the way it is," finished Verna inexorably. "I'm sorry, Pallas, truly. There's a horrid little pushbutton in this mind that plays that phrase off every once in a while no matter what I do. I'm rebuilding the mind as fast as I can; I'll get to it soon. I hope."

"Verna . . . " said Pallas with an air of revelation. "We can speed this thing up. I'm sure we can. Look. These fools won't group in threes. And Ril and Kad can't complete themselves unless their three hosts are emotionally ready for it. Now then." She leaned forward over her teacup. "There's no important difference between *two* groups of *three* and *three* groups of *two.*"

"You really think . . . why, Pallas, that's a *marvelous* idea. You're so clever, dear! Now the first thing we'll have to—"

They both froze in an attitude of listening.

"My word," said Verna. "That's a bad one."

"I'll go," said Pallas. "That's one of the creatures I'm guarding. Ril is in it."

"Shall I come too?"

"You stay here. I'll take a taxi and keep in touch with you. When I'm far enough away I'll triangulate. Keep watch for that signal again. Goodness! What an urgent one!"

She trotted out. Verna looked across at Pallas's untouched teacup. "She left me with the check." A sigh. "Well, that's the way it is."

The news is the artificial satellite program and flying discs . . . three-stage rockets and guilt by association.

Dr. Jonathan Prince was saying, "The world's never been in such a state. Industrialization is something you can graph, and you find a geometric increase. You can graph the incidence of psychoneuroses the same way and find almost the same curve, but it's a much larger one. I tell you, Edie, it's as if something were cultivating our little traumas and anxieties like plowed fields to increase their yield, and then feeding off them."

"But so much is being done, Jon!" his ex-wife protested.

Jon waved his empty glass. "There are 39,000 psychotherapists to how many millions of people who need their help? There's a crying need for some kind of simple, standardized therapy, and people refuse to behave either simply or according to standards. Somewhere, somehow, there's a new direction in therapy. So-called orthodox procedures as they now exist don't show enough promise. They take too long. If by some miracle of state support and streamlined education you could create therapists for everyone who needed them, you'd have what amounted to a nation or a world of full-time therapists. Someone's got to bake bread and drive buses, you know."

"What about these new therapies I've been reading about?" Edie wanted to know.

"Oh, they're a healthy sign to a certain extent; they indicate we know how sick we are. The most encouraging thing about them is their diversity. There are tools and schools and phoneys and fads. There's psychoanalysis, where the patient talks about his troubles to the therapist, and narcosynthesis, where the patient's troubles talk to the therapist, and hypnotherapy, where the therapist talks to the patient's troubles.

"There's insulin to jolt a man out of his traumas and electric shock to subconsciously frighten him out of them, and CO_2 to choke the traumas to death. And there's the pre-frontal lobotomy, the transorbital leukotomy, and the topectomy to cut the cables between a patient's expression of his aberrations and its power supply, with the bland idea that the generator will go away if you can't see it any more. And there's Reichianism which, roughly speaking, identifies Aunt Susan, who slapped you, with an aching kneecap which, when cured, cures you of Aunt Susan too.

"And there's—but why go on? The point is that the mushrooming schools of therapy show that we know we're sick; that we're anxious—but not yet anxious enough, *en masse*—to do something about it, and that we're willing to attack the problem on all salients and sectors."

"What kind of work have you been doing recently?" Edie asked.

"Electro-encephalographics, mostly. The size and shape of brainwave graphs will show a great deal once we get enough of them. And—did you know there's a measurable change in volume of the fingertips that follows brainwave incidence very closely in disturbed cases? Fascinating stuff. But sometimes I feel it's the merest dull nudging at the real problems involved. Sometimes I feel like a hard-working contour cartographer trying to record the height and grade of ocean waves. Every time you duplicate an observation to check it, there's a valley where there was a mountain a second ago.

"And sometimes I feel that if we could just turn and look in the right direction, we'd see what's doing it to us, plain as day. Here we sit with our psychological bottle of arnica and our therapeutic cold compresses, trying to cure up an attack of lumps on the headbone. And if we could only turn and look in the right place, there would be an invisible maniac with a stick, beating us over the head, whom we'd never detected before."

"You sound depressed."

"Oh, I'm not, really," he said. He stood up and stretched. "But I almost wish I'd get away from that recurrent thought of looking in a new direction; of correlating neurosis with a virus disorder. Find the virus and cure the disease. It's panacea; wishful thinking. I'm probably getting lazy."

"Not you, Jon." His ex-wife smiled at him. "Perhaps you have the answer, subconsciously, but what you've learned won't let it come out."

"Very astute. What made you say that?"

"It's a thing you used to say all the time."

He laughed and helped her up. "Edie, do you have to get up early tomorrow?"

"I'm unemployed. Didn't I tell you?"

"I didn't ask," he said ruefully. "My God, I talk a lot. Would you like to see my new lab?"

"I'd love to! Oh, I'd love it. Will it be—all right?"

"All right? Of course it—oh. I see what you mean. Priscilla. Where is she, anyway?"

"She went out. I thought you noticed. With that man who plays the guitar. Irving." She nodded toward the discarded instrument.

"I hadn't noticed," he said. Over his features slipped the poker expression of the consulting psychologist. "Who did you come with?"

"The same one. Irving. Jon, I hope Priscilla can take care of herself."

"Let's go," he said.

Faintly, and with exasperation, Ril's thought came stumblingly through to Ryl and Rul:

"How can a thinking being be so stupid? Have you ever heard a more accurate description of the Pa'ak virus than that? 'Cultivating our little traumas and anxieties like plowed fields to increase their yield, and then feeding off them.' And 'a new direction.' Why haven't these people at least extrapolated the idea of energy life? They know that matter and energy are the same. An energy virus is such a logical thing for them to think of!"

And Rul's response: "They can no more isolate their experiments from their neuroses than they can isolate their measuring instruments from gravity. Have patience. When we are able to unite again, we will have the strength to inform them."

Ril sent: "Patience? How much more time do you think we have before they start to spread the virus through this whole sector of the cosmos? They are improving rockets, aren't they? We should have sent for reinforcements. But then—how could we know we'd be trapped like this in separate entities which refuse to merge?"

"We couldn't," Ryl answered. "We still have so much to learn about these creatures. Sending for reinforcements would solve nothing."

"And we have so little time," Rul mourned. "Once they leave Earth, the Pa'ak pestilence will no longer be isolated."

Ril responded: "Unless they are cured of the disease before they leave."

"Or prevented from leaving," Ryl pointed out. "An atomic war would lower the level of culture. If there is no choice, we could force them to fight—we have the power—and thus reduce their technology to the point where space flight would be impossible."

It was a frightening idea. They broke contact in trembling silence.

They had a drink, and then coffee, and now Irving was leading her homeward. She hadn't wanted to go through the park, but it was late and he assured her that it was much shorter this way. "There are plenty of places through here where you can cut corners." It was easier not to argue. Irving commanded a flood of language at low pitch and high intensity that she could do without just now. She was tired and bored and extremely angry.

It was bad enough that Jon had deserted her for that bit of flotsam from his past. It was worse that she should have walked right past him with her hat on without his even looking up. What was worst of all was that she had let herself be so angry. She had no claims on Jonathan Prince. They were more than friends, certainly, but not any more than that.

"Who's the girl you came to the party with, Irving?" she asked.

"Oh, her. Someone trying to get a job at the plant. She's a real bright girl. Electronics engineer—can you imagine?"

"And—"

He glanced down at her. "And what? I found out she was a cold fish, that's all."

Oh, she thought. So you ditched her because you thought she was a cold fish, and scooped me up. And what does that make me? Aloud she said, "These paths wind around the park so. Are you sure it's going to take us out on the downtown side?"

"I know everything about these woods." He peered. "This way."

They turned off the blacktop walk and took a graveled path away to the right. The path was brilliantly lit by a street-lamp at the crossing of the walks, and the light followed the path in a straight band through the undergrowth. It seemed so safe . . . and then Irving turned off to still another path. She turned with him, unthinking, and blinked her eyes against a sudden, oppressive darkness.

It was a small cul de sac, completely surrounded by heavy undergrowth. As her eyes became accustomed to the dim light that filtered through the trees, she saw benches and two picnic tables. A wonderful, secluded, restful little spot, she thought—for a picnic.

"How do you like this?" whispered Irving hoarsely. He sounded as if he had been running.

"I don't," she said immediately. "It's late, Irving. This isn't getting either of us anywhere."

"Oh, I don't know," he said. He put his arms around her. She leaned away from him with her head averted, swung her handbag back and up at his face. He caught her wrist deftly and turned it behind her.

"Don't," she gasped. "Don't . . ."

"You've made your little protest like a real lady, honey, so it's on the record. Now save us some time and trouble. Let's get to it."

She kicked him. He gasped but stood solidly. There was a sharp click behind her. "Hear that?" he said. "That's my switch-blade. Push a button and zip!—seven inches of nice sharp steel. Now don't you move or make a sound, sweetheart, and this'll be fun for both of us."

Locking her against him with his left arm, he reached slowly up under the hem of her short jacket. She felt the knife against her back. It slipped coldly between her skin and the back of her low-cut dress. "Don't you move," he said again. The knife turned, sawed a little and the back strap of her brassiere parted. The knife was removed; she heard it click again. He dropped it in his jacket pocket.

"Now," he breathed, "doesn't that feel better, lamb-pie?"

She filled her lungs to scream, and instantly his hard hand was clamped over her mouth. It was a big hand, and the thumb was artfully placed so that she couldn't get her mouth open wide enough to use her teeth on it.

"Let's not wrestle," he said, his voice really gentle, pleading. "It just doesn't make sense. I'd as soon kill you as not—you know that."

She stood trembling violently, her eyes rolled up almost out of sight. Her mouth sagged open when he kissed it. Then he screamed.

His arms whipped away from her and she fell. She lay looking dully up at him. He stood straight in the dim light, stretched, his face up and twisted with pain. He had both hands, apparently, on one of his back pockets. He whirled around and her eyes followed him.

There was someone else standing there . . . someone in black. Someone who looked like a high-school teacher Priscilla had once had. Gray hair, thin, wattled face.

Moving without haste but with great purpose, the spinsterish apparition stooped, raised her skirts daintily and kicked Irving accurately in the groin. He emitted a croaking sound and dropped to a crouch, and began a small series of agonizing grunts. The old lady stepped forward as if she were dancing a minuet, put out one sensible shoe and shoved. Irving went down on his knees and elbows, his head hanging.

"Get out," said the old lady crisply. *"Now."* She clapped her hands once. The sound stiffened Irving. With a long, breathy groan he staggered to his feet, turned stupidly to get his bearings and hobbled rapidly away.

"Come on, dear." The woman got her hands under Priscilla's armpits and helped her up. She half-carried the girl over to one of the picnic tables and seated her on the bench. With an arm around Priscilla's shoulders, she held her upright while she put a large black handbag on the table. Out of it she rummaged a voluminous handkerchief which she thrust into Priscilla's hands. "Now, you sit there and cry a while."

Priscilla said, still trembling," I can't," and burst into tears.

When it was over she blew her nose weakly. "I don't . . . know what to say to you. I—he would have killed me."

"No, he wouldn't. Now while I'm alive and carry a hatpin."

"Who are you?"

"A friend. If you'll believe that, child, that's good enough for me and it'll have to be good enough for you."

"I believe that," said Priscilla. She drew a long, shuddering breath. "How can I ever thank you?"

"By paying attention to what I tell you. But you must tell me some things first. How did you ever get yourself mixed up with such an animal? You surely have better sense than that."

"Please don't scold . . . I was silly, that's all."

"You were in a tizzy, you mean. You were, weren't you?"

"Well," sniffed Priscilla, "yes. You see, I work with this doctor, and he and I—it isn't anything formal, you understand, but we work so well together and laugh at the same things, and it's . . . nice. And then he—"

"Go on."

"He was married once. Years ago. And he saw her tonight. And he didn't look at me any more. I guess I'm foolish, but I got all upset."

"Why?"

"I told you. He just wanted to talk to her. He forgot I was alive."

"That isn't why. You were upset because you were afraid he'd get together with her again."

"I—I suppose so."

"Do you want to marry him?"

"Why, I—I don't ... No, I wouldn't. It isn't that."

The old lady nodded. "You think if he married her again—or anyone else—that it would make a big difference in the work you do together, in the way he treats you?"

"I ... don't suppose there would be any difference, no," Priscilla said thoughtfully. "I'd never thought it through."

"And," continued the old lady relentlessly, "have you thought through any other possible course of action he could have taken tonight? He was married to her for some time. He apparently hasn't seen her for years. It must have been a small shock to him to find her there. Now, what else might he have done? 'Goodness gracious, there's my old used-up wife. Priscilla, let's dance.' Is that what you expected?"

At last she giggled. "You're wonderful. And you're right, you are so absolutely right. I have been sil—Oh!"

"What is it?"

"You called me Priscilla. How did you know my name? Who are you?"

"A friend. Come along, girl; you can't sit here all night." She drew the startled girl to her feet. "Here, let me look at you. Your lipstick's smeared. Over here. That's better. Can you button that jacket? I think perhaps you should. Not that it should matter if your bust *does* show, the way you brazen things dress nowadays. There now, come along."

She hurried Priscilla through the park, and when they reached the street, turned north. Priscilla tugged at the black sleeve. "Please— wait. I live *that* way." She pointed.

"I know, I know. But you're not going home just yet. Come along, child!"

"Where are you—we—going?"

"You'll see. Now listen to me. Do you trust me?"

"Oh, my goodness, yes!"

"Very well. When we get where we're going, you'll go inside alone. Don't worry now, it's perfectly safe. Once you're inside you'll do something very stupid indeed."

"I will?"

"You will. You'll turn around and try to leave. Now, then, I want you to understand that you must *not* leave. I shall be standing outside to see that you don't."

"But I—But why? What am I supposed ... where ..."

"Hush, child! You do as you're told and you'll be all right."

Priscilla walked along in silence for a time. Then she said, "All right." The old lady turned to look into the softest-smiling, most trusting face she had ever seen. She put her arm around Priscilla's shoulders and squeezed.

"You'll do," she said.

Henry Faulkner sat in a booth, far from the belly-thumping juke box and the knot of people chattering away at the head end of the bar. Henry's elbows were on the table and his thumbs, fitted carefully into the bony arches over his eyelids, supported the weight of his head. The cafe went round and round like a Czerny etude, but with a horizontal axis. The walls moved upward in front of him and down behind him, and he felt very ill. Once he had forced down three beers, and that was his established capacity; it had bloated him horribly and he'd had a backache in the morning. Tonight he'd had four double ryes.

"There he shtood," he said to one of the blonde girls who sat opposite, "nex' to the conductor, watching the orch'stra, an' sometimes he'd beat time wiz arms. When the last movement ended, th' audience rozhe up as one man an' roared. An' there he shtood, nex' to the conductor—"

"You said that before," said the girls. They spoke in unison, and the pair of them had only one voice, like the doubled leading tone in a major chord.

"There he shtood," Henry went on, "shtill beating time after the music stopped. An' the conductor, wi' *eyes* in his tears—wi' *tears* in his eyes—turned him around so he could *shee* the applause."

"What was the matter with him?" asked the girls.

"He was deaf."

"Who was?"

"Beethoven." Henry wept.

"My God. Is that what you're tying one on about?"

"You said to tell you the sad story," said Henry. "You didn't say tell you *my* sad story."

"Okay, okay. You got money, ain't you?"

Henry lifted his head and reared back to get perspective. It was then that the girl merged and became one; he realized that there had been one all along, in spite of what he had seen. That explained why they both had the same voice. He was extravagantly pleased. "Sure I got money."

"Well, come on up to my place. I'm tired uh sittin' around here."

"Very gracious," he intoned. "I shall now tell you the sad story of my laysted wife."

"What type wife?"

"I beg your pardon? I've never been married."

The girl looked perplexed. "Start over again."

"*Da capo,*" he said, with his finger beside his nose. "Very well. I repeat. I shall now tell you the story of my wasted life."

"Oh," said the girl.

"I have had the ultimate in rejections," said Henry solemnly. "I fell in love, deeply, deeply, deeply, dee—"

"Who with?" said the girl tiredly. "Get to the point and let's get out of here."

"With a string bass. A bull, as it were, fiddle." He nodded solemnly.

"Ah, fer Pete's sake," she said scornfully. She stood up. "Look, mister, I can't waste the whole night. Are you comin' or ain't you?"

Henry scowled up at her. He hadn't asked for her company. She'd just appeared there in the booth. She had niggled and nagged until he was about to tell her all the things he had come here to forget. And now she wanted to walk out. Suddenly he was furious. He, who had never raised his hand or his voice in his whole life, was suddenly so angry that he was, for a moment, blind. He growled like the open D on a bass clarinet and leaped at her. His clawed hand swept past her fluffy collar and got caught, tore the collar a little, high on the shoulder.

She squealed in routine fear. The bartender hopped up sitting on the bar and swung his thick legs over.

"What the hell's going on back there?" he demanded, pushing himself onto the floor.

The blonde said, shrilly and indignantly, exactly what she thought Henry was trying to do.

"Right there in the booth?" said a bourbon up the row.

"That I got to see," replied a beer.

They started back, followed by the rest of the customers.

The bartender reached into the booth and lifted Henry bodily out of it. Henry, sick and in a state of extreme panic, wriggled free and ran—two steps. The side of his head met the bridge of the bourbon's nose. Henry was aware of a dull crunch. There were exploding lights and he went down, rolled, got to his feet again.

The girl was screaming in a scratchy monotone somewhere around high E flat. The bourbon was sitting on the floor with blood spouting from his nose.

"*Get 'im!*" somebody barked.

Powerful hands caught Henry's thin biceps. A heavy man stood in front of him, gigantic yellow mallets of fists raised.

"Hold him tight," said the heavy man. "I'm gonna let him have it."

And then a sort of puffball with bright blue eyes was between Henry and the heavy man. In a soft, severe voice it said, "Leave him alone, you—you bullies! You let that man go, this very minute!"

Henry shook his head. He regretted the movement, but among the other things it made him experience was clearing sight. He looked at the puffball, which became a sweet-faced lady in her fifties. She had gentleness about her mouth and sheer determination in her crackling blue eyes.

"You better stay out of this, Granny," said the bartender, not unkindly. "This character's got it comin' to him."

"You let him go this instant!" said the lady, and stamped a small foot. "And that's the way it is."

"Al," said the heavy man to the bartender, "just lead this lady off to one side while I paste this bastard."

"Don't you put a hand on me."

"Watch your language, Sylvan," said the bartender to the heavy man. He put a hand on the lady's shoulder. "Come over here a sec—*uh!*"

The final syllable was his staccato response to the old lady's elbow in the pit of his stomach. That, however, was not the end of her—literally—chain reaction. She swung her crocus reticule around in a full-armed arc and brought it down on the heavy man's head. He sank to the floor without a whimper. In the same movement she put her other hand swiftly but firmly against Henry's jaw and pushed it violently. His head tipped back and smashed into the face of the man who stood behind him holding his arms. The man staggered backward, tripped, and fell, bouncing his skull off an unpadded bar stool.

"Come along, Henry," said the old lady cheerfully. She took him by the wrist as if he were a small boy whose face needed washing, and marched him out of the cafe.

On the street he gasped, "They'll chase us...."

"Naturally," said the lady. She put two fingers into her mouth and blew a piercing blast. A block and a half away, a parked taxicab slid away from the curb and came toward them. There was shouting from the cafe. The taxicab pulled up beside them. The lady whipped the door open and pushed Henry in. As four angry men shouldered out on the sidewalk, she reached deep into her reticule and snatched a dark object from it. She stood poised for a moment, and in the neon-shot half-light Henry saw what was in her hand—an old-fashioned, top-of-stove flat iron. He understood then why the heavy man had drowsed off so readily.

The lady hefted the iron and let it fly. It grazed the temple of one of the men and flew straight through a plate glass window. The man who was hit went to his knees, his hands holding his head. The other three fell all over each other trying to get back out of range. The lady skipped into the cab and said calmly, "Young man, take us away from here."

75

"Yes, *ma'am!*" said the driver in an awed tone, and let in his clutch.

They jounced along in silence for a moment, and then she leaned forward. "Driver, pull up by one of these warehouses. Henry's going to be sick."

"I'm all right," said Henry weakly. The cab stopped. The lady opened the door. "Come along!"

"No, really, I—"

The lady snapped her fingers.

"Oh, all right," said Henry sheepishly. In the black shadows by the warehouse he protested faintly, "But I don't *want* to be sick!"

"I know what's best," she said solicitously. She took his hand, spread it, and presented him with his long middle finger, point first, as if it were a clinical thermometer. "Down your throat," she ordered.

"No!" he said loudly.

"Are you going to do as you're told?"

He looked at her. "Yes."

"I'll hold your head," she said. "Go on."

She held his head.

Afterward, in the cab, he asked her timidly if she would take him home now.

"No," she said. "You play the piano, don't you, Henry?"

He nodded.

"Well, you're going to play for me." She reached forcefully into her reticule again, and his protest died on his trembling lips. "Here," she said, and handed him an old-fashioned mint.

Priscilla mounted the stairs. She had a "walking-underwater" feeling, as if she were immersed in her own reluctance. She had trod these stairs many times at night—usually downward after a perplexing, intriguing series of experiments. She did not know why she should be returning to the laboratory now, except that she had been ordered to do so. She freely admitted that if it were not for the thin, straight figure in black who waited downstairs, she would certainly be in bed by now. But there was an air of command, of complete certainty, about the old lady who had saved her that was utterly compelling.

She walked quietly down the carpeted hall. The outer door of the lab office was ajar. There was no light in the office, but a dim radiance filtered in from the lab itself, through the frosted panel of the inner door. She crossed to it and went in.

Someone gasped.

Someone said, "Priscilla!"

Priscilla said, "Excuse *me!*" and spun around. She shot through the office and out into the hall, her cheeks burning, her eyes stinging. "He—he—" she sobbed, but could not complete the thought, would not review the picture she had seen.

At the lower landing she raced to the street door, valiantly holding back the tears and the sobs that would accompany them. Her hand went out to the big brass doorknob, touched it—

As the cool metal greeted her hand she stopped.

Outside that door, standing on the walk by the iron railings, radiating strength and rectitude, would be the old lady. She would watch Priscilla come out of the building. She would probably nod her head in knowledgeable disappointment. She would doubtless say, "I told you you would want to leave, and that it would be foolish."

"But they were—" said Priscilla in audible protest.

Then came the thought of trustfulness: "Listen to me. Do you trust me?"

Priscilla took her hand away from the knob. She thought she heard the murmur of low voices upstairs.

She remembered the talk about Jon and his meeting with Edie at the party. She remembered herself saying, "I—just didn't think it through."

She turned and faced the stairs. "I can't, I can't possibly go back. Not now. Even if ... even if it didn't make any difference to me, they'd ... they'd hate me. It would be a terrible thing to do, to go back."

She turned until the big brass knob nudged her hip. Its touch projected a vivid picture into her mind—the old lady, straight and waiting in the lamplight.

She sighed and started slowly up the stairs again.

When she got to the office this time the light was on. She pushed the door open. Jon was leaning against the desk, watching it open. Edie, his ex-wife, stood by the laboratory door, her wide-spaced eyes soft and bright. For a moment no one moved. Then Edie went to Jon and stood beside him, and together they watched Priscilla with questions on their faces, and something like gentle sympathy. Or was it empathy?

Priscilla came in slowly. She went up to Edie and stopped. She said, "You're just what he needed."

The wide dark eyes filled with tears. Edie put her arms out and Priscilla was in them without quite knowing which of them had moved. When she could, Edie said, "You are so lovely, Priscilla. You're so very lovely." And Priscilla knew she was not talking about her red hair or her face.

Jon put a hand on each of their shoulders. "I don't understand what's happening here," he said, "but I have the feeling that it's good. Priscilla, why did you come back?"

She looked at him and said nothing.

"What made you come back?"

She shook her head.

"You know," he smiled, "but you're just not talking. You've never done a wiser thing than to come back. If you hadn't, Edie and I would have been driven apart just as surely as if you'd used a wedge. Am I right, Edie?

Edie nodded. "You've made us very happy."

Priscilla felt embarrassed. "You are giving me an awful lot of credit," she said in a choked voice. "I didn't really do anything. I wish I had the—the bigness or wisdom you think I have." She raised her eyes to them. "I'll try to live up to it, though. I will ..."

The phone rang.

"Now who could that—" Jon reached for it.

Priscilla took it out of his hand. "I'll take it."

Edie and Jon looked at each other. Priscilla said into the phone, "Yes ... yes, it's me. How in the world did you ... Tonight? But it's so late! Will you be there? Then so will I. Oh, you're wonderful ... yes, right away."

She hung up.

Jon said, "Who was it?"

Priscilla laughed. "A friend."

Jon touched her jaw. "All right, Miss Mysterious. What's it all about?"

"Will you do something if I ask you? You, too, Edie?"

"Oh, yes."

Priscilla laughed again. "We do have something to celebrate, don't we?" When they nodded, she laughed again. Well, come on!"

It was easier to carry the chopsticks piano-player with Derek to help, Jane concluded. She watched the rapt faces in the club. The house counted good, and it was going great, but she couldn't help thinking what it would be like if Derek hadn't been so pigheaded about little Henry. She finished her chorus and the piano took it up metronomically, nudged on the upbeats of the authoritative beat of Derek's bass. She looked at him. He was playing steadily, almost absently. His face was sullen. When he got absent-minded he wasn't colossal any more; only terrific.

The piano moved through an obvious C-sharp seventh chord to change key to F-sharp, her key for the windup. She drifted into the bridge section with a long glissando, and disgust moved into her face and Derek's in perfect synchronization as they realized that the pianist was blindly going into another 32 bars from the beginning.

Derek doubled his beat and slapped the strings hard, and the sudden flurry of sound snapped the pianist out of it. Blushing, he recovered the fluff. Jane rolled her eyes up in despair and finished the number. To scattered applause she turned to the piano and said, "Tinkle some. Derek and I are going to take ten. And while you're tinkling," she added viciously, "*practice*, huh?"

She smiled at the audience, crossed the stand and touched Derek's elbow. "I'm going behind that potted palm and flip my lid. Come catch it."

He put his bass out of harm's way and followed her into the office. She let him pass her and slump down on the desk. She banged the door.

"You—"

He looked at her sullenly. "I know what you're going to say. I threw out the best ten fingers in the business. I told you I don't want to talk about it. You don't believe that, do you?"

"I believe it," she said. Her eyes glittered. "Derek Jax, I love you."

"Cut it out."

"I'm not kidding. I'm not changing the subject, either. I love you this much. I'm going to call your hand, kid. I love you so much that I'm going to make you talk about what's with this business of Henry, or I'm going to see you walk out of here with, and into, your doghouse."

"That don't make a hell of a lot of sense, Janie," he said uncomfortably.

"No, huh? Listen, the guy I love talks to me. I understand him enough so he can talk to me. If he won't talk to me, it's because he thinks I won't understand. I think you see what I mean. I love the guy I think you are. If you won't talk about it, you're just not that guy. Maybe that doesn't mean anything to you."

"Could be," he growled. He rose and stretched. "Well, I guess I'll be going. Nice working with you, Janie."

"So long," she said. She went and opened the door.

"By God," he said, "you really mean it."

She nodded.

He licked his lips, then bit them. He sat down. "Shut the door, Janie."

She shut the door and put her head against it. He flashed her a look. "What's the matter?"

She said hoarsely, "I got something in my eye. Wait." Presently she swung around and faced him. Her smile was brilliant, her face composed. The vein in the side of her neck was thick and throbbing.

"Jane … " he said with difficulty, "that Henry—did he ever make a pass at you?"

"Why, you egghead. No! To him I'm something that makes music, like a saxophone. It's you he's interested in. Hell, did you see his face when you came in with your bass this afternoon? He'd rather play to that bass than go over the falls in a barrel with me. If that's all that was on your mind, forget it."

"You make it tough for me," he said heavily. "I'll play it through for you a note at a time. Got a stick?"

She rummaged in the desk drawer and found him a cigarette. He lit it and dragged until he coughed. She had never seen him like this. She said nothing.

He seemed to appreciate that. He glanced at her and half his mouth flashed part of a smile. Then he said, "Did I ever tell you about Danny?"

"No."

"Kids together. Kids get close. He lived down the pike. I got caught in a root one time, swimming in a rock quarry. Danny seemed to know the instant I got tangled. He couldn't swim worth a damn, but in he came. Got me out, too."

He dragged on his cigarette, still hungry, hot and harsh. The words came out, smoking. "There was a lot of stuff ... we played ball, we run away from home, we broke into an ol' house and pried loose a toilet and threw it out a fourth-floor window onto a concrete walk. We done a lot.

"We jived a lot. He had natural rhythm. We used to bang away on his ol' lady's piano. I played trumpet for a while, but what I wanted to do was play string bass. I wanted that real bad.

"We grew up and he moved away. Some lousy job trying to learn cabinet-making. Saw him a couple times. Half-starved, but real happy. I was playing bass by then, some. Had to borrow a fiddle. Wanted my own instrument *so* bad, never had the money. So one day he called me up long distance. Come over. I didn't have no trainfare, so I hitchhiked. Met him at a barrelhouse joint in town. He was real excited, dragged me out to his place. A shack—practically a shanty. When we got in sight of it he started to run. It was on fire."

Derek closed his eyes and went on talking. "We got to it and it was pretty far gone. I got there first. One wall was gone. Inside everything was burning. Danny, he—he screamed like a stung kid. He tried to jump inside. I hung on to him. Was much bigger'n him. Then

I saw it—a string bass. A full-size string bass, burning up. I sat on Danny and watched it burn. I knew why he'd moved out of town. I knew why he took up cabinet-making. I knew why he was so hungry an'—an' so happy. Made the box with his own two hands. We watched it burn and he tried to fight me because I would not let him save it. He cried. Well—*we* cried. Just two kids."

Jane said a single, unprintable word with a bookful of feeling behind it.

"We got over it. We roomed together after that. We done everything together. Crowd we ran with used to kid us about it, and that just made it better. I guess we were about nineteen then."

He squeezed out a long breath and looked up at her with stretched, blind eyes. "We had something, see? Something clean and big that never happened before, and wasn't nothing wrong with it.

"Then I come home one night and he's at the back window staring into the yard. Said he was moving out. Said we weren't doing each other any good. He was in bad shape. Somebody'd been talking to him, some lousy crumb with a sewer mouth and sewer ideas. I didn't know what it was all about. We were still just kids, see?

"Anyway, I couldn't talk him out of it. He left. He was half-crazy, all eaten up. Like the time we watched the bull-fiddle burn up. He wouldn't say what was the trouble. So after he went I milled around the joint trying to make sense out of it and I couldn't. Then I—"

Derek's voice seemed to desert him. He coughed hard and got it back. "—Then I went and looked out the window. Somebody'd wrote our names on the fence. Drew a heart around 'em.

"I never gave a damn what anyone thought, see? But Danny, he did. I guess you can't know how someone else feels, but you can get a pretty fair idea. First I was just mad, and then I pretended I was Danny looking at a thing like that, and I got an idea how bad it was. I ran out lookin' for him.

"Saw him after a time. Up by the highway, staggering a bit like he was half-soused. He wasn't, though. I ran after him. He was waiting for the light to change. There was a lot of traffic. Tried to get to him. Couldn't begin to. He sort of pitched off the curb right under oh my God I can still see it the big dual wheel it run right over his head ... " he finished in a rapid monotone.

Jane put her hand on his shoulder. Derek said, "I didn't know then and I don't know now and I never will know if he was so tore up and sick he just fell, or if he done it on purpose. All I know is I've lived ever since with the idea I killed him just by being around him so much. Don't try to talk me out of it. I know it don't make sense. I know all the right answers. But knowing don't help.

"That's the whole story."

Jane waited a long time and then said gently, "No, Derek."

He started as if he had suddenly found himself in an utterly strange place. Gradually his sense of presence returned to him and he wiped his face.

"Yeah," he said. "Your boy Henry. Danny—he played piano, Janie. I started with him. Danny played piano like nothing that ever lived except this Henry. Everything I ever drug out of a string bass was put in there first by the way he played piano. He used to sit and play like that and every once in a while grin at me. Shy.

"So I walk in here on a guy playing that kind of piano and he grins shy like that when he plays, and besides, here's that *real close* stuff around him like a fog. That Henry's a genius, Janie. And he's a—he's the type of guy they ought to use for a mold to make *people* out of. And he just wants to be near my fiddle. And me. And you want me to keep him around here until he knocks hisself off.

"Janie," he said, with agony in his voice, *"I'm not goin' through that again!"*

Jane squeezed his shoulder. She looked back over the afternoon and evening and words flitted through her mind: "You won't have to lose any sleep over him..." "Looks like you've made a conquest..." "Did he ever make a pass at you?" Aloud she told him, "I've sure said all the right things ... take a swing at me, pudd'nhead."

Derek pulled her hand close against his cheek, and pressed it there so hard it hurt her. She let him do it as long as he wanted. "I love you, Janie," he whispered. "I shoulda told you all that about Danny a long time ago."

"How could you tell till you tried?" she asked huskily. "Let's go on out there before ol' Kitten on the Keys drives all the customers away."

"I can't go in there," said Henry Faulkner in genuine panic.

"You can and you will," said the old lady firmly.

"Listen, there's a man in there who'll throw me out on sight."

"Have I been wrong yet? This is your night to do as you're told, young man, and that's the way it is."

In spite of himself he grinned. They went in through the herculite doors. Janie was just finishing a number. The piano fluffed the last chorus badly. Henry and the old lady stood in the back of the club until Derek and Jane walked off the floor.

"Now," she said briskly, "go on up there and play for me. Play anything you want to."

"But they have a piano player!"

"He's in a pet. Just go up there."

"Wh-what'll I say to him?"

"Don't say anything, silly! Just stand there. He'll go away."

He hesitated, and the lady gave him a small shove. He shambled around the dance floor and diffidently approached the piano.

The pianist was playing a dingdong version of *Stardust*. He saw Henry coming. "You again."

Henry said nothing.

"I suppose you want to take my job again."

Henry still said nothing. The man went on playing. Presently, "You can have it. How anyone can work with a couple sourpusses like that ... " He got off the stool in mid-chorus, leaving *Stardust's* garden gate musically ajar. Henry's right hand shot out and, catching the chord as if it had been syncopated instead of shut off, began molding it like a handful of soft clay. He sat down still playing.

Edie said, "I can't help feeling a little peculiar. This is wonderful, so wonderful—but there are still two of us and one of you."

"Three of us," corrected Priscilla.

"In some ways that's so," said Jon. He swallowed the rest of his

84

drink and beckoned the waiter. "Pris is the best statistician and psychological steno I've ever run across. And you're a genius with the machines. Why, between us we will do research that'll make history."

"Of course we will. But—isn't three a crowd?"

Priscilla said, without malice, "From anyone but you I'd consider that a hint. Don't worry about me. I have the most wonderful feeling that the miracles aren't finished."

"Pris, are you ever going to tell us about the miracles?"

"I don't know, Jon. Perhaps." Her eyes searched the club. Suddenly they fixed on a distant corner table. "There she is!"

"Who?" Jon twisted around. "Well, I'll be damned!"

"What is it?" asked Edie.

"Excuse me," said Jon, and rose. "Someone I've got to see." He stalked over to the corner table and glowered down at its occupants. "May I ask you what you're doing here?"

"Why, Dr. Prince!" said Pallas. "Imagine meeting you here!"

"What are you two doing here at this time of night?"

"We can go where we like," said Verna, smoothing her snowy hair, "and that's the way it is."

"There's no law against a lady having a spot at bedtime," amended Verna.

"You two never cease to amaze me," Jon said, chuckling in spite of himself. "Just be careful. I'd hate to see my prize exhibits get hurt."

They smiled up at him. "We'll be all right. We'll talk to you again later, won't we, Verna?"

"Oh, yes," said Verna. "Definitely. That's the way it is."

Still chuckling, Jon went back to his table. "There sits the damnedest pair of human beings I've encountered yet," he said as he sat down. "Three years ago they were senile psychotics, the two of them. As far as I can determine, they had no special therapy— they were in the County Home, and as mindless as a human being can get and stay alive. First thing you know they actually started feeding themselves—"

"Pallas and Verna!" said Priscilla. "You've mentioned—holy Pete! Are you sure?"

"Of course I'm sure. I'm on the Board out there. You know the case history. They have to report to me every sixty days."

"Well—I—will—be—damned," Priscilla intoned, awed.

"What is it, Pris? I didn't think you'd ever seen them. They've never been to the lab. . . . Say, how did you recognize them just now?"

"Could . . . could you bring them over?"

"Oh, come now. This celebration is only for—"

"I've heard enough to be curious about them," said Edie. "Do invite them, Jon."

He shrugged and returned to the other table. In a moment he was back with the two spinsters. He drew out chairs for them in courtly fashion, and called a waiter. Pallas ordered a double rye, no chaser. Verna smiled like a kitten and ordered scotch on the rocks. "For our colds," she explained.

"How long have you had colds?" he demanded professionally.

"Oh, dear, we don't get colds," explained Verna sweetly. "That's because we drink our liquor straight."

Dr. Jonathan Prince felt it within him to lay down the law at this point. A patient was a patient. But there was something in the air that prevented it. He found himself laughing again. He thought he saw Pallas wink at Priscilla and shake her head slightly, but he wasn't sure. He introduced the girls. Without the slightest hesitation he introduced Edie as "my wife." She colored and looked pleased.

"Listen to that music," breathed Priscilla.

"Thought you'd notice it," said Pallas, and smiled at Verna.

They all listened. It was a modal, moody, rhythmic invention, built around a circle of chords in the bass which beat, and beat, and beat on a single sonorous tone. The treble progressed evenly, regularly, tripped up on itself and ran giggling around and through the steady structure of the bass modulations, then sobered and marched again, but always full of suppressed mirth.

Priscilla was craning her neck. "I can't see him!"

Verna said, "Why don't you go up there, dear? I'm sure he would not mind."

"Oh . . . really not?" She caught Pallas's eye. Pallas gave her one firm nod. Priscilla said, "Do you mind?" She slipped out of her chair and went up past the dance floor.

"Look at her," breathed Edie. "She's got that—that 'miracle' expression again. . . . Oh, Jon, she's *so* lovely."

Jon said, looking at the spinsters, "What are you two hugging each other about?"

Henry looked up from the keyboard and smiled shyly.

"Hello," Priscilla said.

"Hello." He looked at her face, her hair, her body, her eyes. His shyness was there, and no boldness was present; he looked at her the way she listened to his music. It was personal and not aggressive. He moved over on the bench. "Sit down."

Without hesitation she did. She looked at him, too—the hawk profile, the gentle gray-green eyes. "You play beautifully."

"Listen."

He played with his eyes on her face. His hands leaped joyfully like baby goats. Then they felt awe and hummed something. Henry stopped playing by ear. He began to sight-read.

Note followed note followed note for the line of her nose, and doubled and curved and turned back for her nostrils. The theme became higher and fuller and rounded and there was her forehead, and then there were colorful waves up and back for her hair. Here was a phrase for an earlobe, and one for the turn of the cheek, and now there were mysteries, two of them, long and subdued and agleam and end-tilted, and they were her eyes. . . .

Derek came out of the office and stopped so abruptly that Jane ran into him. Before she could utter the first startled syllable, her breath was taken away in a great gasp.

Derek turned and gestured at the music. "You—"

She looked up at him, the furious eyes, the terrified trembling at the corners of his mouth. "No, Derek, so help me God, I didn't ask him to come back. I wouldn't do that, Derek. I *wouldn't*."

"You wouldn't," he agreed gently. "I know it, hon. I'm sorry. But out he goes." He strode out to the stand. Jane trotted behind him, and when they turned the corner she caught his arm so violently that her long fingernails sank into his flesh. *"Wait!"*

There was a girl on the bench with Henry, and as he played he

87

stared at her face. His eyes moved over it, his own face moved closer. His hands made music like the almost visible current which flowed between them. Their lips touched.

There was a tinkling explosion of sound from the piano that built up in fullness and sonority until Jane and Derek all but blinked their eyes, as if it were a blaze of light. And then Henry's left hand picked up a theme, a thudding, joyous melody that brought the few late-owls in the club right to their feet. He no longer looked at the girl. His eyes were closed, and his hands spoke of himself and what he felt—a great honest hunger and new riches, a shy and willing experience with a hitherto undreamed-of spectrum of sensation.

Jane and Derek looked at each other with shining eyes. Jane said, deliberately, "Son, you got a rival," and Derek laughed in sheer relieved delight.

"I'm going to get my fiddle," he said.

When Derek started to play, four people left their table and came up to the piano as if cables drew them. Hand in hand, Jon and Edie stopped close by Priscilla and stood there rapt as she, Pallas and Verna stood at the other end of the bench, their eyes glowing.

And out of the music, out of the bodies that fell into synchronization with the masterful pulse of the great viol, came a union, a blending of forces from each of six people. Each of the six had a part that was different from all of the others, but the shape of them was a major chord, infinitely complete and completely satisfying.

"Ril!"

"Oh, make it formal, KadKedKud!"

"RilRylRul, then . . ."

"If only Mak were here."

"Myk is with us, and Muk. Poor partial things, and how hard they have worked, guarding and guiding with those pitifully inadequate bodies as instruments. Come, Ril; we must decide. Now that we can operate fully, we can investigate these creatures."

Just as they had investigated, compared, computed and stored away observations on industrial techniques, strength of materials, stress and temperature and power and design, so now they took instant and total inventory of their hosts.

RilRylRul found classicism and inventiveness, tolerance and empathy in Henry. In Derek were loyalty and rugged strength and a powerful interpretive quality. In Jane was the full-blown beauty of sensualism and directive thought, and a unique stylization of the products of artistic creation.

KadKedKud separated and analyzed a splendid systematization in Priscilla, a superior grasp of applied theory in Edie, and in Jon that rarest of qualities, the associative mind—the mind that can bridge the specialties.

"A great race," said Ril, "but a sick one, badly infected with the Pa'ak pestilence."

"The wisest thing to do," reflected Kad, "would be to stimulate the virus to such an extent that humanity will impose its own quarantine—by reducing itself to savagery through atomic warfare. There is such a great chance of that, no matter what we do, that it would seem expedient to hasten the process. The object would be to force atomic warfare before space travel can begin. That at least would keep the virus out of the Galaxy, which is what we came here to effect."

"It's a temptation," conceded Ril. "And yet—what a tremendous species this human race could be! Let us stay, Kad. Let us see what we can do with them. Let us move on to other human groups, now that we know the techniques of entry and merging. With just the right pressure on exactly the right points, who knows? Perhaps we can cause them to discover how to cure themselves?

"It will be a close race," worried Kad. "We can do a great deal, but can we do it soon enough? We face three possibilities: Mankind may destroy itself through its own sick ingenuity; it may reach the stars to spread its infection; or it may find its true place as a healthy species in a healthy Cosmos. I would not predict which is more likely."

"Neither would I," Ril returned. "So if the forces are that closely balanced, I have hope for the one we join. Are you with me?"

"Agreed. Myk—Muk ... will you join us?"

Faintly, faintly came the weak response of the two paltry parts of a once powerful triad: "Back in our sector we would be considered dead. Here we have a life, and work. Of course we will help."

So they considered, and, at length, decided.

And their meeting and consideration and decision took four microseconds.

The six people looked at one another, entranced, dazed.

"It's—gone," said Jon. He wondered, then, what he meant by that.

Henry's fingers slid off the keys, and the big bass was silent. Priscilla opened her tilted eyes wide and looked about her. Edie pressed close to Jonathan, bright-faced, composed. Jane stood with her head high, her nostrils arched.

They felt as if they were suddenly living on a new plane of existence, where colors were more vivid and the hues between them more recognizable. There was a new richness to the air, and a new strength in their bodies; but most of all it was if a curtain had been lifted from their minds for the first time in their lives. They had all reached a high unity, a supreme harmony in the music a second before, but this was something completely different, infinitely more complete. "Cured" was the word that came to Jonathan. He knew instinctively that what he now felt was a new norm, and that it was humanity's birthright.

"My goodness gracious!"

Verna and Pallas stood close together, like two frightened birds, darting glances about them and twittering.

"I can't think what I'm doing here," said Pallas blankly, yet aware. "I've had one of my spells ..."

"We both have," Verna agreed. "And that's the way it is."

Jonathan looked at them, and knew them instantly as incomplete.

He raised his eyes to the rest of the people in the club, still stirring with the final rustle of applause from the magnificent burst of music they had heard, and he recognized them as sick. His mind worked with a new directiveness and brilliance to the causes of their sickness.

He turned to Edie. "We have work to do ..."

She pressed his hand, and Priscilla looked up and smiled.

Derek and Jane looked into each other's eyes, into depths neither had dreamed of before. There would be music from that, they knew.

Henry said, with all his known gentleness and none of the frightened diffidence, "Hey, you with the red hair. I love you. What's your name?" And Priscilla laughed with a sound like wings and buried her face in his shoulder.

On earth there was a new kind of partnership of three. And ...

> *The news is new aggression threatens unleashing of atomic weapons. ... President calls for universal disarmament. ... First flight to the Moon possible now with sufficient funds. ... Jonathan Prince announces virus cause of neurosis, promises possible cure of all mental diseases. ...*

Watch your local newspapers for latest developments.

Make Room for Me

"WE SHALL NEVER SEE *him again . . . there will be no more argu-*
ments, no more pleasant thinking with Eudiche," mourned Torth
to the other Titan.

"*Come now. Don't be so pessimistic,"* said Larit, stroking the
machine. *"The idea of dissociation has horrified you, that's all. There
is every chance that his components will fuse."*

"*So involved, so very involved,"* Torth fretted. *"Is there really
no way to send the complete psyche?"*

"*Apparently not. The crystals are of a limited capacity, you know.
If we grow them larger, they cannot retain a psychic particle. If we
sent all three encased particles together, their interaction would break
down the crystals chemically. They must be sent separately."*

"*But—horrible! How can one third of a psyche live alone?"*

"*Biologically, you know perfectly well. Psychologically, you need
only look about you. You will find a single psyche only in each of
our gracious hosts—"*

"*—gracious indeed,"* muttered Torth, *"and gracious they will
remain, or die."*

"*—and each of the natives on the planet to which we sent Eudiche
has but one psyche.*

"*How then can he occupy three of them?"*

"*Torth, you insist on asking questions requiring a higher tech-
nological comprehension than yours to understand,"* replied the
other in annoyance. *"There are closer ties than physical proximity.
Eudiche will avail himself of them. Let that suffice."* More kindly,
he added, *"Eudiche will be all right. Wait; just wait."**

---

*The author apologizes for this poor translation of the Titan personal pronoun,
which, in the original, is singular and plural, masculine and feminine, and has no
counterpart in our tongue.

The statue of Ben Franklin, by the very weight of its greyness, sobered the green sparkle of the campus. At the foot of the benevolent image the trio stood—Vaughn, tiny, with long braids of flaxen hair; Dran, slender and aquiline, and—apart from the others, as usual—Manuel, with heavy shoulders and deep horizontal creases over his thick brows.

Dran smiled at some chattering coeds who passed, then slanted his narrow face toward the semi-circle of stone buildings. "After three years," he said, "I've gotten over being delighted by my own uniqueness—the three miserable years it took me to convince myself that distinction and difference are not synonymous. And now that I'm *of* this place—no longer on the outside looking in, or on the inside looking on, I—"

"Who's so exceptional?" growled Manuel, moving closer. "Aside from the runt here, who never will get the knack of being a human being."

"Are you a specimen of humanity?" asked the girl stormily. "Manuel, I don't expect compliments from you, but I wish you'd try courtesy. Now listen. I have something to tell you. I—"

"Wait a minute," said Dran, "I have something more important, whatever you have on your mind. I've got the answer—for me, any-way—to this whole question of being the same as everyone else and being different at the same time. I—"

"You said it all last night," said Vaughn wearily. "Only you were so full of sherry that you didn't know what you were saying. I quote: 'Vaughn, not only your charming person but your poetry would be a lot more popular if you wouldn't hide behind this closed door of non-aggression and restraint.' Well, I've been thinking about that, and I—"

"Manuel," Dran interrupted, "you've got muscles. Throttle her, will you? Just a little. Just until I can put a predicate on this subject."

"I'd love to get started on that job," grinned Manuel, licking his lips. "Imagine how those wall eyes would pop."

"Keep your hands off me, animal," Vaughn hissed. "Dran, I'm trying to—"

"I will not be stopped," said Dran. With a gesture completely characteristic, he knocked back a strand of his red-gold hair, scattering ashes from his cigarette through it. "Be quiet and listen. You two have held still for a lot of my mouthings and gnashings of teeth about my being a white monkey—the one all the brown monkeys will tear to pieces just because he's different. Well, I have the solution."

"Get to the point," Manuel grunted. "It could be that I got a speech to make, too."

"Not until I've told you—" Vaughn began.

"Shut up, both of you," said Dran. "Especially you, Vaughn. All right. What are we here for?"

"To get a degree."

"We are not. At least, I'm not," said Dran. "The more I think of it, the less I think school teaches you anything. Oh, sure, there are some encyclopaedics that you sponge up, but that's secondary. A school's real function is to teach you how to learn. Period."

"All right—then what about the degree?"

"That's just to convince other people that you have learned how to learn. Or to convince yourself, if you're not sure. What I'm driving at, is that *I'm* sure. I know all I need to know about how to learn. I'm leaving."

There was a stunned silence. Vaughn looked slowly from one to the other. Dran's eyebrows went up. "I didn't expect such a dramatic effect. Vaughn...? Say something!"

"Y—you've been reading my script!" she murmured. Her eyes were huge.

"What do you mean?"

"Why—I've been thinking .. For more than a year I've known what I wanted to do. And this—" she waved a hand at the grey buildings—"this hasn't been it. This ... interferes. And I wanted to tell you about that, and that you mustn't think it means that I've finished learning. I want to learn a world of things—but not here."

Manuel released a short bark of laughter. "You mean you made a great big decision—all by yourself?"

"I'll make a decision about you one of these days, now that I've learned the technique," she spat. "Dran ... what are you going to do? Where are you going?"

"I have something lined up. Advertising—direct mail. It isn't too tough. I'll stay with that for a couple of years. See how the other half lives. The half with money, that is. When I'm ready, I'll drop it and write a novel. It'll be highly successful."

"Real cocky," said Manuel.

"Well, damn it, it will be. With me. *I'll* like it. So far as I'm concerned it will be successful. And what about you, Vaughn?"

"I have a little money. Not much. But I'll manage. I'll write poems." She smiled. "They'll be successful, too."

"Good thing you guys don't have to depend on what anyone else thinks," Manuel grunted. "Me, I do it the way the man wants it done or else."

"But you please yourself doing it," Dran said.

"Huh? I—never thought of it like that. I guess you're right. Well." He looked from Vaughn to Dran and back. They suddenly spoke, almost in unison. "Manuel! What are you going to—" and—"Manuel! What will you do now?"

"Me? I'll make out. You two don't think I *need* you?"

Vaughn's eyes grew bright. Dran put an understanding hand on her shoulder. He said, "Who writes this plot? What a switch! Manuel, of all people, clinging to these walls with the rest of the ivy, while Vaughn and I try our wings."

"Sometimes you characters give me a pain in the back of my lap," said Manuel abruptly. "I hang around with you and listen to simple-minded gobbledegook in yard-long language, if it's you talking, Dran, and pink-and-purple sissification from the brat here. Why I do it I'll never know. And it goes that way up to the last gasp. So you're going to leave. Dran has to make a speech, real logical. Vaughn has to blow out a sigh and get misty-eyed." He spat.

"How would you handle it?" Dran asked, amused. Vaughn stared at Manuel whitely.

"Me? You really want to know?"

"This I want to hear," said Vaughn between her teeth.

"I'd wait a while—a long while—until neither of you was talking. Then I'd say, 'I joined the Marines yesterday.' And you'd both look at me a little sad. There's supposed to be something wrong with coming right out and saying something. Let's see. Suppose I do it the way Vaughn would want me to." He tugged at an imaginary braid and thrust out his lower lip in a lampoon of Vaughn's full mouth. He sighed gustily. "I have felt . . ." He paused to flutter his eyelashes. "I have felt the call to arms," he said in a histrionic whisper. He gazed off into the middle distance. "I have heard the sound of trumpets. The drums stir in my blood." He pounded his temples with his fists. "I can't stand it—I can't! Glory beckons. I will away to foreign strands."

Vaughn turned on her heel, though she made no effort to walk away. Dran roared with laughter.

"And suppose I'm you," said Manuel, his face taut with a suppressed grin. He leaned easily against the base of the statue and crossed his legs. He flung his head back. "Zeno of Miletus," he intoned, "in reflecting on the cromislon of the fortiseetus, was wont to refer to a razor as 'a check for a short beard.' While shaving this morning I correlated 'lather' with 'leather' and, seeing some of it on my neck, I recalled the old French proverb, 'Jeanne D'Arc,' which means: The light is out in the bathroom. The integration was complete. If the light was out I could no longer shave. Therefore I can not go on like this. Also there was this matter of the neck. I shall join the Marines. Q. E. D., which means thus spake Zarathusiasm."

Dran chuckled. Vaughn made a furious effort, failed, and burst out laughing. When it subsided, Manuel said soberly, "I did."

"You did what?"

"I joined the Marines yesterday."

Dran paled. Manuel looked at him in open astonishment. He had never seen Dran without an instant response before. And Vaughn clutched at his arms. "You didn't! You couldn't! Manuel . . . Manuel . . . the uniform . . . the pain . . . you'll be *killed!*"

"Yup. But slowly. In agony. And as I lie there in the growing dark, a sweet thought will sustain me. I'll never again see another line of your lousy poetry. For Christ's sake!" he bellowed suddenly. "Get off that tragic kick, stupid! I'll be all right."

"What did you go and do a thing like that for?" Dran asked slowly.

"What are you and the reptile leaving for?" Manuel returned. "The same thing. This place has taught me all it can—for me. I'm going where I'll know who's my boss, and I'll know who takes orders from me. What I'll wear, where I'll live—someone else can decide that. Meantime I'll work in communications, which I'd be doing anyway, but someone else will buy the equipment and materials."

"You'll be caged. You'll never be free," said Vaughn.

"Free for what? To starve? Free to argue with salesmen and land-lords? Nuts. I'll go and work with things I can measure, work with my hands, while you two are ex-prassing your tortured souls. What would you like to see me do instead? Take up writing sonnets that nobody'll ever read? Suppose I do that, and *you* go join the Marines."

Dran touched Vaughn's arm. "He's right, Vaughn. What he's doing would be wrong for you, or for me, but it's right for him."

"I don't ... I don't know what to do," she mourned.

"I do," said Manuel. "Let's go eat."

"We are parasites," said the Titan, "which is the initial measure of our intelligence."

Torth said, "Our intelligence doesn't make it possible for us to survive on Titan."

"It's an impasse. The very act of settling the three components of our psyche into the brains of the natives gives us a home—and shortens the life of the native."

"Wouldn't that be true of the bipeds on the third planet?"

"To a degree," admitted the other. "But they are long-lived—and there are three billion of them."

"And how would we affect them?"

"Just as we affect the natives here."

Torth made the emanation which signified amusement. "That should make them very unhappy."

"You speak of a matter of no importance," said the other irritably. "And it is not true. They will be as incapable of expressing unhappiness as anything else." He applied himself again to the machine, with which he was tracking the three crystalline casings which carried Eudiche on his Earthward journey.

After dinner they went to a concert. They sat in their favorite seats—the loges—and waited, each wrapped in his own thoughts. Dran stared at the dusty carved figures under the ceiling. Manuel sketched busily—a power-operated shock absorber, this time. Between them Vaughn sat, withdrawn and dreamy, turning night-thoughts into free verse.

They straightened as the conductor appeared and crossed the platform, amid applause which sounded like dead leaves under his feet. When he raised his baton, Vaughn glanced swiftly at the faces of the other two, and then they pressed forward in unison.

It was Bach—the *Passacaglia and Fugue in C Minor.* The music stepped and spiralled solemnly around them, enclosing them in a splendid privacy. They were separate from the rest of the audience, drawn to each other. Manuel and Dran moved slightly toward Vaughn, until their shoulders touched. Their eyes fixed unmoving on the orchestra.

At the last balanced, benevolent crescendo they rose together and left, ahead of the crowd. None of them cared to talk, strangely. They walked swiftly through the dark streets to a brightly lit little restaurant several blocks from the Academy.

In a high-walled booth, they smiled to each other as if acknowledging a rich secret. Then Vaughn's eyes dropped; she pulled at her fingers and sighed.

"No effusions from you, please," said Dran—possibly more coldly than he intended. "We all felt it, whatever it was. Don't mess it up."

Vaughn's gaze was up again, shocked. Manuel said, with an astonishing gentleness, with difficulty, "I was—somewhere else, but you were with me. And we all seemed to be—to be walking, or climbing ..." He shook his massive head. "Nuts. I must be thirsty or something. What do you want, runt? Dran?"

Vaughn didn't answer. She was staring at Dran, her violet eyes dark with hurt.

"Speak up, chicken. I didn't mean to crush you. I just didn't feel like listening to an iambic extravagance. Something happened to all of us."

"Thanks f-for crediting me with so little sensitivity that you think I didn't feel it. That you think I'd spoil it!"

"Not too little sensitivity. Too much—*and* out of control. I'm sorry," Dran relented. "Let's order." He turned to Manuel, and froze in surprise at the look in the other's face. It was a look of struggling, as if unwelcome forces were waking within him, disturbing the rough, familiar patterns of his thinking.

Joe passed, flashy, noisy, wide open for hurt. The trio had often discussed Joe. Superficially, he was pushing into their group because of Vaughn, who appeared to make him quite breathless. Dran had once said, however, that it went deeper than that. Joe could not abide a liaison that he couldn't understand. Joe called, "Hi! As I live and bleed, it's the internal triangle. Nice to see you, Vaughn. When am I going to do it on purpose instead of by accident?"

"Is this drip necessary?" Manuel muttered.

"I'll see you soon, Joe," Vaughn said, smiling at him. "We have a class together tomorrow. I'll talk to you about it then." Her nod was a warm touch, and a dismissal. Joe appeared about to speak, thought better of it, waved and went away.

"That impossible idiot," growled Dran. "A more quintessential jerk I have yet to meet."

"Oh, Dran! He's not bad! Just undeveloped. Of course, he isn't one of *us,* but he's fun all the same. He reads good poetry, and he's quite a—"

Manuel brought his hand down with a crash. *"That's* what I was after. 'One of us.' What do you mean, 'one of us?' Who joins this union? I'm not 'one of us.' You two have more in common than you have with me."

Vaughn touched his hand. "Manuel," she said softly. "Oh, Manuel! Why, everyone links us together. I—I know I do. So much so that until now I didn't think it required questioning. It's something you accept as natural."

Dran's eyes brightened. "Wait, Vaughn. Let's not call it natural. Let's examine it. See what we get. I've been chewing on it since the business with the music tonight anyway."

Manuel shrugged. "Okay. What do the runt and I share after all? You and I can agree on politics, and we have one or two mechanical interests. But you, Vaughn—you ..." He wet his lips. "Hell!" he exploded. "You're—useless!"

"I can ignore that," said Vaughn, very obviously ignoring nothing, "because you are only trying to hurt me."

"Hold on," said Dran easily. "I think this is worth an effort to avoid that kind of emotional smokescreen. You particularly, Manny. You sound resentful, and I don't know that you have anything to resent."

"She makes me mad, that's all. Look—there are a lot of useful things in the world—lock washers .. cotter pins. But this—this dame! You couldn't use her for a paperweight. She's a worm trying to be a snake. You can't approach her logically. I can get to you that way, Dran, though I'll admit the going gets a little swampy sometimes."

"Perhaps this thing we have," said Vaughn softly, "is more than emotion, or intellect, or any of those things."

"Here we go again," snorted Manuel.

"A mystic entity or something?" Dran chuckled. "I doubt it. But there is something between us—all of us. It isn't limited to any two. We all belong. I'm not sure of what it's for, or even if I like it. But I'm not prepared to deny it. You aren't either, Manny."

"Manuel," said Vaughn urgently. She reached across and touched him, as if she wanted to press her eager words into him. "Manuel—haven't you ever felt it even a little? Didn't you, tonight? Didn't you? In your own terms.... Manuel, just this once, I'd like to know honestly, without any sneers."

Manuel glowered at her, hesitated, then said, "What if I have?" truculently. In a gentler tone, he added, "Oh, I have, all right. Once or twice. It—like I said, damn it, it makes me mad. I don't like getting pushed around by something I don't understand. It'll probably stop when I get away from here, and good riddance to it."

Vaughn touched her knuckles to her teeth. She whispered, "To me, it's something to treasure."

Dran grinned at her. "If you like it it's got to be fragile, hm?

Vaughn, it isn't. And I think Manny's in for a surprise if he thinks distance is going to make any difference."

"I have hopes," Manuel said sullenly.

Dran spread his hands on the table and looked at them. "Vaughn stands in awe of this—this thing we have, and to Manuel it's like a dose of crabs. Excuse me, chicken. Far as I'm concerned, it's something that will bear watching. I can't analyze it now. If it gets weaker I will be able to analyze it even less. If it gets stronger it will show its nature no matter what I do. So I'm going to relax and enjoy it. I can say this much ..." He paused, frowning, searching for words. "There is a lowest common denominator for us. We're all way off balance. And our imbalances are utterly different in kind, and negligibly different in degree."

Vaughn stared dully. Manuel said, "Huh?"

Dran said, more carefully, "Vaughn's all pastels and poetry. Manuel's all tools and technology. I'm—"

"All crap and complication," said Manuel.

"Manuel!"

Dran laughed. "He's probably right, Vaughn. Anyway, we're all lopsided to the same degree, which is a lot, and that's the only real similarity between us. If we three were one person, it'd be a somebody, that's for sure."

"It'd be an insect," Manuel scowled. "Six legs." He looked at Vaughn. "With your head. No one'd know the difference."

"You're ichor-noclastic," said Dran. Vaughn groaned. Manuel said, "That was one of those puns. The only part I got was the 'corn'. Where the hell's the waiter?"

"Why Eudiche?" Torth fretted. "Why couldn't they send someone else?"

"Eudiche is expendable," said the other parasite shortly.

"Why? His balance is so perfect ..."

"Answer restricted. Go away. One-third of his psyche has found a host and is settling in. The observations are exceedingly difficult, because of the subtlety of Eudiche's operations. And you are most exasperating. "

For the third time in a week, Vaughn was lunching with Joe—a remarkable thing, considering that in the two years since her departure from the University she had seen less and less of old acquaintances. But after all—Joe was easy to be with because she didn't have to pretend. She could be as moody as she chose. He would patiently listen to her long and misty reflections, and let her recite poetry without protest. The meetings did not hurt her, and Joe seemed to enjoy them so. . . .

But Joe had something to offer this time, rather than something to take. As the waitress took their dessert order and left, he gently placed a little plush box beside her coffee cup. "Won't you consider it at all?" he asked diffidently.

Her hand was on the box, reflexively, before she realized what it was. Then she looked at him. Thoughts, feelings, swirled about each other within her, like petals, paper, dust and moths in a small sudden whirlwind. Her eyes fixed on his shy, anxious face, and she realized that she had seldom looked directly at him .. and that he was good to look at. She looked at the box and back at him, and then closed her violet eyes. Joe as a suitor, as a potential lover, was an utterly new idea to her. Joe as a bright-faced, carefully considerate *thing* was not Joe with hands, Joe with a body, Joe with habit patterns and a career and toothpaste and beneficiaries for life insurance. She felt flattered and bewildered and uncertain, and—warm.

And then something happened. It was as if an indefinable presence had raised its head and was listening. This alien attentiveness added a facet to the consideration of Joe. It made the acceptance or rejection of Joe a more significant thing than it had been. The warmth was still there, but it was gradually overlaid by a—a knowledge that created a special caution, a particular inviolability.

She smiled softly then, and her hand lifted away from the box.

"There's nothing final about an engagement," Joe said. "It would be up to you. Every minute. You could give me back the ring any time. I'd never ask you why. I'd understand, or try to."

"Joe." She put out her hand, almost touched him, then drew it back. "I . . . you're so *very* sweet, and this is a splendid compliment.

But I can't do it. I— If I succeeded in persuading myself into it, I'd only regret it, and punish you."

"Umm," mused Joe. His eyes were narrowed, shrewd and hurt. "Tied up, huh? Still carrying the same old torch"

"The same—" Vaughn's eyes were wide.

"That Dran Hamilton character," said Joe tiredly, almost vindictively. He reached for the ring box. "Part two of the unholy trio—"

"*Stop it!*"

It was the first time he had seen her gentle violet eyes blazing. It was probably the first time they ever had. Then she picked up her gloves and said quietly, "I'd like to go now, Joe, if you don't mind."

"But—but Vaughn—what did I—I didn't mean any—"

"I know, I know," she said wearily. "Why, I haven't even thought about them for a long time. For too long. Perhaps I should have. I— *know* I should have. Joe, I have to go. I've got to get out of here. It's too small. Too many people, too many cheap little lights. I need some sun."

Almost frightened, he paid the check and followed her out. She was walking as if she were alone. He hesitated, then ran to catch up with her.

"It's a thing that you couldn't understand," she said dully when he drew alongside. She did not look up; for all he knew she may have been talking before he reached her. She went on, "There were three of us, and that's not supposed to be right. Twos, and twos, and twos, all through literature and the movies and the soap operas. This is something different. Or maybe it isn't different. Maybe it's wrong, maybe I'm too stupid to understand. . . . Joe, I'm sorry. Truly I am. I've been very selfish and unkind." There was that in her voice which stopped him. He stood on the pavement watching her move away. He shook his head, took one step, shook his head again, and then turned and plunged blindly back the way he had come.

"You're getting old," said Torth maliciously.

"Go away," said the other. "With two particles assimilated and the third about to be, matters have reached a critical point."

"*There is nothing you could do about it no matter what happened,*" said Torth.

"*Will you go away? What did you come for, anyway?*"

"*I was having an extrapolative session with another triad,*" Torth explained. "*Subject: is the Eudiche experiment a hoax? Conclusion: it could be. Corollary: it might as well be, for all it has benefited our race. I came for your comments on that. You are an unpleasant and preoccupied entity, but for all that you are an authority.*"

The old one answered with angry evenness: "*Answers: The Eudiche experiment is no hoax. It will benefit the race. As soon as Eudiche has perfected his fusion technique, we shall emigrate. Our crystalline casings are dust-motes to the bipeds of the third planet; our psychic existence will be all but unnoticeable to them until we synthesize. When we do, they will live for us, which is right and just. They will cease thinking their own thoughts, they will discontinue their single-minded activities. They will become fat and healthy and gracious as hosts.*"

"*But observations indicate that they feed themselves largely by tilling the soil, that they combat the rigors of their climate by manufacturing artificial skins and complex dwelling shelters. If we should stop all that activity, they will die off, and we—*"

"*You always were a worrier, Torth,*" interrupted the other. "*Know, then, that there are many of them and few of us. Each of us will occupy three of them, and those three will work together to keep themselves fed and us contented. The groups of three will be hidden in the mass of bipeds, having little or no physical contact with one another and remaining largely undetected. They will slaughter as they become hungry; after all, they are also flesh-eaters, and the reservoir of unoccupied bipeds will be large indeed. If, after we get there, the bipeds never plant another seed nor build another dwelling, their own species will still supply an inexhaustible supply of food purely by existing to be slaughtered as needed. They breed fast and live long.*"

Torth saluted the other. "*We are indeed entering upon an era of plenty. Your report is most encouraging. Our present hosts are small, few, and too easy to kill. I assume that the bipeds have somewhat the same minuscule intelligence?*

"The bipeds of the third planet," said the other didactically, "have mental powers several hundred times as powerful as do those we have dominated here. We can still take them over, of course, but it will be troublesome. Look at the length of time it is taking Eudiche. However, the reward is great. Once we have disrupted their group efforts by scattering our triads among them, I can predict an eternity of intriguing huntings and killings in order for our hosts to feed themselves. Between times, life will be a bountiful feast of their vital energies.

"Now, leave me, Torth. As soon as the final part of Eudiche's triad is settled in, we can expect the synthesis, by which he will come into full operation as an entity again. And that I want to observe. He has chosen well, and his three seeds are sprouting on fertile soil indeed."

"You have been uncharacteristically polite and helpful," conceded Torth. He left.

Dranley Hamilton drank the highball with the cold realization that it was one too many, and went on talking cleverly about his book. It was easy to do, because for him it was so easy to define what these fawning critics, publishers, club-women and hangers-on wanted him to say. He was a little disgusted with his book, himself, and with these people, and he was enjoying his disgust immensely, purely because he was aware of it and of his groundless sense of superiority.

Then there was a sudden, powerful agreement within him, compounded of noise, heat, stupidity and that last highball, which made him turn abruptly, to let a press-agent's schooled wisecrack spend itself on his shoulder blades as he elbowed his way through the room to the terrace doors. Outside, he stood with his arms on the parapet, looking out over the city and thinking, "Now, that didn't do me any good. I'm acting like something from the Village. Art for art's sake. What's the matter with me anyway?"

There was a light step behind him. "Hello, Dranley Hamilton."

"Oh—it's you." He took in the russet hair, the blend of blendings which she used for a complexion. He had not noticed her before. "Do you know I have hung around this literary cackle-factory for the past two hours only because you were here and I wanted to get you alone?"

"Well!" said the girl. Then, with the same word in a totally different language, she added, "Well?"

He leaned back against the parapet and studied her tilted eyes. "No," he said finally. "No. I guess I was thinking of somebody else. Or maybe even something else."

Her real defenses went up in place of the party set. "Excuse *me!*" she said coldly.

"Oh, think nothing of it," he responded. He slapped her shoulder as if it were the withers of a friendly horse, and went back to the reception. *That was lousy,* he thought. *What's the matter with me?*

"Dran," It was Mike Pontif, from his publisher's publicity department. "You got that statement up about your next novel?"

"Next novel?" Dran looked at him thoughtfully. "There's not going to be a next novel. Not until I catch up on .. something I should be doing instead." At the publicity man's bewildered expression, he added, "Going to bone up on biology."

"Oh," said the man, and winked. "Always kidding."

Dran was not kidding.

Manuel crumpled up the letter and hurled it into the corner of the communications shack. He shouldered through the door and went out on the beach, his boots thudding almost painfully down on the rough white coral sand. He drove his feet into the gritting stuff, stamping so that the heavy muscles of his thighs felt it. He scooped up the stripped backbone of a palm frond and cut at the wet sand by the water's edge as he walked, feeling the alternate pull of shoulders and chest.

He needed something. It wasn't women or liquor or people or solitude. It wasn't building or fighting or laughter. He didn't even need it badly. What he did want badly was to find out what this gentle, steady, omnipresent need was. He was sick of trying this and that to see if it would stop this infernal tugging.

He stopped and stared out to sea. The thick furrows across his forehead deepened as he thought about the sea, and the way people wrote about it. It was always alive, or mysterious, or restless, or something. Why were people always hanging mysterious qualities on what should be commonplace? He was impatient with all that icky business.

"It's just wet salt and distance," he muttered. Then he spat, furious with himself, thinking how breathless the runt would be if she heard him say such a hunk of foolishness. He turned and strode back to the shack, feeling the sun too hot on the back of his neck, knowing he should have worn his helmet. He kicked open the screen door, blinked a moment against the indoor dimness, and went to the corner. He picked up the letter and smoothed it out.

> *"From some remembered world*
> *We broke adrift*
> *Like lonely stars*
> *Divided at their birth.*
>
> *For some remembered dream*
> *We wait, and search*
> *With riven hearts*
> *A vast and alien earth ..."*

With the poem in his hand, Manuel glared around at useful things—the transmitter, the scrambler, the power supply. He looked at worthwhile things—the etched aluminum bracelets, the carved teak, the square-knotted belt he had made. And he looked at those other things, so meticulously machined, so costly in time and effort, so puzzling in function, that he had also made without knowing why. He shook the paper as if he wanted to hurt it. Why did she write such stuff? And why send it to him? What good was it?

He carried it to the desk, ripped out his personal file, and put it away. He filed it with Dran Hamilton's letters. He had no file for the runt's stuff.

When she concluded that she loved Dran, Vaughn wrote and said so, abruptly and with thoroughness. His answering telegram made her laugh and cry. It read:

NONSENSE, CHICKEN! ROMANTIC LOVE WRONG DIAGNOSIS. I
JUDGE IT A CONVENTIONAL POETIC IMPULSE BETTER CONFINED
TO PAPER. A CASE OF VERSE COME VERSE SERVED. TAKE A COLD
SHOWER AND GO WRITE YOURSELF A SONNET. BESIDES, WHAT
ABOUT MANUEL? HE ARRIVES, INCIDENTALLY, NEW YEAR'S EVE
AND INTENDS MEETING ME AT YOUR HOUSE. OKAY?

Dran arrived first, looking expensive and careless and, to Vaughn,
completely enchanting. He bounded up the front steps, swung her
off her feet and three times around before he kissed her, the way he
used to do when they were children. For a long while they could say
nothing but commonplaces, though their eyes had other things to
suggest.

Dran leaned back in a kitchen chair as if it were a chaise longue
and fitted a cigarette to a long ivory holder. "The holder?" he chattered. "Pure affectation. It does me good. Sometimes it makes me
laugh at myself, which is healthy, and sometimes it makes me feel
fastidious, which is harmless. You look wonderful with your hair
down. Never pin it up or cut it again. Manuel's just turned down a
commission. He ought to arrive about six, which gives us plenty of
time to whirl the wordage. I liked your latest poems. I think I can
help you get a collection published. The stuff's still too thin in the
wrong places, though. So are you."

Vaughn turned down the gas under the percolator and set out
cups. "You do look the successful young author. Oh, Dran, I'm *so*
glad to see you!"

He took her hand, smiled up into her radiant face. "I'm glad too,
chicken. You had me worried there for a while, with that love
business."

Vaughn's eyes stopped seeing him for a moment. "I was—silly,
I suppose," she whispered.

"Could be," he said cheerfully. "I'll tell you, hon—I like women.
Without question there's a woman somewhere on earth that will
make me go pitty-pat, quit drinking, write nothing but happy endings, and eat what's given to me instead of what I want. Maybe I've

already met her and don't realize it. But one thing I'm sure of is that you're not that woman."

"What makes you so sure?"

"The same thing that makes you sure of it. You had a momentary lapse, it seems, but—come now; do you love me?"

"I wish Manuel would get here."

"Isn't that irrelevant?

"No."

Then the coffee boiled over and the thread was lost.

They talked about Dran's book until Manuel arrived. The book was a strange one—one of those which captivates or infuriates, with no reader-reactions between the extremes. There were probably far more people who were annoyed by it than not, "which," said Dran, "is one of the few things the book has in common with its author."

"That remark," laughed Vaughn, "is the first you have made which sounded the way your picture in the *Literary Review* looked. It was awful. The decadent dilettante—the bored and viceful youth."

"It sells books," he said. "It's the only male answer to the busty book-jacket, or breast seller. I call it my frontispiece pose; separate but uplifted."

"And doubly false," snapped Vaughn. When he had quieted, she said, "but the book, Dran. There was one thing in there really worth mentioning—between us. The thing the critics liked the least."

"Oh—the dancer? Yes—they all said she was always present, never seen. Too little character for such a big influence."

"That's what I meant," said Vaughn. "I know and you know—and Manuel? We'll ask him—that the dancer wasn't a person at all, but an omnipresent idea, a pressure. Right?"

"Something like that cosmic search theme that keeps pushing you around in your work," he agreed. "I wonder what Manuel's counterpart is. It would have to be something he'd turn on a lathe."

Vaughn smiled. And then there was a heavy tread on the porch, the front door flew open, and the room was full of Manuel. "Hi, Dran. Where's the runt? Come out from under the furniture, you little—oh. There you are. Holy cow," he bellowed. "Holy sufferin' sepoys! You've shrunk!"

Dran threw up his hands. "Sepoys. Foreign background. Authentic touch."

Vaughn came forward and put out a demure hand. "I haven't shrunk, Manuel. It's you. You're thicker and wider than ever."

He took her hand, squeezed it, apologized when she yelped, rubbed his knuckles into her scalp until she yelped again, and threw himself onto the divan. "Lord, it's cold. Let's get going. Do something about this New Year's Eve and welcome home and stuff."

"Can't we just stay here and talk awhile?" asked Vaughn in rumpled petulance.

"What's the matter, runt?" Manuel asked in sudden concern, for Vaughn's eyes were filling.

Dran grinned. "I come in here, ice-cold and intellectual, and kiss the lass soundly. You come flying through the door, Lochinvar, shake hands with her and then proceed to roll her around like a puppy. Like the song says—try a little tenderness."

"You be quiet!" Vaughn almost shouted.

"Oh, so that's what you want." He strode across to Vaughn, brushed aside her protecting arms, and kissed her carefully in the exact center of the forehead. "Consider yourself smootched," he growled, "and we'll have no more of this lollygagging. Vaughn, you're acting like an abandoned woman."

Vaughn laced her anger with laughter as she said, "Abandoned is right. Now wait while I get my coat."

"I brought something back with me," Manuel said.

They were at a corner table at Enrique's, immersed in the privacy of noise, lights, and people. "What is it?" asked Vaughn. "Something special in costume jewelry?"

"Always want gilding, don't you, lily? Yes, I have the usual cargo. But that's not what I mean."

"Quell your greed," said Dran. "What is it, Manny?"

"It's a . . ." He swizzled his drink. "It's a machine. I don't know what it is."

"You don't—but what does it do? What's it made of?"

"Wire and a casting and a machined tube and ceramics, and I built it myself and I don't know what it does."

"I hate guessing games," said Dran petulantly.

Vaughn touched his arm, "Leave him alone, Dran. Can't you see he's bothered about it?" She turned quickly to the Marine, stroked the ribbons on his chest. "Talk about something else if you want to. What are these for?" she asked solicitously.

Manuel looked down at the ribbons, then thumbed the catch and removed them. He dropped them into Vaughn's hand. "For you," he said, his eyes glinting. "As a reward for talking like a hot damned civilian. I won't need 'em any more. My hitch is up; I'm out."

"Why, Manuel?"

"It's ... I get—spells, sort of." He said it as if he were confessing to leprosy or even body odor. "Trances, like. Nobody knows about it. I wanted to get out from under before the brass wised up."

Vaughn, whose terror of "the ills our flesh is heir to" amounted to a neurosis, gasped and said, "Oh! What is it? Are you sick? What do you think it is? Don't you think you ought to have an examination right away? Where does it hurt? Maybe it's a—"

Dran put an arm around her shoulders and his other hand firmly over her mouth. "Go on, Manny."

"Thanks, Dran. QRM, we call that kind of background noise in the Signal Corps. Shut up, short-change. About those spells ... everything seems to sort of—recede, like. And then I work. I don't know what I'm doing, but my hands do. That's how I built this thing."

"What sort of a thing is it?"

Manuel scratched his glossy head. "Not a gun, exactly, but something like it. Sort of a solenoid, with a winding like nothing you ever dreamed of, and a condenser set-up to trigger it."

"A gun? What about projectiles?"

"I made some of those too. Hollow cylinders with a mechanical bursting arrangement."

"Filled with what?"

"Filled with nothing. I don't know what they're supposed to hold. Something composed of small particles, or a powder, or something.

It wouldn't be an explosive, because there's this mechanical arrangement to scatter the stuff."

"Fuse?"

"Time," Manuel answered. "You can let her go now. I think she's stopped."

Dran said, "Manny, I've got the charge for your projectiles." He raised his hand a fraction of an inch. Vaughn said, "Let me *go!* Dran, let me go! Manuel, maybe you ate too much of that foreign—"

Dran's hand cut her off again.

Manuel said, "Like holding your hand over a faucet with a busted washer, isn't it?"

"More like getting a short circuit in a Klaxon. Vaughn, stop wriggling! Go on, Manny. I might as well tell you, something like it has happened to me. But I'll wait until you've finished. What about the fuse timing?"

"Acid vial. Double acting. There's an impact shield that pops up when a shell is fired, and a rod to be eaten through which starts a watch-movement. That goes for eight days. As for the acid—it'd have to be something really special to chew through that rod. Even good old Aqua Regia would take months to get through it."

"What acid are you using?"

Manuel shook his head. "That's one of the things I don't know," he said unhappily. "That acid, and the charge, and most of all what the whole damned thing is for—those things I don't know."

"I think I've got your acid too," said Dran, shifting his hand a little because Vaughn showed signs of coming up for air. "But where are your specifications? What's the idea of making a rod so thick you can't find an acid to eat through it?"

Manuel threw up his hands. "*I* don't know, Dran. I know when it's right, that's all. I know before I rig my lathe or milling machine what I'm after." His face darkened, and his soft voice took on a tone of fury. "I'm sick and tired of getting pushed around. I'm tired of feeling things I can't put a name to. For the first time in my life I can't whip something or get away from it."

"Well, what are you going to do?"

"What *can* I do? Get out of the service, hole up somewhere, finish this work."

"How do you know it won't go on for the rest of your life?"

"I don't know. But I know this. I know what I've done is done right, and that when it's finished, that'll be the end of it," said Manuel positively. "Hey—you better turn her loose. The purple face goes great with the hair, but it's beginning to turn black."

Dran released Vaughn, and just then the bells began to ring.

"Old one—"

The other turned on Torth. "Get out. Get out and leave me alone. Get out!"

Torth got.

The bells. . . .

"Not now," smiled Vaughn. "Not now. I'll give you rascals the punishment you deserve next year sometime." She reached out her arms, and they came close to her. She kissed Manuel, then Dran, and said, "Happy New Year, darlings."

The bells were ringing, and the city spoke with a mighty voice, part hum, part roar, part whistle, part scream, all a unison of joy and hope. *"Should auld acHappy-Nooooo Yearzhz-z-zh-h-h . . ."* said the city, and Manuel pulled Vaughn closer (and Dran with her, because Dran was so close to her) and Manuel said, "This is it. This is right, the three of us. I quit. Whether I like it or not don't matter. I got it and I'm stuck with it. I . . ."

EUDICHE!

No one said that. No one shouted it out, but for a split second there was a gasping silence in the club, in the floors above and the floors below, as three abstracts coalesced and a great subetheric emanation took place. It was more joyous than all the joy in the city, and a greater voice than that of all the other voices; and it left in a great wave and went rocketing out to the stars. And then someone started to sing again, and the old song shook the buildings

". . . and never brought to mind . . ."

113

"It's done!" said the old one.

Torth replied caustically. "I appreciate the news. You realize that not one of us on Titan could have missed that signal."

"Eudiche has succeeded," exulted the old one. "A new era for our race ... on his next transmission we will start the emigration.

"And you had doubts of Eudiche."

"I did—I did. I admit it. But it is of no moment now—he has overcome his defection."

"What is it, this defection?"

"Stop your ceaseless questions and leave me to my joy!

"Tell me that, decrepit one, and I shall go."

"Very well, Eudiche was imbalanced. He suffered from an overbroadening of the extrapolative faculty. We call it empathy. It need not concern you. It is an alien concept and a strange disease indeed."

Eudiche left, still in three parts, but now one. He stopped at the railroad station for a heavy foot-locker, and at a hotel for a large suitcase. And in the long ride in a taxi, Eudiche thought things out—not piecemeal, not single-mindedly in each single field, but with the magnificent interaction of a multiple mind.

"Is it certain that everything will fit together?" asked the mechanical factor.

"It certainly should. The motivation was the same, the drive was almost identical, and the ability in each case was of a high order," said the intellectual.

The aesthetic was quiet, performing its function of matching and balancing.

The mechanical segment had a complimentary thought for the intellectual. "That spore chest is a mechanical miracle for this planet. Wasn't it grueling, without a full mechanical aptitude to help?"

"The bipeds have wide resources. Once the design is clear, they can make almost anything. The spores themselves have started lines of research on molds, by the way, that will have far- reaching effects."

"And good ones," murmured the aesthetic. "Good ones."

Far away from the city Eudiche paid the driver and the intellectual told him to come back in the morning. And then Eudiche struck off through the icy fields, across a frozen brook, and up a starlit slope, carrying with him the spore case, the projector, and the projectiles.

It was cold and clear, and the stars competed with one another—and helped one another, too, the aesthetic pointed out: " . . . for every star which can't outshine the others seems to get behind and help another one be bright."

Eudiche worked swiftly and carefully and set up the projector. The spores were loaded into the projectiles, and the projectiles were primed with the acid and set into the gun.

The aesthetic stood apart with the stars, while the mechanical and the intellectual of Eudiche checked the orbital computations and trained the projector. It was exacting work, but there was not a single wasted motion.

The triggering was left to charge for a while, and Eudiche rested. The aesthetic put a hand to the projector—that seeking hand, always, with her, a gesture of earnestness.

"Back to Titan, and may the race multiply and grow great," she intoned. "Search the spaces between the stars and find Titan's path; burst and scatter your blessings at his feet."

The condensers drank and drank until they had their fill and a little over—

Phup! It was like the popping of a cork. Far up, seemingly among the stars, there was a faint golden streak, gone instantly.

"Reload," said the intellectual

Two worked; the third, by her presence, guided and balanced and added proportion to each thought, each directive effort. Eudiche waited, presently, for the projector to charge again. "Earth . . ." crooned the aesthetic. "Rich, wide, wonderful Earth, rich with true riches, rich in its demonstrations of waste . . . wealthy Earth, which can afford to squander thousands upon thousands of square miles in bleak hills on which nothing grows . . . wealthy Earth with its sea-sunk acres, its wandering rivers which curiously seek everything of interest, back and forth, back and backwards and seaward again, seeking in the flatlands. And for all its waste it produces magnificently, and magnificently its products are used. Humans are its products, and through the eyes of humans are seen worlds beyond worlds ... in the dreams of the dullest human are images unimaginable to other species. Through their eyes pour shapes and colors and a hungry hope that has no precedent in the cosmos."

"Empathy," defined the intellectual: "The ability to see through another's eyes, to feel with his finger-tips.

"To know fire as the feathers of a Phoenix know it. To know, as a bedded stone, the coolth of brook-water ..."

Phup!

"Reload," said the intellectual

In its time the second projectile followed, and then a third and a fourth.

"This is the machine," old Torth said to the youngster. "It was monopolized, long ago, by a caustic old triad who has since died. And may I join him soon, for it troubles me to be so old."

"And what was the machine for?"

"One Eudiche was analyzed into his three components and sent to that star there.

"It's a planet."

"Youth knows too much, too young," grumbled Torth.

"And why was Eudiche sent?"

"To test the sending; to synthesize himself there; and to prepare for mass emigration of our kind to the planet."

"He failed?"

"He failed. He took over three inhabitants successfully enough, but that was all. He had empathy, you know."

The youngster shuddered. "No loss."

"No loss," repeated Torth. "And then the reason for invasion was removed, and no one bothered to use the machine again, and no one will."

"That was when the molds came?"

"Yes, the molds. Just as we came out of space so long ago, as crystalline spores, so these molds arrived on Titan. At that time, you

*know, we possessed all Titans and reproduced faster than they did.
We had to expand."*

"It is not so now," said the youngster with confidence.

*"No," said Torth. "Happily, no. The products of the molds—
and the molds grow profusely here—worked miracles with the metabolism of our hosts. They reproduce faster and they live longer."*

"And will they never overpopulate Titan?"

*"Not in our time, not in any predictable time. Titan can support
billions of the little creatures, and there are only a few thousand
today. The rate of increase is not that great. Just great enough to
give us, who are parasites, sufficient hosts."*

"And—what happened to Eudiche?"

"He died," said Vaughn. Her voice was shocked, distraught in the
cold dawn.

"He had to die," said Dran sorrowfully. "His synthesis was complete in us three. His consistency was as complete. His recognition
of the right to live gave him no alternative. He saved his own race
on its own terms, and saved—spared, rather—spared us on human
terms. He found what we were, and he loved it. Had he stayed here,
he and his progeny and his kind would have destroyed the thing he
loved. So he died."

The grey light warmed as they started down the hill, and then
the dawn came crashing up in one great crescendo of color, obliter-
ating its pink prelude and establishing the theme for the sun's gaudy
entrance. Drunk with its light, three people crossed the frozen brook
and came to the edge of the road.

At last Manuel spoke. "What have we got here?"

Dran looked at the satchels, at Vaughn, at Manuel. "What have
you got?"

Manuel kicked his foot locker. "I've got the beginnings of a space
drive. You've got a whole new direction in biological chemistry.
Runt—Oh my god, will you look at that face. I know—poems."

"Poems," she whispered, and smiled. The dawn had not been like
that smile.

The taxi came. They loaded their cases in and sat very close together in the back.

"No one of us will ever be greater than any other," Dran said after a time. "We three have a life, not lives. I don't know anything yet about the details of our living, except that they will violate nothing."

Vaughn looked into Manuel's face, and into Dran's. Then she chuckled, "Which means I'll probably marry Joe."

They were very close. Dran again broke the silence. "My next book will be my best. It will have this dedication:

"What Vaughn inspires, I design, and Manuel builds."

And so it came about.

Poor Joe.

Special Aptitude

As we approach the year 2300, the most popular parlor game seems to be picking the Man of the Century. Some favor Bael benGerson because he rewrote the World Constitution, and some hark back to Ikihara and his work on radiation sickness. More often than not, you'll hear Captain Riley Riggs nominated, and that comes pretty close to the mark.

But it misses—it misses. I'm just an old space-hound, but I know what I'm talking about. I was communications officer with Riggs, remember, and even if it was all of sixty years ago I remember it as if it was last month. The Third Venus Expedition, it was, and the trip that changed the face of the Earth. That was the space voyage that brought back the Venus crystals, and made you and you into the soft and happy butterflies you are today. Things were different in the old days. We knew what it was to put in a solid five-hour workday, and we had no personal robots the way everyone has now—we had to put our clothes on by ourselves in the morning. Well, it was a tougher breed then, I guess.

Anyway, my bid for the Man of the Century was on that ship, the old *Starlure*—but it wasn't Riggs.

They were a grand crew. You couldn't want a better skipper than Riggs nor a better mate than Blackie Farrel. There was Zipperlein, the engineer, a big quiet man with little eyes, and his tube techs, Greaves and Purci—a wilder pair of fire-eaters never hit black space. And there was Lorna Bernhard, the best navigator before or since. She was my girl, too, and she was gorgeous. There were two other women aboard—a ray analyst by the name of Betty Ordway and Honey Lundquist, the damage control officer. But they were strictly from blueprints and homely to boot.

And for comic relief we had this character Slopes. He was shipped because of some special training in the Venus crystals. I don't know why they bothered to put him aboard. Any development work on the crystals would have to be done on Earth when—*if*—we got back. I guess they figured there was room for him, and maybe he'd be needed to locate the crystals or something. Meanwhile, he was useless. We all thought he was and we told him about it often enough to keep him reminded.

Not that he was a nuisance to anybody. It was just that he was funny. A natural comic. I don't mean the kind who slips an anti-gravity plaque under the tablecloth and switches it on when somebody sets down the soup, and I don't mean the life-of-the-party who sticks a brace of fluorescent tubes under his collar and pretends he's a Martian. This Slopes was just automatically funny to have around. He wasn't quite big enough, see, and though he wasn't homely, he also wasn't good-looking enough to do himself any good. His voice wasn't quite deep enough or loud enough to be completely heard. . . . I guess the best way to say it is to call him an Almost; a thorough-going Almost. And the difference between Almost and Altogether—at least in Slopes—was very funny to ship out with, and he had it in every department.

None of us knew him before he came aboard, which he did two hours before blast-off in civilian clothes. That was his first mistake, though why I should call it a mistake . . . after all, he was a civilian technician. Even so, all the rest of us were from one or another of the Services, and we just naturally had something on him from the start. Purci, the Number Two Tube Man, was lounging in the alley-way when Slopes stepped off the cargo-lift with his gear, and he sized the man up right now. Purci was tall, loose-jointed, relaxed, deadpan. He took Slopes aft (down, that is, since the *Starlure* stood upright on her tail-vanes when she was aground) and showed him where to stow his gear. The locker Purci gave him happened to be the garbage port, which scavenged out automatically when we hit the ionosphere. There was no real harm in that—there was plenty of gear in the slop-chest which almost fit him, and at least he looked halfway "regulation." But he sure was funny. The look on his face when he went to that garbage port six hours out was indescribable. I have to laugh now thinking about it. And for the rest of the trip all he had to do was ask where anything was, and someone'd say, "Look in the garbage!" and the whole crew would lay back and roar.

Probably the most fun we had was at "turnover," when we stopped accelerating and went into free fall. For Slopes's benefit the artificial gravity was left off, and all hands but Zipperlein, who was at the drive controls, gathered in the wardroom to watch. Word had passed to everyone but Slopes as to just when the gravity would cut out, and believe me, it was a tough job to keep from busting out laughing and spoiling the whole deal. We all sprawled around hard by a stanchion or a bolted-down table so we'd have something solid to grab when the time came. Slopes came in and sat by himself near the chow-chutes, innocent as a babe. Greaves sat with one hand cupping his wrist watch and his eyes on the sweep second hand. About three seconds short of turnover, he barked, "Slopes! Come over here, huh?"

Slopes blinked at him. "Me?" He uncrossed his legs and got to his feet, timidly. He had taken about two steps when the drive cut off.

I guess nobody ever gets really used to turnover. Your stomach gives a delicate little heave and the semicircular canals in your inner ear rebel violently. You tense yourself, all over, to the cramping point, and get no end confused because, though you know you're falling, you don't know which way—and anyhow, your reflexes expect a swift and sudden impact (because you're falling) and there just isn't any impact, so your reflexes feel foolish. Your hair drifts out every which way, and through and through, completely separated from your intense panic, is the *damnedest* feeling of exhilaration and well-being. They call it Welsbach's Euphoria. Psychological stuff. Anxiety relief with the gravityless state.

But I was talking about Slopes.

When Zipperlein cut the drive, Slopes just went adrift. His advancing foot touched and lightly scraped the floor instead of making a good solid pace. He flung his arms backward, I guess because he thought he was falling that way, and as his shoulders checked the arm motion, they were carried down while his feet went up. He did a slow-motion half-somersault and would have gone all the way around if his feet hadn't touched the overhead and stopped his rotation. He hung in midair with his head down and his feet up, with nothing to hang on to, and with the powerful feeling that, though the blood ought to be rushing to his face, it wasn't. All of a sudden, everything around him acted like *up,* and there wasn't any *down* left anywhere. He grabbed wildly toward the bulkhead, the overhead, the door—things he knew he couldn't reach. After that he subsided, trembling, and by that time the rest of us had recovered from the weird impact of turnover—after all, we'd all felt it before—and we could enjoy the fun.

"I said, 'Come here'!" Greaves snapped.

Slopes sort of flailed at the air and jigged with his feet. It made no never mind—he just stayed where he was, head down and helpless. We roared. He flapped his lips a couple of times, and then said, real strained, *"Mmmph. Mmmph."* I thought I'd die.

"Don't be so standoffish," said the Lundquist chick, the damage control officer. "Come on down and give us a kiss."

Slopes whispered, "Please ... please."

Betty Ordway said, "Make him say 'pretty please.' " We laughed.

"Reckon maybe he don't like us," I piped up. "Come on down and join the crowd, Slopesy."

Somebody said, "Hold out some garbage," and everybody laughed again.

Zipperlein came in, hand over hand. "Looky there," he said in his big, fat, flatulent voice. "Man can fly."

"Got his head in the clouds," said the skipper. Everybody laughed again—not because it was funny—because it was the skipper.

"Please," said Slopes, "get me down. Somebody get me down."

Greaves said, "I like a shipmate that can stand on his own two feet. Slopes, I asked you real polite-like to come on over and be sociable."

Zipperlein laughed. "Oh—you want him?" He went from the door to the scuttlebutt, from the wardroom table to a lighting fixture, one hairy hand after another, until he could reach Slopes's foot. "Greaves wants you," he said, and shoved.

Slopes spun end over end. He began to wail, "Ow-*oo!* Ow-*oo!*" as he turned. Spinning, he went from one end of the wardroom to the other toward Greaves. Greaves was ready for him, his hands firm to a banister-bar, his feet doubled up. When Slopes reached him, he planted his feet in Slopes's back and booted him, spinning no longer, upship toward the Captain. Riggs gave him a shoulder and shunted him over to me. I butted him back to Greaves. Greaves reached but missed him, and he hit the bulkhead with a crunch. Weight is one thing—you can get rid of that. Mass is something else again. Slopes's hundred and fifty-odd pounds were all with him, at high velocity, when he hit the wall. He hovered near it, whimpering.

"Zip," said the Captain, "Turn on the grav plates. This could go on all day."

"Aye," said the engineer, and swarmed out.

I'd been hanging on to Lorna, partly because I knew she'd have hold of something solid, and partly because I just liked to hang on to her. "Ace," she said to me, "whose idea was this?"

"Guess."

"Ace," she told me, "you know what? You're a skunk."

"Ah, climb off," I grinned. "You should see what they did to me when I was a cadet."

She turned to look at me, and there was an expression I'd seen in her eyes only twice before. Both times she and I had been strangers. She said, "I guess you learn something new every day. Even about people you know pretty well."

"Yep," I said, "and it's a blessing. You can look at the stars just so long on these trips, and then you can watch just so many visitape recordings. After that you need something to relieve the monotony. I think we all owe Slopes a rousing vote of thanks. He's a very funny man."

She said something then but I didn't get it. Everyone was laughing too hard. Zipperlein had cut in the artificial gravity and Slopes had thumped to the floor, where he writhed, hugging it to him as if he loved it, which of course he did. Everyone does coming out of free fall.

Oh, we had a time that evening. I'll never forget it.

There was a lot of chit-chat aboard about our mission. Now that we have Venus crystals by the hundreds of millions, it's not easy to tell you just how valuable they were sixty years ago. The Second Venus Expedition had picked up two of them, and both were destroyed in the tests that determined their characteristics. The first was shattered purposely—nobody knew at that time that it was different from any other crystal—so it could be chemically analyzed, a solution prepared, and new crystals grown. But Venus crystals just don't grow. The second crystal was subjected to some high-frequency resonance tests. Someone got a little too experimental with the frequencies and the crystal blew up. Data on the explosion showed that what we had just had in our hands, but didn't have any more, was the key to broadcast power—power so plentiful that everyone could have it practically for free. The power we already had, since the technique for fissioning copper atoms had been developed. But broadcasting it was something else again, unless a tight beam could be aimed from power plant to receiver and kept that way, even if the receiver was on an automobile or a 'copter and dodging. The Venus crystal could do that job—vibrating to power frequencies and sending back radiations that would guide in the power beam. Get enough of those crystals and we could do away with millions of miles of transmission wire, and convert it to enough fuel to power Earth for a couple of centuries. Don't forget, mankind has been laying a network of copper over the world for going on four hundred years, and there's lots of it.

So for a fuel-hungry Earth, these crystals were top priority. And the only thing that stood in our way—aside from getting to Venus— was the Gabblers.

The First Venus Expedition discovered the Gabblers, and left them respectfully alone. The Second Expedition discovered that the Gabblers had a stock of the precious crystals—and got chased the hell out after picking up two. It was our job to bring back a whole slew of the crystals, Gabblers or no Gabblers. Although our orders ran to a bucketful of fine detail, the essence of them was: "Treat with the Gabblers and get crystals. If the Gabblers won't play—get the crystals anyway."

"I hope we can get them peacefully," Lorna would say. "Humans have destroyed and killed enough."

And I'd tell her, "It don't matter one way or the other, kid. Gabblers aren't *people.*"

"They're civilized, aren't they? Almost?"

"They're savages," I'd snort. "And monsters as well. Keep your sympathies for nice smooth hungry human beings like me."

Then she'd slap my hands away and go back to her computers. Once Slopes asked me about the Gabblers. "Are they really humans?"

"Humanoids," I told him shortly. He made me a little uncomfortable to talk to, somehow. I mostly enjoyed his comedy. "They walk on two legs, and they have hands with an opposed thumb, and they wear ornaments. That's all they use the crystals for. But they breathe ammonia instead of oxygen and have Lord knows what kind of metabolism. Why, Slopesy? Figuring on rootin' in their garbage?"

"I was just asking," he replied gently. He put on his timid almost-smile and went aft. I remember laughing at the thought of him up against a couple of Gabblers—the most terrifying object in history since some ancient tale-teller dreamed up the Gryphon. All but two of the crew of the *Starbound,* the Expedition Two ship, had thrown down their packs and run for their lives at the very sight of a Gabbler. The other two had faced them out until the Gabblers started to scream. The psychologists had a lot to say about that noise. It was too much for any normal human being. One of the two men broke and ran, and no shame attaches to him for that. The other was cut off from the ship, and stood paralyzed with fear while the Gabblers screamed and trumpeted and pounded the earth with their scaly fists until it shook. He fired one shot in the air—he had sense enough not to risk wounding one of the enraged creatures—to frighten them off. Perhaps it did. All he remembers is a redoubled bedlam—such a gush of furious animal noise that he passed out cold on the spot.

When he came to they'd gone. The two crystals were lying near him; he picked them up and ran blindly for the ship. It took eight months of the world's most advanced psychotherapy to straighten him out, and they say he's not quite normal yet, though he's lived to be an old man. What fantastic psychic emanations the Gabblers used as weapons was not known, but the idea of Slopes up against them really tickled me.

The watches passed quickly enough with him aboard to keep us amused. I'll never forget the night Greaves slipped a spoonful of head-mastic, the damnedest adhesive that has ever been developed, into one of his sandwiches. Slopes bit into it and right then his upper teeth were welded to his lower teeth. He ran around in circles, whimpering, with half a sandwich sticking out of his face, flapping his hands uselessly. It was a riot. The stuff was quite harmless—it's chemically inert, and it yields readily to a little low-grade beta radiation, which breaks down the molecular cohesion. But we didn't radiate him until we were good and ready. I wish you could have seen the fun.

We forgot about Slopes when we broke atmosphere on Venus, though I rigged the infrared view-screens for Lorna—they're a little cleaner than radar in ammonia fog—and she took us in as neat as you please. We located the spot where the *Starbound* had landed by feeding a photo-map of the scene into the automatic pilot and matching it to the view screen.

Lorna threw the nose up and flipped the controls to the gyros. Tail-first we drifted down, sitting on a diminishing pillar of fire, while Lorna's eyes were glued to the echo-gauge which indicated the solidity of the footing under the ship. Once let one of these space-hoppers fall on its side and you could call yourself marooned. We didn't have antigravity drive in those days. It was real primitive stuff. All the dash and daring's gone from you young 'uns.

There's not much to tell about Venus. It was as unappetizing and useless then as it is now—except that somewhere out there were the crystals we had come for. Through the ports we could see nothing but fog. Through the radar and infrared screens we saw rolling country, crags, pale blue vegetation, and an occasional treelike growth far larger than such things ought to be.

We had to sit tight for twelve hours or so while the ground under us cooled and the chemical mish-mash of fixed and unfixed nitrogen, nitric acid, ammonium nitrate, ozone, and water stirred up by our landing worked itself out. Most of us slept. I don't think Slopes did, though. He traveled from the infrared to the radar apparatus, fore, aft, left, above, and below screens. He even haunted the blank, fog-frosted portholes, peering into the swirl of heat and chemical reaction, straining his eyes and his heartbeat for little glimpses of that meaningless Venusian landscape. And it was Slopes who roused us.

"Gabblers!" he jittered. "Come look! Captain Riggs! Captain Riggs!"

He was as excited as a ten-year-old, and I've got to admit it was catching. We crowded around the screens.

Out among the rocks and pale blue bushes two hundred meters from the ship were moving things which, in spite of our careful indoctrination, made us gasp and turn away. They were bigger than men— I hadn't figured on that, for some reason. They were much bigger. As for the rest ... I have a vision of yellow fangs, angry red eyes, and gray-green scales that is vivid enough—I'd as soon not talk much about it.

"Let's have some sound," said the skipper. I went into the communications shack and cranked up an amplifier. I switched in an exterior microphone and plugged the output into the intercom. The ship filled with background noises of an alien planet—a hollow wind-sound, startling because the fog seemed so still; birdlike squeaks and screams, distant and different; and over it all, the repulsive chatter and back-chatter of the Gabblers—the sound that had given them their name. It was an insane sound, hoarse and seemingly uncontrolled. It ranged harshly up and down the scale, and it differed rather horribly from the yammering of apes in that it seemed to carry consistent intelligence.

"Tubes!" barked the Captain. "Break out the suit stores and walkie gear. Sparks, stand by your shack. I want separate recordings of each suit transmitter. Navigator, tend the screens. Four volunteers here by the exit port. Jump."

Now, I don't want to run down the courage of the Space Service. It might be nice to say that everyone aboard clicked his heels and said, "At your command, sire!" On the other hand, when I was telling you about the *Starbound* men who broke and ran when they saw the Gabblers, I think I made it clear that under the circumstances they carried no shame with them. Riggs asked for four volunteers; he got two: Purci, who, without dramatics, genuinely did not give a damn, and Honey Lundquist, who I suppose wanted to be noteworthy for something besides being as homely as a blue mud fence. Me, I was glad I'd been assigned to my communications equipment and had no decision to make. As for the rest who didn't volunteer, I don't blame them. Not even Slopes, though I still thought it was a fine idea for him to face up a couple of hungry Gabblers, just for the comedy of contrast.

Riggs made no comment. He just stripped and got into space harness, the other two following. The rest of us helped them pull on the skin-tight rig and clamp down the globular transparent helmets. They tested their air and their communications, and then went to the inside gate of the airlock. I opened it for them.

"We're going to make contact," said Riggs stonily. His voice came from the intercom speakers rather than directly from him. It was eerie. "We'll try to make it peaceful first. So no side arms. I'm taking a pencil gun, just in case. You two stay close together and behind me. We'll stay hard by the ship, and under no circumstances let ourselves get cut off. Check communications."

"Check!" yelped Purci.

"Check!" whispered Honey Lundquist.

The skipper marched into the lock with the other two close behind him. I rumbled the gate shut behind them, and opened the outer lock with the remote control. All hands left aboard dived for the viewscreens.

The Gabblers, twenty or thirty of them, stuck close to the bush. Although we could not see the skipper and his volunteers yet, it was immediately evident that they had been seen. The Gabblers came out with a rush, and a more terrifying spectacle these old eyes have not seen. In the intercom, I heard Purci say, "Ugh!" and Honey say, "Eeek!" The Captain said, "Steady," in an unsteady voice. Behind me, there was a faint *thunk* as Betty Ordway passed out. I let her lie and went back to my screen.

As if by common agreement, the bulk of Gabblers halted at the crest of the gentle slope between us and the brush, and three of them came forward together, one ahead and two behind. The rest set up such a roaring that the giant trees visibly quivered. It was just about then that the skipper moved far enough out to be visible, with Honey and Purci close behind him. They stopped, and the three advancing Gabblers stopped, and, incredibly, the crowd at the top of the hill doubled its noise. I couldn't help it—I turned down the gain control on the outside mike. I couldn't stand it. Lorna thanked me. Slopes wiped his face, working the handkerchief around his eyes so he wouldn't miss anything.

There was a moment's tension—I don't mean silence; the gabbling kept up at that astounding volume, but nothing moved. When movement started, it was awfully fast.

The Captain raised both arms in what he obviously felt was a gesture of peace. Judging by what happened the Gabblers took it as a deadly insult. They went straight up in the air, all three of them, and hit the ground running. They traveled in great bounds, yowling and roaring as they came, and behind them the mass of their followers started down the slope. Over the racket I heard Honey Lundquist scream. The three spacesuited figures looked very tiny down there at the approach of that wave of bellowing giants. I saw one of the three go down in a faint. Riggs yelled a futile, "Halt or I fire!" and aimed the pencil gun. One volunteer scooped up the limp form of the other, draped it across the shoulders of the space suit, and began lumbering toward the ship. Riggs aimed, fired, turned, and ran without waiting to see what his shot had accomplished.

It was Slopes who leaped to the lock control and pressed his nose to the vision port to make sure all three were safely inside, and then slammed the outer door. He switched on the air-replacement pump that would get rid of the ammonia gas in the lock, and dived back to the screens.

There was a cluster of Gabblers around the one Riggs had shot. The noise was fiendish. I went to the shack and turned down the volume again, but you could actually hear that racket through your feet on the deck plates.

The inner-lock gate slid open, and a very pale-faced skipper stepped out. Behind him were his volunteers—Honey Lundquist looking winded, and Purci draped over her shoulders. "He fainted," she said unnecessarily and dumped him in our arms.

We rolled him into a corner and kept our eyes on the screens. "Anyway, I got one of them," breathed Riggs.

"No, you didn't, Captain," said Slopes. Sure enough, the prostrate Gabbler was sitting up, weaving his massive tusked head from side to side and shrieking.

"Are they bullet-proof?" Greaves mouthed.

"No," Slopes said devastatingly. "The skipper shot him smack on that crystal he had around his neck."

Captain Riggs groaned. "And that's about as close we'll get to those crystals this trip," he predicted morosely. "They never told me it was going to be like this. Why in time didn't they send a battle cruiser?"

"To kill off these creatures and loot their bodies for their ornaments?" asked Lorna scornfully. "We've come a long way in the last thousand years, haven't we?"

"Now that's not the way to look at it," I began, but Riggs cut in, "You're right, you're right, Lorna. Unless we get them to cooperate, we'll spend years in finding out how they make the crystals. Or where they mine them. And we haven't got years. We've got about four more days."

See, sixty years ago a ship could fuel for just so much blasting. A trip was timed for the closest transit of the planets. To leave Venus and chase after Earth as the planets drew apart again in space was out of the question. Now, of course, with power to throw away, it happens every day.

We got Purci out of his suit and revived him. We were all ready to swear that he'd had some secret weapon used on him. He didn't scare easily. It was probably just his particular response to that particular level of noise—a completely individual thing. But at the moment we were ready to believe anything of the Gabblers.

The ship began to tremble.

"They're attacking us!" yelped Greaves.

But they weren't. There were more than ever of them. The entire slope was covered with bulky, scaly, horribly manlike monsters. They were all gabbling away insanely, and in great numbers they'd squat down and pound on the ground with their mallet-like fists.

"Working theirselves up into a frenzy," Zipperlein diagnosed. "Skipper, let's blast off. We're what you might call underequipped for this sort of stuff."

Riggs thought. "We'll stick it out for a while," he said finally. "I'd like to feel I'd done everything I could—even if it's just sitting here until we have to leave."

I had my doubts, and from the looks of them, so had the others. But no one said anything. The ship trembled. We went and had chow.

About thirteen hours before blast-off time I was staring glumly into a screen at the swarm of Gabblers when I sensed someone beside me. It was Slopes. He'd been left pretty much alone in the past three days. I guess everyone was too depressed and nervous to want fun.

"Look at 'em," I growled, waving at the screen. "I don't know whether it's the same ones or whether they've been working in relays to keep the hassle going all this time. You'd have to be a Venusian to tell one from another. I can't tell 'em apart."

He looked at me as if I'd just told him where the crown jewels were hid, and walked off without a word. He began pulling off his clothes. None of us paid any attention. If we thought anything at all, I guess we figured he was going to take a shower. Before any of us knew what was happening, he'd skinned into a space suit and was clamping on the helmet.

"Hey! Slopes! Where do you think you're going?"

He said something but I couldn't hear. I reached back and flipped on the intercom, which would pick up his suit radio. He repeated his remark, which was simply, "Out." He stepped into the airlock and slid the door shut.

Riggs came pounding out of the control room. "Where's that crazy fool go—" He went for the airlock, but the red light over it blazed, indicating that the chamber was now open to the outside, and Slopes was gone.

"Get on his beam," Riggs snapped, and grabbed a mike from my bench. "Slopes!" he roared.

I punched buttons. Slopes's voice came in, far more calm and clear than I had ever heard it before.

"Yes, Captain."

"Get back in here!"

"I'm going to try for those crystals."

"You're trying for some suicide. Get back here. That's an order!"

"Sorry, Captain," said Slopes laconically. Riggs and I stared at each other, amazed. Slopes said, before the Captain could splutter out another word, "I have an idea about these Gabblers, and I'm the only one qualified to carry it out."

"You'll get killed!" Riggs bellowed.

"I will if I'm wrong," said Slopes's quiet voice. "Now, if it's all the same to you, I'll switch off. I have to think."

Riggs was filling his lungs when he saw Slopes's radio-response indicator wink out on the board. The breath came out in a single obscene syllable.

All hands went to the screens, in which Slopes was just visible walking away from the ship. "Qualified!" I snorted. "What the hell is *he* qualified for?"

"Humanity," said Lorna. I didn't know what she meant by that. Her face was white and strained as she watched the screen.

The Gabblers went into a flurry of activity when they saw him. They crowded forward, practically stepping on one another to get at him. Three or four of the fastest raced out to him, screaming and clashing their tusks. As if to gloat over his helplessness, they circled him, leaping and yammering, occasionally dropping to drum powerfully on the ground with their fists. Then suddenly one of them picked him up, held him high over its head, and raced up the slope with him. The mob parted and closed again behind the creature, and the whole scaly crowd followed as Slopes was borne up out of sight in the blue underbrush.

"Of all the ways in the world to commit suicide," breathed Purci. Honey Lundquist began to sob.

"It isn't suicide," said Lorna. "It's murder. And you murdered him."

"Who?" I demanded. "Me?"

"Yes, you," she flared, "you and all the rest of you. That poor little tyke never hurt anyone. You did the rottenest thing that can be done to a human being—you persecuted him for what he was, and not for anything he'd done. And now he proves himself man enough—human enough—to give his life for the mission we've all failed on."

"If he went out there to get killed," said Betty Ordway with icy logic, "it's suicide, not murder. And if his going out there had anything to do with getting the crystals, I don't see it."

"I didn't see you giving him a tumble," said Honey smugly.

Lorna didn't try to fight back. "I didn't really know what he was until just now," she said ashamedly, and went to her quarters.

"We ought to go out after him," said Greaves. Everyone just let that remark lie there. Riggs said, "We blast off in eleven-point-three hours, whatever," and went into the chart room. The rest of us stood around trying not to look at one another, feeling, *Maybe we were a little hard on the guy,* and *damn it, we never did him any harm, did we?*

It hit all of us at the same second, I think, that after three days of incessant babbling and ground-thumping, it was deadly quiet outside. Everybody started to talk and shut up after two syllables. And I think we all began to understand then what Lorna had been driving at.

It was Purci who said it for us, softly, "He didn't want to come back into this ship. He didn't want to go back to Earth. He didn't belong anywhere, because no one ever bothered to take him in. And I guess he just naturally got tired of that."

I don't think fifty words were spoken—outside the line of duty—in the next ten hours.

It couldn't have been more than ninety minutes before blast-off when we heard the Gabblers coming back. Heads came up one by one.

"They want another bite to eat," someone said. Someone else—one of the girls—swore abruptly.

I threw power into the screens. The underbrush was alive with Gabblers, swarming toward the ship. "Skipper!" I called "blast off, huh? And singe the scales off'n them."

"You could keep your big stupid fat mouth shut," said Lorna. It was barely a whisper, but I'll swear you could hear it all over the ship. *"They're bringing back Slopes!"*

She was right. She was so right. With his legs wrapped around the neck of a capering Gabbler, his face slightly blue because of a dwindling oxygen supply in his suit, and a wide grin, Slopes rode up to the ship, followed and surrounded by hundreds of the scaly horrors. The Gabbler he rode knelt, and Slopes climbed stiffly off. He waved his hand, and a full fifty of the creatures dropped to their haunches and began pounding the dirt with their fists. Slopes walked wearily toward the ship, and four Gabblers followed him, each carrying a bulky bundle on its head.

"Port open?" someone managed to say. I checked it. It was.

There were heavy thumps in the port, and a nerve-rackingly close blast of Gabbler chatter. Then the red light went out and we heard the whine of the air-transfer pump.

At last the door slid open. We fell all over each other to get his helmet and suit off. "I'm hungry," he said. "And I'm awful tired. And I swear I'll be deaf for life."

We rubbed him down and wrapped him up and fed him hot soup. He fell asleep before he was half finished. About then it was blast-off time. We secured him in his bunk and lashed his four big bundles down and, after a couple of short puffs to warn the Gabblers back, we reached for the stars.

In the four bundles were eight hundred and ninety-two perfect Venus crystals. And on the return trip we tried so hard to make up to Slopes for what he'd been through all his life that we actually began to be jealous of each other. And Slopes—he was no longer an

Almost. He was very definitely an Altogether, with a ring to his voice, with a spring to his step.

He worked like a slave on those crystals. "They've *got* to be synthesized," was all he'd say at first. "Humanity and the Gabblers must be kept apart." So—we helped him. And bit by bit the story came out. The nearer he got to analyzing the complex lattice of those crystals, the more he'd say. So before we reached Luna we found out what he'd done.

"Those Gabblers," he said. "You had them figured wrong. That's the damn thing about a human being—anything he doesn't understand, he fears. That's natural enough—but why does he have to assume that every emotion he causes in a strange animal means the animal is going to attack?

"Just suppose you're a small animal—say a chipmunk. You're hiding under a table eating cake crumbs and minding your own business. There's a half-dozen humans in the room and one of them is droning on about a traveling farmer and a salesman's daughter. He reaches the punch line and everybody laughs. But what about Mr. Chipmunk? All he knows is that there's a great, explosive roar of animal sound. He all but turns himself inside out with fright.

"That's exactly what happened with human beings and the Gabblers. Only the humans were the chipmunks, for a change."

Someone exploded, "You mean those lizard-apes was *laughing* at us?"

"Listen to him," said the New Slopes. "How indignant can you get? Yes, I mean exactly that. Human beings are the funniest things the Gabblers have ever seen in their lives. When I went out to them they carried me off to their village, called in neighbors for miles around, and had themselves a ball. I couldn't do anything wrong. Wave my arm—they roared. Sit on the ground—they doubled up. Run and jump—they lay down and died."

Suddenly he shoved aside his work and spoke from down deep inside himself. "That hurts, somehow, doesn't it? Humans shouldn't be laughable. They've got to be the kings of creation, all full of dignity and power. It's inexcusable for a human being to be funny unless he tries to be. Well, let me tell you something—the Gabblers gave me something that no human being ever was able to give me—a sense of *belonging* to humanity. Because what you people went through when the Gabblers first rushed up to you, laughing, is what I've been going through all my life. And it's never going to happen again. Not to me; for thanks to the Gabblers I know that all you superior joes are just as funny as I am.

"The Gabblers are gentle, grateful people. They enjoyed the show and they showered gifts on me. When I indicated that I liked crystals, they went out and got more crystals than I could carry.

"And I'm just as grateful, and that's why these crystals are going to be manufactured so cheaply on earth that there will never be another Venus Expedition for them. Don't you see? If mankind ever makes close contact with a race that laughs at them on sight—mankind will exterminate that race."

On second thought, maybe they shouldn't nominate Slopes as Man of the Century. Maybe he wouldn't like for the Gabblers to get that much publicity. And besides, he's a stinker. He married my girl.

The Traveling Crag

"I KNOW AGENTS who can get work out of their clients," said the telephone acidly.

"Yes, Nick, but—"

"Matter of fact, I know agents who would be willing to drop everything and go out to that one-shot genius's home town and—"

"I did!"

"I know you did! And what came of it?"

"I got a new story. It came in this morning."

"You just don't know how to handle a real writer. All you have to do is—you what?"

"I got a new story. I have it right here."

A pause. "A new Sig Weiss story? No kidding?"

"No kidding."

The telephone paused a moment again, as if to lick its lips. "I was saying to Joe just yesterday that if there's an agent in town who can pry work out of a primadonna like Weiss, it's good old Crisley Post. Yes, sir. Joe thinks a lot of you, Cris. Says you can take a joke better than—how long is the story?"

"Nine thousand."

"Nine thousand. I've got just the spot for it. By the way, did I tell you I can pay an extra cent a word now? For Weiss, maybe a cent and a half."

"You hadn't told me. Last time we talked rates you were overstocked. You wouldn't pay more than—"

"Aw, now, Cris, I was just—"

"Goodbye, Nick."

"Wait! When will you send—"

"Goodbye, Nick."

It was quiet in the office of Crisley Post, Articles, Fiction, Photographs. Then Naome snickered.

"What's funny?"

"Nothing's funny. You're wonderful. I've been waiting four years to hear you tell an editor off. Particularly that one. Are you going to give him the story?"

"I am not."

"Good! Who gets it? The slicks? What are you going to do: sell it to the highest bidder?"

"Naome, have you read it?"

"No. I gave it to you as soon as it came in. I knew you'd want to—"

"Read it."

"Wh—now?"

"Right now."

She took the manuscript and carried it to her desk by the window. "Corny title," she said.

"Corny title," he agreed.

He sat glumly, watching her. She was too small to be so perfectly proportioned, and her hair was as soft as it looked, which was astonishing. She habitually kept him at arm's length, but her arms were short. She was loyal, arbitrary, and underpaid, and she ran the business, though neither of them would admit it aloud. He thought about Sig Weiss.

Every agent has a Sig Weiss—as a rosy dream. You sit there day after day paddling through oceans of slush, hoping one day to run across a manuscript that means something—sincerity, integrity, high word rates—things like that. You try to understand what editors want in spite of what they say they want, and then you try to tell it to writers who never listen unless they're talking. You lend them money and psychoanalyze them and agree with them when they lie to themselves. When they write stories that don't make it, it's your fault. When they write stories that do make it, they did it by themselves. And when they hit the big time, they get themselves another agent. In the meantime, nobody likes you.

"Real stiff opening," said Naome.

"Real stiff," Cris nodded.

And then it happens. In comes a manuscript with a humble little covering note that says, "This is my first story, so it's probably full of mistakes that I don't know anything about. If you think it has anything in it, I'll be glad to fix it up any way you say." And you start reading it, and the story grabs you by the throat, shakes your bones, puts a heartbeat into your lymph ducts and finally slams you down gasping, weak and oh so happy.

So you send it out and it sells on sight, and the editor calls up to say thanks in an awed voice, and tells an anthologist, who buys reprint rights even before the yarn is published, and rumors get around, and you sell radio rights and TV rights and Portuguese translation rights. And the author writes you another note that claims volubly that if it weren't for you he'd never have been able to do it.

That's the agent's dream, and that was Cris Post's boy Sig Weiss and *The Traveling Crag*. But, like all dream plots, this one contained a sleeper. A rude awakening.

Offers came in and Cris made promises, and waited. He wrote letters. He sent telegrams. He got on the long distance phone (to a neighbor's house, Weiss had no phone).

No more stories.

So he went to see Weiss. He lost six days on the project. It was Naome's idea. "He's in trouble," she announced, as if she knew for sure. "Anyone who can write like that is sensitive. He's humble and he's generous and he's probably real shy and real good-looking. Someone's victimized him, that's what. Someone's taken advantage of him. Cris, go on out there and find out what's the matter."

"All the way out to Turnville? My God, woman, do you know where that is? Besides, who's going to run things around here?" As if he didn't know.

"I'll try, Cris. But you've got to see what's the matter with Sig Weiss. He's the—the greatest thing that ever happened around here."

"I'm jealous," he said, because he was jealous.

"Don't be silly," she said, because he wasn't being silly.

So out he went. He missed connections and spent one night in a depot and had his portable typewriter stolen and found he'd forgotten to pack the brown shoes that went with the brown suit. He brushed his teeth once with shaving cream and took the wrong creaking rural bus and had to creak in to an impossibly authentic small town and creak out again on another bus. Turnville was a general store with gasoline pumps outside and an abandoned milk shed across the road, and Cris wasn't happy when he got there. He went into the general store to ask questions.

The proprietor was a triumph of type-casting. "Whut c'n I dew f'r you, young feller? Shay—yer f'm the city, ain't cha? Heh!"

Cris fumbled vaguely with his lapels, wondering if someone had pinned a sign on him. "I'm looking for someone called Sig Weiss. Know him?"

"Sure dew. Meanest bastard ever lived. Wouldn't have nought to dew with him, I was you."

"You're not," said Cris, annoyed. "Where does he live?"

"What you want with him?"

"I'm conducting a nation-wide survey of mean bastards," Cris said. "Where does he live?"

"You're on the way to the right place, then. Heh! You show me a man's friends, I'll tell you what he is."

"What about his friends?" Cris asked, startled.

"He ain't got any friends."

Cris closed his eyes and breathed deeply. "Where does he live?"

"Up the road a piece. Two mile, a bit over. That way."

"Thanks."

"He'll shoot you," said the proprietor complacently, "but don't let it worry you none. He loads his shells with rock salt."

Cris walked the two miles and a bit, every uphill inch. He was tired, and his shoes were designed only to carry a high shine and make small smudges on desk tops. It was hot until he reached the top of the mountain, and then the cool wind from the other side make him feel as if he were carrying sacks of crushed ice in his armpits. There was a galvanized tin mailbox on a post by the road with S. WEISS and advanced erosion showing on its ancient sides. In the cutbank near it were some shallow footholds. Cris sighed and started up.

There was a faint path writhing its way through heavy growth. Through the trees he could see a canted shingle roof. He had gone about forty feet when there was a thunderous explosion and shredded greenery settled about his head and shoulders. Sinking his teeth into his tongue, he turned and dove head first into a tree-bole, and the lights went out.

A fabulous headache was fully conscious before Cris was. He saw it clearly before it moved around behind his eyes. He was lying where he had fallen. A rangy youth with long narrow eyes was squatting ten feet away. He held a ready shotgun under his arm and on his wrist, while he deftly went through Cris's wallet.

"Hey," said Cris.

The man closed the wallet and threw it on the ground by Cris's throbbing head. "So you're Crisley Post," said the man, in a disgusted tone of voice.

Cris sat up and groaned. "You're—you're not Sig Weiss?"

"I'm not?" asked the man pugnaciously.

"Okay, okay," said Cris tiredly. He picked up his wallet and put it away and, with the aid of the tree trunk, got to his feet. Weiss made no move to help him, but watchfully rose with him. Cris asked, "Why the artillery?"

"I got a permit," said Weiss. "This is my land. Why not? Don't go blaming me because you ran into a tree. What do you want?"

"I just wanted to talk to you. I came a long way to do it. If I'd known you'd welcome me like this, I wouldn't've come."

"I didn't ask you to come."

"I'm not going to talk sense if I get sore," said Cris quietly. "Can't we go inside? My head hurts."

Weiss seemed to ponder this for a moment. Then he turned on his heel, grunted, "Come," and strode toward the house. Cris followed painfully.

A gray cat slid across the path and crouched in the long grass. Weiss appeared to ignore it, but as he stepped by, his right leg lashed out sidewise and lifted the yowling animal into the air. It struck a tree trunk and fell, to lie dazed. Cris let out an indignant shout and went to it. The cat cowered away from him, gained its feet and fled into the woods, terrified.

"Your cat?" asked Weiss coldly.

"No, but damn if—"

"If it isn't your cat, why worry?" Weiss walked steadily on toward the house.

Cris stood a moment, shock and fury roiling in and about his headache, and then followed. Standing there or going away would accomplish nothing.

The house was old, small, and solid. It was built of fieldstone, and the ceilings were low and heavy beamed. Overlooking the mountainside was an enormous window, bringing in a breathtaking view of row after row of distant hills. The furniture was rustic and built to be used. There was a fireplace with a crane, also more than ornamental. There were no drapes, no couch covers or flamboyant upholstery. There was comfort, but austerity was the keynote.

"May I sit down?" Cris asked caustically.

"Go ahead," said Weiss. "You can breathe, too, if you want to."

Cris sat in a large split-twig chair that was infinitely more comfortable than it looked. "What's the matter with you, Weiss?"

"Nothing the matter with me."

"What makes you like this? Why the chip on your shoulder? Why this shoot-first-ask-questions-afterward attitude? What's it get you?"

"Gets me a life of my own. Nobody bothers me but once. They don't come back. You won't."

"That's for sure," said Cris fervently, " but I wish I knew what's eating you. No normal human being acts like you do."

"That's enough," said Weiss very gently, and Cris knew how seriously he meant it. "What I do and why is none of your business. What do you want here, anyhow?"

"I came to find out why you're not writing. That's my business. You're my client, remember?"

"You're my agent," he said. "I like the sound of it better that way."

Cris made an Olympian effort and ignored the remark. *"The Traveling Crag* churned up quite a stir. You made yourself a nice piece of change. Write more, you'll make more. Don't you like money?"

"Who doesn't? You got no complaints out of me."

"Fine. Then what about some more copy?"

"You'll get it when I'm good and ready."

"Which is how soon?"

"How do I know?" Weiss barked. "When I feel like it, whenever that is."

Cris talked, then, at some length. He told Weiss some of the ins and outs of publishing. He explained how phenomenal it was that a pulp sale should have created such a turmoil, and pointed out what could be expected in the slicks and Hollywood. "I don't know how you've done it, but you've found a short line to the heavy sugar. But the only way you'll ever touch it is to write more."

"All right, all right," Weiss said at last. "You've sold me. You'll get your story. Is that what you wanted?"

"Not quite." Cris rose. He felt better, and he could allow himself to be angry now that the business was taken care of. "I still want to know how a guy like you could have written *The Traveling Crag* in a place like this."

"Why not?"

Cris looked out at the rolling blue distance. "That story had more sheer humanity in it than anything I've ever read. It was sensitive and—damn it—it was a *kind* story. I can usually visualize who writes the stuff I read; I spend all my time with writing and writers. That story wasn't written in a place like this. And it wasn't written by a man like you."

"Where was it written?" asked Weiss in his very quiet voice. "And who wrote it?"

"Aw, put your dukes down," said Cris tiredly, and with such contempt that he apparently astonished Weiss. "If you're going to jump salty over every little thing that happens, what are you going to do when something big comes along and you've already shot your bolt?"

Weiss did not answer, and Cris went on: "I'm not saying you didn't write it. All I'm saying is that it reads like something dreamed up in some quiet place that smelled like flowers and good clean sweat ... Some place where everything was right and nothing was sick or off balance. And whoever wrote it suited that kind of a place. It was probably you, but you sure have changed since."

"You know a hell of a lot, don't you?" The soft growl was not completely insulting, and Cris felt that in some obscure way he had scored. Then Weiss said, "Now get the hell out."

"Real glad to," said Cris. At the door, he said, "Thanks for the drink."

When he reached the cutbank he looked back. Weiss was standing by the corner of the house, staring after him.

Cris trudged back to the crossroads called Turnville and stopped in at the general store. "Shay," said the proprietor. "Looks like a tree reached down and whopped ye. Heh!"

"Heh!" said Cris. "One did. I called it a son of a beech."

The proprietor slapped his knee and wheezed. "Shay, thet's a good 'un. Come out back, young feller, while I put some snake oil on your head. Like some cold beer?"

Cris blessed him noisily. The snake oil turned out to be a benzocaine ointment that took the pain out instantly, and the beer was a transfusion. He looked at the old man with new respect.

"Had a bad time up on the hill?" asked the oldster.

"No worse'n sharing an undershirt with a black widow spider," said Cris. "What's the matter with that character?"

"Nobuddy rightly knows," said the proprietor. "Came up here about eight years ago. Always been thet way. Some say the war did it to him, but I knew him before he went overseas and he was the same. He jest don't like people, is all. Old Tom Sackett, drives the RFD wagon, he says Weiss was weaned off a gallbladder to a bottle of vinegar. Heh!"

"Heh!" said Cris. "How's he live?"

"Gits a check every month. Some trust company. I cash 'em. Not much, but enough. He don't dew nahthin. Hunts a bit, roams these hills a hull lot. Reads. Heh! He's no trouble, though. Stays on his own reservation. Just don't want folks barrelin' in on him. Here comes yer bus."

"My God!" said Naome.

"You're addressing me?" he asked.

She ignored him. "Listen to this:

Jets blasting, Bat Durston came screeching down through the atmosphere of Bbllzznaj, a tiny planet seven billion light years from Sol. He cut out his super-hyper-drive for the landing ... and at that point a tall, lean spaceman stepped out of the tail assembly, proton gun-blaster in a space-tanned hand.

'Get back from those controls, Bat Durston,' the tall stranger lipped thinly. 'You don't know it, but this is your last space trip.' "

She looked up at him dazedly. "That's Sig Weiss?"

"That's Sig Weiss."

"The same Sig Weiss?"

"The very same. Leaf through that thing, Naome. Nine bloody thousand words of it, and it's all like that. Go on—read it."

"No," she said. It was not a refusal, but an exclamation. "Are you going to send it out?"

"Yes. To Sig Weiss. I'm going to tell him to roll it and stuff it up his shotgun. Honey, we have a one-shot on our hands."

"That is—it's impossible!" she blazed. "Cris, you can't give him up just like that. Maybe the next one ... maybe you can ... maybe you're right at that," she finished, glancing back at the manuscript.

He said tiredly, "Let's go eat."

"No. You have a lunch."

"I have?"

"With a Miss Tillie Moroney. You're quite safe. She's the Average American Miss. I mean it. She was picked out as such by pollsters last year. She's five-five, has had 2.3 years of college, is 24 years old, brown hair, blue eyes, and so on."

"How much does she weigh?"

"34B," said Naome, with instant understanding, "and presents a united front like a Victorian."

He laughed. "And what have I to do with Miss Tillie Moroney?"

145

"She's got money. I told you about her—that personals ad in the *Saturday Review*—remember? 'Does basic character ever change? $1000 for authentic case of devil into saint.'"

"Oh my gosh yes. You had this bright idea of calling her in after I told you about getting the Weiss treatment in Turnville." He waved at the manuscript. "Doesn't that change your plans any? You might make a case out of *The Traveling Crag* versus the cat-kicking of Mr. Weiss, if you use that old man's testimony that he's been kicking cats and people for some years. But from my experience," he touched his forehead, which was almost healed, "I'd say it was saint into devil."

"Her ad didn't mention temporary or permanent changes," Naome pointed out. "There may be a buck in it. You can handle her."

"Thanks just the same, but let me see what she looks like before I do any such thing. Personally, I think she's a crank. A mystic maybe. Do you know here?"

"Spoke to her on the phone. Saw her picture last year. The Average American Miss is permitted to be a screwball. That's what makes this country great."

"You and your Machiavellian syndrome. Can't I get out of it?"

"You cannot. What are you making such a fuss about? You've wined and dined uglier chicks than this."

"I know it. Do you think I'd have a chance to see her if I acted eager?"

"I despise you," said Naome. "Straighten your tie and go comb your hair. Oh, Cris, I know it sounds wacky. But what doesn't, in this business? What'll you lose? The price of a lunch!"

"I might lose my honor."

"Authors' agents have no honor."

"As my friend in the general store is wont to remark: Heh! What protects you, little one?"

"My honor," replied Naome.

The brown hair was neat and so was the tailored brown suit that matched it so well. The blue eyes were extremely dark. The rest well befit her Average Miss title, except for her voice, which had the pitch of a husky one while being clear as tropical shoals. Her general air was one of poised shyness. Cris pulled out a restaurant chair for her, which was a tribute; he felt impelled to do that about one time in seven.

"You think I'm a crank," she said when they were settled with a drink.

"Do I?"

"You do," she said positively. He did, too.

"Well," he said, "your ad did make it a little difficult to suspend judgment."

She smiled with him. She had good teeth. "I can't blame you, or the eight hundred-odd other people who answered. Why is it a thousand dollars is so much more appealing than such an incredible thought as a change from basic character?"

"I guess because most people would rather see the change from a thousand dollars."

He was pleased to find she had the rare quality of being able to talk coherently while she laughed. She said, "You are right. One of them wanted to marry me so I could change his character. He assured me that he was a regular devil. But—tell me about this case of yours."

He did, in detail: Sig Weiss's incredible short story, its wide impact, its deep call on everything that is fine and generous in everyone who read it. And then he described the man who had written it.

"In this business, you run into all kinds of flukes," he said. "A superficial, tone-deaf, materialistic character will sit down and write something that positively sings. You read the story, you know the guy, and you say he couldn't have written it. But you know he did. I've seen that time after time, and all it proves is that there are more facets to a man than you see at first—not that there's any real change in him. But Weiss—I'll admit that in his case the theory has got to be stretched to explain it. I'll swear a man like him simply could not contain the emotions and convictions that made *The Traveling Crag* what it is."

"I've read it," she said. He hadn't noticed her lower lip was so full. Perhaps it hadn't been, a moment ago. "It was a beautiful thing."

"Now, tell me about this ad of yours. Have you found such a basic change—devil into saint? Or do you just hope to?"

"I don't know of any such case," she admitted. "But I know it can happen."

"How?"

She paused. She seemed to be listening. Then she said, "I can't tell you. I . . . know something that can have that effect, that's all. I'm trying to find out where it is."

"I don't understand that. You don't think Sig Weiss was under such an influence, do you?"

"I'd like to ask him. I'd like to know if the effect was at all lasting."

"Not so you'd notice it," he said glumly. "He gave me that bouncing around after he wrote *The Traveling Crag,* not before. Not only that . . ." He told her about the latest story.

"Do you suppose he wrote that under the same circumstances as *The Traveling Crag?*"

"I don't see why not. He's a man of pretty regular habits. He probably—wait a minute! Just before I left, I said something to him . . . something about . . ." He drummed on his temples. ". . . Something about the *Crag* reading as if it had been written in a different place, by a different person. And he didn't get sore. He looked at me as if I were a swami. Seems I hit the nail right on the thumb."

The listening expression crossed her smooth face again. She looked up, startled. "Has he got any . . ." She closed her eyes, straining for something. "Has he a radio? I mean—a shortwave set—a transmitter—diathermy—a fever cabinet—any . . . uh . . . RF generator of any kind?"

"What in time made you ask that?"

She opened her eyes and smiled shyly at him. "It just came to me."

"Saving your presence, Miss Moroney, but there are moments when you give me the creeps," he blurted. "I'm sorry. I guess I shouldn't have said that, but—"

"It's all right," she said warmly.

"You hear voices?" he asked.

She smiled. "What about the RF generator?"

"I don't know." He thought hard. "He has electricity. I imagine he has a receiver. About the rest, I really can't say. He didn't take me on a grand tour. Will you tell me what made you ask that?"

"No."

He opened his mouth to protest, but when he saw her expression he closed it again. She asked, "What are you going to do about Weiss?"

"Drop him. What else?"

"Oh, please don't!" she cried. She put a hand on his sleeve. "Please!"

"What else to you expect me to do?" he asked in some annoyance. "A writer who sends in a piece of junk like that as a followup to something like the *Crag* is more than foolish. He's stupid. I can't use a client like that. I'm busy. I got troubles.

"Also, he gave you a bad time."

"That hasn't anyth—well, you're right. If he behaved like a human being, maybe I would take a lot of trouble and analyze his trash and guide and urge and wipe his nose for him. But a guy like that—nah!"

"He has another story like the *Crag* in him."

"You think he has?"

"I know he has."

"You're very positive. Your ... voices tell you that?"

She nodded, with a small secret smile.

"I have the feeling you're playing with me. You know this Weiss?"

"Oh, no! And I'm not playing with you. Truly. You've got to believe me!" She looked genuinely distressed.

"I don't see why I should. This begins to look real haywire, Tillie Moroney. I think maybe we'd better get down to basics here." She immediately looked so worried that he recognized an advantage. Not knowing exactly what she wanted of him, he knew she wanted something, and now he was prepared to use that to the hilt. "Tell me about it. What's your interest in Weiss? What's this personality-alteration gimmick? What are you after and what gave you your lead? And what do you expect me to do about it? That last question reads, 'What's in it for me?'"

"Y-you're not always very nice, are you?"

He said, more gently, "That last wasn't thrown in to be mean. It was an appeal to your good sense to appeal to my sincerity. You can always judge sincerity—your own or anyone else's—by finding out what's in it for the interested party. Altruism and real sincerity are mutually exclusive. Now, talk. I mean, talk, please."

Again that extraordinary harking expression. Then she drew a deep breath. "I've had an awful time," she said. "Awful. You can't know. I've answered letters and phone calls. I've met cranks and wolves and religious fanatics who have neat little dialectical capsules all packed and ready to make saints out of devils. They all yap about proof—sometimes it's themselves and sometimes it's someone they know—and the proof always turns out to be a reformed drunk or a man who turned to Krishna and no longer beats his wife, not since Tuesday ... " She stopped for breath and half-smiled at him and, angrily, he felt a warm surge of liking for her. She went on, "And this is the first hint I've had that what I'm looking for really exists."

She leaned forward suddenly. "I need you. You already have a solid contact with Sig Weiss and the way he works. If I had to seek him out myself, I—well, I just wouldn't know how to start. And this is urgent, can't you understand—urgent!"

He looked deep into the dark blue eyes and said, "I understand fine."

She said, "If I tell you a ... story, will you promise not to ask me any questions about it?"

He fiddled about with his fork for a moment and then said, "I once heard tell of a one-legged man who was pestered by all the kids in the neighborhood about how he lost his leg. They followed him and yelled at him and tagged along after him and made no end of a nuisance of themselves. So one day he stopped and gathered them all around him and asked if they really wanted to know how he lost his leg, and they all chorused YES! And he wanted to know if he told them, would they stop asking him, and they all promised faithfully that they would stop. 'All right,' he said. 'It was bit off.' And he turned and stumped away. As to the promise you want—no."

She laughed ruefully. "All right. I'll tell you the story anyway. But you've got to understand that it isn't the whole story, and that I'm not at liberty to tell the whole story. So please don't pry too hard."

He smiled. He had, he noticed in her eyes, a pretty nice smile. "I'll be good."

"All right. You have a lot of clients who write science fiction, don't you?"

"Not a lot. Just the best," he said modestly.

She smiled again. Two curved dimples put her smile in parenthesis. He liked that. She said, "Let's say this is a science fiction plot. How to begin . . ."

"Once upon a time . . ." he prompted.

She laughed like a child. "Once upon a time," she nodded, "there was a very advanced humanoid race in another galaxy. They had had wars—lots of them. They learned how to control them, but every once in a while things would get out of hand and another, and worse, war would happen. They developed weapon after weapon—things which make the H-bomb like a campfire in comparison. They had planet-smashers. They could explode a sun. They could do things we can only dimly understand. They could put a local warp in time itself, or unify the polarity in the gravitomagnetic field of an entire solar system."

"Does this gobbledegook come easy to you?" he asked.

"It does just now," she answered shyly. "Anyway, they developed the ultimate weapon—one which made all the others obsolete. It was enormously difficult to make, and only a few were manufactured. The secret of making it died out, and the available stocks were used at one time or another. The time to use them is coming again—and I don't mean on Earth. The little fuses we have are flea-hops. This is important business.

"Now, a cargo ship was traveling between galaxies on hyperspatial drive. In a crazy, billion-to-one odds accident, it emerged into normal space smack in the middle of a planetoid. It wasn't a big one; the ship wasn't atomized, just wrecked. It was carrying one of these super-weapons. It took thousands of years to trace it, but it has been traced. The chances are strong that it came down on a planet. It's wanted.

"It gives out no detectable radiation. But in its shielded state, it has a peculiar effect on living tissues which come near it."

"Devils into saints?"

"The effect is ... peculiar. Now ..." She held up fingers. "If the nature of this object were known, and if it fell into the wrong hands, the effect here on Earth could be dreadful. There are megalomaniacs on Earth so unbalanced that they would threaten even their own destruction unless their demands were met. Point two: If the weapon were used on Earth, not only would Earth as we know it cease to exist, but the weapon would be unavailable to those who need it importantly."

Cris sat staring at her, waiting for more. There was no more. Finally he licked his lips and said, "You're telling me that Sig Weiss has stumbled across this thing."

"I'm telling you a science fiction plot."

"Where did you get your ... information?"

"It's a science fiction story."

He grinned suddenly, widely. "I'll be good," he said again. "What do you want me to do."

Her eyes became very bright. "You aren't like most agents," she said.

"When I was in a British Colony, the English used to say to me, every once in a while, 'You aren't like most Americans.' I always found it slightly insulting. All right; what do you want me to do?"

She patted his hand. "See if you can make Weiss write another *Traveling Crag*. If he can, then find out exactly how and where he wrote it. And let me know."

They rose. He helped her with her light coat. He said, "Know something?" When she smiled up at him he said, "You don't strike me as Miss Average."

"Oh, but I was," she answered softly. "I was."

TELEGRAM

SIG WEISS   JULY 15
TURNVILLE

PLEASE UNDERSTAND THAT WHAT FOLLOWS HAS NOTHING
WHATEVER TO DO WITH YOUR GROSS LACK OF HOSPITALITY.
I REALIZE THAT YOUR WAY OF LIFE ON YOUR OWN PROPERTY
IS JUSTIFIED IN TERMS OF ME, AN INTRUDER. I AM FORGET-
TING THE EPISODE. I ASSUME YOU ALREADY HAVE. NOW TO
BUSINESS: YOUR LAST MANUSCRIPT IS THE MOST UTTERLY
INSULTING DOCUMENT I HAVE SEEN IN FOURTEEN PROFES-
SIONAL YEARS. TO INSULT ONE'S AGENT IS STANDARD OPER-
ATING PROCEDURE: TO INSULT ONESELF IS INEXCUSABLE AND
BROTHER YOU'VE DONE IT. SIT DOWN AND READ THE STORY
THROUGH, IF YOU CAN, AND THEN REREAD THE TRAVELING
CRAG. YOU WILL NOT NEED MY CRITICISM. MY ONLY SUGGES-
TION TO YOU IS TO DUPLICATE EXACTLY THE CIRCUMSTANCES
UNDER WHICH YOU WROTE YOUR FIRST STORY. UNLESS AND
UNTIL YOU DO THIS WE NEED HAVE NO FURTHER CORRE-
SPONDENCE. I ACCEPT YOUR SINCERE THANKS FOR NOT SUB-
MITTING YOUR SECOND STORY ANYWHERE.

CRISLEY POST

Naome whistled. "Really—a straight telegram? What about a
night letter?"

Cris smiled at the place where the wall met the ceiling. "Straight
rate."

"Yes, master." She wielded a busy pencil. "That's costing us
$13.75, sir," she said at length, "plus tax. Grand total, $17.46. Cris,
you have a hole in your head!"

"If you know of a better 'ole, go to it," he quoted dreamily. She
glared at him, reached for the phone and continued to glare as she
put the telegram on the wire.

In the next two weeks Cris had lunch three times with Tillie
Moroney, and dinner once. Naome asked for a raise. She got it, and
was therefore frightened.

Cris returned from the third of these lunches (which was the day after the dinner) whistling. He found Naome in tears.

"Hey ... what's happening here? You don't do that kind of thing, remember?"

He leaned over her desk. She buried her face in her arms and boohooed lustily. He knelt beside her and put an arm around her shoulders. "There," he said, patting the nape of her neck. "Take a deep breath and tell me about it."

She took a long, quavering breath, tried to speak, and burst into tears again. "F-f-fi-fi ..."

"What?"

"F—" She swallowed with difficulty, then said, *"Fire of Heaven!"* and wailed.

"What?" he yelled. "I thought you said *'Fire of Heaven.'*"

She blew her nose and nodded. "I did," she whispered. "H-here." She dumped a pile of manuscript in front of him and buried her face in her arms again. "L-leave me alone."

In complete bewilderment, he gathered up the typewritten sheets and took them to his desk.

There was a covering letter.

> *Dear Mr. Post: There will never be a way for me to express my thanks to you, nor my apologies for the way I treated you when you visited me. I am willing to do anything in my power to make amends.*
>
> *Knowing what I do of you, I think you would be most pleased by another story written the way I did the Crag. Here it is. I hope it measures up. If it doesn't, I earnestly welcome any suggestions you may have to fix it up.*
>
> *I am looking forward very much indeed to meeting you again under better circumstances. My house is yours when you can find time to come out, and I do hope it will be soon. Sincerely, S. W.*

With feelings of awe well mixed with astonishment, Cris turned to the manuscript. *Fire of Heaven*, by Sig Weiss, it was headed. He began to read. For a moment, he was conscious of Naome's difficult and diminishing sniffs, and then he became completely immersed in the story.

Twenty minutes later, his eyes, blurred and smarting, encountered "The End." He propped his forehead on one palm and rummaged clumsily for his handkerchief. Having thoroughly mopped and blown, he looked across at Naome. Her eyes were red-rimmed and still wet. "Yes?" she said.

"Oh my God yes," he answered.

They stared at each other for a breathless moment. Then she said in a soprano near-whisper: *"Fire of . . ."* and began to cry again.

"Cut it out," he said hoarsely.

When he could, he got up and opened the window. Naome came and stood beside him. "You don't read that," he said after a time. "It . . . happens to you."

She said, "What a tragedy. What a beautiful, beautiful tragedy."

"He said in his letter," Cris managed, "that if I had any suggestions to fix it up . . ."

"Fix it up," she said in shaken scorn. "There hasn't been anything like him since—"

"There hasn't been anything like him period." Cris snapped his fingers. "Get on your phone. Call the airlines. Two tickets to the nearest feederfield to Turnville. Call the Drive-Ur-Self service. Have a car waiting at the field. I'm not asking any woman to climb that mountain on foot. Send this telegram to Weiss: Taking up your very kind offer immediately. Bringing a friend. Will wire arrival time. Profound thanks for the privilege of reading *Fire of Heaven*. From a case-hardened ten-percenter those words come hard and are well earned. Post."

"Two tickets," said Naome breathlessly. "Oh! Who's going to handle the office?"

He thumped her shoulder. "You can do it, kid. You're wonderful. Indispensable. I love you. Get me Tillie Moroney's number, will you?"

She stood frozen, her lips parted, her nostrils slightly distended. He looked at her, looked again. He was aware that she had stopped breathing. "Naome!"

She came to life slowly and turned, not to him, but on him. "You're taking that—that Moron-y creature—"

"Moroney. What's the matter with you?"

"Oh Cris, how could you?"

"What have I done? What's wrong? Listen, this is business. I'm not romancing the girl! Why—"

She curled her lip. "Business! Then it's the first business that's gone on around here that I haven't known about."

"Oh, it isn't office business, Naome. Honestly."

"Then there's only one thing it could be!"

Cris threw up his hands. "Trust me this once. Say! Why should it eat you so much, even if it was monkey-business, which it isn't?"

"I can't bear to see you throw yourself away!"

"You—I didn't know you felt—"

"Shut up!" she roared. "Don't flatter yourself. It's just that she's … average. And so are you. And when you add an average to an average, you've produced NOTHING!"

He sat down at his desk with a thump and reached for the phone, very purposefully. But his mind was in such a tangle at the moment, that he didn't know what to do with the phone once it was in his hands, until Naome stormed over and furiously dropped a paper in front of him. It had Tillie's number on it. He grinned at her stupidly and sheepishly and dialed. By this time, Naome was speaking to the airlines office, but he knew perfectly well that she could talk and listen at the same time.

"Hello?" said the phone.

"Ull-ull," he said, watching Naome's back stiffen. He spun around in his swivel chair so he could talk facing the wall.

"Hello?" said the phone again.

"Tillie, Weiss found it he wrote another story it's a dream he invited me down and I'm going and you're coming with me," he blurted.

"I beg your—Cris, is anything the matter? You sound so strange."

"Never mind that," he said. He repeated the news more coherently, acutely conscious of Naome's attention to every syllable. Tillie uttered a cry of joy and promised to be right over. He asked her to hang on and forced himself to get the plane departure from Naome. Pleading packing and business odds and ends, he asked her to meet him at the airport. She agreed, for which he was very thankful. The idea of her walking into the office just now was more than he could take.

Naome had done her phoning and was in a flurry of effort involving her files, which had always been a mystery to Cris. She kept bringing things over to him. "Sign these." "You promised to drop Rogers a note about this." "What do you want done about Borilla's scripts?" Until he was snowed under. "Hold it! These things can wait!"

"No they can't," she said icily. "I wouldn't want them on my conscience. You see, this is my last day here."

"Your—Naome! You can't quit. You can't!"

"I can and I am and I do. Check this list."

"Naome, I—"

"I won't listen. My mind's made up."

"All right then. I'll manage. But it's a shame about *Fire of Heaven.* Such a beautiful job. And here it must sit until I get back. I did want you to market it."

"You'd trust me to market that story?" Her eyes were huge.

"No one else. There isn't anyone who knows the market better, or who would make a better deal. I trust you with it absolutely. After you've done that one last big thing for me—go, then, if you'll be happier somewhere else."

"Crisley Post, I hate you and despise you. You're a fiend and a spider. Th-thank you. I'll never forget you for this. I'll type up four originals and sneak them around. Movies, of course. What a TV script! And radio . . . let's see; two, no—three British outfits can bid against each other . . . you're doing this on purpose to keep me from leaving!"

"Sure," he said jovially. "I'm real cute. I wrote the story myself just because I couldn't get anyone to replace you."

At last she laughed. "There's one thing I'm damn sure you didn't do. An editor is a writer who can't write, and an agent is a writer who can't write as well as an editor."

He laughed with her. He bled too, but it was worth it, to see her laughing again.

The plane trip was pleasant. It lasted a long time. The ship sat down every 45 minutes or so all the way across the country. Cris figured it was the best Naome could do on short notice. But it gave them lots of time to talk. And talking to Tillie was a pleasure. She was intelligent and articulate, and had read just as many of his favorite books as he had of hers. He told her enough about *Fire of Heaven* to intrigue her a lot and make her cry a little, without spoiling the plot for her. They found music to disagree about, and shared a view of a wonderful lake down through the clouds, and all in all it was a good trip. Occasionally, Cris glanced at her—most often when she was asleep—with a touch of surmise, like a little curl of smoke, thinking of Naome's suspicions about him and Tillie. He wasn't romancing Tillie. He wasn't. Was he?

They landed at last, and again he blessed Naome; the Drive-Ur-Self car was at the airfield. They got a road map from a field attendant and drove off through the darkest morning hours. Again Cris found himself glancing at the relaxed girl beside him, half asleep in the cold glow of the dash lights. A phrase occurred to him: "undivided front like a Victorian"—Naome's remark. He flushed. It was true. An affectation of Tillie's, probably; but everything she wore was highnecked and full-cut.

The sky had turned from grey to pale pink when they pulled up at the Turnville store. Cris honked, and in due course the screen door slammed and the old proprietor ambled down the wooden steps and came to peer into his face.

"Heh! If 'tain't that city feller. How're ya, son? Didn't know you folks ever got up and about this early."

"We're up late, dad. Got some gas for us?"

"Reckon there's a drop left."

Cris got out and went back with the old man to unlock the gas tank. "Seen Weiss recently?" he asked.

"Same as usual. Put through some big orders. Seen him do that before. Usually means he's holing up for five, six months. Though why he bought so much liquor an' drape material and that, I can't figure."

"How'd he behave?"

"Same as ever. Friendly as a wet wildcat with fleas."

Cris thanked him and paid him and they turned up the rocky hill road. As they reached the crest, they gasped together at the sun-flooded valley that lay before them. "Memories are the only thing you ever have that you always keep," said Tillie softly, "and this is one for both of us. I'm ... glad you're in it for me, Cris."

"I love you, too," he said in the current idiom, and found himself, hot-faced, looking into a face as suffused as his. They recoiled from each other and started to chatter about the weather—stopped and roared together with laughter. He took her hand and helped her up the cutbank. They paused at the top. "Listen," he said in a low voice. "That old character in the store has seen Weiss recently. And he says there's no change. I think we'd better be just a little bit careful."

He looked at her and again caught that listening expression. "No," she said at length, "it's all right. The store's outside the ... the influence he's under. He's bound to revert when it's gone. But he'll be all right now. You'll see."

"Will you tell me how you know these things?" he demanded, almost angry.

"Of course," she smiled. Then the smile vanished. "But not now."

"That's more than I've gotten so far," he grumbled. "Well, let's get to it."

Hand in hand, they went up the path. The house seemed the same, and yet ... there was a difference, an intensification. The leaves were greener, the early sun warmer.

There were three grey kittens on the porch.

"Ahoy the house!" Cris called self-consciously.

The door opened, and Weiss stood there, peering. He looked for a moment exactly as he had when he watched Cris stride off on the earlier visit. Then he moved out into the sun. He scooped up one of the kittens and came swiftly to meet them. "Mr. Post! I got your wire. How good of you to come."

He was dressed in a soft sport shirt and grey slacks—a startling difference from his grizzled boots-and-khaki appearance before. The kitten snuggled into the crook of his elbow, made a wild grab at his pocket-button, caught its tail instead. He put it down, and it fawned and purred and rubbed against his shoe.

Weiss straightened up and smiled at Tillie. "Hello."

"Tillie, this is Sig Weiss. Miss Moroney."

"Tillie," she said, and gave him her hand.

"Welcome home," Weiss said. He turned to Cris. "This is your home, for as long as you want it, whenever you can come."

Cris stood slack-jawed. "I ought to be more tactful," he said at length, "but I just can't believe it. I should have more sense than to mention my last visit, but this—this—"

Weiss put a hand on his shoulder. "I'm glad you mentioned it. I've been thinking about it, too. Hell—if you'd forgotten all about it, how could you appreciate all this? Come on in. I have some surprises for you."

Tillie held Cris back a moment. "It's here," she whispered. "Here in the house!"

The weapon—here? Somehow he had visualized it as huge—a great horned mine or a tremendous torpedo shape. He glanced around apprehensively. The ultimate weapon—invented after the planet-smasher, the sun-burster—what incredible thing could it be?

Weiss stood by the door. Tillie stepped through, then Cris.

The straight drapes, the solid sheet of plate glass that replaced the huge sashed window; the heavy skins that softened the wide-planked floor, the gleaming andirons and the copper pots on the fieldstone wall; the record-player and racks of albums—all the other soothing, comforting finishes of the once-bleak room—all these Cris noticed later. His big surprise was not quite a hundred pounds, not quite five feet tall—

"Cris . . ."

"Naome's here," he said inanely, and sat down to goggle at her.

Weiss laughed richly. "Why do you suppose you and Tillie got that pogo-plane cross country, stopping at every ball-park and cornfield? Naome got a non-stop flight to within fifty miles of here, and air-taxi to the bottom of the mountain, and came up by cab."

"I had to," said Naome. "I had to see what you were getting into. You're so—impetuous." She came smiling to Tillie. "I am glad to see you."

"Why, you idiot!" said Cris to Naome. "What could you have done if he—if—"

"I'm prettier than you are, darling," laughed Naome.

"She came pussyfooting up to the house like a kid playing Indian," said Weiss. "I circled through the woods and pussyfooted right along with her. When she was peeping into the side window, I reached out and put a hand on her shoulder."

"You might have scared her into a conniption!"

"Not here," said Weiss gravely.

Surprisingly, Tillie nodded. "You can't be afraid here, Cris. You're saying all those things about what might have happened, but they're not frightening to think about now, are they?"

"No," Cris said thoughtfully. "No." He gazed around him. "This is—crazy. Everybody should be this crazy."

"It would help," said Weiss. "How do you like the place now, Cris?"

"It's—it's grand," said Cris. Naome laughed. She said, "Listen to the vocabulary kid there. 'Grand.' You meant 'Peachy,' didn't you?"

"Cris didn't laugh with the others. "Fear," he said. "You can't eliminate fear. Fear is a survival emotion. If you didn't know fear, you'd fall out of windows, cut yourself on rocks, get hunted and killed by mountain lions."

"If I open the window," Weiss asked, "would you be afraid to jump out? Come over here and look."

Cris stepped to the great window. He had not known that the house was built so close to the edge. Crag on crag, fold after billow, the land fell down and away to the distant throat of the valley. Cris stepped back respectfully. "Open it if you like," he said, and swallowed, "and somebody else can jump. Not me, kiddies."

Sig Weiss smiled. "Q.E.D. Survival fear is still with us. What we've lost here is fear of anything that is not so. When you came here, you saw a very frightened man. Most of my fears were "might-be" fears. I was afraid people might attack me, so I attacked first. I was afraid of seeming different from people, so I stayed where my imagined difference would not show. I was afraid of being the same as people, so I tried to be different."

"What does it?" Cris asked.

"What makes us all what we are now? Something I found. I won't tell you what it is or where it is. I call it an amulet, a true magic amulet, knowing that it's no more or less magic than flame springing to the end of a wooden stick." He took a kitchen match from his pocket and ran his thumbnail across it. It flared up, and he flipped it into the fireplace. "I won't tell you where or what it is because, although I've lost my fear, I haven't lost my stubbornness. I've lived miserably, a partial, hunted, hunting existence, and now I'm alive. And I mean to stay this way."

"Where did you find it?" Tillie asked. "Mind telling us that?"

"Not at all. A half mile down the mountain there was a tremendous rockfall a couple of years ago. No one owns that land; no one noticed. I climbed down there once looking for hawks' eggs. I found a place ...

"How can I tell you what that place was like, or what it was like to find it? It was a brush-grown, rocky hillside near the gaping scar of the slide, where the crust of years had sloughed away. Maybe the mountain moved its shoulder in its sleep. There were flowers—ordinary wildflowers—but perfect, vivid, vital. They lived long and hardily, and they were beautiful. The bushes had an extraordinary green and a fine healthy gloss, and it was a place where the birds came close to me as I sat and watched them. It was the birds who taught me that fear never walked in that place.

"How can I tell you—what can I say about the meaning of that place to me? I'd been a psychic cripple all my life, hobbling through the rough country of my own ideas, spending myself in battle against ghosts I had invented to justify my fears, for fear was there first. And when I found that place, my inner self threw away its crutches. More than that—it could fly!

"How can I tell you what it meant to me to leave that place? To walk away from it was to buckle on the braces, pick up the crutches again, to feel my new wings molt and fall away.

"I went there more and more. Once I took my typewriter and worked there, and that was *The Traveling Crag.* Cris never knew how offended I was, how invaded, to find that he had divined the existence of that place through the story. That was why I turned out that other abortion, out of stubbornness—a desire to prove to Cris and to myself that my writing came from me and not from the magic of that place. I know better now. I don't know what another writer would do here. Better than anything he could conceivably do anywhere else. But it wouldn't be the *Crag* or *Fire,* because they could only have been mine."

Cris asked, "Would you let another writer work here?"

"I'd love it! Do you mean to ask if I want to monopolize this place, and the wonders it works? Of course not. One or another fear or combinations of fear are at the base of any monopoly, whether it's in industry, or in politics, or in the area of religious thought. And there's no fear here."

"There should be some sort of a—a shrine here," murmured Naome.

"There is. There will be, as long as I can keep the amulet. I found it, you see. It was lying right out in the sun. I took it and brought it here. The birds wouldn't forgive me for a while, but I've made them happy here since. And here it is and here it will stay, and there's your shrine."

Fear walked in then. It closed gently on Cris's heart, and he turned to look at Tillie. Her eyes were closed. She was listening.

A hell of an agent I turned out to be, he thought. How much I was willing to do for Weiss, how much for all the world through his work! By himself he found himself, the greatest of human achievements. And I have done the one thing that will take that away from him and from us all, leaving only the dwindling memory of this life without fear—and two great short stories.

He looked at Tillie again. His gaze caught hers, and she rose. Her features were rigidly controlled, but through his mounting fear Cris could recognize the thing she was fighting. She surely understood what was about to happen to Weiss and to the world if she succeeded. Her understanding versus her ... orders, was it?

Cris had sat in that incredible aura, listening to the joyous expression of Sig Weiss's delivery from fear, and he had thought of killing. Now, he realized that part of her already thought as he did, and perhaps ... perhaps ...

"Sig, can we look around outside?" Cris had stepped over to Tillie almost before he knew he wanted to.

"You own the place," said Weiss cheerfully. "Naome and I'll stir up some food. You've had a nice leisurely trip. I wonder if you realize that Naome spent fourteen hours on a typewriter before she took that long hop? *Fire of Heaven's* well launched now, thanks to her. Anyway, she deserves food."

"And a golden crown, which I shall include in the next pay envelope. Thank you, Naome. You're out of your mind."

"Thank you," she twinkled.

Cris led Tillie out, and they walked rapidly away from the house. "Not too far," she cautioned. "Let's stay where we can think. We're in a magic circle, you know, and outside we'll be afraid of each other, and of ourselves and of all our ghosts."

He asked her, "What are you going to do?"

"I shouldn't have got you into this. I should have come by myself."

"I'd have stopped you then. Don't you see? Sig would have told me. Even with whatever help you have, you couldn't have succeeded in getting the weapon on the first try. He's too alert, too alive, far too jealous of what the 'amulet' has given him. He'd have told me, and I'd have stopped you, to save him and his work. You made me an ally, and that prevented me."

"Cris, Cris, I didn't think that out!"

"I know you didn't. It was done for you. Who is it, Tillie? Who?"

"A ship," she whispered. "A space ship."

"You've seen it?"

"Oh, yes."

"Where is it?"

"Here."

"Here, in Turnville?"

She nodded.

"And it—they—communicate with you?"

"Yes."

He asked her again. "What are you going to do?"

"If I tell you I'll get the weapon, you'll kill me to save Weiss, and his work, and his birds, and his shrine, and all they mean to the world. Won't you, Cris?"

"I will certainly try."

"And if I refuse to get it for them—"

"Would they kill you?"

"They could."

"If they did, could they then get the weapon?"

"I don't know. I don't think so. They've never forced me, Cris, never. They've always appealed to my reason. I think if they could control me or anyone else, they'd have done it. They'd have to find another human ally, and start the persuading process all over again. By which time Weiss and everyone else would be warned, and it would be much more difficult for them."

"Nothing's difficult for them," he said suddenly. "They can smash planets."

"Cris, we don't think as well as they do, but we don't think the way they do, either. And from what I can get, I'm sure that they're good—that they will do anything they can to spare this planet and the life on it. That seems to be one of the big reasons for their wanting to get that weapon away from here."

"And what of their other aims, then? Can we take all this away from humanity in favor of some cosmic civilization that we don't know and have never seen, which regards us as a dust-fleck in a minor galaxy? Let's face it, Tillie: they'll get it sooner or later. They're strong enough. But let's keep it while we can. A minute, a day of this aura is a minute or a day in which a human being can know what it's like to live without fear. Look at what it's done for Weiss; think what it can do for others. What are you going to do?"

"I—Kiss me, Cris."

His lips had just touched hers when there was a small giggle behind them. Cris whirled.

"Bless you, my children."

"Naome!"

"I didn't mean to bust anything up. I mean that." She skipped up to them. "You can go right back to it after I've finished interrupting. But I've just got to tell you. You know the fright Sig tried to throw into me when I got here last night? I'm getting even. I found his amulet. I really did. It was stuck to the underside of a shelf in the linen closet. You'd have to be my size to see it. I swiped it."

Tillie's breath hissed in. "Where is it? What did you do with it?"

"Oh, don't worry, it's safe enough. I hid it good, this time. Now we'll make him wonder where it is."

"Where is it?" asked Cris.

"Promise not to tell him?"

"Of course."

"Well, it's smack in the innards of one of his pet new possessions. You haven't been in the west room—the ell he calls a library—have you?"

They shook their heads.

"Well, he's got himself a great big radio. I lifted the lid, see, and down inside among the tubes and condensers and all that macaroni are some wire hoops, sort of. This amulet, it's a tiny thing—maybe four inches long and as wide as my two thumbs. It's sort of—blurry around the edges. Anyway, I stuck it inside one set of those hoops. Cris—you're green! What's the matter?"

"Tillie—the coil—the RF coil! If he turns that set on—"

"Oh, dear God . . ." Tillie breathed.

"What's the matter with you two? I didn't do anything wrong, did I?"

They raced into the house, through the living room. "In here!" bellowed Cris. They pounded to the west room, getting into each other's way as they went in.

Sig Weiss was there, smiling. "Just in time. I want to show you the best damn transceiver in—"

"Don't! Don't touch it—"

"Oh, a little hamming won't hurt," said Sig.

He threw the switch.

There was a loud click and a shower of dust.

And silence.

Naome came all the way in, went like a sleepwalker to the radio and opened the lid. There was a hole in the grey crinkle-finished steel, roughly rectangular. Weiss looked at it curiously, touched it, looked up. There was a similar hole in the ceiling. He bent over the chassis. "Now how do you like that! A coil torn all to hell. Something came down through the roof—see?—and smashed right through my new transmitter."

"It didn't go down," said Cris hoarsely. "It went up."

Naome began to cry.

"What the hell's the matter with you people?" Sig demanded.

Cris suddenly clutched Tillie's arm. "The ship! The space ship! They wouldn't let it go off while they're here!"

"They did," said Tillie in a flat voice.

"Will somebody please tell me what gives here?" asked Sig plaintively.

Through a thick silence, Tillie said, "I'll tell it." She sank down on her knees, slowly sat on the rug. "Cris knows most of this," she said. Don't stop to wonder if it's all true. It is." She told about the races, the wars, the weapons of greater and greater destructiveness and, finally, the ultimate weapon, and its strange effect on living tissue. "Eight months ago, the ship contacted me. There was a connection made with my nerve-endings. I don't understand it. It wasn't telepathy; they were artificial neural currents. They talked to me. They've been talking ever since."

"My amulet!" Sig suddenly cried. "Sit down," said Tillie flatly. He sat.

Cris said, "I thought you required some physical contact for them to communicate with you. But I've been with you while you were communicating, and you had no contact."

"I hadn't?" She began to unbutton her blouse at the throat. She stopped with the fourth button, and gently drew out a metal object shaped somewhat like a bulbous spearhead with a blunt point. It glittered strangely with a color not quite that of gold and not quite of polished brass. It seemed to be glazed with a thin layer of clear crystal.

"Oh-h-h," breathed Naome, in a revelatory tone.

Tillie smiled suddenly at her. "You minx. You always wondered why I never wore a V-neck. Come here, all of you. Down on the rug."

Mystified, they gathered around. "Put your hands on it." They did so, and stared at each other and at their hands, waiting like old maids over a Ouija board. "It hurts a tiny bit at first as the probes go in, but it passes quickly. Be very still."

A strange, not unpleasant prickling sensation came and went. There was a slight shock, another; more prickling.

Testing. Testing. Naome Cris Sig Tillie . . .

"Everybody get that?" asked Tillie calmly.

Naome squeaked. "It's like someone talking inside my sinuses!"

"It said our names," said Sig tautly. Cris nodded, fascinated.

The silent voice spoke: *Sig, your amulet is gone and you have lost nothing.*

Tillie, you have been faithful to your own.

Naome, you have been used, and you have done no wrong.

Cris, we have observed that it takes superhuman understanding to guide and direct work you cannot do yourself.

Reorient your thinking, all of you. You insist that what is lethal or cosmically important must be huge. You insist that anything which transcends a horror must be greater horror.

The amulet was indeed the ultimate weapon. Its effect is not to destroy, but to stop useless conflict. At this moment there is a chain reaction occurring throughout this planet's atmosphere affecting only one rare isotope of nitrogen. In times to come, your people will understand its radiochemistry; it is enough for you now to know that its most significant effect is to turn on the full analytical powers of the mind whenever fear is experienced. Panic occurs when analysis is shut off. Embarrassment occurs when fear is not analyzed. Hereafter, no truck-driver will fear to use the word 'exquis-

ite,' no propagandist will create the semblance of truth by repeating falsehoods, no human group will be able to instill fears about any other human group which are not common to the respective individuals of the groups. There will be no fear-ridden movements of securities, and no lovers will be with each other and afraid to state their love. In large issues and in small ones, the greater the emergency the greater will be the stimulation of the analytical powers.

That is the meaning and purpose and constitution of the ultimate weapon. To you it is a gift. There are few races in cosmic history with a higher potential than yours, or with a more miserable expression of it. The gift is yours because of this phenomenon.

As for us, our quest is as stated to you. We were to seek out the weapon and bring it back with us. We gave it to you instead, by manipulation of your impulses, Naome, and yours, Sig, with the radio. Earth needs it more than we do.

But we have not failed. The radio-chemistry of the nitrogen-isotope reaction and its catalyses are now widely available to us. It will be simplicity itself for us to recreate the weapon, and the time it will take us is as nothing ..

... For we are a race which commands the fluxes of time, and we can braid a distance about our fingers, and hold the Alpha and Omega together in the palms of our hands.

"The probes are gone," said Tillie, after a long silence.

Reluctantly, they removed their hands from the communicator, and flexed them.

Cris said, "Tillie, where is the ship?"

She smiled. "Remember? 'You insist that what is cosmically important must be huge.'" She pointed. "That is the ship."

They stared at the bulbous arrowhead. It rose and drifted toward the door. It paused there, tilted toward them in an obvious salute, and then, like a light extinguished, it was gone.

Naome sprang to her feet. "Is it all true, about the propaganda, the panic, the—the lovers who can speak their minds?"

Naome said, "Testing. Testing. Sig Weiss, I love you."

Sig picked her up and hugged her. "Come on, all of you. I want to walk clear down to the corners and have a beer with the old man. I want to tell him something I've never said before—that he's my neighbor."

Cris helped Tillie up. "I think he stocks some real V-type halters."

Outside, it was a greener world, and all over it the birds sang.

Excalibur and the Atom

IN A FACE that was a statement of strength, two deep lines formed parentheses. They enclosed a mouth that was a big gentleness. Into the mouth he thrust the soggy end of the pretzel stick he had been dunking in his coffee. He grunted. The classified ad read:

Lose something? Or maybe you want something found. Or maybe you just want something. Convince me it exists, pay my expenses, and I'll charge you a fee for finding it. Hadley Guinn, HE 6-2420.

"A hell of a way to get business," he said to the coffee container. It had two flyspecks and a brown stain that together looked like a grinning rat. "Go ahead," he growled. "Laugh."

She came in then, straight through the waiting room into his office. "Hadley Guinn?" She had a voice to go with olive skin, the kind with a glow under it.

"You read signs on doors?"

"I still have to ask questions. You forgot to wear your dog-tag." She came forward and sat down. She moved across the floor as if she were on tracks. She sat down as if she were folding wings.

"Have a wet pretzel?"

"Thanks, no. I just threw one away." She regarded him evenly. She had not smiled, she had not raised a brow or arched a nostril. She was everything in the world that was completely composed. She was about twenty, with blue-black hair. Her blue eyes didn't belong with that complexion at all. They didn't belong with her age either. They were wise eyes. They were ten thousand years old. She wore a black dress with a built-on cape around her shoulders and a neck-line down to here. She used a brown-red lipstick that went with the skin but not at all with the eyes or the dress. On her it looked fine.

"Reckon it'll rain tomorrow?" he asked eventually.

She took the remark at face value. "Not in Barenton."

"Where's Barenton?"

"Sorry" she said. "Classical reference. There's a hawthorne bush there."

"Would that be the one you're beating around?"

The thick lashes did not bat. "You can find anything?"

"I'm near enough to being legal to be able to handle the language," he said. He quoted: " 'Convince me it exists ...' "

"I see. If it's too much trouble, you're not convinced."

He quoted: " ' ... pay my expenses ...' "

"Mmm. And then the fee comes automatically."

"When I find it. You examine more clauses than the guy who manicures for Clyde Beatty."

She said, deadpan, "That job really gives one pause."

His appreciation was in his eyes and in the parentheses. He left it there. "It was nice of you to drop in, Miss Jones."

"Morgan," she said.

He drained the container, crushed it, filed it in the wastebasket. He swept the remaining pretzel sticks into the drawer. "Lunch time's over," he explained. "Shall we dance?"

"Not while we have to watch our steps ... What's your special signal that means you're about to go to work?"

"I answer a businesslike question."

She nodded. "Want to find something for me?"

He waited.

She said, coolly, "Want to find something for me if I convince you that it is, and pay your expenses?"

He said nothing.

"In advance?"

"Certainly," he said.

"Very well. I'm looking for a stone. It's a big one—seven or eight karats. Not a diamond. A diamond looks like a piece of putty beside it. It glows in the dark."

"Where is it?"

She shrugged.

"Well, is it loose, or in a ring, or what?"

"It's on a cup. It looks like gold, but it isn't. The cup holds about a quart, and it has a five-sided pedestal and a five-sided foot."

He closed his eyes, looked at the mental picture her words drew, and said, "Got a lead?"

"There's a man in town who almost had it once. His name's Percival."

Guinn reached under the desk and scratched his lower shinbone. "You mean the Caveman?"

"That's the man."

"Hell. He doesn't have any use for baubles. He doesn't even believe in money."

"You meet all kinds of people," she said gently.

"All right. I'll go see him. What else do you know about this cup?"

"What do you want to know?"

"Where did it come from? Where was it last seen? Why do you want it?"

"No one knows where it came from. The stone is supposed to have come from the sky. The cup was made in the Middle East more than two thousand years ago. It's been seen only twice, and that was too long ago to bother about. I do know it's been seen near here. As for why I want it . . ." The wise eyes looked deep into his. "I want it very badly," she whispered.

The intensity of her gaze, of her voice, gave him a genuine shock. It was the first break in her incredible composure and he hadn't been ready for it.

"I'll look for it," he said.

She stood up. "Here's five to start with."

He watched her open her purse. "Five? Don't knock yourself out, Miss Morgan."

"There'll be more when you need it," she said. She put five bills down on the desk. They were C-notes.

"It's that important?" he asked.

"At least that important," she said soberly.

"Guys get killed over things that important."

"Lots of guys have gotten killed over this." She looked at him for a moment. "Shall I pick up those bills now?"

"Allow me," he said graciously. He scooped them, stacked them, fingered his smooth brown wallet out of his hip pocket and slipped the money into it. "Now tell me more."

She looked him straight in the eye and shook her head very slowly, twice. Her eyes, her wise eyes, slid in their long sockets as her head moved. "It's your cooky, Guinn."

He shrugged. "You're just going to make me use up more of your expense money. What's your first name?"

"Morgan."

"All right, if you don't want to tell me. Where can I get in touch with you?"

"For the time being," she said coolly, "I'll worry about that." She stood up. "Be careful."

"Should I really be careful?"

"I keep telling you," she said, "this job isn't just difficult." She turned and walked out.

When she got to the outer door, he called her: "Miss Morgan!"

"Yes?"

"Goodbye."

She set the shoulder strap of her bag and passed the doorknob from one hand to the other as she sidled through it. "You're so formal," she said, and was gone.

Guinn sat staring at the door. His face was completely impassive; he was suddenly conscious of it, that he was imitating hers. He grunted loudly, spread one big hand and drummed the desk top, once.

He saw the girl called Morgan crossing the sidewalk. He knew how women walked. He'd never seen one move like this. He wondered some things about her and then felt his wallet without taking it out. He bent it; his sensitive fingers could feel it crackle. They were nice new bills.

He shook his head and went back to the desk. From the second drawer he took a shoulder harness and strapped it on. In the middle drawer were two guns. He took the dull-gray .32 and slipped the magazine out. He ejected the shell that was in the breech, pressed it into the magazine and, holding the cocking-piece back, twisted the breech-block and broke the gun. He sighted the bore to the window, nodded, and deftly put the gun together again, returning the top cartridge to the breech. He dropped it into the holster, picked up the other gun, thought for a moment and then put it back. It clinked. He bent, peered, palmed out a four-fifths of rye. He sighted it exactly and as carefully as he had the gun-bore, then put it back in the drawer.

He went to the door, felt for his keys, thumbed the spring catch. The bolt shot out with a disapproving *tsk!* He pulled at his square chin, returned to the desk, opened the middle drawer again and found an unpaid telephone bill in a well-thumbed envelope. He took out his wallet, put three of the C-notes in with the bill, and dropped the envelope back in the drawer. He felt the bottle staring at him, muttered, "If that's the way you feel," and resentfully drank from it. There were only a couple of fingers left. Then he went out and slammed the door behind him.

It wasn't quite two o'clock.

There was a two-year-old station wagon on the street that looked as if it had run two hundred thousand miles and rolled sidewise the last four. A lean youth sat on the front fender with his feet on a fireplug. On the pavement by the plug were four dog-eared cheesecake magazines.

Guinn asked him, "What goes, Garry? You take the pledge?"

The youth looked down at the magazines. "Those I don't need," he said, and flashed a sudden, loose-lipped grin. He had clumped hair that looked like the oozings at the top of a cotton-bale, and steel-gray eyes that were very pale pink all around the edges. "I just seen a chick, hey. She has hair like this, see," and he made a motion as if he were saluting with both hands at once, "and it's so black it's blue. She's stacked like wheatcakes, but with honey. Mostly, she's got a face like a pyramid."

"You mean a sphinx."

"Same thing. So why should I look at pictures? Hey—you know her, hey?"

Guinn reached in through the window of the station wagon and opened the door. "A client." He got in.

Garry trotted around the street side, grasped the window frame, and pulled. The door opened and sagged. He got in, lifted the door and pulled it until it latched, and tramped on the starter. The motor responded instantly and quietly. "Yeah, huh," said Garry enthusiastically. "What's she want?"

Guinn said shortly, "Just because this wagon's a dog doesn't mean you have to keep it by a hydrant all the time. Let's go."

The car moved forward. Garry said, "Is she—"

"Take the hill road and turn off at the Spur."

Garry nodded. "Will she—"

"I changed the subject twice," said Guinn.

Garry tightened his lips and raised his eyebrows in a facial shrug. Guinn sat silently, his big hands lax on his knees, his eyes on the road.

After a time he said, "I mean that about the fireplugs."

"Well," said Garry, "I got to have some place to put my feet."

"Put 'em in your pockets."

About two miles further on Garry asked, "Now, how am I going to do that and keep my pants on?"

The two lines at the corners of Guinn's mouth deepened. Suddenly he straightened. "Slow down."

There was a girl on the road, hobbling painfully along toward them. Guinn said, "That kid's hurt ... no; busted a heel off. Stop, Garry."

He leaned out. "Something wrong, sister?"

She made no effort to approach the car. "I'm all right." She wore a strapless sun-back dress that flared out at the hips. She was a copper blonde with angry green eyes. Her left hand clutched the top hem of the dress; in her right she held a limp handbag made of the same purple linen as her dress.

"The hell you are," said Guinn. He peered at her. "Don't I know you? Your name's ... Lynn."

She sighed and crossed the road shoulder. "That's right. I deal off the arm at Crenley's Cafeteria. You're that detective in the Miles Building."

"What's the matter?"

The slight identification seemed to make a large difference. She came close to the car. She wiped her brow with the back of the hand that held the bag. "It's real hot," she said with a small smile, as if apologizing for the weather. "Oh, I just guessed wrong. Day off, fellow says it's a nice day for a spin, get 'way out in the country, and suddenly I get an offer. Or walk." She shrugged, clutched tighter at her neckline. "I walked."

"There was some wrestling," said Guinn.

"Uh-huh. Tore my dress, the stinker. For that I wiped off his collarbone with his ear.

"Good." He looked at his watch. "I don't have much time to run you back in. Have to spend most of the afternoon up on the Spur. But I should be back in town before seven. You're welcome to come along."

She hesitated, looked down the hot, dusty road toward the town and then at the inviting shade inside the station wagon. Then, "Why not?" she said. "I'm off till tomorrow. Gosh, thanks, Mr. Guinn."

He reached back and opened the door and she climbed in. Garry let in the clutch. Lynn said, "That feels good, that breeze."

Guinn fumbled in the glove compartment. "There ought to be— yeah—here it is." His hand closed on a small plastic case which he passed back to the girl. "Sorry I don't seem to stock your color."

"Wh—Oh! A needle and these little rolls of thread. You are a Boy Scout!"

"Yeah, huh," muttered Garry.

Lynn said, "Don't look around, will you? I'm not ... not wearing anything under this, and if I'm going to sew it from the inside I'll have to pull it right down."

"Go ahead," said Guinn.

They bowled along in silence through the hot afternoon. The right-hand wheels rumbled on the shoulder, sang again on tarmac. They rumbled again. Guinn looked up sharply to see Garry's eyes fixed on the rear-view mirror. He reached up and turned it on its swivel and with the same movement snapped his thumbnail so hard on the bridge of Garry's nose that tears came to the driver's eyes. Neither man said a word, and Lynn was apparently too busy to notice.

They turned off on the Spur road and began to climb. At the second hairpin the blacktop ceased. At the fourth there were no more retaining walls. At the seventh the road had yielded up its last cottage driveway and was a two-track meander through neglected hilltop fields. In the middle of one of these Garry stopped the car.

"More?"

"Go ahead," said Guinn.

"You know," said Garry resignedly, and inched over the track until the car poked its battered snout into woods. Garry glanced at Guinn, who sat as if in deep thought and gave no orders. The car moved through underbrush and there, abruptly, was the track again, winding through the woods.

"Oh, how lovely!" said Lynn.

It was certainly restful; an underwater-green light, sun-spangled in shifting patches of gold.

"Whoa."

There was a glitter of chrome ahead, as offensive as a belch in a theater audience. Garry braked. Guinn stared thoughtfully at the low-slung Town-and-Country convertible which blocked the track a hundred shaded yards ahead, and at the gray rock outcropping beyond it. There was a flash of white; a baby goat curvetted on the rocks, then another and another.

"Pull 'way over," said Guinn. "Far enough so that Chrysler can get out if it wants to. But keep your eye on him."

There was a sound from Lynn—a quickly checked almost-syllable. Guinn swung around.

She was staring at the convertible, sitting bolt-upright, and her green eyes were round. "What is it, Lynn?"

"I could be wrong, but I think that's the—the fellow who—"

"We'll take care of him."

"Oh, please. I don't want any trouble."

Garry turned around and said jovially, "Oh, it won't be any trouble, miss."

He tooled the car between the trees and got it off the road. Guinn watched him narrowly. He'd known that combination of joviality and slitted eyes from 'way back. "Garry—"

"I don't like to see women pushed around," said Garry. He switched off.

Guinn got out, closed the door, leaned his elbows on the window ledge. "Lynn . . ."

She took her apprehensive eyes from the convertible. "Mmm?"

"You'll be all right with Garry. He's harmless. He likes to look, but he's afraid to touch." He thumped Garry's shoulder. "If anyone shoots at you," he told him, "try to catch the slug in your head, where it won't make any difference."

Garry laughed with the same ominous cheerfulness. "How soon'll you be back?"

"Shortly." He turned away and struck into the woods at about forty-five degrees away from the road.

He worked his way carefully, keeping a constant watch on the convertible and on the area between it and the rocks. Nothing moved. There was no one in sight in or around the Chrysler when he drew abreast of it. He made no attempt to get closer, but moved steadily toward the rocks. Once he stopped and listened. He made another fifty feet and stopped again. There was a high, thin cry, faint and close. It sounded like a hoarse-voiced three-year-old child repeating a single vowel sound: *Ei-ee! Ei-ee!*

He stepped into the clearing around the rocks. Out of the corner of his eye something dark flashed out of sight around a projection in the gray stone.

Guinn slid back into the brush and waited. He reached inside his jacket and fingered the butt of his .32.

The black thing barely showed, disappeared again.

Hollow, faint, near, insistent came the childlike *Ei-ee . . . ei-ee . . . ei-ee . . .*

Guinn lifted his gun, kicked off the safeties, crouched lower.

Explosively, the black thing leaped out into the open. Guinn's breath caught in his throat and he quelled the trigger reflex of his right hand by an enormous application of will. A black goat kid pranced into the open, ran and leapt high over some invisible obstacle created in its own fantastically playful imagination, hit the ground with all four feet together, back arched, head down. It gave an infantile snort and raced away, its little hooves making astonishingly soft little sounds on the rocks, like a cat's feet on parquet flooring.

"Percival!" Guinn called.

Ee-ee ... ei-ee ...

From the woods came the sound of a starter. Not the station wagon, for the motor turned over all of four times before it caught, a delay that Garry wouldn't stand for in anything he drove. Must be the Chrysler.

Guinn hesitated only a second, recalled that Garry was between the Chrysler and the outside world, then stepped out into the clearing. He heard the convertible grind into reverse, cut into low and then a dwindling second. He shrugged and moved across to the rocks and around them, swiftly and watchfully. Nothing moved. Somewhere a goat bleated, and another answered.

Then there was a wide cave-mouth.

"Percival?"

No answer, except that repetitive, high-pitched cry.

Guinn ducked into the cave and sprang to one side, feeling for that silhouetted second like a towed artillery target. A sixth sense told him there was nothing human inside. He shut his eyes tight as if to squeeze the residual sunlight out of them like some dazzling juice.

At last he could see. Book rack. A hard mattress on the scrupulously leveled and swept clay floor. Goatskins. And back in the corner, something small and white that wept and wept.

He crossed, knelt beside it. It was a newborn goat kid, a day or so old, its wobbly and beseeching head stretched toward the light.

He patted its neck and it slapped his wrist with a tongue as rough

as a finishing rasp. Then he flicked his gaze over the cave again. He
ran his hand over the books, glanced at their titles. Krishnamurti,
Malory, Tennyson, Gibrahn, Swedenborg. White's *The Sword in the
Stone,* C.S. Lewis's *That Hideous Strength.* Theosophy, anthropol-
ogy, *Ancient British Landmarks.*

"Busy boy," he muttered. He turned to the mattress, touched it.
It was wet.

He could detect, as he bent over it, the acrid not unpleasant odor
of fresh clean perspiration. He threw off the shaggy goatskin. Under
it the mattress was sopping. But this wasn't perspiration.

It was blood.

"*Ei-ee . . .*" mourned the kid.

"Hold tight, baby," he soothed. He knelt and scrutinized the floor
carefully in the band of sunlight which streamed in through the cave-
mouth.

"Um-hm!" Blood again; a spot, a starred droplet, a smear. Once
he had seen them it was easy enough to follow them outside ("I'll
be back, baby," he told the kid), across the clearing, through a band
of woodland (where, on a flat rock, there was a full scarlet hand-
print) and into the meadow behind the outcropping.

The goats were there, massed together like a bed of flowers, their
heads all turned toward him, their eyes like shining seeds. He stopped,
and here a head fell, and there, and one by one they began to graze
absently. But none of them wandered far from the still figure on the
grass.

He went to it and the goats fell back before him, warily and
attentive.

Percival lay face downward on the grass. Guinn knew it was Percival because of the single length of white linen wrapped around his
waist, and because of the tumbled gray shoulder-length hair. The
hair had blood on it.

He turned the body over, and Percival moaned. He wasn't dead,
and that, under the circumstances, was a pity.

Guinn took out his carefully folded display handkerchief, shook
it open, and wiped out the blood-filled eyes. "It's Hadley Guinn,"
he said softly. "You'll be all right now."

"Mo," whispered Percival. No one could have made an 'n' sound from a mouth and tongue in that condition.

"Who did it?"

Percival breathed deeply, twice, and his eyes began to glaze. Guinn shook him, almost roughly. "You've got to tell me who did this to you." He turned the handkerchief, dabbed very gently at the tattered mouth.

Slowly the eyes regained some life. "Gwim?"

"Guinn, yes; Hadley Guinn. I'll help you, Percival. Who did this to you?"

"Gwim ... g o o' boy, Gwim." He coughed. Guinn caught the blood. "Who ... fent ... oo?"

Guinn closed his eyes and ran over forty possibilities. Then, "Who sent me? Never mind that, Percival, man. Tell me, you've got to tell me—"

Percival tossed his head impatiently. "Who? Who?"

"All right. It was a dame called Morgan."

The painful distortion of the wrecked mouth might have been a smile. Percival nodded. "Gh-h-issen ..."

Guinn translated this as listen ... "I'm listening, Percival," he said softly.

Percival's gnarled hand came up, pointed. The sharp old index finger dug into his knee to punctuate the crippled, halting speech. "... Hynd guh ghuid umgh-ozhiush ..."

Watching those tortured eyes, Guinn felt grief and panic mount. He tried. He tried desperately hard. "Wait: you say hy ... hie ... fi ... *find* ... guh ... duh ... the? *The. Find the.* Find the what, Percival?"

"Ghuid ... Dhuid ..."

"Doo-id? D ... Druid?" Is it *Druid*, Percival?"

Percival nodded weakly, rapidly. His hand patted Guinn's knee as if in vast approval. "Um ... amgh-ozhiush."

"Amgh ... Amgrozihi-ess ..."

Percival spread his hand in a helpless gesture. Guinn said, "Was that close? Is that almost it, Percival? *Amghrozhi-ess?*"

Percival nodded weakly. Guinn could all but see his soul leaving his body. "Who did it? Who, Percival—who?"

"M-m-m . . ."

"Please, please . . . try."

"Mugh-gug."

"Mur . . . murdered. Murdered. Yes, Percival—who did it?"

"M-m-m . . ."

Guinn put the great head down softly and stood up. He hurt. He hurt away down inside where his roiling anger lived—way under anything he could control.

He hurt enough to measure his wonderment when as a kid with a dog he had run into Percival and his goats; when he used to sit in the cave and hear that great rolling voice tell tales of ancient times, and the gods men worshipped when the world was younger, when faith had the place that knowledge has now. There were great tales of the future, too, when the reverence now given knowledge will be replaced by understanding.

He hurt enough to measure his delight when Percival would gravely give him his choice of goat's milk or turnip juice to drink, and when the hermit gave him a great white ram's skin for his own. (It lay over the foot of his bed to this day.)

He hurt enough to measure his shame when as an enlightened teenager he had been part of a gang that went up to jeer and throw mud at the "nekkid looney." (For Percival lived naked in the warm weather and in goat-skins in the cold, always courteously donning his strip of linen when anyone came by.) They'd taken pictures and had themselves a hell of a laugh over it; and Guinn couldn't live with it and went up to apologize, and the hermit greeted him as a friend.

Percival was part of the mountain—part of the world. He was part of a very real world of rocks and flowers, wind and winter and eternal wildness—a world on which chrome and neon and nuclear energy and power politics grew like acne on a great calm face. He had never done harm to a living soul. He had never sought a human being out nor turned one away. He was on the mountain when Guinn was born and he should have been there when Guinn died, because he was part of the eternity that every man should have, somewhere, to turn to when he needs it.

Something died and was born in Guinn as he stood looking down at the great torn face. "Take care of him," he said to the goats. "I'll send somebody up . . ."

From the cave the kid cried and cried.

"Oh, yes, baby. You've got it just right."

He scooped up a startled nanny and headed for the cave. As he reached the entrance he heard a shot from the woods.

"Sorry, lady," he said. He flung the nanny through the cave-mouth with one fluid sweep of his two arms, hoping against hope that she and the kid would get together, and sprinted for his car.

As he passed the place where the Chrysler had been parked there was another shot, and the moan of the Town-and-Country's motor. He pounded up to the station wagon just in time to see the convertible break through the underbrush and disappear into the meadow.

Lynn was gone. Garry lay beside the car. There was a hole in the side of his head and another at the back, and he was very bloody.

Guinn was around at all largely because he had the knack of selecting priorities among simultaneous emergencies, and because, having been born with the knack, he'd spent most of his life developing it.

When he knelt beside Garry's body he knew he had feelings about it, but he filed them away for later. The priority he noticed immediately was a smell and a sound; a steady trickle of liquid on dead leaves, and the acrid fumes of gasoline.

He dropped to his belly and looked under the car. A stream of gas the size of a pencil lead was flowing out of the tank. He pulled himself up by a doorhandle, opening the door as he moved, scooped up the rear seat and got a folding bucket from under it, and ran around to shove it under the tank. He felt the hole, a jagged oval rip cut by a .32 or something larger.

"Don't go away," he said to Garry.

He opened the right rear door, pulled at the scarred upholstery. It came off its snap-fasteners with a sound like teeth going into peanut brittle. In the shallow space between upholstery and the outer panel were row on row of parts, neatly clipped with spring clamps. There were spark plugs, three spare distributor caps, ignition wire and a number of other things that it's better to have and not need than need and not have.

Guinn's hands were a blur. He found what he was looking for: spider-expansion bolts and washers, and a screwdriver. He dove under the car, slipped the bolt through the washer and a gasket, and forced the bolt into the hole in the tank. He spun it with the screwdriver with a palm-on-palm technique he had learned in his wartime stretch in an aircraft factory, until the spider inside spread and the washer seated tightly over the hole. The he wrenched off the tank cap and slopped in the fuel which had been caught in the bucket.

The whole operation had taken somewhat over ninety seconds.

Guinn hurled the bucket, screwdriver and upholstered panel into the back of the station wagon. He lifted Garry swiftly and gently and spread him out on the seat behind the driver's. There were cargo straps. He whipped one around Garry's chest, one around his thighs, and cinched them down. He took one precious moment to touch the youth's head with big, sensitive fingers, feeling carefully between the two holes. He pursed his lips worriedly, slid under the wheel and kicked the motor over. A patient rear fender took yet another wound-stripe as he slithered the car around, caromed off a tree, and headed out. He leaned forward, his hands placed lightly at "ten and two" like a racing driver's. He let the wheel shimmy through his fingers, and he drove.

Two shots. Garry got one. The gas tank got the other. The man who had cut up Percival's face had Lynn. Hadley Guinn was out to get that man.

On the third hairpin turn he craned over the edge as his wheels kicked stones out into space. Down below him he saw a dust cloud. He let his foot give four more ounces to the accelerator.

On the fourth turn he actually saw the convertible taking the last straightaway into the Spur road. Guinn groaned. He had two more hairpins to negotiate.

Or had he? The road zig-zagged down the mountain face, but that didn't necessarily mean he had to ...

This far down the hill, the grade flattened out. From this stretch there was about a four-to-one slope to the road below. From that road the grade was a mere thirty degrees or so.

"So what the hell," he growled, and pulled on the wheel.

For an endless second he had strictly a bird's-eye view all across the windshield. Then the front end came swooping downward. There was a nasty crunch as the road shoulder ground into the muffler pipe under the car's center of gravity, and then he was off the road, headed down the slope.

There wasn't time to think. There was just time to fight. He locked the brakes when the machine would slide straight, let it roll when it wanted to turn. He diddled the brakes and outguessed the wheel. A small avalanche accompanied him, and a rising cloud of dust joined hands with the growing dusk to make seeing tough.

Then the front wheels hit the shallow ditch of the next level of the switchback road. There was a harrowing snap as the bumper bulldozed into the ditch and broke off, and then the car was slanting across the road and down again off the other side. The underside took another blow, though not as severe this time, as the car levered over the edge. And once more the nightmare of rolling too fast and not sliding straight enough.

There was no appreciable ditch at the bottom, and it was a black-top road. Guinn hauled the wheel over and the rubber screamed as he gunned down the Spur road. Looking across country he could see the convertible streaking along the township highway that would take it across the river and into the city.

Guinn bore down to the floor, and the station wagon laid its ears back and went. With it, it carried an unholy din of scraping metal which suddenly ceased as the muffler and exhaust stack tore loose and skittered into the ditch. The car bellowed with an open throat. Guinn nodded grimly. Made to order; he could crowd six or seven miles more per hour out of the old dog without that manifold back pressure.

He took the turn into the township road altogether too fast, and had the rear end into and out of the ditch on the far side of the turn. And then he was on the straightaway, and with the convertible a distant beetle ahead of him. He glanced back at the mountain, grinned tightly as he saw the long scar of his tracks straight down its naked face. He'd gotten a half-mile jump on the Chrysler by short-circuiting those two hairpins.

He checked ahead for traffic and then twisted to look back at Garry. The youth lay limp and pale in his straps. The bleeding seemed to have stopped for the time being. Guinn prayed that his probing fingers had been right.

Glancing ahead again, he felt a leap of joy as he saw that he was gaining on the convertible. Traffic was light, happily, and there was nothing between him and the other car. He pulled out the choke lever a tiny fraction and did his best to put his foot through the floorboards. He took his right hand off the wheel, fingered his gun out of its holster and wedged it between his right buttock and the seat.

Suddenly he stiffened, peered. The convertible was just about to gain the bridge, which carried the road on its own level as steep banks fell to the water below. And at the other end of the bridge, coming toward them, was the great hulking mass of a lowboy trailer carrying a fifty-ton power shovel. The bridge was wide enough for two lanes of ordinary traffic, but getting the Chrysler past it was going to be a trick.

He saw a single flicker of the convertible's brake lights, and then its driver apparently decided to bull through. Guinn saw the lowboy tractor lumbering as far over to his side of the bridge as it could, and the trailer reluctantly following. The swelling sides of the shovel's cab bulged far over the center-line of the roadway.

The brake lights flared again. The convertible would clear the tractor and probably the side of the shovel, but the rear end of the trailer was still slightly angled across the road.

The convertible braked, and braked again, and each time a huge bite was taken out of the distance between Guinn and his quarry. He was less than two hundred feet behind when it happened.

The Chrysler found its opening and hurtled through. It must have nipped the back corner of the lowboy the lightest of touches, and it was all but scraping the guard rail on the right. In that split second the right-hand door of the Chrysler opened. It was rear-hinged door; the wind flipped it wide. Its edge struck the guard rail and broke it off—and a slim figure in purple rose in the air and arched over the rail.

"Lynn!"

In the same instant he had to wrench his wheel right, then left to get through the same gap, a blessed inch or two wider now as the trailer straightened out on its side of the roadway. It had all happened so fast that the lowboy crew probably saw none of it, except two cars driving too damn fast.

Now Guinn *really* had a priority to choose.

He could go after his man and run him to earth—with the idea that Lynn might be hurt—drowned or crushed—in that wild leap over the rail. Or he could swing right at the end of the bridge, where an underpass connected with the River Road, and try to save her—knowing that the Chrysler would be miles away.

He peered at the license plate and knew he wouldn't forget it. He realized, too, that with Lynn out of the Chrysler, half his reason for catching it was gone. Of course, catching Percival's murderer was reason enough, but—

He cursed, and as he swept off the end of the bridge, pulled right. The convertible arrowed ahead.

Down under the first pier of the bridge, Guinn pulled up. He glanced worriedly at Garry. "You'll just have to wait, son," he murmured.

He slipped his gun back in its holster and ran down to the water's edge. His first searching look was upward, at the roadway above. There was no sign of a body on the rail or on the second pier, seventy-five feet or so out in the river. She'd fallen clear, then. And on the upstream side. And then he saw her—the merest glimpse of water-darkened copper blonde hair, the flash of an arm against the brown stone of the pier.

He kicked off his shoes, shoved his gone in one and his wallet in the other, ran down a flight of stone boat-landing steps and plunged into the river.

He swam strongly out to the pier, wondering how he could have been so stupid as to have left his jacket on, figuring what the hell, it was a tropical and not very unwieldy; no point wasting it now. He gained the pier almost under the bridge, for the current ran fairly strongly here. He pulled himself up on its platform-like surface, which was only a foot or so above water level, and walked squishily to the upstream end.

She was there, clinging weakly to the stone, breathing in deep gasps. When she saw him she yelped. "Oh!" She took in some water, coughed violently. He knelt and grasped her wrist.

The coughing subsided. "Mr. Guinn . . ." She pushed her hair back. One side of her face and one shoulder were scarlet. "I didn't . . . see you come up. I was . . . just getting my wind back . . . before I . . . tried to make . . . the bank."

"Are you all right?"

"Oh, sure, except I . . . hit awful hard . . . I'm—Mr. Guinn, I'm mother naked!"

"That was a smart move."

"It wasn't a move! Strapless dress and no bra and . . . when I hit I just skinned right out of it! Shoes and all . . . Even my . . . Oh, this is awful!"

"I've got news for you," said Guinn, his eyes twinkling. "I've seen the like before."

"I'm terribly sorry about it," she said surprisingly. "But . . . I got away from him, didn't I?"

"That you did. Don't talk now. Get your wind back and I'll give you a tow in. We've got to get to a hospital, but quick."

"Hospital? I'm—"

"Not you. Garry."

"He's—he's dead!"

"Not him. The slug slipped in under his temple and skinned around his big thick skull and came out over his ear, near the back. Concussion, maybe, but I don't think there's a fracture."

"Oh, come on." She turned immediately shoreward with long competent strokes.

Guinn let her get out into the stream and then dove after her, coming up a little ahead. He swam with a side-stroke, watching her. She suddenly coughed again.

"Thought it was too soon," he said. "Float."

"Oh, I'm all—"

"Float," he said. Submissively, she did. He got a hand under her chin and towed her, his long legs supplying a powerful scissor kick, his free hand gathering armloads of distance. Lynn lay back, completely relaxed, filling her lungs gratefully. Again the current carried them downstream a little way and they had to work their way up the stone embankment to the landing.

"Please go ahead," she said. "I'm not prissy, but—"

"Don't fret," he said kindly. He scrambled up the steps and went to where he had left his shoes. Lynn hesitated, then ran up the steps and started toward the car, which was parked out of sight of the riverside roadway under the bridge. She was perhaps halfway there when there was a flash and a roar from the road. A heavy calibre slug nicked a small sapling at Lynn's elbow. She squeaked.

"This way," snapped Guinn. "Jump!"

She ran to him; he motioned her past so that the first bridge pier was between her and the source of the shots. Guinn dropped back to the stone steps, backed down them until he had cover.

It was growing dark as reluctantly as any early summer night will. Guinn's eyes passed the car parked on the other side of the River Road twice before he noticed it looming in the shadow of a dogwood tree.

It was the Chrysler.

He took careful aim and snapped two shots at it. There was a distinctly audible gasp, then a moan. Guinn sprinted toward it. A bullet struck the ground at his feet and another tugged at his sleeve. He fired and hit the dirt. Before he could so much as raise his head the starter whinnied, the motor caught, and the car moved off. It turned and sped up the ramp to the bridge level. Guinn fired once more, stood fuming for a moment, and then went back to the girl. She was flattened against the river side of the pier.

"It's okay now," he said. He turned and went to the station wagon. She followed. "Was that my ardent swain?" she asked in a shaken voice.

He got in the car and opened the other door for her. "It was." He took off his jacket, wrung it out over the ground, shook it, and handed it across to her. She put it over her shoulders and climbed in. "He must have had an attack of second thought. Wondered if you had killed yourself or not. Came back to see. You showed up nicely against the dark river. He couldn't see the station wagon, and didn't notice me in this brown suit. It must have been a big surprise to him to get lead thrown back at him. Who is he, anyway?"

"I don't know him, really. His name's Mordi. He came into the—"

"Morty?"

"Mordi. He came into the hash house a few times. Dark. Dresses well. Very quiet." She shuddered. "I'll look out for those quiet ones after this. Steel traps ... dynamite sticks ... they're nice and quiet, un-*til.*"

He started the motor, backed, turned, and got onto the River Road. She said suddenly, "Mr. Guinn ..."

"Mmm?"

She hesitated. Then, "Mind if I take this off again? You'll think I'm terrible, but it's so clammy. And it's warm this evening and somehow it doesn't seem to matter. Though I don't know how I'll ever get out of the car in town."

"Go ahead," said Guinn. "It's getting dark. The passing parade will think you're still in that strapless job. You're right—it matters as much as or as little as you let it. When we get to the hospital I'll see if there isn't a nurse's uniform I can swipe for you."

She peeled off the jacket and draped it over the seat between them. She crossed her arms and rubbed her shoulders for a moment, then sat demurely with her hands on her lap.

He said, "You took a hell of a chance with that high-dive."

"Not so much," she said. "I used to swim there a lot. The channel's real deep between the bank and that second pier, and I knew that. I noticed the way that car door opened when I was with him this afternoon. I knew it would slam wide open if I just opened it a little and I was waiting my chance. When he had to swing so near the rail to pass that trailer—that was it. I got my feet under me and dove right off the seat. I used to go off there all the time. It's forty-two feet," she added.

"At about forty-two miles an hour, just then," he said: "Lucky you didn't break your back."

"Well, I didn't."

He glanced at her admiringly. "Do you have to work at that hash-house?"

"It's a job."

"You've got a better one if you want it."

"With you? Do you mean it?"

"Yup."

"Oh, I'd love it. I'd just love it."

A conquest, thought Guinn.

She said, "I could maybe see him every day."

"See who?"

"Garry."

Not my conquest, he thought, and allowed himself one of his rare grins. "He's a good kid."

"He's the bravest man I've ever known! Why, when that man came up out of the woods like that . . ."

"Tell me about it."

"I was a little afraid of him at first, Garry I mean," she said. "The way he was looking at me. Then he started to talk. I never heard anybody talk the way he does. Not as if I was a girl. Just as if I was . . . well, people. About the car and you and jet aircraft and banana cream pie and the National League. It was . . ." She paused. "Anyway, we heard the other car start. Garry put a hand on my arm and said not to worry. That was all, just 'Don't worry.' I wish I could tell you how—safe—it made me feel.

"The car came up, and sure enough it was him—Mordi, the man

I'd been riding with before I met you. He looked out at us and then stopped his car. He leaned out for a long time and looked at me and at Garry and the station wagon, and then he got out and came up to us. I never saw such cold eyes on a human being in my life, and they shouldn't be, they're not the right color to be so cold.

"Garry got out and they stood looking at each other. Finally Mordi said, 'Nobody cuts in on me, cottonhead.'

"Garry said, 'Beat it, cottonmouth. Nothing around here belongs to you.'

"So the man said to me, 'He's so wrong, ain't he, sugar?'

"And I said, 'He's so right.'

"He came up close, then, and told me I was going back with him. I just shook my head. Then Garry said, 'That'll do for now, tailor-dummy. Goodbye again.' And he reached inside his jacket. When he did that, Mordi pulled out a gun and shot him in the head."

Guinn's eyes seemed to get smaller. "Garry never carries a gun," he said. "I'll have to tell him some things about raising on a three-card straight."

"He's too honest to get away with a bluff," said Lynn.

"Oh," said Guinn. The smile appeared again.

Lynn said, "He reached in and got my wrist. I didn't know he was going to pull so hard, so suddenly. He hauled me out and I was flat on my face before I knew what was happening. Then he hit me." She put her hand behind her neck, stroked. "I guess I went out, and I didn't come to all at once, either. Everything was sort of dreamy for the longest time."

"I know that punch," said Guinn.

"I was in his car," she continued. "He wasn't. I heard another shot. I remember thinking he must have gone back to finish Garry. Or maybe you."

"Shot a hole in my gas tank," said Guinn.

"Oh. Well, before I was completely out of it, we were charging down the hill. He drove very fast. He laughed at me. He's crazy ... what'd he want to kill a man over me for?"

"I don't want to take a compliment away from a lady," said Guinn, "but it wasn't over you. He killed somebody up there, and we were the only ones who'd seen him around. He knew what he was doing. That's why he came back just now to make sure you were out of the running. He seems to've missed me altogether. I guess while I was catfooting over toward the rocks on one side, he was sneaking back on the other."

She shuddered. "He laughed at me," she said. "He-he touched me, too."

"I'll speak to him about that sometime soon," said Guinn.

The county hospital was just outside the city limits, across the highway from forest land. It was quite dark when they reached it. Guinn pulled up across the road from the big brick pylons which flanked the entrance to the hospital drive.

"Out," he said.

She looked at him, wide-eyed. "What?"

He chuckled. "Cheer up. I'm not pulling a Mordi on you. Has it occurred to you that I've got to drive up to the emergency ward, floodlights and all, and that a couple of interns will be out to tote Garry in? Of course, I could explain that I'm helping you home from a floating crap game where you lost your shirt . . ."

She opened the door. "Hurry back," she said.

He watched her cross the road shoulder and enter the woods. He shrugged into his damp jacket. It was clammy, but would cover his holster. Then he pulled into the drive. He turned at the parking court, wondering about the mental processes of landscapers who built graceful curves into a road which so often would have life or death at the end of it, and swung in under the brightly-lit port-cochere.

A grizzled guard hobbled over to him, peered. "Had Guinn! Back again?"

"With a customer. Get a couple of butchers out here with a stretcher, will you, Jerry?"

He followed the old man in and went over to the registration window. "Hello, Cheryl."

A blonde woman with a face like the most comfortable of sofa pillows looked up through the glass. When she saw him she smiled. It was like the kind of lamplight that goes with that kind of pillow. "Hadley!"

"I brought Garry in," he said bluntly. "Someone creased his head." She rose. "Is he—"

"Doesn't look too bad. But I'd like to know right away. I'm on a case. Will you take care of the gunshot report for me?"

"Oh, yes." She got out the form, slid it through to him.

He signed it on the bottom line. "One more thing. I know you people do the best you can, but I'd like you to think up something even better for Garry. Whatever he needs, hear? I mean anything."

He got his wallet out and thumbed through its inside compartment. An expression of almost stupid astonishment slackened his features.

Cheryl said, "What is it, Hadley? You been robbed?"

"No ..." His eyes came back to earth. "No, Cheryl, I should say not." He pulled bills out of the wallet.

C-notes. Five of them.

He closed his eyes. There was that center drawer of his desk. In it, the telephone company's envelope. In the envelope, three of the C-notes the Morgan chick had given him. Five minus three left two. There ought to be two hundred in the wallet. There were five.

"What is it, Hadley?"

He looked at her. "Just trying to figure out whether or not I'd tipped a waiter. Here." He slid two of the bills through the hole. They settled to her disk like a couple of pigeons on a roof. That's extra, over the bill. I got more."

"You don't have to—"

"I do have to. I just want to know he's a bit more than all right. Uh ... you don't have to talk to him about it."

She smiled. "The way you treat him, he thinks you hate him." She picked up the money.

"So he keeps on trying hard to make me happy. If he thought I was happy, why should he bother?"

"You're a softy, Hadley Guinn."

"You're a pretty hard character yourself." He winked at her. "Oh. Cheryl—"

"Yes, Had."

"Can you dredge me up a nurse's uniform? Not the starched job—one of those lab wraparounds."

"What on earth for?"

"My Sunday school's putting on a pageant," he explained. "I'm to be Florence Nightingale."

"Idiot. What size?"

"About Miss Roark and a half." Miss Roark was the trim one in the super's office.

"Sure, Hadley." She went through a door at the back of the office. Guinn turned. They were bringing Garry in. He looked very white. Guinn followed the interns into the receiving ward. A tired man with wakeful eyes waved the interns toward an examining table. "Hello, Jim."

The doctor thumped his shoulder. "Good to see you. That's your Number One boy, isn't it? Garry what's-his-name?"

"Yeah. Can you give me a verdict quickly. I got to go."

"What happened to him?"

The doctor bent over Garry's head while Guinn told him. Then he rolled Garry's lids back, peered at the eyes. He put on his stethoscope and prodded around with it.

"He might need a transfusion. Concussion possibly. Shock certainly. He might have trouble with the hearing on that side for a while. He's a lucky boy."

"How long will the transfusion take me?"

"No time at all. Not for you, Guinn. He's Type B, you're A. Don't worry about it. We have lots in the bank. You won't do."

"You can tell by my astral vibrations?"

The doctor laughed. "I can tell by memory. The last time you two gave blood for the Red Cross he asked me what your blood type was, and swore a blue streak when he found out his was different. He thought he might be useful to you some time."

"Hell." Guinn looked at the still face. "Take care of him, Jim."

"Sure." He bent over the patient again. Guinn read that one casual syllable all the way through, and in it found what sort of care Garry was going to get. He said, "Thanks, Jim," and went out.

Cheryl was waiting for him with a neatly folded paper package. "Hadley . . ."

"Oh, thanks, Cheryl. The uniform." He took it.

She said, "I think I ought to tell you. There was someone here today boning through the hospital records. Yours especially."

"Looking for what? That bone operation?"

She shook her head. "That's in the journals—how they picked a .44 slug piece by piece out of your bone marrow. No, Hadley, the birth records."

His face went absolutely expressionless. "Who was it?"

"A girl. A really beautiful girl."

"Probably from a matrimonial agency trying to answer some maiden's prayer. What kind of authority did she have?" Cheryl recoiled at the way the last words grated out. Guinn touched her shoulder. "Sorry. Well?"

"She had identification from the State Census. Strictly kosher. I just thought you ought to know." Her eyes were very soft. "Hadley, it makes more difference than it should to you. Not the investigator. You know."

"My birth records. Yes, I know. Maybe it does. It makes a difference to any of us." He looked down at the package, crinkled the paper. "Hey, I got to get out of here. Thanks for everything, Cheryl."

"For nothing, honey. Hadley, I won't ask you about your business, but if you've got to go near any more gun fights, let's not have any more hospital cases on your side. Hm?"

He went to the door, waved. "I'll be good." She cared. She gave a damn. It's fine to know somebody gives a damn. "By the way, what was the name of the nosy chick?"

Cheryl said, "Morgan."

Hadley steered through the pylon-guarded entrance, wheeled across the highway, and stopped. He waited.

Nothing happened.

He slid across the seat and peered into the black wall of the forest. Nothing.

He got back behind the wheel. He lit a cigarette. That took a little time. He opened the package, wadded up the paper and tossed it back over the seat, unfolded the crisp white dress and draped it over the seat next to him. That took some time too.

She didn't come.

He uttered a sudden snort of disgust. Of course! The lights. He shifted, angled the car close in to the ditch, and shut off the lights and motor.

It was very quiet out there. The forest slept, but for all its sleep it was alive with little creaks and whisperings. He climbed out, and something made him close the door very quietly.

There was no wind. Somewhere a train uttered a two-toned cry, and the mountains threw it back like a wailing wall. The hospital was a gold-checkered garment tossed carelessly on a hassock, with the checks showing randomly back, up, across. The emergency entrance blazed defiantly at the patient blackness, and from the whole structure came a hum of power; machines turning, water running, life flowing, coming in, going out.

The woods had their low, live sound, too, but it was at odds with the hospital and everything it represented. The forest had its light, too.

It took Guinn a while to see the light, because his pupils were still tensed from the brilliance of the receiving ward. It was not firelight, and it wasn't a flashlight. It looked like the third or fourth reflection of a welder's arc, but without an arc's flicker. Nor was it steady, like a magnesium flare; it waxed and waned irregularly, like the sound of a crowd at a prize fight. And it was very, very dim.

Guinn hesitated. Had Lynn seen the light? Probably. She had been very alone and very watchful, crouching naked in the dark. Had she then gone to investigate? It could be. She had more guts than most regiments. If he went in there, he might miss her. If she got to the car and he wasn't there, would she wait for him?

What else?

He reached in the window, got his keys out of the ignition and the dress from the front seat. His clothes were still damp, but the night was very warm. He folded the dress and tucked it inside his jacket, on the right side. Then he headed for the brush.

The thicket just over the ditch was like an ancient boxwood, tangled and impenetrable. He cast to the right until he found what looked like an opening. He had to fight the branches, and he did so quietly. He got through, and found himself in a patch of wood that was very like virgin forest—a solid roof overhead and very little underbrush. He could see the light much better now, waxing and waning through the stark trunks. The going was good, and the possibility of Lynn's being back here made a lot more sense. The first thing she would have done would be to get through the hedge; after that, the light must have beckoned her strongly.

He forged ahead, unconsciously taking on the sliding stride of a natural woodsman, finding and avoiding projecting roots and rocks. His eyes were wide; he felt that an infrared picture would show his pupils almost as big as his irises. Bigger, maybe. His lips twitched at the fantastic thought, and he switched it out of his mind.

He began to hear the voice.

There is a passage in Ravel's *Bolero* where the composer, either through a thorough scientific knowledge of vibratory physics or instinctively, under the guidance of his trained ears, gives the great droning solo theme to the clarinet, and adds a piccolo part. That piccolo, on paper, is sheer nonsense. It plays the same theme at the same intervals, but in a different and totally unrelated key. It makes almost as little sense on the piano. Orchestrated, it creates one of the most astonishing effects known to music. Its compulsion, as it restates the already hypnotic theme, is indescribable—and largely a function of the psychological susceptibilities of the listener. In acoustical terms, what is happening is that the clarinet, more than most instruments, projects harmonics with its basic tone. Ravel's amazing treatment uses a piccolo, which is very stingy with its overtones, to reinforce the usually inaudible fifth harmonic of the clarinet.

The effect is that of a new voice, never heard before, speaking with the familiar tones of a friend.

This little-known piece of musicology flashed through Guinn's mind as he heard the voice. The analogy was an exact one, for that was precisely what was happening, except that the voice which stated the basic tone was something more than human. It was certainly a single voice, but it had the quality of a great many ranges, from the highest tenor to the most shattering *basso profundo,* all speaking in unison. The second voice, the one pitched in a disharmony that served to reinforce a single one of the qualities of the main voice—that second one was familiar. In the rare moments that his acute ear could tune it away from its accompanying diapason, Guinn knew that he had heard those full, high, sweet tones before.

Something began to bother him. He had moved forward a hundred feet before he realized what it was. His legs; the voice; the light—they were meshing too closely in their movements. Furiously, he identified it; he was walking in time to a beat which was created by the sound and the changing light. Not that they changed with any predictable regularity. Far from it. But as if they were part of some incredibly complex, rigidly fixed ritual, they touched and fled from and syncopated a basic beat—a beat faster than a quiet heart, forcefully held slower than a frightened and guarded one. He broke stride, fiercely defending his independence.

The light seemed to have its source in a circular area of the forest floor, and the voice was born somewhere in the light. The ground rose gently as he walked; suddenly, then, he saw it all.

There was a dip in the forest, a saucer-like depression thirty yards or so across. As he reached its lip, the entire scene below was revealed to him, suddenly, completely, as if a great curtain had parted.

A tremendous oak stood in the center of the depression. Its mighty spread had waned off anything but moss that had tried to grow around it, so that there was a smooth clearing around it. Standing at its base was the biggest man Guinn had ever seen.

He was standing in the clearing, his face upturned, his arms out toward the oak. He looked like an old oak himself. His skin was dark brown, his face gnarled, his arms knotted and powerful. They stretched out like winter limbs from the dazzlingly white sleeveless robe which covered him from his shoulders to his bare feet. The light-source was his robe, and his lips were the source of the great voice.

Behind him knelt Lynn, sitting on her heels, with her back arched and her hands on the ground behind her. Her head was up, her tangled, fine hair thrown back. Her teeth shone and her eyes blazed. Her lips moved. The second, harmonic voice was hers, in its highest register. It was modulated exactly to his magnificent chanting; she spoke so perfectly in concert with him that they might both have been controlled by the same mind, like two pipes of an organ under the knowing hand of a master.

The chant at first seemed wordless. Guinn slowly realized it was not. It was a series of syllables, most of them long drawn vowel sounds without diphthongs, like those in an Irish brogue. They were separated by unearthly consonants, staccato and clean. The language was like nothing he had ever heard, but it was good to listen to.

He stood there for uncounted moments, forgetting to breathe, completely entranced. There was an intensity to the light which changed with the quality of the sounds, and there was a quality to the light which changed with the sounds' pitch. It was a thing which had to be experienced to be understood, and once that understanding occurred, it was inexpressible.

The huge dark man dropped one of his massive hands to the wide white belt that was clasped around his waist. From it he drew a long, slightly curved dagger that gleamed like gold. He held it point upward in both hands. Guinn followed his gaze, and saw that it was pointed at a cluster of dark green leaves and white berries on the tree-trunk. The dagger began to move upward toward it.

This, later, was the most inexplicable thing of all to Guinn. For at no time did the man change his position. He did not lose his grasp on the knife; he kept both hands on its hilt. The tree did not move. Yet—

The knife went out and up, slowly and steadily. It reached the trunk of the oak, turned and sliced off the clump of glossy green. The man, standing twenty feet away from the tree, had bridged the gap between him and a growth twelve feet from the ground. His arms had not stretched; in no way did he seem out of proportion. In fact, the movement seemed utterly right. Guinn felt that he had seen a movement in a new direction, and that he could not be surprised. He seemed to have known of that direction for a long time but never had bothered to look that way before.

The plant fell. One of the great brown hands was there before it, caught it, laid it on the moss before the knotted feet.

Then the man turned, stood facing outward, away from the tree. Lynn's body turned as he turned, and now she knelt with her back toward him, her arms down, her long slim hands palm-upward on the ground.

Guinn's eyes flicked to the hand holding the knife, to the smooth white back bowed before him. He reached into his left armpit and eased the .32 out.

Shockingly, the chant stopped. The silence was deafening, unbearable. The light was unchanging, muted. There was a great expectancy in the wood.

He looked around the clearing. So compelling had been the tableau by the oak that he hadn't taken in the edges of the scene at all.

The bushes around the depression looked as if they were filled with rhinestones—with emeralds, rubies—with ... *eyes!*

And they were eyes. The low branches held silent birds, their little heads turned sidewise so that one eye could take in the scene. From a tree-fork at his shoulder hung the luxuriously dressed form of a raccoon, which stared fixedly at the big man. Guinn looked down. What he had thought was a small stump was a fox, not six feet away from him. Its black, wet nose tossed delicate spangles of light as it pressed its head down and forward toward the oak. On the ground in front of it—almost between its paws—was a chipmunk, staring brightly, and holding its deft small hands together in frozen ecstasy.

There was a deep crooning. Guinn looked back at the dark man. He had not moved, but the sound came from him. And Lynn's high, sweet supplement was there too; he could see the flexing of her ribcage as she drew breath between the mesmeric phrases.

Something moved at the lip of the depression, forty-five degrees across from Guinn's viewpoint, and directly in front of Lynn.

One ... no, two big brown rabbits came toward her. They did not hop. They moved belly-down, like stalking cats. It affected Guinn almost more than anything else had. The animals were in the throes of some strange supplication, and their completely uncharacteristic gait caused a deep pain in him somewhere.

They reached the girl, and lay down, one across each of her hands. She lifted them. They drooped, motionless except for their hind legs, which were taut, stiff, quivering in rapid spasm.

Still singing, Lynn rose to her feet and brought the rabbits to the big man. Guinn realized how big he was. Lynn was a tall girl, but her head barely reached the level of the man's heart. The rabbits were large ones—eight- or nine-pound jacks; but both, lying side by side, barely covered the huge dark hand from thumb-base to fingertips.

Holding both rabbits in one hand, the man turned to face the tree again. Lynn was suddenly silent. The man shouted four crackling syllables, and with a single sweep of his golden dagger, sliced off the rabbits' heads.

The muscles of Guinn's jaw crackled audibly. He became conscious of a long-forgotten fact—that his automatic was in his right hand. He raised it, took the barrel in his left, held it while he released the cramped right fingers and flexed them until he felt they could be trusted. Then he grasped the molded grip again, got his index finger under the guard.

The big man was moving now, holding the twitching bodies downward. Dark blood was spouting, and with it he was sprinkling the roots of the tree. As Guinn brought his gun hand up, the man disappeared around the tree.

The huge shadow of the tree moved opposite the light source, sweeping across the clearing like a monstrous hand brushing away flies. And at its touch the animals scattered like flies, an approaching, passing, receding wave of squeaks and squawks, whimpers, growls, hoots and rustlings. Behind the passing shadow the tree-limbs moved and their leaves fluttered, and the underbrush whipped and thrashed. Before it, the forest was spangled with the gleaming of their fixed eyes.

Then the big man rounded the trunk, still holding the carcasses. Their blood dripped now instead of spurting, and he held them close to the roots and moved slowly.

When his circuit was completed he stopped, dropped the rabbits, and turned toward Lynn, who stood watching him tensely, her lips parted, her head up. And Guinn brought up his gun and fired. He aimed over the man's left shoulder, purposely high.

The man's hand came up in unison with Guinn's. Just behind the crash of Guinn's gun came a distinct *thunk!*

And Guinn found himself gaping down at that laughing dark face—laughing so that the leaves shivered—and following the movement of the small object being tossed in the huge hand.

The giant had caught Guinn's bullet not only in his hand, but between his thumb and forefinger.

You're acting like a rube, he snarled at himself. The hand is quicker than the eye—even the private eye. He tightened his grip on himself, on his gun. "Sorry to interrupt," he said into the echoing silence that followed the giant's laughter, "But the lady was with me."

"You interrupted nothing," said the giant pleasantly. "We were quite finished."

"Who are you?" Guinn snapped.

The man looked at him thoughtfully. "You know who I am."

"I do?"

"You do. When you admit that you do, you'll seek me out. Until then ..." He made a courtly gesture, a sort of casual salute. Then the light—went out.

Guinn bit his tongue and cursed. The darkness had hit his eyeballs like a physical blow, and he literally sagged under the impact. He stood in the blackness, shaking, sweating, waiting.

Gradually there was a leaf-torn sky again, the dim presence of tree trunks. Somewhere a mouse squeaked. Overhead he heard the tiny, unlubricated sound of a bat. A breath of wind passed, and the forest seemed to exhale quietly.

"Lynn . . ."

"Yes, I'm here."

"Is he—"

"He's gone." He heard her feet as she left the mossy carpet and crossed dead leaves. She was climbing toward him. He put out his hand. It touched her body; soft, warm, unafraid. His throat was dry and burning and his flesh was cold and clammy. He found her hand and said again, "Are you all right?"

"Oh, yes."

"Where is he?" he whispered. "He must be standing down there."

"He isn't," she said positively. "He's gone."

He peered down into the blackness, and abruptly there was a sort of flow, a warm radiation of comfort and relaxation. There was proportion and reality in the world again. "Yes," he said, surprising himself. "He's gone."

Hand in hand they followed the glow, the mechanical hum of the hospital, which was now visible. "Lynn, what happened?"

"I saw the light," she said quietly. "I went to see. I think I was afraid at first. I thought if I knew what the light was I wouldn't be afraid any more, so I went to look. He was . . ."

She fell behind as they passed between close-set trees, then caught up and took his hand again. "He was—waiting for me. It was as if I knew him, knew what to do . . . You saw, didn't you?"

"Yes. Lynn, what was it for? Who is he?"

She was silent as they worked their way through the blackness. She was quiet for so long that he squeezed her hand and said, "Well?"

She said, "If you're around somebody a whole lot—your brother or someone you go to school with or something—do you suddenly stop and say 'What's your name?' It was sort of like that. No, I never saw him before. I never did those things before. But it didn't occur to me to ask any questions."

He said, because he wanted to know, "He didn't touch you?"

"Oh, no!"

"I believe," said Guinn, "that two things and two things get you four things. I believe that every effect has a cause, and every reaction is there because of some action." He paused, and then said almost plaintively, "I've got to believe that, Lynn!"

She chuckled. She was certainly not laughing at him. She reached her other hand over and patted his wrist. "Hard guy," she said.

They reached the hedge. Guinn fumbled along it for an opening. He stopped suddenly. "I plumb forgot." He reached inside his jacket and got the nurse's uniform, shook it out. "This won't look like Fifth Avenue," he said apologetically.

"What is—Oh! A dress! Thank you . . ." She shrugged into it, and as she buttoned the belt, she said, "I didn't feel naked until you handed me that."

In an obscure way, he felt like apologizing. He didn't. He said, "I didn't feel you were." He turned to the hedge, added, "You suppose I'm getting old?"

"Do you suppose I'm getting brazen?"

It was the right answer. Something was going on here—some shift in perspective, some new element in the atmosphere. "Come on."

They broke through and emerged into the highway some hundred yards below the parked station wagon. They walked silently, each deeply immersed in thought. Lynn spoke once: "Is Garry—"

"He's going to be all right."

"I knew that," she said wonderingly. "I seem to've known that all along. Remember when I got into the car, when he was lying on the seat? I didn't do anything for him. I barely even looked at him. I didn't have to; I *knew* he was all right."

Then they reached the car, got in. Guinn found his keys, started the car. They pulled into the highway and moved off toward the town. It wasn't easy to talk against the roar of the unmuffled exhaust, and they didn't try too hard. Lynn gave him her address, and when they reached the town he found it without trouble. He pulled up in front of it. It was frame house with a vine-covered porch and a picket fence. There was a sign on a post in the lawn that said ROOMS TRANSIENT PERMANENT.

Lynn got out. Guinn leaned across the seat and looked up at her. "I owe you an outfit."

"You do not. I owe you a whole lot more."

"A clout on the neck?"

"I got hit much harder than that," she twinkled. "Shall I come to your office tomorrow?"

"Call me," he said. Her face seemed to fall a trifle. He said, "I meant what I said about that, Lynn. Square yourself with your boss at the cafe."

"Thanks. Oh, thanks so much."

"I'm ahead." He waved his hand and started the car. He had to turn it around, and he sped past her place again she was still on the porch, tiptoe on her bare feet, waving.

Guinn parked the car in front of his building and sagged for a moment. He felt as if he had earned the luxury of letting his back bend for a few seconds. He thought.

He thought about Lynn, and about the extraordinary scene in the wood, about the man in the convertible who shot at girls and flayed off the skin on people's faces, strip by strip. He thought back and back through his day's work until he got to lunch time, where it started. The Morgan girl and her vagueness and her fantastic expense money. He took out his wallet.

In it were five one-hundred-dollar bills.

He sat very quietly, with his eyes closed.

She'd given him five centuries. He'd put three in the drawer before he left. At the hospital he'd found he had five left, not two. He'd given two hundred to Cheryl. Now he had five left instead of three.

He thought, there are two kinds of things going on around here. One is the kind of thing I understand, and the other is the kind of thing I don't understand.

Is that simple enough? he asked himself.

It should be.

I understand about guys who make rough passes at girls. I understand about guys who torture people to get information from them. I even understand about girls who have guts enough to dive out of a moving car over the railing of a forty-foot cliff.

But I don't understand about men who can coax rabbits out to have their throats cut, and can pluck a .32 slug out of the air. I don't understand a guy who makes a chanting and somehow controls a girl's voice to synchronize with it like that. And I especially don't understand about this money.

Guinn sat up a little straighter: He knew he would be better off if he forgot the things he couldn't understand. He also knew that he couldn't. What he could do was seal them up in the back of his mind. Maybe he'd find the bridge between the known and the unknown; maybe some silly little piece of evidence would show up that would be the missing link. Until then, he wasn't going to beat his brains out.

He swung the door open, pulled out the ignition key, dropped it in his pocket and climbed out. He stretched. He felt tired. He kicked the car door closed and went into the building.

Old George, the night elevator man, was asleep on a battered rung chair, his Adam's apple still pretending it was a chin, and chewing. Guinn walked up the two flights. He was glad to be back. He thumbed out his door key and let himself into the dark waiting room, crossed to the inner office, turned on the light.

"Hello," somebody said gravely.

He stood dangling his key stupidly. He was stiff with shock. Shock was a vise on his abdomen, a clamp on his heart, a quick-freeze on his lungs. He didn't show it.

"Please shut it. There's a draft," said the girl called Morgan.

Guinn tossed the key, caught it, put it away. He crossed the office and got behind the desk and sat down. He glowered at her. She sat where she had been before. Her legs were crossed and her hair gleamed and she still had the most exquisite mouth he had ever seen. Her skin was still young and her eyes ancient. Instead of the caped dress, she now wore a lime-colored number with a demure little white collar buttoned under her chin. There was another button an inch above her waistline. Between the two buttons the material separated, no wider than a finger, all the way down. This was a garment with something to say, and it made its points.

"I'd like a progress report," she said.

He snorted and reached for the phone, dialed. While he waited for the connection, he glared at her. If she had grinned at him he would have thrown the phone at her. She didn't grin. She watched him levelly, and waited.

"Sam," Guinn said into the phone. "Yeah, I know it's late. Look, I want you climb into your jalopy and take a trip. No—not tomorrow; now! Don't say that, chum. You know I wouldn't call you if it wasn't important. Okay, then ... That's better.

"I want you to get up to Percival's cave. Yeah. No, he won't. Somebody knocked him off today. Damn you, would I kid about a thing like that? All right then. Sorry, I knew him a long time. Anyway, the wagon's come and gone by now, but his goats are still up there. I want you to round 'em up and take care of them. Yeah. And don't forget to milk the nannies. They've missed one milking already, maybe two, and that's no good. It hurts 'em.

"Right. All right, Sam. You're okay, you short-tempered old scut. Stay with 'em; I'll be up in the morning. Sam—thanks."

He put the phone down, took out his wallet, got out the five bills, dropped them on the desk, and pushed them across the desk with a pencil eraser. "Here."

She lowered her lids to look at the money. Her lashes almost touched her cheeks. When she was asleep they probably did. "What's that for?"

"It's your money. I don't want it. I don't want your case, either."

She nodded, almost placidly.

She picked up the money, opened the chartreuse and black handbag she carried, and dropped the money into it. "That's not all the money you've gotten from me, is it?"

"I gave you five."

Her gaze dropped to the desk. He cursed suddenly, viciously, ripped the drawer open and got the telephone bill. The old envelope tore in two as he pulled the banknotes out of it.

Three bank notes. C-notes.

He looked up at her, his face frozen. "The hand," he said, "is quicker than the—" He stopped, because he remembered saying, or thinking, the same thing just recently. This afternoon, or was it—

She took the money and put it away in her purse. She asked, without smiling, without frowning either: "Why don't you want the case?"

He said, "I wouldn't be so foolish as to accuse you of sending me up on the Hill when you did just so old Percival would get what he got. But it figures the same way. I'll never live so long that I'll forget this afternoon—or the fact that you had something to do with it."

"How do you figure that?"

He reached behind him and switched on a hot plate. He swizzled the pot that stood on it to see how much water was in it. Satisfied, he turned back to her. "You've been asking questions about this stone, this cup, or whatever it is. Some hood figured it was valuable, went after it. Percival got—Miss Morgan, do you know what was done to him?"

"I can imagine."

He snorted. "The hell you can."

She considered him in her expressionless way. "I take it you're going to drop the whole thing, then."

"I didn't say that. I said I didn't want your case. How far I chase down my own affairs is up to me."

Her expression changed, but there was no saying exactly how. It wasn't in the eyes, the mouth. It was, if anything, something inside. But now she looked pleased.

He was annoyed. "I gave you the money," he said pointedly. When she simply sat, watching him, he said, "And tomorrow I change that lock."

"Locks mean nothing to me," she said.

"They do to me, if they're mine. Miss Morgan, I think I'm taking up too much of your time."

"Oh, no." She shook her head solemnly.

He rummaged into his desk, found a jar of instant coffee and some restaurant-style containers. He spooned the powder into a container, switched off the hot plate, and poured steaming water into the coffee. He sat stirring it, looking at her. He didn't offer her any.

From his top right-hand drawer he got a handful of pretzel sticks. Dunking one, he stuck the end into his mouth.

"This is where you came in," he said.

She nodded.

"Damn it!" he exploded. "What are you after?"

She said, "Wouldn't it be better with rye?"

He had the container to his lips as she spoke. His nostrils distended. There's a distinctive odor to strong black coffee with a dollop of rye in it—and this had it.

Guinn's first reaction was to drop it; his second to throw it. His third was to drink it. He did none of these things. He put it down with a consciously controlled rock-steadiness. He selected a pretzelstick carefully and dunked it. It tasted of rye. He finished it slowly, wiped his hand across his mouth, and took out a cigarette. As he clawed a book of matches up from the desk, the girl raised one hand from her lap and pointed a finger at him. Something like a swift butterfly of flame whisked across from the finger to his cigarette, and was gone. He drew back violently, followed by a faint curl of tobacco smoke. He automatically dragged on the cigarette. It was lit, and the unexpected gout of smoke made him cough. He thought he smelled ozone.

"Do something else casual," said the girl, as quietly and offensively as ever. "I can keep this sort of thing up all night."

"Okay," he said harshly. "What's your story, Miss Morgan?"

"Look in your wallet."

"I know what's in the wallet."

"You do?"

A dangerous light came into his eyes. Silently he took out his wallet, opened it, drew out five one-hundred dollar bills and put them and the wallet down side by side on the desk.

"Very good." He wet his lips. I guess this means that the two yards I left at the hospital for Garry are phoney—if they're there at all. I'm beginning to like you, Miss Morgan."

"No," she said quickly. "They're real. They're all real."

"They come from some place."

"They come from people who won't miss it—or who shouldn't have it."

"How?"

"You wouldn't understand." There was no effrontery in her voice; she was stating a flat fact.

"I'm a pretty understanding guy," he said.

She rose and came close to the desk. She smelled of vanilla, and, faintly, of mignonette. She glanced back at the chair and gestured slightly. It slid across to her. It must have been lifted a fraction of an inch off the floor, because it made no sound. She sat in it and said, "Do you think you're going crazy?"

"No," he said positively. "If that's what you're after, you've done everything wrong."

"How so?"

He stretched out his legs. "I don't know that you've earned a lecture on the secrets of my success. But I don't mind telling you that I can be puzzled but not mystified. If I throw that switch, the hotplate lights up. I understand that. If Einstein tells me that light can only go just so fast, I don't understand it, but I accept it. If another five yards shows up in that wallet I won't understand it—" His fist came down with a crash—"and damn if I accept it. Now, quit your skylarking around, or—"

"Or?"

He shrugged, suddenly, and smiled. "Or make sense."

The smile, apparently, worked. She smiled too, and it was the first time. He'd seen a lot of wonderful things today, but nothing like this.

"Pour us a drink, and I'll talk sense."

"I haven't got any liq—" he began, and then caught the bare suggestion of an amused crinkle at the corners of her age-old eyes. He opened the top drawer, then remembered what he had done with the bottle. He scooped it up out of the wastepaper basket and held it up. It had about two fingers in it. He raised his eyebrows resignedly and found a couple of shot-glasses under "G" in the filing cabinet. He poured. There was just enough to fill both glasses, and when he put the bottle down there was about two fingers of liquor surging around the bottom.

They lifted their glasses. It didn't look like any rye he had ever seen. It had gold flecks which were in constant, dazzling motion, and it seemed to have an elusive blue cast to its gleaming amber. Her glass touched his, and one of her fingers, and he experienced a distinct and pleasant shock.

He drank.

For a split second he thought he had swallowed nothing at all, so smoothly did it go down. Then his earlobes warmed up like radiant heaters, and there came a feeling in his throat as if it had grown an internal pelt of finest mink.

"This you get for nothing?"

She shook her head. "From nothing. But it isn't easy."

"It's worth the trouble." He poured again. "Talk."

She lowered her eyes for a moment, then said, "I've been looking for you for a long time."

"I thought it was a stone you were looking for."

"Oh, it is. But you're the only man who can find it."

"There're a lot of private eyes."

"There's only one like you."

He turned on her suddenly. "You were smelling around the hospital records."

She nodded. "I had to find something out."

"Did you?"

"Yes."

"Now you know why I'm so lucky."

"What do you mean?"

"You know the old stories about the seventh son of a seventh son," he said harshly. "Well, like a guy called Geosmith once said, I'm the seventh bastard of a seventh bastard."

"Why do you make jokes that hurt you?"

"I like to be the first one to make 'em. You get your nose rubbed in a thing like that."

"And things like your real name?"

"You did snoop."

"I had to know."

"Why? To find that stone?"

"Yes," she said. "You have it."

"Not unless you planted it on me, like this cabbage." He flicked the banknotes with his fingernail.

"You can be ever so sure I didn't," she said seriously. "I want it too badly. I just want to . . ." Her fingers curled. She had long slender, strong fingers. ". . . to hold that cup. Just to hold it in these two hands."

He looked at her tense face wondering where all the cold poise had gone. "Well, it ought to be a snap. I have it, you want it. Tell me where I've hidden it and I'll hand it over."

"I can't tell you where it is. You've got to find it yourself."

"I thought you were going to talk sense."

She sighed. "Has it dawned on you yet that this is a slightly unusual case?"

He glanced again at the money. "Seems so."

"Then you have to take what comes as sense. Guinn, is a radio set magic?"

"Not to me it isn't."

"But it would be to a bushman."

"Mmm. So now I'm a bushman. I see what you mean. You're using my own arguments on me. If there's anything I don't understand in all this, it's because I don't have the background for it. Don't worry, I'm not going to get superstitious."

"All right. But a lot of this is going to demand new thinking—a new kind of thinking from you."

"Do it to me."

"All right. You went up on the Hill today. You picked up a girl called Lynn. She'd had some trouble with a man named Mordi. When you got to Percival, you found him in terrible shape. He talked to you and then died. When you got back to your friend Garry, you found him wounded by this same Mordi. You then—"

"Now, wait. Were you there?"

"No."

"Then—"

"It was just something you had to go through."

"What are you talking about?"

"Shall I start again from the beginning? You are a very special person, Hadley Guinn. You, and only you can find that cup. And the stone on it. Unless and until you find out who you are, you won't know where that cup is or how to find it. You can't be told—it's absolutely essential that you figure it out for yourself. In order to be able to figure it out, you've got to go through certain things. You'll keep on going through these things until you do figure it out—or die in the attempt. You already have all the evidence you need, but you won't look in the right direction. You've got a psychological block as big as a house that keeps you from it. You'll have to find it, or die. And if you're going to find it, it damn well better be soon!"

"Suppose I don't?"

"We ... you ... won't have to worry any more."

"I'm not worried now."

"Yes you are."

He studied his hands. "Yeah," he grunted. "You're right about that." He thought for a moment. "Those things I have to ... go through. You mean like finding old Percival that way?"

She nodded. "And everything else that's happened since I walked in here."

"Sort of ... staged?"

"You can call it that."

He pushed back his chair and stood up, looming over her like a cliff. "Did you have something to do with it?"

"Something."

"With what happened to Percival? To Garry?" His voice was rich with self-control.

She looked up at him with perfect composure. "Percival volunteered."

"Volun—for that!"

"He knew who you were. He's known for years. He's watched over you and guided you more than you'll ever know. He knew what you were before I did—and I've known it for a long time. As for Garry, what happened to him had to happen, because you had to feel just that way about something. You're in a bigger play than you think you are. Now, sit down and stop blowing up like a sea squab, or I'll stick a pin in you and bust you."

Slowly, he sat down. "You better talk some more."

"I will. Lynn was in it for the same reason. Don't you see? Percival was the symbol of a lot of large issues to you. I don't have to draw you a diagram about them. They all came to a focus in him, and with his death they came front and center."

"Did he have to die that way?" growled Guinn.

"He did." She held up a commanding hand. "I told you—I'm 'talking sense', just as you asked me to. Damn you, you'll hold still for it. Garry is something you protect and teach, and he matters very much to you on those terms. You saved his life by your quick thinking, taking the car down the mountain face that way, getting him to the hospital in time—"

"You'll remember I stopped on the way."

"That was on the agenda. You had a choice to make, and you gave it to Lynn. You let her danger be more important to you than either Mordi or Garry's life."

"I suppose that strip act was part of it."

"Of course it was! You had to see how she reacted to you under circumstances that would have had her hysterical with anyone else. She trusted you because she could trust you—because you are you."

"Go on." His eyes were closed, his vision turned inwards.

"Cheryl," said the girl. "Someone who cared. Doctor Jim. Someone you trusted. And the ritual of the oak. Something you had to see."

"Why that?"

"Because, with a mind that refuses to see anything that isn't

216

straight cause and effect, you had to witness effects with causes you'll never understand—and trust your own eyes! The same goes for the money and this liquor. Pour me some more, by the way."

There wasn't much in the bottle—only a couple of fingers. Resignedly, he poured, and filled his own glass.

"Miss Morgan," he said carefully, "you are very beautiful and you have a great bag of tricks. But your story is as full of holes as a yard of cheesecloth. I don't know what you're after, but from where I sit you're a rich bitch with a warped sense of humor and an army of spies. Shut up!" he barked as her extraordinary eyes flamed with indignation.

"I still think Percival died because you've been wandering around yammering about some secret treasure he's supposed to've been on to. That's the kind of story that gets believed about eccentrics like him who've never given a hoot about money. I think you're responsible for his murder because of it. I don't know but what you hired Lynn to help you pull the wool over my eyes, to slip extra money into my wallet, to pull that fancy performance in the woods. I haven't figured out yet how half this sleight-of-hand was pulled, but I will. I'll sweat some of it out of Lynn and dope the rest out for myself."

"Why, you—"

"If that fairy story of yours was true, that this whole thing was scripted out to put me through some paces, it'd mean outside circumstances that widen to where you couldn't have had a damn thing to do with them. What about the timing of that lowboy trailer— was that arranged?"

"Yes!"

He snorted. "The effect that old Percival had on me when I was a kid?"

"Yes!"

Sarcastically, he said, "The old oak tree growing just there?"

"Yes, yes, *yes!* All of it! How can I make you understand? Every-thing—the big things, like your being born when you were, like the building of the bridge just where it was, just that width—and the little things—like old Joe being asleep when you got here, so that even when you were tired you climbed the steps rather than bother him. Like the first phone call you made being an arrangement to take of Percival's goats. You're you, damn it; but today, you've had to be more you than ever before. In every way that's important because you've got to realize who you are!"

Her intensity was like the radiation from a cherry-red ingot, a thing to narrow the eyes, against which to throw up futile hands. He shook his head in bewilderment. "Why do you go on with this?" he asked in genuine curiosity. "What's in it for you? Lady, how crazy can you get?"

She wrung her hands. "I can't tell you who you are," she mourned. "I can't, I can't ... because if I did, that little wrinkle in your silly head would kink up and switch out all the circuits. You've been holding that knowledge locked up in your stubborn skull for years, and you won't look at it. You're born to the part, bred to it, trained for it, and you won't make the simple admission to yourself." She knitted her brows. Her full lower lip sucked in and her white teeth came down on it. She lowered her head and sat tensely, and a crystal tear welled out under her long lashes and lay twinkling on her high dark cheekbone.

He went to her and put a hand on her shoulder. "You've had a tough time, Miss Morgan," he said. His voice shook, and he realized with a shot of fury that her breakup had affected him more profoundly than he thought he was capable of.

She took his hand and pressed it against her wet cheek. "You're such a wonderful fool," she said brokenly.

He didn't know how his hand slid from her cheek to her throat. Her head came up abruptly and he found his eyes inches away from hers. Down, down in her eyes something glowed and called and promised. In those incredible eyes was a hunger, a yearning, and an overwhelming gladness fighting, fighting to emerge.

He stood like that for minutes. Finally he said hoarsely, "This won't gain you a thing. It won't make me believe a word of that.... .of yours." The word he used was filthy, viciously used.

"I know," she whispered. "It doesn't matter. It doesn't matter ..."

And so the full spectrum was completed, and he was himself more than he had ever been before.

Lynn yawned. The office was swept. The files were in order, the furniture dusted, the waiting room davenport vacuumed and plumped, the paneling oiled. The bills were paid. The phone almost never rang, and when it did all she could do was note the caller's name and promise that Mr. Guinn would call back when he returned.

"Hey—Had! Are you—" There was a step.

Lynn leapt to her feet, smoothed her hair, and ran to the waiting room.

He was there, tall, stooped, a patch on his temple and a clump of bandage on his neck looking like a misplaced tuft of his cotton hair.

"Garry! Garry—oh!"

She was in his arms before he knew it. She hugged him until he grunted, put him away at arms' length, ran eager rapid fingers over his lips and cheeks.

"Wait a minute, hey—" he spluttered. He colored violently. "Lynn, I was hoping . . . I was thinking of some way to maybe see you again sometime . . . I didn't figger that—Gee. Hey."

"You idiot, you fool you," she crooned. "Darling, sit down. You must be tired. I thought you'd be in the hospital for another week. I've missed you so! You don't know, you just—oh, Garry, am I making a fool of myself? Am I?"

"Gosh," he said. "I don't think so." He put his hands awkwardly on her shoulders. "I think this is all right."

She spun in close to him, put her cheek on his chest. His heart was going like a riveting gun. They sat on the davenport and at last he kissed her.

At length he came up for air. "Ain't felt like this since I won the sack race at the county fair," he said. "Where's Had?"

"I don't know," she said.

"You working here now?"

She nodded. "He wanted me to, since that day. You know. He

told me to call him and I did and he wasn't there. I felt real bad. And about ten in the morning old Sam came around. He brought me a note from Mr. Guinn and the keys. He said Mr. Guinn had sent him up to take care of Percival's goats—"

"He would," said Garry.

"Yes, and Mr. Guinn had come up early in the morning and told him to go."

"What did the note say?"

"I'll show you." She skipped into the office, opened a file drawer and came out with a rumpled piece of paper. "I'll read it."

" 'I've got some thinking to do. I'll be back shortly after I arrive. Don't look for me. Here are the keys. Straighten up the place for me. You'll find money in the top drawer of the desk. If you find any bills, pay them. If you get any calls, stall them. Take fifty a week for yourself and give Garry anything he needs.' Garry, I'm to give you anything you need."

"Haw!" grinned Garry. "He thinks of everything. That all?"

"No. 'If you see that Morgan girl, tell her I still don't believe her, but . . .' Here the writing gets all squiggly. ' . . . but I'll keep looking until I find what she's after. And I almost think I might.' That's all."

"Have you seen the girl?"

"No. She hasn't so much as called. Who is she?"

"The most . . ." He flushed. "I like you better," he said lamely. "You just better!"

"I bet I know where he is," said Garry. "Though maybe he wouldn't want to hang around there now. Still . . ."

"Where?"

"Still up there with the goats. He used to say that if ever he got mixed up in too much detail, that was the place to go. Said nobody could think little things up there."

"That's where we'll start looking," said a voice, and it laughed.

Garry and Lynn sprang apart, and then Lynn cowered up close against Garry.

Standing in the doorway was a dark, spare man with cold black eyes. His left arm was in a splint, though not in a sling. His jacket was draped over his left shoulder, and its drape gave him a chilling, vampire look. In his right hand was a heavy automatic.

"Mordi!"

"The whole thing suits me fine," said Mordi. "Nothing's going sour this time, buster. I want to be the first to congratulate you. You got a chick that will look at you, and I got a gun that will look at the chick. There's nothing you can do so fast that I can't—" He described the process of shooting Lynn in terms that made Garry's lips go white.

"What do you want?"

"Same thing your boss wants. Either I get it first or he does. If he does, I get it right afterward. Come on, lovebirds. We're taking a trip." His black eyes slitted. "And look, little smarty, you better just follow my instructions and not pull another fast one, because I'm not holding this gun for fun."

Garry took a step toward him and Lynn flung her arms around him. "Garry, don't, don't ..."

Guinn threw the old book aside and stretched. "Morning, Matty," he smiled.

The nanny stretched her long neck further inside the cave. *"Eh-eh-eh!"* she answered.

"Okay, okay."

He rolled off the goat-hair mattress and stooped to go through the entrance. The nanny skipped away from him and stopped again a few feet out in the clearing. *"Eh-eh."*

"I'm coming, honey."

He followed the goat through the neck of woods to the meadow. "Oh, for Pete's sake! Can't you stay out of trouble? You want to grow up to be a detective?" He strode over to the ruins of an ancient fieldstone wall. Tangled in a whip-vine was a week-old kid. Its clumsy thrashings had brought it under a flat stone which had fallen across a rock and a stump in such a way that the little animal was caught, painlessly, but effectively, under the stone with its legs spraddled out and its silly head springing up out of the shrubbery like a barrage balloon. "Up you come," said Guinn, heaving the rock away. He picked up the kid and freed its legs from the vine. It bawled shrilly, and the nanny fretted impatiently beside him. He set the kid down and it staggered to the nanny and hooked on to a teat with exaggerated smackings and droolings and a series of frantic, contented little grunts. Guinn chuckled and walked away.

The mist was a sea which had turned the hills into a wind-borne archipelago. There had been sun up here for two hours, but the valleys were still submerged, asleep. Guinn breathed the good air and let his gaze reach and reach into the indeterminate area where mist and sky met. Eight days of this had brought a great peace and purpose to him, and for forty-eight hours now he had even forgotten that he was out of cigarettes.

The goats were company and a modicum of trouble, anchoring him to a duty. The sky and the stars and the sun and rain were things he could drift in, but the goats never let him lose himself. It was a good place to be, a good way to be.

And the books . . .

"...There was a man spawned by the powers of darkness, born of a virgin, destined to be the antichrist. And the virgin Blaise told her confessor, who believed when others would not, and baptized the child, taking him from the control of his dark father . . ."

"... asleep under a rock in Barenton in Brittany amongst the hawthornes. And when the rain fails them, then do the peasants call to him, and strike the rock, and he calls down succor for the thirsty land."

(What was it he had heard about Barenton? Oh yes; when that Morgan girl had first come in: "Reckon it'll rain tomorrow?" and she had said, not in Barenton." And he had asked, "Where's Barenton?" and she had said "Sorry. Classical reference. There's a hawthorne bush there.")

"... a precious stone is brought to earth by angels, and committed to the guardianship of a line of kings. It is self-acting and food-providing, and the light issuing from it extinguishes the light of candles. No man may die within eight days of beholding it, and the weeping maiden who bears it retains perennial youth . . ."

(So if there's a drought at Barenton, he's no longer under the stone ...)

He went back into the cave to read some more. Lovely, lovely stuff, those legends. What had turned him from them?

(The echoes in his mind, the jeering kids at school. The smug young substitute teacher who had labeled his desk after an absence "The Siege Perilous"—the old name given the empty place at a great table when a knight was out searching for the ... for the ...)

Before noon he heard the scuttle of hooves and the sharp snort of the big billy called Bucko.

He ran outside. Bucko was on the high bluff behind the cave. Guinn scrambled up the rocks. "Easy, Bucko," he said. Bucko turned to him and back toward the forest, his great head high, his heavy horns curving down and back so that the tips all but touched his massive shoulders.

Guinn stood up and peered. He could see nothing, hear nothing—wait; there was a sound. A distant groan, a complex sound.

It was the whining of a car in low gear, travelling rough ground so that the driver's foot bounced on the accelerator.

The sound came closer. Guinn automatically reached for his armpit and cursed. His gun was in the cave with his clothes. He hadn't had them on in four days; why bother? The goats didn't mind ...

He turned to go down when a brilliant flash caught his eye—the sun on chrome. Then he knew that by the time he gained the cave again the car would be in the clearing. Strangers or friends—fine. He could put something on and come out to greet them. But if this visitor were no stranger, and no friend ...

He'd take his chances out here in the open.

The car pulled into the clearing. Guinn knelt behind the gray peak of rock that jutted up like a chimney, and froze. From the ground he would look like another conformation of the rocks silhouetted against the bright sky.

The car door opened. It was a Nash sedan. Garry was driving. He got out and walked straight away from the car for perhaps ten feet when, at a low growl from the car, he stopped. He stood still, trembling. Even from that distance Guinn could see the sweat standing out on his forehead.

The rear door opened. Lynn got out. Her face was chalky, and her red-gold hair was vivid against it. She was staring straight ahead, and her eyes were as round as an auger-hole.

Behind her came Mordi, crouching, watchful. He kept an automatic steadily on the girl. Guinn could hear his voice clearly as it grated, echoed among the rocks.

"All right, cottonhead. Peek inside. If he's there, call him out."

Garry stood still, and the torment on his face was indescribable.

The automatic barked, and a slug whined twice in a crazy double ricochet. Garry whirled. Lynn snatched at her skirt, whimpering. She fingered a bullet hole in her skirt, low on her hip. "No!" she cried to Garry. "It didn't touch me!"

"The next one will," promised Mordi faithfully. "Go on, cottonhead."

Garry stalked forward like a zombie. Mordi closed with Lynn, putting the muzzle of his gun against her back. They followed.

Garry stooped and disappeared in the cave. He was out in a moment. "He isn't there."

"He's been there," said Mordi.

"No."

"You're a liar." He shoved Lynn so hard with the gun that she stumbled. Mordi stood back until she was on her feet again. Then he snapped, "Inside, Sister!" He pushed her roughly into the opening. "You," he said to Garry, "stand right where you are, where I can see you. One step any way, and I start shooting." He ducked into the cave.

Guinn was suddenly conscious of pain in his hands, and he took them off the rock. One fingernail was broken and bleeding. He looked down. Garry was standing stiff and trembling in the clearing in front of the cave-mouth. Guinn thought of leaping down from the rock, landing on Garry, bearing him away from the cave-mouth, and then realized that it wasn't Garry that Mordi would start shooting at.

He looked around frantically.

There was a movement in the wood.

Someone, palefaced, slender, stood in the shadows. Clad in a mottled green cloak, she was all but invisible. When his eyes rested on her face, it relaxed visibly, as if she had been standing in an agony of tension, waiting for him to see her.

"Morgan!"

(The memory flitted through his tortured mind. "What's your first name?" "Morgan." "All right, if you don't want to tell me.")

"Morgan ..." he breathed. "Morgan le Fay ..."

She nodded. She raised something in her hands—a three-foot clump of evergreen with yellow-green flowers, a cluster of white berries ...

("... and when the missal shall be found upon the oak, then shall the Druid sever it with a golden knife. And sacrifice shall be made, the living blood feeding the roots of the tree ...")

She stepped out into the clearing at the side of the outcropping, and with one clean sweep of her arm, she threw the mistletoe.

Guinn stood, stretched, and caught it. Two fierce thoughts collided in his mind. The first was that this was no time for kissing games; he'd a damn sight rather had an automatic rifle than this shrubbery. The other sprang from the remembered passage in Percival's old book: *"... when the missal shall be found upon the oak, then shall the Druid ..."*

Druid. The Druid.

Percival had muttered, through his tattered tongue, something about the Druid. The one Guinn was to find. The one who had a golden knife, who had said "When you admit you know me, you shall seek me out."

His name! What in time was his name?

The hawthorne bush ... under a flat stone in Barenton, in Brittany, he sleeps. ... But there is a drought in Brittany. He sleeps no longer.

Percival's bloody wreck of a mouth floated before his eyes. *"Amghozhiush ..."*

"Amgro—Ambrozhi—*Ambrosius. Merlin Ambrosius!*"

In his mind, he screamed it, over and over.

Hollowly, Mordi's voice boomed out below. "You lying bastard! He was here! His clothes, his gun—I'll teach you to lie to me!"

The automatic roared once and again. Coming from the cave, it sounded like artillery. Garry put his arms out, and on his face was an expression of delighted amazement that distorted itself into a tormented, rubbery grimace. "But, Lynn," he said softly. He looked down at his chest, and suddenly there were two bright splotches on his shirt. Chin on chest, he vomited blood on the splotches and toppled.

A horrible garble of sound came from the cave—Mordi's roar of laughter and Lynn's terrible shriek. She bolted out into the open. Mordi was after, on her in two bounds. He twisted one arm behind her until she fell to her knees, then struck her on the back of the neck with his splinted forearm. She collapsed without a sound.

Guinn uttered a low growl—precisely the sound made by a furious mastiff. He tensed and sprang—

And he couldn't move.

He looked up.

Standing beside him, with one gigantic arm extended and an expression of perfect calm on his dark face, stood the Druid—the man he had seen cut the mistletoe from the oak tree.

"You called me," he said. His tones rang, but somehow Guinn knew he couldn't be heard by Mordi.

"Let me go," said Guinn between his teeth. "Damn you to hell, let me go!"

The Druid was not touching him, but there was no question of the fact that the paralysis came from that extended arm. "Stand up," said the giant.

Slowly, Guinn stood up. "Let me go," he said again. "Garry's dying!"

"He will die if you do not do as I say," said the giant.

Guinn gritted his teeth and, as if moving in a heavy fluid, turned and glanced down. Mordi was working over Garry, lifting him, dragging him. He could hear Garry's bubbling breath and weak coughs.

Peering down, Guinn saw him prop the dying man in a sitting position at the cave-mouth, facing in.

"A lung job," gasped Mordi. "You'll go slowly, buster. Which is
good. There's something I'll want you to watch."

He went out into the clearing and picked up Lynn's limp form—
both wrists in one hand, a twist under her so that she was draped
over his right shoulder. He half carried, half dragged her into the
cave. There was the sound of tearing cloth. "We'll get this out of the
way, hey, smarty?"

Garry tried to speak, but blood choked him.

Guinn whimpered in frustration as the invisible power drew at
him, turned him around to face the great, calm, kindly face of the
Druid.

"Your Quest," said Merlin Ambrosius. "There is nothing more
important than your Quest. End your search and you shall have your
heart's desire."

The calm power flowed into him from that huge face. Suddenly,
without effort, he understood. He understood it all, from all its beginnings to its incredible present to all possible endings. He put up his
hands and closed his eyes.

There was a flow from the Druid to his whole being, and an
answering flow up through the rocks from the core of the earth itself.
There was an emanation from everything that lived around him—
the trees, the grass, the silent goats that stared up at him as once
oxen stared up at a Star. Butterflies sank to the earth and were still,
and all the birds were with him, silently striving.

In his empty hands he felt a weight. He pulled his mind together and
threw it all into a mighty effort; and his thumbs curled over something carven, and there was a high center of gravity there, so that he
must balance what he held.

Then he knew it was done, and that out of himself and the earth
and all things which had ever lived, the Search he had made all his
life (most of it unwittingly) was over. He and his substance had been
the assembly point for the thing which had left its mysterious mark
on all histories and all myths.

He opened his eyes, and was not dazzzled by its light, though it was far brighter than that of the high sun.

It was a chalice, apparently filled with wine. It was infinitely graceful, and each curve and carven line had a basic meaning.

There was a clinking and a rustle, and a weight on his shoulders, and a mighty, comforting burden around his waist. He found himself clad in golden chain-mail, marvelously made. It was covered by a long white silken surplice, and it blazed in the light of the unbelievable stone set in the cup.

"Will you yield it to me?" asked Merlin. His great dark eyes were full of years and hunger and ... and supplication. There was no power in him to take this cup.

Guinn turned, looked down. Garry sagged against the rocks.

But Guinn was free now. He leaped. He had one brief glimpse of Merlin's pleading hands, and then he struck the ground jarringly.

"Mordred!" he cried in a great voice. "Come out!"

The answer was a shot that roared from the open throat of the cave. Guinn saw, to his amazement, a .45 slug appear in midair three inches away from the cup he still held, and, flattening, fall to the ground.

Mordi had apparently fired before he looked, for he now came out of the cave. His clothes were disheveled and his dark face was flushed. "Well, well. If it isn't the pure boy himself, all dressed up for Sunday. All right—give it here."

From the corner of his eye, Guinn saw Morgan moving forward, like a stalking cat.

"Throw down that gun," said Guinn.

Mordi laughed. He raised the gun and sighted it carefully at Guinn's forehead, and pulled the trigger.

The gun bucked in his hand.

He stared at it, unbelievingly. It was melting. It was falling together like a water-filled balloon with a fast leak. It flowed and dripped down and ran between his fingers. There was no heat. It simply melted.

He looked up, saw Morgan. She had a strange, luminous smile on her face, and was looking up at the peak of the rock. Mordi looked up too.

Merlin stood there, his arms folded. "Would you kill the bearer of the Grail?"

Mordi cursed. He shook his fist at the giant and bellowed: "I, Mordred pen Dragon, of the true line of the Kings of pen Dragon, Guardians of the Grail, I am your master, Merlin Ambrosius, and you are committed to my service. I command you to deliver it to me!"

Morgan gasped. Guinn, startled, looked at her. "It's true, it's true," she keened. Tears streamed down her face.

"Quickly," she said. She ran to him. "Give me the Grail. You can't kill while you hold it." He hesitated only a fraction of a second, and then thrust it into her hands. Her face matched the Grail's radiance as she took it.

Mordi made a lunge for her, but she skipped back out of the way, and that was when Guinn's fist hit him. It bowled him right off his feet and up against the rock.

Guinn leaped on him. Mordi, with his back to the rock, lashed out with both feet and caught Guinn on his mailed chest. Guinn went flying backwards, to land in a tangle of surplice and chain, with his heavy two-handed sword twined into the heap. Mordi leaped on him, kicked at his head. Guinn ducked, and the heel of Mordi's shoe cut a long crease in his scalp. Guinn rolled over, got his feet under him and tossed the surplice back out of the way. He advanced on Mordi.

"Merlin, your protection!" screamed Mordi.

"To my sorrow," said the giant, and his voice was like the theme of a dirge. He threw up his hands.

Guinn loosed a straight right that had all the power of his blood, bones and hatred behind it.

And it was as if there were a wall of plexiglass between him and Mordi. The fist bounced off nothingness, and the diverted blow threw Guinn down on one knee. His arm tingled to the shoulder. He bobbed to his feet and circled, warily. He rushed, and was again warded off.

"Now this," said Mordi, "is real fun." He dropped his hands. "Come in again, brother bastard. Did I ever tell you how many guys tried to be your father?"

From the cave-mouth, Garry coughed, and from the sound of it, it would be about his last. Morgan, carrying the Grail, darted to him, pulled his head back, thrust the glowing chalice in front of his glazing eyes. Over her shoulder she cried, "Your sword! Use your sword!"

The sword, to Guinn, was no more than a nuisance. He hadn't had time to look at the buckle nor to fumble with it, or he would have shucked it off to get it out of the way. But so far Morgan had been right. He backed off and drew the sword. Merlin and Morgan, having seen such things done before with skill, must have been appalled. Guinn had to run it out of the scabbard hand under hand down the blade before he could get it all the way out.

He got his hands on the long hilt, and the weapon seemed to take on a life of its own. Mordi staggered back a pace or two and raised his arms.

"Merlin—protect me!"

The glittering blade went up, back, and to one side, and came forward in a screaming arc.

"Protect me—"

"Against *Excalibur?*" said the giant, his great voice shaking with laughter. And then the blade struck Mordi's neck and passed through it as if it had been a puff of smoke.

The body stood upright for fully two seconds, a pulsing fountain of blood replacing the head. Then it fell. The head rolled over twice and stopped at Guinn's feet, the eyelids batting flirtatiously, the tongue running in and out like that of a rude little boy.

Merlin came down from the crest. Guinn did not see him do it. It was as if he had disappeared from the top and reappeared at the bottom. Perhaps that was the case.

From his robe he produced a silver chain. He held out a hand to Morgan, and she came to him, walking mechanically, and stopped before him with her head down.

"On the day the Grail passes from the guardianship of the pen

Dragons," Merlin intoned, "Morgan le Fay, called the Wild, shall be chained and given into slavery."

He cast one end of the chain to Morgan's slender wrist. It nestled there as if drawn by some magnetism, and by some marvel that Guinn did not understand, formed what appeared to be a broad silver link about her wrist.

"We don't have slaves," Guinn said stupidly.

Morgan knelt at his feet. "She is yours if you wish it," said Merlin.

Leaning on his great sword, Guinn reached and took the chain. "Stand up, Morgan," he said. "You embarrass me." He tugged at the chain. "Merlin, take this thing off her."

Merlin sighed. "As you wish." He made the slightest of gestures and the chain fell away. "But I warn you—she is called the Wild for good reason. She is that which appears to be something else. She is the very source of the term 'fey.'"

"Wild I may be," said Morgan in a low voice, "but I feel I shall be tamed for this one's lifetime—yes, and all his others."

Guinn walked to the cave-mouth and knelt by Garry. "He's still alive! If only we could get him to a doctor!"

"There will be time," said Morgan, with a peculiar quirk to her mouth.

There was a moan from the cave. Guinn bent and peered in. He turned and took the Grail from Morgan. "Give her a hand," he said, and turned away.

Merlin stood looking hungrily at the Grail. "May I drink?"

Guinn looked at him quizzically. "I don't know, Merlin," he said honestly. "I'm going to need a whole mess of indoctrination here. I don't know what I should or shouldn't do."

"It will do nothing but good, believe me."

"Can't you wait a bit?"

"Ay." Merlin heaved an enormous sigh. "But after waiting near two thousand years, it isn't easy."

Lynn stumbled out of the cave. Her clothes were torn, and there were ugly fingernail scratches on her shoulders. She flung herself on Garry and lay in a twisted ecstasy of tortured sobs.

Morgan knelt and held her. "Give her the Grail," she said urgently to Guinn. "Make her walk with it while she weeps. While she weeps!"

Guinn gently lifted the sobbing girl. "Lynn, honey. Here. Here— take this."

Lynn strained toward Garry. Guinn tilted her face up and only then did she see his shining armor and great sword. She blinked in surprise. And then the radiance of the Grail suffused her. She put out her hands blindly and he gave it to her.

"Here, dear," called Morgan from a short distance.

Her sobs gradually subsiding, Lynn walked to her and gave her the chalice. Morgan took it, narrowed her eyes, and suddenly the astonished Lynn was arrayed in a beautifully draped Grecian dress.

"Now, what was that for?" asked Guinn.

Merlin smiled. "Don't you remember the qualities of the Grail? 'The weeping maiden who bears it shall retain perennial youth.' Morgan is a woman with the values and compassions of a woman."

"Oh, yes," said Guinn devoutly, remembering his last meeting with Morgan. "Merlin, help me out of this hardware."

"So be it," said Merlin. He reached out and took the sword, and the golden chain-mail vanished, surplice and all.

"Hey!" Guinn yelped, and dove into the cave. He found his clothes and pulled them on.

"How do you feel, boy?"

They were in the car, working gently down the switchback road toward the town. Garry lay on the wide back seat, with his head on Lynn's lap. Morgan and Guinn were in front. (Merlin, who scorned any mechanical transportation, was left behind "to take care of the goats," he had said. Morgan had explained to him that old Sam would find the goats in an empty lot near his place in town. "You'll understand how, one day.")

Garry grinned weakly. "I feel pretty damn itchy," he said. "But I'm gonna be all right."

Guinn glanced quickly at Morgan and she nodded. "He will be. No man can die within eight days once he's seen the Grail."

Guinn glanced into the rear-view mirror again. There was no doubt of the fact that Garry was alive and chipper.

"Okay," he said, "I've been in the dark altogether too damn much. Let's have it. Where did all this start?"

She smiled, and touched his shoulder. "It's a big thing and requires big thinking, darling."

"I can try."

She settled back in her seat. "Well, first, you've got to get used to the idea of a race of beings so enormous, so powerful, that you can't fully comprehend them. You just have to know they're there."

"Gods?"

"Do ants think elephants are gods? Do birds think locomotives are gods? By all means believe in God, but if you do, do Him the justice to believe that he is a God to the Great Beings as well."

"Theology later," said Guinn. "Go on."

"When it became evident that this planet would support such as we, the Great Ones supplied guidance for us. They put it on Earth and went on. It is not their custom to stop and watch a civilization grow. They do what they do in order to prevent imbalances that might disrupt little corners of the universe. Once a race in this very system blew up its planet, you know. Their balances prevent that. Or they should. And now they will again."

"What is this—guidance?"

"A permeating, controlling force for each of the great basics of life: growth and decay. A better way of putting it is the anabolism and the catabolism which together comprise metabolism. There is a force that builds and a force that destroys; one that delivers heat and one that absorbs it. It's light and dark. It's *yin* and *yang*, the oldest symbol known to man—a circle divided in two by the S-shaped line inside of it, one half light, one half dark."

"Good and evil."

"No!" she said explosively. "Not that! Good and evil are erroneous human concepts that derive from the terrible mistake that was made here."

"What mistake?"

"Mythology contains many a mention of it, though few regard it as the disaster it was. You see, only one of these forces has been fully operating on earth. The other is crippled, subdued."

"What happened?"

Morgan wrinkled her brow. "First, let me explain what the effect of this imbalance is. If you put a cup on a table, and extend your hand to pick it up, you are moving directly toward an established aim. If you shove your arm all the way, as far as it will go, you'll push the cup all the way across and send it crashing to the floor on the other side. Yet no one can deny that your force was applied to the desired end, in the right direction, with the correct motivations.

"There is nothing evil or dangerous or harmful on this planet except excess. There's no such thing as a deadly poison; there's just too much of a poison. Too much pleasure is pain; too much fear (a fine survival characteristic) or too much anger (and that's another) means madness."

"I think I see. Then which of these powers was crippled?"

"The power of darkness—destruction—anabolism."

"You're out of your head! This planet's loaded with it!"

She shook her head sagely. "It's building—building gone out of control. It's the cause of technology's outstripping the spirit. Every nation that smashes every other nation does it through a desire to construct something—a political philosophy, an empire, a personal fortune or a personal power. It's construction that's killing us off. It's cancer!"

"I never thought of it that way."

"Humans don't. How can they? They're born to it. But that can all be changed. It's up to you."

"Me?"

"You. Only you have the power to give the Grail to Merlin."

"What has that to do with it?"

"Remember your reading about him? What was his parentage?"

"He was—he was born of a virgin."

"That's right. That is the way the guidances are placed on a planet.

Merlin's the antichrist—yes. But don't recoil from that word. I tell you it has nothing to do with evil—everything to do with balance."

"What would the world be like with that force in it?"

"That requires a whole new system of thought. It's hard to put into human language. Have you ever heard of someone committing a crime for his own benefit?"

"All the time."

"Well, try to imagine a culture in which it would be impossible to construct that sentence, because 'crime' and 'benefit' couldn't exist in the same idea-sequence!"

He was quiet for a long time. At last he said, "Mankind as a unit of free things, eh? Each with the full consciousness of the whole species?"

She shrugged. "Action is a light force, inhibition a dark one. The name you have for rational inhibition is conscience. Imagine all mankind with a cohesive conscience, and you'll get the picture."

Guinn wet his lips. "And what about you? And the Druids?"

"There's a long word for me. I'm a metempsychotic. I get transferred complete from one body to another, with complete memory. That's how I can do the things I do. None of it's magic. It's just that for me there have been no dark ages. It's all soundly scientific. The money in your wallet? A kind of teleportation. The chair that moved by itself? Telekinesis.

"The same thing's true of the Druids. 'Druid' isn't the name of a religious sect, by the way; it's a title, like 'chancellor' or 'minister'. They're metempsychotics too, but for the dark powers. I'm neutral. I imagine I'm a sort of recording device for the Great Ones."

"And how did the one force get crippled?"

"These guidances are put among humans in human terms. The antichrist was baptized! His mother confessed her visitation to a man who had the power to do it. And that is Merlin—fully possessed of the dark powers, but unable to use them for their intended purposes!"

"And the Grail?"

"Pure and simple, a power source. That jewel is a reservoir of vital energy. It was left in charge of a line of kings—the most cohesive form of authority at that time—and of them, the revered Arthur pen Dragon . . . I hope I'm not knocking over any childhood idols."

"Not mine," said Guinn sullenly.

"King Arthur was a petty, self-righteous little martinet with a weak mind and a strong arm. He fell in accord with a renegade Druid who got him to turn the Grail completely to the powers of light. It shouldn't be denied them, of course; but neither should it be monopolized. The Grail itself, in its symbolized chalice form, was put into an immaterial form, keyed to the very special aura of a certain kind of man, a man *who couldn't exist as long as the dark powers were crippled!*

"So we—Merlin and I—searched until we found suitable material, and then made what environmental changes we could until we got one. You. Percival almost made it, but not quite. He wasn't—well—dirty enough."

"Thanks."

"It's been tough sledding. Merlin had to keep his powers under forced draft by any means he could. That ritual you saw is one of the ways. The combination of auras of hypnotized animals, a virgin, oak, mistletoe and fresh-killed mammals is a tremendous recharge. With the Grail it won't be necessary."

"And Mordi?"

"A madman. Happened to be a genealogist and found that he was of the true pen Dragon stock—the last of the pure line, most fortunately. Got to fooling around with old rituals and found that the Druids, even Merlin himself, were bound to him. He wanted the Grail as a personal power-source—which, God knows, it certainly is."

Guinn drove thoughtfully for a while. Then, "I called him Mordred."

Morgan laughed. "There may be more pattern behind this than anyone—even Merlin and I—know. For we have a Gareth and his Lynette; we had a Percival, the good man who almost had the Grail. And Mordred, the deputy King who turned so evil."

"There was a gasp from the back seat. Lynn said, "Mordi—he saw the Grail. He'll live eight days?"

"At least," said Morgan cheerfully. And Guinn, holding the wheel, saw a flash of that bodiless head, blinking and tonguing up at him. Then he thought of Gary propped up against the cave entrance, dying, and watching ... and he drove without speaking.

"So it's up to you, chum," said Morgan. "Give Merlin the Grail, and restore some balance to this rock, or don't, and we'll keep on building Babel."

"Excalibur and the atom, is that it? Wait. The atom bomb is a disruptive dark-power device if anything ever was. Right?"

"Right," said Morgan. "A feeble victory for Merlin's side. It's the H-bomb we're worried about. That's *fusion*—that's building. Darling, if you give Merlin the Grail, that damned thing ... won't ... work!"

Garry said, weakly, "Hey, boss. Just who are you?"

When Guinn didn't answer, Morgan laughed and said, "He's Hadley Guinn. He got his last name from the only name anyone knew his mother by. It was Guinevere. He called himself Hadley because he got sick and tired of getting kidded about his real name." She hugged him. "In a couple thousand years, he'll get over that."

Guinn took a deep breath and said it, all by himself—the one word that had been anathema to him all his life, that had poisoned the whole Round Table legend for him.

"Galahad," he said. "By God, I'm Galahad, that's who I am!"

And when they test the H-bomb, you'll know what he decided.

The Incubi of Parallel X

IT'S SMALLER, GARTH thought as he lay on his belly on top of the hill and looked down, through carefully parted branches, at Gesell Hall. The Hall had towered over him when he was a child, last year, last week, last night, in his dreams. And now, at the moment he had schooled himself for, waited for since the day his world had ended, he could feel no thrill, no triumph—only it's smaller.

The great building, with its rambling wings, its twisted, broken power receptor antennae, its yellow weed-grown courts, lay as if in the hollow of some mighty neck, with a cliff and a mountain shoulder shrugging it into its crowded, cluttered, sheltered state.

I should have known, he thought. I was only a kid when I left— when the Ffanx—

He lost himself in the restimulated dream, the clear mental picture of his toy spaceship, hovering in midair on a pillar of koolflame fire, and his child's dream of worlds, and then the shrill thunder of jets—real jets, Ffanx jets—which had brought an end to his dream and his childhood and his world.

Garth Gesell slipped a long-fingered hand under his abdomen and hauled out a knobby root which rowelled him. *It was there,* he thought, *right there by the main building. The Ffanx came, and I ran around to the front and through the double doors, and right in to Dad and Mooley. And the roof came down, and Mooley, the cat, ran through fire and was naked and agonized, and then there was Dad's head with a splinter through the bridge of his nose and the end of it in a ruined eye, talking to me ... talking out of a mountain of rubble, out of torture, out of gentleness and greatness, asking me to save a race and a world and a system ...*

Well, he was back. Not back home, for this was enemy territory now. All the backslid, savage world was enemy territory for anyone

238

who ventured out of his settlement, and Garth's adopted village was many a long day's march behind him. Behind him, too, were years of growth and training and of living with the nagging, driving force of his childhood promise to his father: I shall open the Gateway.

"I shall open the Gateway." He said it aloud, intensely, in a deep re-dedication to his father's wish. And then he threw himself violently to one side.

His watchful subconscious, his trained hearing, were a shade too slow to avoid the blow completely. The short, stubby spear whacked him painfully between the shoulder-blades instead of burying itself in his back. He rolled back over it, snatching it up as he rolled, and bounced to his feet in a single fluid motion, striking upward with the spear. He got a quick impression of a tall, wide, golden figure which, without moving its feet, bent gracefully aside to avoid the spear's hungry point. Then there was a sharp blow on Garth's wrist and the spear went flying end over end into the undergrowth.

Garth stood, shaken and helpless, grasping his wrist, and looked up into the easy smile of the stranger.

"Move fast, don't you?" said the man. He had a broad, clean-cut face and the rasping, rapid speech of a Northerner. He stood with his thick legs apart, the knees slightly flexed. Garth had the impression that from that stance the man could move instantly in any direction, including straight up. "But not fast enough for Bronze," the man added.

Garth understood the name and the reason for it—the golden skin and yellow hair, the rivet-studded belt and boots were obviously a personal trade-mark. In his hand Bronze held a polished throwing-stick, the source of the stubby, bullet-like spear. He slowly whacked the end of it into a wide, horny palm as he studied Garth. "What are you after?"

Garth thumbed over his shoulder at the crumbling building down in the green hollow. "What do you call that place?"

"Gesell."

"I am Gesell too."

Bronze's face turned into a mask. He stepped past Garth, dropping his throwing-stick into the quiver of spears which hung behind his right shoulder. He stooped and picked up Garth's weapon and handed it back to him.

Garth carefully avoided saying, "Thanks."

"I heard you say you'd open the Gateway."

Garth nodded.

Bronze said, "Could I help you?" and in that moment Garth knew he'd won. He suppressed a smile. "I don't need help," he said.

"You might," said Bronze.

Garth shrugged as if he didn't care. In reality, he cared a great deal. He had known for a long time that he'd have to recruit some help, and he liked the looks of those big shoulders, and of the obvious skill that had gone into the man's trappings and weapons. "What's it to you if I open the Gateway?"

Bronze licked his lips. Then, with no attempt to conceal his motives, he said, "There's women in there. Thousands of 'em. The best, the smartest on this world or off it." He paused. "I come here all the time. I sit up here and look down at the Hall and try to figure a way in." He spread his big hands. "If you were trying to stop me from getting to those women, I wanted to kill you. If you can help me get to them, I'm on your side. All the way. See?"

"Fair enough," said Garth, and let the grin come through this time. "Not enough women around here for you?"

"Not enough women in the whole damn world. Seven in Prellton—that's my village—and a hundred men. Over the hill there, in Haddon's Town, there's twice as many women and three times as many men."

"So you want the Gateway open so you can cut loose with the whole lot of 'em?"

"Me?" cried Bronze. "No, man, I just want one. Just one woman, all for me."

"I see you're a reasonable man," said Garth, smiling. "You can go with me."

Bronze looked as if Garth had given him a kingdom, and a pair of wings to boot. "I heard of you Gesells."

"You heard of my father," said Garth.

"They still tell stories about him."

If there has to be a shrine, there's bound to be a legend, thought Garth. "Why didn't you try breaking into the Hall?"

"Some tried, one time or another," said Bronze. He cast a quick, fearful glance down into the hollow. "They're all dead."

"That's what I heard." Garth studied Bronze thoughtfully. "Ever see it happen?"

"Once." Bronze swung his spear quiver off his shoulder and squatted on the bank, running the spears nervously through his thick fingers as he spoke, testing their points, their grooved hafts. "I was to watch, me and Rob O'Bennet and his fighting-boys. Flan of Haddon's Town and his men got the main assault because they have the larger settlement. We were to storm down and back them once they'd breached the Hall." He paused and wet his lips. His amber eyes were haunted. "Two Guardians the Hall had, then as now—two only, just two against the two hundred of us. Flan's boys raised a yell you could hear over the mountain, and charged. Not a sign of life from the Hall until they were half across the court there—" he pointed— "and then the Guardians stepped out, one from the north corner, one from the south, by the little door. There was blast of green fire the like of which words won't handle." Bronze covered his eyes as he spoke. "I saw it stretch between the two Guardians for a half second, and then I was dazzle-blinded.

"When I could see again my brave boys were gone, leaving me writhing my burned eyes into the grass here. And down there in the court lay Flan and thirty-eight of his boys, smoking and black."

He paused while the terrifying picture died behind his eyes. "Afterward," he said, "a party of us went over to Haddon's Town to see if so many dead hadn't left a widow for us, but they had the place well-stockaded."

Garth made no comment. "Tell me what you know of the Guardians."

"I'll tell you little enough," said Bronze. "But if I said what I'd heard I'd be talking a month or more. All you ever see of them is that pointed cowl and the long habit that goes to the ground. Some say they're men and women—or were. Some say they're monsters from the other side of the Gateway."

"We'll soon see," said Garth.

"You're a Gesell," said Bronze, his voice hoarse with suppressed excitement. "You can just walk in like a guest."

"I can not," said Garth shortly. "I hate to disappoint you, Bronze, but a lot of water has gone over the dam since the Ffanx conquered us. My father built the Gateway twenty years ago, thinking that it would guard those women for the month or so it took to smash the Ffanx. They killed my father and closed the Gateway. And by then the world was a ruin, with the women gone and the men fighting over the handful who were left, and the secret of the Gateway locked up in the brain of an eight-year-old child. And now the Hall is a shrine, and the guards are Guardians, science is magic and each part of the world fights every other part."

"What are you saying? You can't just walk in, and you a Gesell?"

"Everything's changed," said Garth patiently. "I've listened to every traveler's tale, read every record—there are damned few enough—and it all comes to the one stupidity: I am the only man alive who can open the Gateway, and those dedicated fools down there will kill me on sight if I go near it."

"How do I know you're a Gesell?" said Bronze, in reawakened suspicion.

"You don't," said Garth. Without looking up or turning, he made one sudden, brief movement. The tube seemed to leap from his right holster into his hand. "Look, Bronze."

Bronze's face went stony. "What is it? What is that thing?"

Garth pressed the stud on the side of the tube. A beam of light leaped from the tube to bathe Bronze's terrified face. The big man cried out, and then sat frozen, eyes shut in terror. Garth turned it off and dropped it back into the holster. "My name is Gesell," he said conversationally, "but I don't give a hub-forted damn if you believe it or not."

"What was it?" What did it do? That light, that white light—"

"Just light," said Garth, and laughed. He slapped the big man on his meaty shoulder. "Stop your chattering."

"You shouldn't 'a done that," said Bronze hoarsely. "You didn't have to scare me like that, Gesell. I said I'd help. I wasn't backing out. I believe you."

"Good. Now shut up and let me figure this out."

They stood at the crest of a wooded slope that fell away almost vertically to the clearing below. The Hall stood in the center of the clearing, and beyond it was another rise—the mountain shoulder itself, not quite as high as the elevation on which they hid. The weed-grown court offered no shelter except a couple of giant trees, one of which towered over the central building. One thick branch held a mighty, protective arm over the low roof. Garth stared at it and at the opposite slope.

"Bronze!"

Bronze was by him, almost crowding him in his eagerness to serve. "What, Gesell?"

"Just how good are you with that womera of yours?"

"Good enough, Gesell. I once killed a deer at ninety yards."

"How many?"

"Seventy," said Bronze, finding himself fixed by Garth's deep eyes. He gulped and grinned.

"It's damn near a hundred and fifty over to the top of the bluff— see it there, the sheer rock straight over the Hall?"

"Uh-huh. I could peg a spear over there. Wouldn't hit too hard, though."

"Could you put it exactly there?"

Confidently, Bronze made a ring of his thumb and forefinger. "I could put it through that."

"Show me."

Bronze selected a spear and fitted the butt of it to the cup-shaped hook in the end of his throwing stick. He tested the ground under his feet, glanced overhead to check for overhanging brush, and moved a little to the left. For a moment he stood poised, fixing the oppo-site cliff with a hypnotic eye. Then he moved. His arm was a blur, and the stick itself was invisible. It all but crackled as it cleft the air.

For a brief moment Garth lost sight of the spear altogether. Then his quick eye caught its flicker just before it stopped, deep-buried in a tree-trunk at the lip of the rock cliff. He held his breath, and in a second or so he heard, through the warm afternoon air, the soft, solid *thunk* of its impact.

Incredible! He thought. He said, boredly, "Not too bad. I'd hate to depend on that thing if there was any wind, though."

Garth threw off his belt. He stood up in a single garment, a skin-tight shorts-and-tunic combination of midnight blue, with a narrow white stripe all the way around under his armpits and another just below his waistline. Raising his arms he felt along this line and drew out a small ring, which he slid along the stripe. It was, judging by the wide eyes and slack mouth, Bronze's first view of a slide fastener.

Garth repeated the movement with a second ring on the lower stripe, and drew off the center portion of his tunic over his head— a single, resilient tube of soft, thin fabric. He ran its edge through his fingers, stopped, and carefully picked out a thread, which he worked free. Ignoring the astounded Bronze, he began to unravel the material.

"What you doing?"

Garth said, "Make yourself useful. I want you to sweep the ground clean—really clean—some place where it's solid. I want an area six by six feet without so much as a straw on it, with clear air above it. Get to it."

Willing and mystified, Bronze did as he was told. By the time Garth had thirty feet of thread cleared, the area was ready and Bronze, panting, was back at Garth's side. Garth took pity on him—he was obviously about to burst with curiosity. He held up the thread. "Break off a piece for me, Bronze boy."

Bronze took the end of the thread, wrapped it around his fists, and—"Wait!" laughed Garth.

He picked up two heavy pieces of tree branch, unwound the thread from the big unresisting fists, and took a couple of turns of the thread around each piece of wood, leaving about six inches of thread between them. "Now try it," he said. "Grip the wood, not the thread."

Puzzled, Bronze grasped the two pieces of wood and pulled. The thread went taut with a musical twang which rose in pitch as Bronze pulled. A look of utter amazement crossed his broad face. He relaxed, turned the two pieces of wood so that he wound up more thread and had only two inches between them. He set his back against a tree, knotted his jaw, and, with his great hands close to his chest, began to pull. His triceps swelled until the stretched skin shone. His body moved visibly away from the tree that he leaned against as his scapular muscles bunched and crawled.

There was a muffled crackling from his shoulders, and Garth stepped forward in alarm. Then one of the pieces of wood gave. The thread sliced through it like a scythe through a stand of wheat, and Bronze stood gasping, staring foolishly at the cleancut stub of branch in his hand. The thread fell away, unstretched, unbroken.

"I gave you the wood," Garth grinned, "because it would've sliced through your paws."

"What Ffanx stuff is that?" gasped Bronze.

"That isn't Ffanx stuff; it's strictly human. Molecularly condensed fibre spun under massive ion bombardment, if that makes any never mind to you. It has linear cohesion in the order of six tons test and eight and a half tons breaking strain. And it has no rotary cohesion at all."

"Yeah," said Bronze, "but what is it?"

"It's what you're going to tie to a spear and fire over the gulch for me. Now let's get busy and flake it out here. There's four hundred yards of it in this shirt. Half that should be enough. We'll give it a little more."

For two hours, as the afternoon shadows grew long, they worked, laying the thread meticulously in a series of small coils. Each turn of each coil lay flat and obedient. Slowly, the coils began to carpet the cleared area. They talked little, except toward the end of the laborious job. Finally—"That should do it," Garth said.

Bronze straightened up and punched himself in his aching kidneys. "I'm hungry."

"Feed us," said Garth.

Bronze took up his quiver and throwing-stick without a word, and glided away through the underbrush. Within a quarter of an hour he was back, carrying two large rabbits. One had a ragged hole through the head just behind the eyes, and the other was still impaled through the ribcage and heart by one of the stubby spears. Bronze squatted down, pulled out a worn knife, and with the swift casualness of long practice, gutted and skinned one of the animals and handed the warm and dripping quarters to Garth.

"Now listen to me," Garth said with his mouth full. "I don't know for sure who those Guardians are. But this I do know for sure—that green fire you saw doesn't come from them. It comes from under the ground—an energy field activated by something they carry under those long robes ... Why do I bother to explain anything to you?"

"I'm listening," grunted Bronze, spitting out a piece of gristle.

"All right. Now get this, it takes two Guardians, both on the line of those underground cables, to set off that fire. But *it takes two of them to do it*. Do you understand? If I can get one of them out of the way, you can jump the other one without any danger."

"Uh?" Bronze wiped rabbit blood off his chin.

"Are you following this? I'm going to leave you in a minute, and I want to know I can depend on you. Are you going to take my word for it—that you can tackle a Guardian without danger of getting burned?"

Bronze looked at him. "You said I could, didn't you?" he asked simply.

Garth let the grin come through again. "I think we're going to make it, Bronze boy," he said. "Now here's the plan."

The night was cool and still, but Garth, naked except for his belt, his boots, and the briefest of shorts—which were all that was left of his tunic—was warm and slick with sweat as he completed the long, silent climb to the top of the bluff. He filled and emptied his lungs in deep, open-throated gasps as he felt his way along the lip of the sheer rock wall of the cliff. He found the bald spot and the tree into which Bronze had sunk his test spear that afternoon.

He stepped behind the tree in which Bronze's spear still stuck, and, reaching around it with his flashlight in his hand, sent a quick, white beam up the trunk.

Then he waited.

There was a crescent moon in the sky, a chunky moon that urgently wanted to be gibbous. Somewhere a katydid cried for the grease like the proverbial squeaky wheel, and a tree-toad plucked away at its piano-wire heartstrings. Over the brink was blackness—eighty feet or better, straight down—and then, away from the cliff's shadow, a hundred yards from the base of the bluff, stood the arched shadow of the great tree with its limb stretched out over the main building like a giant frozen in a gesture of benison.

Where was Bronze? The opposite hill was a featureless mass of shadow and shifting moonlight. Was he there, sighting carefully on the place where he had seen Garth's gleam of light? Or was he gone, freed from the spell of wonderment and awe that Garth had put on him, strolling back toward his village to spend tonight and the rest of his musclebound life with idle speculation about the time he almost helped to open the Gateway?

The katydid and the treefrog suddenly were more than Garth could bear. With a snort of impatience he stepped from behind the tree. Immediately there was a whining whisper that crescendoed closer—air fanned his nose and eyes, and something slammed into the tree trunk. He went to his knees, staring up into blackness and then, in spite of himself, laughed. "I hope I've used up all my dumbness for tonight," he thought ruefully. He had known the impossibility of Bronze's hitting the tree again, especially in the dark—and had almost stepped out of the shelter of the tree-trunk in time to catch the spear with his silly head.

The spear hadn't stuck in the tree, for he had cautioned Bronze to bury the point in a piece of heartwood; he'd never have been able to pull it out of the tree, and, to do what he had to do, the thread-end must be free.

He fumbled about for the spear and found it. From his belt-pouch he drew a pair of molded gloves, thin, light, impenetrable, made of the same condensed matter as his tunic. Slipping them on, he picked up the spear and purely by touch found the thread. He brought it in hand over hand, yards of it, until suddenly it jerked sharply, twice, in his grip. He grinned. That was Bronze's "Good luck!"

Taking a bight of the thread, he walked once around the tree, thrust the loop of the bight under the main part where it would be pinched between that part and the tree-trunk. A slight tug on the free end would cast the line adrift.

He took a deep breath and walked to the cliff-edge. Everything depended on his estimates of the distances involved.

This is it, he thought. Carefully he took the thread at the point his measurements had brought him to, and tied it to the back of his belt. He knelt and swept a space on the ground, and carefully recoiled the line so it would flake away freely. Then he went to the edge of the cliff, reached up over his head, and got his gloved hands on the anchored part of the line, where it passed tautly from tree to tree across the hollow. He watched then, and tried not to think.

The buildings were dark, except for a dim orange light in the main Hall. He could see a flickering, an occasional movement as if restless figures inside passed and re-passed the light.

What the hell was Bronze doing over there? Had he forgotten what he was supposed to do next? The big, stupid, slow ...

From the other side of the canyon came a titanic crashing as a boulder went bounding down the slope, and with it a blood-chilling yell that echoed and re-echoed and faded repetitively off into the distance. It sounded like a score of lost souls calling and answering from strategic points up and down both sides of the valley.

What a set of pipes! Garth thought, and stepped off the cliff.

He could feel the rod-hard, stretched thread humming in his hands as the gentle night wind stroked it. He hung for a moment, then put one hand before the other. And again. And again. His body began to swing forward and back as he went along the line. He swore under his breath and checked the movement by a swift, synchronized run-and-stop, run-and-stop with his hands.

His shoulders began to ache and he tried to forget it. He hung by one hand for a moment and allowed himself the luxury of bringing the other arm down, flexing the fingers. Hand over hand over hand over hand ...

He put his hands together and crossed the wrists, so that his body turned to look back the way he had come. The shadowed cliff he had left was already distant, one with the hill-blackness that surrounded the buildings. He went on. Before and below him, the great tree came closer and closer and closer as he inched along. Too close?

He swung along, arms all but numb, shoulders an agony, hands reduced to two stiffly disobedient hooks that grasped, released, grasped, released, with greater and greater reluctance.

There was some sort of commotion by the building. Someone called out. A Guardian? At that moment he couldn't have defined a Guardian, and wouldn't have cared. The universe was one hand after another.

It came! He had watched for it each second, and when it came it took him totally by surprise. There was the faintest of tugs at his belt as the free end of the line drew tight, and then, far behind him, the thread whipped away from the tree he had left.

He dropped like a nighthawk.

The ground struck his knee a single, stunning blow and then he was hurtling upward toward the eaves of the Hall. He reached the top of his swing and all the strain was suddenly gone from his arms. For a single, terrifying split-second he was afraid his cramped hands would not let go. Then he was free of the line. He concentrated his whole being into keeping his balance, flexing his knees.

The dark roof came up and took him. He gathered the shock in his thigh-muscles, turned one shoulder down and rolled.

Then for a long, luxurious minute he lay still and rested.

After Bronze shoved the boulder over the edge and roared his terrible challenge into the night, he scuttled like a frightened rabbit through the dark tunnel of a trail that angled down the slope. "Crazy, crazy," he muttered. It couldn't work, that crazy plan of Gesell's. It was marvelous, heroic, brilliant, but—crazy. And he, Bronze, was crazy too, to think of helping. He'd go home. He'd had enough— enough to tell all Prellton about for the rest of his life.

But in spite of his thoughts, his legs carried him cautiously down the slope to the deadly courtyard of Gesell Hall.

"Line," said a low voice.

It was the cowled figure of a Guardian, waiting quietly in the moonlight to unleash hot green death.

"Now I'm going home," thought Bronze, quite coldly and rationally. He stayed where he was.

Then he saw the other Guardian, moving as if on a track—slowly, steadily, with no hint of a leg-motion—just an inhuman glide. Snails move like that. Centipedes. The stories of monsters from the other side of the Gateway suddenly flooded into his mind.

Bronze saw something else. If the second Guardian moved farther out, away from the Hall, he, Bronze, would be in a straight line between the two of them—

There was an abrupt, intense feeling in his stomach, as if his dinner rabbit had come to life again and had hopped. He rose to his feet. His mouth was dry.

The second Guardian was now out of sight, still moving toward that point which would bracket Bronze in verdant flame.

"Line," said the second voice, and then came the first of the two greatest shocks of Bronze's life.

With a glare of bright white light, a face appeared in midair—twenty feet off the ground—in front of the blank wall of the building.

"Guardian!" sang a deep, organlike voice.

The face was Garth Gesell's.

"Gesell!" gasped a Guardian. Sobbing, he ran toward the light. The other followed slowly. Bronze could begin to see, in the nimbus of light from the radiant face, Gesell's whole body. It hung in the air, perhaps a third of the way down the wall, with one arm thrust forward. The other hand seemed to be behind his back.

"Stop!" intoned the voice. "Remove your habits, Guardian, for I have returned!"

The Guardian from the left faltered, stopped. He stripped off his robe and cast it aside. The other followed suit. The two naked figures moved toward the building, like sleepwalkers. And as they did so, the shining face slid slowly and majestically to the ground. The Guardians fell to their knees and bowed to the earth at his feet. The light disappeared.

"Bronze?" Garth spoke quietly, but the syllable snapped Bronze out of his awed reverie. He leapt to his feet and sprinted across the wide court, to receive his second mighty shock.

250

Garth stood erect against the wall, and Bronze realized the stiffness of utter exhaustion in his stance. "Watch 'em," Garth whispered, and turned his flashlight on the two reverent figures.

One of them was a girl.

The long-tethered wild horses reared up in Bronze's brain. There was an explosion of desire that jolted him to the marrow. He bent quickly and took her arm. "Stand up, you."

She did.

She looked at him from wide, untroubled eyes. She made no attempt to cover herself or to cower. She met his gaze, and simply waited.

There were two kinds of women on Earth—the Escaped, and the Returned. The Escaped had been passed over by the hunting Ffanx—by chance, by luck, by sheer animal cunning on the part of the women or the men who hid them. They had been fair game for the Ffanx while the Ffanx ruled Earth, and they were fair game for any of the hundred-odd men who were left to compete for each of them.

And of the Earth's few women, perhaps one in a thousand was Returned. Almost invariably the Ffanx had slaughtered the women. But once in a long, long while they let the woman go. Why, no human ever understood. Perhaps it was capriciousness, perhaps it was done for experimentation. But in the rough ethic of a heterogeneous, dark-age society—all that was left of Earth culture after the Ffanx had conquered and then were destroyed in their turn—these women were sacrosanct. They had paid. Their very existence on the planet was a narrative and a dirge; they were the walking sorrow of Earth. And they were not to be touched. It was all that could be done for their loss and their loneliness. They knew it, and they walked without fear.

The wild horses within Bronze settled. They gentled, quieted, as if some firm, known hand had touched their flaring nostrils.

"Sister," he said, "I'm sorry."

She barely inclined her head. She turned then to Garth and said in a low voice, "What can we do for the master?"

Garth sighed. "I have come a long way. My friend and I need

rest. Guard as you always have, and in the morning there will be a new day, and nothing will ever be the same again for any of us."

The girl touched the shoulder of the other Guardian. "Come."

He rose. He was a slender, dark-browed youth with the wild frightened eyes of a chipmunk. He had white flesh and stick-like arms, and a very great dignity. "Master," he said to Garth. In his tone was subservience, but an infinitely proud sense of service rather than a humble one. He and the girl went into the building.

"Sexless," said Bronze. It was an identification only, there was no scorn.

Garth said, "I'm tired."

"You sleep. I'll watch," said Bronze.

"You can sleep too," said Garth. "We're in, Bronze. Really in."

"Bronze . . ."

The big man was on his feet, weapons in hand, before Gesell's voice had ceased. He cast about the room, saw no immediate menace, and crossed to the bed. "You all right?"

Garth stretched luxuriously. "Never better, though I feel as if my shoulder-joints needed oiling . . . what's for breakfast?"

Bronze went to the door and flung it open, filling his mighty lungs to shout. He didn't. The girl was standing there, waiting.

Garth saw her. "Come in—Good Lord, girl, you must be freezing!"

"I haven't had your permission . . ." she said gravely.

"Go dress. And tell the other Guardian to put on some clothes. What's your name?"

"Viki."

"What's his name—that other Guardian?"

"Daw, Master."

"Good. My name's not Master. It's Garth, or Gesell, whichever suits you. This is Bronze. Is there anything to eat?"

"Yes, Garth Gesell."

Garth pursed his lips. Her intonation of his name was infinitely more adoring, even, than her "Master." He said, "We'll be out in a minute. I want you to eat with us, do you understand? You and the other, both."

"A great honor, Garth Gesell." She smiled, and it did wonders for the fine-drawn austerity of her face.

She waited a moment, and when Garth apparently had nothing more to say, she left. She backed to the door.

Breakfast was an acutely uncomfortable affair. They ate at a small square table in the hall under the portrait of the first Gesell. It might have been a picture of Garth five or ten years older. They had always looked alike.

Viki, now dressed in the conventional short flowing tunic fastened only by a wide belt, sat demure and quiet, speaking only when spoken to, and screening her constant gaze at Garth with her long lashes. Daw stared straight ahead out of round, permanently astonished eyes, and tried hard, apparently, to avoid looking directly at Gesell. Bronze grinned broadly at Garth's discomfiture and ignored the prim looks of the two Guardians.

Garth waited until the meal was finished, and then put his palms down on the table. "We have work to do."

They turned to him so raptly and obediently that for a moment he lost his train of thought. Bronze looked as if he was about to laugh. Garth shot him a venomous look and said to the Guardians, "But I want you to talk first. I've been away a long time. I want the history of this place as you know it, especially where it concerns the Gateway."

Viki and Daw looked at one another. Garth said, "Come on, come on—"

Daw composed himself, folded his hands on the edge of the table, and cast his eyes down. "In the year of the Ffanx," he intoned, "on the meadows of Hack and Sack, there appeared a blue light shaped like a great arched doorway, filled with a flickering mist."

"We trust in Gesell," muttered Viki.

"And there came from this archway a creature as long as a hand and as heavy as four times its mass in lead castings. It sniffed at the air, and it took up some soil, and it lifted a box which it held to its head, and it smelled out our women. It called, then; and out of the archway came more of its kind in the hundreds of thousands, wearing strange trappings and bringing machines to work evil. And these were the Ffanx."

"We trust in Gesell," murmured the girl.

Garth opened his mouth to speak, and closed it abruptly. He had a quick ear, and he had rapidly caught the cadences of Daw's voice. No one speaks like that naturally. This wasn't a report, it was a singsong ritual.

"At first the world wondered, at first the world laughed at the Ffanx. For the Ffanx were so tiny, and their ships were like toys, and they spread over Earth without harming a soul, and submitted to capture and acted like comical dolls. They covered the planet and when they were ready—they struck."

He put his head down on his folded hands as he spoke the last two words. Viki droned, "We trust in Gesell."

Daw straightened up and now his voice deepened. His eyes were wide, and fixed on nothing in the room. As he spoke, Garth found himself fascinated by the almost imperceptible motion of Bronze's shaggy head as it nodded in time to the dactylic beat of Daw's speech.

"They struck at our women. They found them in homes and in caves and in churches: killed them by millions. Their weapons were hammers of force from the sky, inaudible sounds that drove strong men to kill their own daughters and slaughter themselves. And then the foul Ffanx would sweep in their bodies.

"And sometimes they herded them, flashing about in their sleek little airships, smashing the men and propelling the foot-weary women along to great pens in the open. They walled them about with their fences of force and destroyed all attacks from outside, and then at their leisure they killed all our females, this one today and then that one, and two or two thousand tomorrow. And Earth saw its blackest, its sorriest day . . .

"Earth was united in madness."

"We trust in Gesell."

"Gesell was a giant who lived on a hill, a worker of wonders who turned from his works to the solving of problems for Earth. Of all men on Earth, he alone learned the nature of Ffanx and the land whence they came and the spell he could cast to destroy them. It was he who devised a retreat for the women that not even Ffanx could detect. He set up a Gateway and passed women through it—women with beauty and women with mind, and any and all of the women with child who could come to the Gateway.

"And the Earth had turned savage, and men lost their reason and stormed up the hill of Gesell, and they tried to pass into the gateway and get to the women. With some it was hunger, with some it was cowardice. So Gesell, all unwilling, constructed defenses, appointed the Guardians, gave instructions to kill all who came in attack, be they human or Ffanx."

"We trust in Gesell."

"And this is the Word of Gesell:

" 'Guard the Gateway with your lives. Make no attempt to open it, or the Ffanx will find it and take the treasure it hides. When the time is right, the women will open the Gateway themselves—or I or another Gesell will open it from this side. But guard it well.'

"That is the Word of Gesell, and the end of his word; and he alone knows if there was to be more; for that was the end of Gesell. The Ffanx came and killed him, but dying, he cast a great spell and they died. They died on two worlds and the menace is done with. And Earth is in darkness and waits for Gesell to return, and the Gateway to open. And meanwhile the Word of Gesell is the hope of the world:

"Guard the Gateway."

Daw's voice died away. Bronze sat as if mesmerized. Viki's lips moved silently in the response.

Garth slapped his hand down suddenly, shockingly. "This is going to hurt," he gritted. "Daw, where did that—that recitation come from? Where did it start?"

"It's the Word of Gesell," said Daw, wonderingly. "Everybody—"

"We repeat it morning and night," Viki interposed, "to strengthen us in our duty."

"But whose phrases are they? Who made it up?"

"Garth Gesell, *you* must know ... or perhaps you are testing us."

255

"Will you answer the question?"

"I learned it from Daw," said Viki.

"I learned it from Soames, who had it from Elbert and Vesta, who were taught by Gesell himelf."

Garth closed his eyes. "Elbert ... Holy smoke! He was the ..." He stopped himself in time. He remembered Elbert—a dreamy scholar with whom his father used to have long and delightful philosophical discussions, and who, at other times, pushed a broom around the laboratories. Garth began to see the growth of this myth, born in the poetic mind of a misfit.

He looked into their rapt faces. "I'm going to tell you the same story that you told me," he said flatly, "but without the mumbo-jumbo."

"Gesell was my father. He was a great man and a good one. He was *not* nine feet tall, Bronze. And—" he turned to the Guardians— "he was not a 'worker' of spells.

"Now to your legend. 'The meadows of Hack and Sack' are swampland just south of what used to be, before the Ffanx came, the greatest city on Earth. The real name is Hackensack. The blue arch wasn't magic, it was science—it was the same thing as the Gateway itself, though of a slightly different kind.

"The Ffanx were small and heavy because they came from an area where molecular structure is far more compressed than it is here. And they struck at our women for a good reason. It wasn't viciousness and it wasn't for sport. It was, to them, a vital necessity. And that necessity made it useless to think of driving them off, defeating them. They had to be *destroyed,* not defeated. I won't go into the deeper details of inter-dimensional chemistry. But I want you to know exactly what the Ffanx were after—you'll understand them a lot better.

"There is no great difference, physically, between men and women. I mean, bone structure, metabolism, heart and lung and muscular function are different in quality but not in kind. But there is one thing that women produce that men do not. It's a complex protein substance called extradiol. One of its parts is called extradiol *beta-prime,* and is the only way in which human extradiol differs from that of other female animals. With it, they're women. Without it, they're nothing... cold, sexless ... ruined.

"So it was this substance that the Ffanx were after. You've heard the tales of what they wanted. Women. But they didn't want them as women. They were after *extradiol* for the best reason on Earth or off it:

"It made them immortal!"

Bronze's jaw dropped. Viki continued to gaze raptly at Garth. Daw's heavy brows were drawn together in an expression that looked more like fear and worry than perplexity.

"Think about that for a minute. Think of what would happen if we of Earth found a species of animal which carried a substance which would do that for us ... we'd hunt it ruthlessly and mercilessly."

"Wait a minute," Bronze said. "You mean that these Ffanx couldn't die from a spear-wound?"

"Lord, no—they weren't immortal in that sense. Just from old age which, in any species, is a progressive condition caused by dysfunction of various parts—particularly connective tissue. A complicated extract of human extradiol *beta* would restore the connective tissues of the Ffanx and keep them healthy for thirty of our years or more. Then another shot would keep 'em that way, and so on."

"Just where is the Ffanx world?" asked Daw, and then colored violently as if embarrassed by the sound of his own voice.

"That's a little difficult to explain," said Garth carefully. "Look, suppose that door—" he pointed to an interior doorway—"opened into more than one room. You can almost imagine it; say you'd have to go through the door from an acute angle to get into the first room, go straight through to get into a second. You might call the second world Parallel X.

"The Gateway and the blue arch at Hackensack were doorways between worlds—between universes. These universes exist at the same time in the same space—but at different vibratory rates ... I don't expect you to understand it, no one really does. The theory's an old one. No one gave it much consideration until the Ffanx got here."

257

Bronze asked, "If it's a doorway, like you say, why didn't the Ffanx find the way in to the world where the women went?"

Garth smiled. "Remember the doorway there? Suppose you were quite familiar with the way that door opened to one of two rooms. Then supposing I came along and pointed out that instead of going straight in or turning left, you could go *up* and find yourself in still a third room. It's like that. The Ffanx just never thought of going into their inter-dimensional arch in the particular direction that would wind them up in the Gateway world.

"There was always the possibility that the Ffanx *might* think of it, though, and you can bet that the women were warned and were ready to fight. But to get back to the story—I have to tell it all to you so you can understand what we're going to do next; and I will have you understand it, because I don't want help from people who just take orders, I want help from people who think.

"All right, let's go on. I'm trying to give you an idea of what my father was—a man who worked and worried and made mistakes and was happy and frightened and brave and all the other things you are.

"He was a scientist, a specialist in molecular structure. In the early days of the invasion he got hold of a couple of Ffanx. You'll remember that they weren't attacking then. My Dad was the only man who was ever able to communicate with them, and he did it without their realizing what he was doing. A specialist in condensed matter can produce a lot of weird effects. One of the things he found out was that thought itself is a vibration very similar to the brain-waves of a Ffanx-type mind; that is, the currents that produced thought in their brains could be changed directly into waves his instruments could detect and translate. He got no details, but he did get some broad concepts. One of them was that the blue arch was the only exit that they had ever made from their world; they had never traveled to other planets in their universe. Another was the nature of their quest on Earth. When he found that out, he killed his specimens, but by then it was too late.

"He took those little bodies apart literally atom by atom. And he found out how to destroy them. It was simple in itself, but hard to get to, an isotope of nitrogen which, if released in their world, would set up a chain reaction in their atmosphere. Due to the differences between the molecules of the two universes—they have a table of elements just like ours, but denser—their atmospheric hydrogen could be commuted to free hydrogen and arsenic tri-hydride, with a by-product of nitrogen ions that would kick off the reaction again and again ... I see I'm talking gobbledegook. Sorry.

"Suffice it to say that my father knew what would destroy the Ffanx, but he had to make it himself. By that time the Ffanx had destroyed communications and the world was in chaos. It took time, as he knew it would. So he built the Gateway.

"He got the idea from the Ffanx' own blue arch, which he had seen from a distance. He took careful readings on that strange blue light and guessed what it was. And in trying to build another like it—I think he planned to invade them where they didn't expect it—he stumbled on the Gateway.

"It gave a weird red-orange light instead of a blue one, and the atmosphere on the other side was breathable, which the Ffanx world's was not—they had to wear helmets and carry an air-supply while they were on Earth. He went through and looked the place over. There was timber and water and, as far as he could find out, no civilization or dangerous animals—just insects and some little rabbit-like creatures so tame they could be caught by hand. And he got the idea of using it as a sanctuary for the world's women while he worked on the weapon that would destroy the Ffanx.

"You know the rest of that story—how the women came, all he could send word to—and then how he had to build defenses against the panic-struck, woman-hungry mobs that stormed this place.

"I was just a boy of eight when Dad finished the weapon. It was an innocent-looking eight-inch capsule filled with compressed gas. He planned to go up to Hackensack, traveling at night and hiding in the daytime, and set up a projector to peg it into the blue arch.

"The day after he showed it to me the Ffanx came ... I'm convinced they didn't know how near they were to the thing that would wipe them out. I'll never know why they came just then ... maybe there was a party of women on the way up the canyon. Anyway, a flight of their little ships appeared, and they let go one of their force-beams on the lab-building—I guess because it was the nearest to the canyon-trail—and stove the roof in. Dad was crushed and the building burned."

Garth took a deep breath. His eyes burned. "I spoke to him while he died. Then I left, with the capsule."

"So it was you who put the poison through the blue arch," said Bronze. "I'd always heard it was Gesell."

"It was Gesell," said Viki devoutly.

"I did, yes. Anyway, when that capsule burst in their world, they had a fine arseniated atmosphere. The hydrogen they breathed was arsenic tri-hydride within minutes after it got to their bloodstreams. I don't know how long it took to kill off every last one of them on their planet, but it couldn't have been long. And it got all the Ffanx here, too. They all had to go back to renew their air supplies. I don't think we'll ever hear of a living Ffanx again."

"And where have you been all these years?"

"Growing up. Studying. Dad's orders. He was the most foresighted man who ever lived. He couldn't be sure of just what would happen in the near future, but he knew what the possibilities were, and acted on all of them. One of the things he did was to prepare a hypnopede—it's a gadget that teaches you while you sleep—no bigger than your two fists. It was designed for me, in case anything happened, and it covered the basic principles of the Gateway, and a long list of reference books. I lived with that thing, month after month, and when I was old enough to move around safely under my own power I began to travel. I went to city after city and pawed through the ruins of their libraries and boned up on all of it—atomic theory, strength of materials, higher math, electronics—until I could begin to get experimental results."

He looked around the table. "Are you people ready to give me a hand with the Gateway?"

"We took a vow—" said Viki. Garth interrupted her. "Let's have none of that!"

Viki continued with perfect composure. "We took a vow to serve Gesell through life and past death, and I see no reason to change it. Do you, Daw?"

"I agree." Daw's face was strained. Garth thought for a second that Daw was going to argue the point. But perhaps he was wrong . . .

"Good," said Garth. "Now—when the Ffanx destroyed the laboratory, they smashed the Gateway generators, as you know. I think I can restore them. With your help I know I can."

"Hey wait," said Bronze. "What about that prediction that the women would open it from the other side?"

"They're supposed to have the facilities," said Garth. "There's just one piece of evidence we have that proves we've got to do it— they haven't opened the Gateway."

"Why not, d'you suppose?"

Garth shrugged. "Afraid to, maybe. Maybe something's happened to them. Who knows? Let's find out."

Viki spoke up, timidly. "Garth Gesell—it's been years since they went through. Will they be . . . I mean, do you suppose there are . . ." She floundered to a halt.

"Even women in their late thirties and forties can do some good to the world now," Garth answered. "And don't forget—many of them were with child. There'll be new blood for Earth. However, one of the most important considerations is the women themselves. Among them were some of the best brains on Earth. Architects and doctors, and even a machine-tool designer. But the biggest treasure of all is Glory Gehman. She was my Dad's friendly enemy—almost as good as he was in his specialty, and a lot better in several more. If she's still alive, she'll do more to get the world back on its feet than any thousand people alive today. You'll see . . . you'll see. Come on, let's get to work!"

The days that followed were a haze of activity. Garth traced the old power-supply, and to his delight found it in prime condition. It had been used for little but the Guardians' flame, all other equipment having been pretty well smashed or gone into disuse. The super-batteries which fed it were neo-tourmaline, a complex crystal that had the power of storing enormous quantities in its facets. Garth's first task was to restore the great sundishes which charged the crystals. His father had designed them to replace the broadcast power that he had used before he developed the condensed-matter crystal.

The Guardians—Garth had abandoned that term, but Bronze still insisted on using it—worked like beavers—Viki worshipfully and silently, Daw in a feverish way which puzzled Garth and angered Bronze. Bronze himself had to be watched to keep him from bossing the others. Garth kept him under control by doubting aloud whether he could do this or that, or by wondering if he was strong enough to move this over to there. "You think I can't," Bronze would mutter, and attack the task as if it were a deadly enemy.

Twice Garth called them all into the new laboratory and announced that the Gateway was ready. The first time nothing happened when he threw the switch, and it took him eight days to trace out the circuits and to test the vibratory controls. The second time a sheet of cool orange flame leaped into being, quivered and flickered for a moment, and then collapsed.

At each of these occasions Bronze berated Garth for letting the Guardians see it. "Here you got them thinking you're a superman," he said disgustedly, "and then you let them watch you pull a blooper."

Garth was alone in the makeshift laboratory when he succeeded. He had bent to replace a crystal which was a few thousandths of a cycle out of phase, and he turned back to the Gateway apparatus— and there it was.

Quietly, noiselessly, it hung there, so beautiful it made him gasp, so welcome he could hardly believe his eyes. It was red-orange at the bottom, shading to gold at the top.

He spun to the switch. It was still open. Then he realized that his synchronization of the quartz frequency-crystals and the tourmaline power-crystals was so perfect that the Gateway had come of its own accord. He had known that the phenomenon was self-sustaining, he hadn't known that it was self-starting.

He closed the switch as a safety-measure, and stood looking at the Gateway. "Got it," he muttered. And he could all but feel his father's presence with him, dark eyes glowing, his hand ready with the reward the boy used to prize so highly—the warm clasp of a shoulder.

Garth glanced at the door, thinking of Bronze and the others. Then he shrugged. "Let 'em sleep. They'll need it."

He stepped through the Gateway.

In her small cell Viki slept lightly. She was dreaming about Gesell, as she often did. Her early training with old Soames had been partly hypnopedic, and like most sleep-training, it tended to be restimulated by sleep itself. Part of it pictorialized itself as a dream of the main foyer in Gesell Hall, where the great portrait of Gesell hung. She seemed to be watching the picture, which refused to be a picture of the elder Gesell, but of Garth. And as she watched, the long, white-browed face began to turn pale. The face was composed, but the eyes conveyed a worriment that grew into terror and then into agony. As she stared at it, frozen, the dream picture suddenly ripped down the middle with a sound she was never to forget as long as she lived.

She bounded out of bed and stood gasping in the middle of the floor. Her sense of presence returned to her. She glanced around her and then bolted for the door.

In a silent panic she raced for the laboratory, threw the door open.

Between the tall grid-electrodes over which Garth had slaved for so many weeks there was a sheet of flame. Viki stared it, awed, and then realized what was so very strange about it; it radiated no heat. She approached it cautiously.

On the floor by the lower frame of the apparatus lay a human hand.

She knew that hand. Heaven knows she had spent enough mealtimes watching its deft movement from under her lowered lashes. She had seen it probing the complexities of the apparatus often enough, and had marveled at its skilled strength.

"Garth Gesell ..." she moaned.

She stooped over the hand and only then did she realize that it was thrust through the flame as if through a curtain.

She seized it and pulled. She saw the forearm, the elbow ... "Bronze!" she screamed. She set her small bare feet against the lower frame and lifted and pulled.

Garth Gesell's body slid out. It was flecked with blood. Blood flowed slowly from his nostrils and ears. His lifeless face held just the expression of terror and agony she had seen in her dream. His flesh was mottled and his lips were blue.

She screamed again, a wordless cry of fury at the fates rather than one of fear. She flipped the body over on its face, turned the head to one side, put her fingers in the unresisting mouth and drew the tongue forward. Then she knelt with her left knee between his thighs and began to apply artificial respiration. "Bronze!" She called again and again, with each measured pressure of her sure hands.

Bronze appeared at the door, looking like a war-horse, his nostrils dilated, his muscular chest gleaming with sweat. "What is— what are you doing to him?" He strode forward, his big hand out to pluck her away from Gesell.

She put her head back and said "Stop." It was said quietly but with such intensity that he halted as if he had run into a wagon-tongue in the dark. Daw came in, rubbing his eyes.

She ignored the men. She lay down on the floor beside Garth and put her face next to his.

"Viki!" said Daw in horror. "Your vows . . ."

"Shut up," she hissed, and put her mouth against Garth's.

Bronze said, "What the hell's she . . ."

"Leave her," said Daw in a new voice.

Bronze's startled expression matched Daw's natural one.

Bronze followed his gaze. Exactly in synchronization, Viki's cheeks and Garth's expanded and relaxed. In the sudden silence, they could hear the breath whistle in Viki's arched nostrils.

"Gesell . . ." whispered Viki hoarsely. She put her mouth against Garth's again.

Suddenly his head jerked back. Feebly, he coughed.

"She did it," muttered Bronze. "Viki—you did it."

Viki rolled like a cat and bounded to her feet. She dipped her hand in a waterbucket and sloshed the freezing mass into the middle of Garth's back. He gasped, a great gulping inhalation, and began to cough again. "Get alcohol," said Viki tightly.

They rolled Garth over and Daw lifted his head. They forced a few drops of ethyl alcohol into Garth's mouth. He shuddered.

"Somebody kissed me," he said. He lay back, breathing deeply. "The ... Gateway ... women are dead. It's no use."

"What was it?" asked Daw. "Was the air poisonous?"

"No ... it was all right—what there was of it. There just wasn't enough. I don't know what caused it, but something has used up most of the air in that world. I passed out before I'd gone any real distance. And the women ..."

"Didn't you see any signs of them?"

"Not a thing. The world seemed empty. Parallel X ..."

There was a silence. Then Garth asked, "Well—where do we go from here?"

Daw suddenly leaped to his feet. "Gesell!" he cried. "Great Gesell, forgive me!"

Garth looked up at him curiously. "Daw I've told you a thousand times not to call me—"

"You!" spat Daw. "You—impostor! You apostate! You're the devil! You came here in the guise of the great Gesell in order to invade the sanctuary of Gesell's women. No Gesell would tire, no Gesell would fail. No Gesell would respond to the clutches of a female."

Bronze was on his feet. "Now, listen, you—"

Daw threw out his skinny arms dramatically. "Go on—kill me; I deserve a hundred deaths for my failure as a Guardian. But I die in defense of Gesell and his works. It's the least I can do." He suddenly flew at Bronze. "Kill me now—kill me!"

Bronze put out one mighty arm and caught the front of Daw's tunic. Daw flailed away helplessly. His arms were far shorter than Bronze's, and all he could do was to rain blows on the iron biceps and kick feebly at the man's boots.

"What shall I do?" said the amazed Bronze. "Shall I squash him?"

"Don't harm him," said Garth. "But I guess you better put him to sleep."

Bronze brought his free hand up and over and put a hammerlike blow on the very top of Daw's head. The little Guardian went limp.

Bronze draped him across the crook of his elbow like a spare blanket.

"What about you?" he said to the girl.

Viki stared up at him out of wide eyes and turned to Garth. "I serve Gesell."

Garth said tiredly. "There seem to be three Gesells around here. My Dad, who's dead. Me. And some sort of King Arthur-type myth. Which one are you serving?"

"Only you," she breathed. She rose gracefully, cast a look of utmost scorn at the feebly twitching Daw, excused herself and left the room.

"Let her go," said Garth to Bronze.

"She's liable to blow up the joint," protested Bronze.

"I think not."

"You can be wrong, Garth Gesell."

Garth grinned wryly. "You know that, and still you stick around. I wish these dedicated charmers felt the same way. I just can't live up to what they want me to be."

"Maybe you can't," growled Bronze. "But you should. I told you and told you you should." He hefted Daw. "What'll we do with this?"

"Try to talk some sense into him."

"Let me twist his head off first. Then you can put the sense in with a trowel."

Garth chuckled. "That won't be necessary. I know what's wrong with him. Bronze, many people who take readily to dedicated service do it only because it's a substitute for ordinary living, which they don't want to face. That isn't by any means true of all of 'em, but it is of our boy here. Life these days isn't easy, I don't have to tell you that. As a Guardian, Daw had an even, dependable existence where he knew what he had to do and knew exactly how to do it. He saw no reason why that should ever change. And then I came along and reduced him to the level of a guy who is changing his environment a lot now so that it can be changed still more later, and he didn't like it."

"That sounds good. Now can you pound that all into his head with one wallop? Or shall I stand guard over him for a year or so while you lead him by the hand out of a swamp he made himself to wallow in?"

"Easy, easy," said Garth ruefully.

"Dammit, you need it," growled Bronze. "Something's wrong with the Gateway world. Something was wrong with your idea of walking into Gesell Hall that day I met you, but that didn't stop you." Bronze wet his lips. "I guess I'm a little bit like that Daw, after all. You got to be what I think you should be before I'll play along with you."

They found Viki in the laboratory, staring at the Gateway, which flamed and flickered coldly in its frames. Garth and Bronze ranged up beside her.

"If we could only move around in there," said Garth. "If we could only know what happened to the air-pressure."

"The Ffanx did it," said Viki.

"Let him do the thinking, sister," said Bronze with the odd combination of bluntness and courtesy he affected with her.

"There are no more Ffanx, Viki," said Garth. "If I'm sure of anything, I am sure of that."

"I know that," said Viki. "I mean that the Ffanx moved from dense air into rarefied air—you said so."

Garth struck himself a resounding wallop on the forehead. "Bronze," he said in an awed tone of voice, "she has the brains."

"Huh?"

"Air helmets! Here I was so defeated that I couldn't see the one thing that was staring me in the face. Come on. The machine shop!"

The helmets they turned out in the next few days were makeshift but serviceable. Using the domed tops of aluminum pressure tanks and a series of welded bands, and a tightly-gasketed piece of plexiglass, they had the basic design. Soft, thick edging of foam rubber sealed the shoulder, chest and back. The air supply was liquid air passed through a tiny but highly efficient chemical heater. "We want no oxygen drunks on this trip," Garth explained.

They locked Daw up in the north storeroom. Garth tried to talk to him but found him completely intractable. He was like a man in a trance. He would speak only to the original Gesell, using his name to call down maledictions on the heads of the impostors.

"What shall we take with us?"

They stood before the Gateway—Bronze impatient and excited, Garth thoughtful, Viki her reserved, willing self. Green floodlights and a smoke generator had been strategically placed on the defense line in the canyon, keyed to the detectors so that any intruder would be badly frightened if he came onto the Court. It was defense enough for the short time they planned to be away.

"My spears," said Bronze.

"No," Garth said. "Take this instead." He tossed over his old blaster. "It's more compact. I mean no insult to that throwing arm of yours, little man, but the blaster has a little more range."

"Thanks." Bronze turned it over admiringly. "Did I ever tell you that if you hadn't been carrying this when I first met you I'd have knocked you off? I never met a man with one before."

Garth laughed. "I hadn't had charges for it for more than four years. It was good protective coloration. But there are plenty of charges now. Viki—"

"I have my dagger. And an extra air tank."

"Good. I'll take two extra tanks. That ought to hold us.

"Now here's the plan. We have no radio. I was able to weld in some thin plates to my helmet—I should be able to hear in there. I don't think you two will be able to unless you touch helmets. I won't be able to hear you but I can hear outside sounds. So once we get in there, we're pretty much on our own. All I can say is—keep together and don't go too far. Mind you, this is just a preliminary recon patrol. Later we can go back in with more and better equipment. Ready?"

Bronze raised a thumb and forefinger in the ancient sign.

"Right!" Viki nodded tensely.

Garth wheeled, settled his helmet down on its shoulderpieces. The others followed suit.

Then Garth plunged through the Gateway.

The three huddled together as they emerged from the Gateway.

They found themselves on a stony plain that stretched out and away as far as the eye could reach. There were the looming shadows of distant, tremendous mountains. The rocks were soft and coarse, and of the same orange-to-gold shading that characterized the Gateway.

Garth glanced around at the Gateway, and understood how in his previous visit he had missed it. It flickered and flamed as dimly as a candle in the sunlight. He touched his two companions and pointed back at it. They nodded, and he knew they understood the need for caution. In that wilderness of boulders, it would be easy to lose it completely.

He recalled the first Gateway, his father's, which had debouched on a flat plain, smaller than this. There had been rocks here and there, but nothing like the monstrous, crumbling boulders which surrounded them now. He wondered, as he had many times in the past few days, if the elder Gesell's specifications had been wrong in some subtle way, and if this was, as Bronze had suggested, a different dimensional world from that to which the women had been sent. In the maze of advanced mathematics involved in the construction of a Gateway, any small slip might have far-reaching results.

His thought broke off sharply. Through the two thin discs welded into the sides of his helmet he could hear a high-pitched, shattering roar. He looked up—

It was a helicopter—but such a machine as a mad aeronautical engineer might dream of in a nightmare!

It was huge and it was slow. It was altogether too slow. Its great blades had a radius of nearly two hundred feet. It settled downward much faster than it seemed to, for its size was so deceptive; the vanes rotated no faster than the wings of an ancient Dutch windmill.

It came to rest a hundred yards away. Its size was incredible. As it rested on the ground, the roof of the fuselage was all of eighty feet from the ground. The door opened.

Garth swept the helmets of the other two against his with one motion. They contacted with a deafening clang.

"Hide!" he barked. "In the rocks ... get out of sight!"

He turned and dove for shelter. Just to his right a huge flat rock, which had apparently once stood on edge, leaned over at about eighty degrees. Under it was just enough space for him to slide into with his helmet protruding.

He looked first for his companions. Bronze was huddled behind a round boulder. Viki was running back toward the Gateway, zigzagging in a panic-struck search for adequate shelter. He saw her trip and fall, and an airtank went bounding away from her shoulder. She rose groggily to her feet and tried to run again.

Garth looked back toward the helicopter. What he saw confirmed the surge of fear he had experienced as its door had opened.

Four women approached with great leaping strides. They were dressed in odds and ends—a ragged halter, a smooth tunic, a slashed skirt. Each was dressed differently and casually. One carried a monstrous knobbed club. All were belted and had long daggers. Around the neck of the leader was a black chain from which swung a mighty jewel, which glowed and sparkled in the universally orange-gold light. The jewel was brilliantly, shockingly green—the characteristic glittering green of neo-tourmaline. But Garth had never seen a crystal of that size. It was gem-cut, and must have been all of forty inches from crown to apex. And the woman carried it comfortably at the end of its ten-foot stick-like mounting, on its chain with links the size of anchor-cable, because she herself was seventy-five feet tall.

Garth was conscious of a pounding in his ears. At first he thought it was the earth-shaking tread of the four giantesses—for the other three were almost as tall as the first. Then he realized that the pounding was caused by the simple fact that in his shock he had forgotten to breathe.

He turned and looked for his companions. Bronze was slack and awed, gaping skyward at the leader's tremendous head. Viki was nowhere to be seen—

And neither was the Gateway. It was gone.

The leader stopped not twenty yards away, and bent, scanning the ground, fingering her jeweled pendant. Her face was distant, composed and cool. She was very beautiful, with long-lashed eyes and high-arched brows and a complexion like unveined marble.

"Bronze!" Garth screamed, for the second woman, a blonde with masses of flowing golden hair, had circled, and was behind Bronze as he stared up at the leader. The blonde raised her club, a thirty-foot mass that must have weighed all of a ton. She spoke—a deep, unintelligible strumming. Bronze, of course, could not hear Garth's cry of warning.

The leader straightened up and glanced at the blonde. She said something equally incomprehensible—the frequency of their voice-tones was down in the subsonic—and the blonde reluctantly put down the club.

And then, to Garth's horror, the leader bent and shot out a mighty hand. Bronze tried to scuttle aside, but the hand closed on him, lifted him high in the air.

Then it was that Garth recognized the giantess. He knew he had seen that cool, beautiful face before—long, long before, when he was a child.

Bronze squirmed and fought that gigantic grip. Garth saw him twist free, ball up and kick with both feet at the huge thumb. He slipped out of the grasp when the hand had carried him forty feet in the air. The giantess fell to one knee and reached out, catching him deftly. She held him up before her great calm face and watched him squirm.

Bronze suddenly struck out with both hands, twisted to one side, and got his hand on the blaster.

"*Don't Don't*" screamed Garth. He knew what that blaster could do at short range. But his raging was useless, he could not be heard.

The giantess fumbled for a second and then, with her left hand, brought up the pendant by its stick-like handle. She held the jewel close to Bronze as if it were a strange magnifying glass.

Bronze whipped the blaster out and up, and just as it bore on the huge, calm face, the great thumb moved on a stud on the handle of the jewel-mounting.

A blaze of green fire reached out from the jewel and enveloped Bronze's chest, turning to dazzling white where it struck him. The jewel deepened in color and seemed to thicken, to grow more solid.

The magnetic buckles of Bronze's helmet harness suddenly parted, and the internal pressure did the rest. The helmet popped off his head and flew up and around, swinging by the one back strap that was caught between his waist and the imprisoning hand.

Then the blaster spoke.

"Don't!" screamed Garth uselessly. "That's Glory Gehman!"

But instead of the shattering roar he expected, his earplates detected only a muffled f-f-ft! A weak tongue of fire, perhaps ten or twelve inches long, flickered wanly from the bore of the blaster, and then faded. Bronze writhed once, then went limp.

The great figure that looked like Glory Gehman held Bronze up like a tiny limp doll and called to the other women. They crowded around. The blonde reached with long, delicate fingers and lifted up the dangling helmet, pointed at Glory Gehman's ears. Garth noticed for the first time that her ear pendants were made of Ffanx helmets, or rather a tremendously oversize version of them. The leader shook her head and laughed, and gently forced Bronze's helmet back on his head. Holding her face very close, as if she were threading a needle in bad light, she set the buckle-magnets back in their grooves and gently tested the air-lines. Then the leader walked off toward the helicopter, while the other three resumed their search of the ground.

Garth's eye caught a glint of metal a few yards away—the spare airtank Viki had dropped. But of Viki there was no sign, and gone, too, was the Gateway.

Garth Gesell was alone on this earth, a pygmy hiding under a rock like a beetle, while he was being hunted by colossi obviously bent on destroying his kind.

A great bare foot pressed the earth close to him. He could hear the stones crackle. He crept farther back in the narrow fissure which held him. He knew that the next step the giantess took might be on top of that flat rock, and that would be then end of Gesell on any world save for a revered memory.

And a fat lot of good the reverence would do him as he lay crushed under a rock.

"For Gesell," sang Daw as he hooked the cable around the frame of the Gateway. Then something struck his back and side and sent him sprawling. He kept his hold on the cable as he fell, and part of him was gratified to feel it catch on the frame. He knew it had contacted, and he knew it without looking at the Gateway for the flickering gold light was abruptly gone.

He rolled and came up on one knee.

Lying on the floor, doubled up in pain as she nursed a bleeding foot, was Viki. She squeezed her eyes as tight as they would shut; even through the thick transparent plastic of her helmet Daw could see the silent tears she forced out.

She sat up and looked around her, then sprang to her feet and leaped to the framework. That brought her up against the rear wall of the laboratory. She stood for a moment feeling it with incredulous fingers, then turned and stepped out again.

Apparently it was only then that she saw Daw.

She slid the magnetic buckles apart and wrenched off her helmet. Her hair and eyes were wild.

"Daw. The Gateway!"

"A false Gateway for a false Gesell," intoned Daw.

She looked around at the dead framework again, and then at Daw. "What are you doing here?"

"The hand of Gesell freed me for his good works," said Daw. "I found a weak spot in the ceiling of the storeroom. Now, more than ever, I know the truth and reason behind my act. For you were spared, sister, spared from your own infamies, and saved, as a sworn Guardian, for the true Gesell."

She looked at him, bewildered.

He explained to her, patiently, exultantly. "You were led to return from the company of evil, just as I obeyed Gesell's command to do away with the false Gateway."

"Return? I didn't return!" she said frantically. "I fell. I was running, looking back and up at—at—" She closed her eyes and shuddered. "And then I hurt my foot, and fell ... Daw, what has happened to the Gateway?"

"Gone," he said, and smiled. "And good riddance. Come, sister. Let us go to the great portrait and receive more messages."

"Daw, we've got to fix it! He's in trouble. They'll kill him, they'll kill him!"

"You confirm it. Death to the impostor. It is Gesell's will!"

Understanding dawned on Viki. "You closed it?"

He bowed his head. "It was the wish of Gesell. I am but a poor instrument ..."

She was on him like a tiger-cat. "You fool. You crazy, blind fool! Show me what you did. We've got to fix it. We've got to, Daw. Garth Gesell is the true Gesell, don't you understand? And he'll die in there if we don't help him!"

"That Gateway," said Daw in stentorian tones, "is a falsehood, a devil's trick. When Gesell wants it to open he will open it, without wires and crystals and steel. As a Guardian I shall see the end of this contraption, and never again will I be duped." He turned, his eyes blazing, and caught up a sledgehammer. "Never again will there be a Gateway in Gesell Hall until Gesell himself opens it!"

"Daw you're mad! Stop!"

He stalked past her. She took one step after him and stopped. She saw the hooked piece of cable Daw had dropped. She leapt forward, caught up the free end, and as Daw raised the hammer high over his head, his right foot placed itself near the hook.

Viki stepped to one side, to be sure of a good contact, and pulled the cable violently. The hooked end caught Daw's ankle, whipped it out from under him. He staggered, lost control of the hammer. The twelve-pound head fell toward him. He lurched aside and it caught him on the shoulder. He fell heavily, trying to turn. His jaw cracked against the stone floor.

He lay still, uttering a series of tortured sounds as he tried to pull himself together.

Viki stood over him like an avenging angel, waiting.

Daw rolled over, sat up. His hand went quiveringly to his shoulder. He looked up at her out of round, bloodshot eyes.

"Guardian ..." he said.

"Help me fix the Gateway, Daw," she said.

"You're misled, sister."

"I won't discuss it with you. And don't start that cant about my sacred duty. Get up!"

Daw rose and fixed her with his mad eyes. "I am counseled by Gesell," he said painfully, "and now I counsel you."

She closed her eyes in a visible effort at self-control. "Are you going to help me?"

"Why do you pursue this folly? What is the compulsion of this—this Garth?" The last word came out with contempt.

"I love him," she said.

There was a crashing silence. It was the silence of utter shock—the silence of death itself, for indeed nothing moved, not even breath.

Finally Daw's suddenly white lips moved, slackened, moved again. "You love him," he whispered. "You?"

She was just as pale. "We all have our own kind of cowardice," she said. "Bronze once told me what Garth Gesell thought of your madness. He said you were a Guardian because you had retired from a real world. You've gone mad trying to save the old ways for yourself. You can doom the world to the new savagery if by doing it you can return to patrolling the Court and humbling yourself before the portrait."

Daw half raised his arms as if to ward off her hot words. He kept his eyes fixed on her, and when she stopped he said only,

"You're Escaped!"

"Yes!" she cried, "Damn you! You never knew, did you? One of the rules you made up for yourself was that only the poor robbed hulk of a woman, with her womanhood completely gone, could become a Guardian. It's what you chose to believe and what I let you believe. I told you we all have our form of cowardice. Mine was to pretend I was Returned. I stole the privilege of those poor creatures who had been discarded by the Ffanx. I lived with them and learned their ways. They walk in safety all over the world, and I took their coloration. And when the chance came to hide further under the cowl of a Guardian, I took it. I let myself sleep safely here. But I'm awake now ..." Her lower lip became full, and her eyes grew very bright. "... awake and I love him, I love him, I love him ..."

She lapsed into silence. She heard Daw grind his teeth.

"Slut!" he said hoarsely. "To think that for these years I've been living next to a—a—" In his mounting rage he stopped using words, and instead uttered a series of creaking, dripping animal sounds.

"Now that we know what we are, Guardian," she said coldly, "Let's fix the Gateway."

"I am the Guardian and I am the Gateway, and in me alone is the trust, the duty, the fidelity, the—"

Suddenly he was upon her, raging. Gone was the last vestige of control. Gone was the carefully schooled impersonality of Guardian behavior, gone was the deeply conditioned, pitying reverence for the woman Returned.

His wild leap bowled her off her feet. They rolled over and over on the floor. Daw didn't strike out at her with fists; he clawed. He pulled her hair and her clothes. He raked his fingernails down her body, twisted her, grasped and clutched and pawed.

At first she tried to get away, to protect herself. She writhed and scrambled and fell and pushed at him. Suddenly he was kneeling by her, both hands full of her hair, both arms stiff, pinning her head down to the floor. The pain of her scalp turned to terror—a rowelling primitive terror that was like nothing she had ever known in intensity. And in the briefest moments it was surpassed by another, new emotion. She had been afraid before, in her life, but this was something different.

For as he bent over her, brought his face close to her, she looked up into his eyes. They were round, staring, veined and toned with red. His jaws were open, and his bitten, bloody tongue flashed insanely in and out. Blood and froth splashed on her face, and at its touch, this transcending new emotion overtook her like a great flood-tide.

It was more than horror. It was disgust and revulsion raised to a peak almost impossible to contain. In one great surge she rose. She felt her hair tear away with a kind of savage joy. How she found the holds she never was to know, but one slim hand fastened into the side of Daw's neck and the other on his thigh. She sprang straight up under him with her feet solidly planted and every dyne of energy in her healthy legs, back and shoulders behind the movement. Daw's body went straight up.

When the weight came off her hands he was nearly at arm's length over her head. She dug in her nails and kept her grip, and as he began to fall she pulled hard with her left hand, which was on his neck. Head down he hurtled, with all her convulsive strength speeding him on his way. He struck . . .

For a long time she stood like a cast-iron statue, her unseeing eyes on the thing which lay there, its misshapen head all but concealed, twisted grotesquely under the scrawny body. Then she became dimly conscious of an ache that became a pain that became a roaring agony—the knotting muscles in her calves, cramping with the onset of nervous shock. She tottered backwards, brought up against the wall.

She crouched there, breathing in great open-throated gasps. Suddenly she began to cry—high, squeaky crying that tore her throat and burned her eyes. She cried for a long time.

But the next day, and the next and the next, found her working.

Garth lay under the rock, his heart beating suffocatingly, but his eyes studying the amazing spread of calloused flesh that was the giant foot. Another came down beside it, and the first one lifted and kicked over a massive boulder nearby. Garth felt his sheltering rock vibrate alarmingly. He bunched his shoulders and waited.

At last the feet moved away. He edged out and lay prone, hardly daring to lift his head. The three women were working away from him, scanning the ground carefully. He got on all fours and scuttled backward into the shadow of a projecting rock, pulled himself to his feet and looked around.

The Gateway was gone. Viki was gone—probably through the Gateway, he surmised. Bronze was gone—captured certainly, dead probably. He wondered what that green fire had been. It looked like neo-tourmaline, but the rays had not burned Bronze's body, at least not as far as he had been able to see. It was a little like the damper crystals that his father had developed, to capture and store energy.

But a crystal as big as that, with the pulling power it must have, couldn't be turned on a human being without out snuffing out the man's tiny store of electro-chemical.

"Bronze . . ." he said aloud.

Big, bluff, faithful Bronze, with his quick temper and his hammer-thinking. Garth got a flash of memory—Bronze's face when Garth had pulled him up short, pointed out some end result of Bronze's impulsiveness. He used to get a puzzled, slightly hurt expression on his broad face, but he always began nodding his head in agreement before he had figured out if Garth was right or not.

Garth's eyes felt hot. Then, with a profound effort of will, he shut his mind to his regrets and concentrated on his surroundings.

Moving carefully, he worked his way over to the spare tank that Viki had dropped. He worried it in between the two tanks he already carried. He'd live a little longer with it. "Though what for," he muttered, "I wouldn't know." He gave a last, despairing glance to the site of the Gateway and began to move toward the distant helicopter.

A hundred feet away he found a leaf—a tremendous thing, eleven feet long and nearly five feet broad at its widest. He picked it up gratefully. It was very light and spongy. He pulled the stem over his shoulder and walked through the rocks, dragging it. The leaf was almost exactly the color of the soil, and ideal camouflage. All he need do would be to drop it flat and pull it over himself.

He was two-thirds of the way to the plane when a thudding from the earth warned him. He looked back and saw the three women coming rapidly. They seemed to be sauntering, but their stride was twenty to twenty-five feet, and they covered ground at a frightening pace. He dropped and covered himself. The steps came nearer and nearer, until he wondered how the earth itself stood up under that monstrous tread. Then they were past. He got up. They walked with their heads up, talking their booming syllables. They were obviously searching no longer.

He began to run. He had no choice except to stay with these creatures. What he would do, where he would go if they took off, he simply did not know.

They climbed into the cabin, one by one. He could see the landing gear—tremendous wheels as tall as a two-story house—spread as they took the weight of the giants.

There was a belly-thumping cough and the incredible rotor-blades began to turn.

Garth flung down his leaf and ran straight toward the ship, trusting to luck that he wouldn't be seen. When he was under the slow-whirling tips of the rotor he still had what seemed an impossible distance to run. He found some more energy somewhere and applied it to his pumping legs.

A tire lost the swelling at the base that indicated weight-bearing. It lifted free. Garth swerved slightly and made for the other. It leapt upward as he approached. He ran despairingly under it. Only the nose-wheel was left. Without slackening speed he rushed it. Fortunately it was smaller than the others—the rim of the wheel was only about as high as his collarbone when the tire rested on the ground. But it was off the ground when he got there. He grunted with effort and made a desperate leap.

His outthrust arm went through the lightening hole just as the wheel jerked upward. He crooked his elbow grimly as his momentum swung his flailing legs under the tire. Then he got his other arm through the hole. It was just big enough for his head and the upper part of his shoulders. The air-tanks kept him from wriggling further.

Then, to his horror, he saw the strut above him fold on a hinge.

The wheel was retractable!

He had to turn his whole body to look upward through his helmet-glass, and somehow he managed it. He had no way of gauging how deep the wheel recess was. Was it deep enough to accept the wheel—and him too?

He looked down.

It would have to be deep enough ... the craft was a hundred feet up and rising rapidly!

He doubled up and got one toe on the edge of the lightening hole. He could just grasp the fork of the wheel. He swarmed up it, caught the other arm of the fork and lay belly down on the top part of the tire-tread. Then the wheel was inside, and the great bayflaps swung closed. The inside of the recess touched his back, squeezed, and stopped.

He couldn't move, but he wasn't crushed.

It was night.

Garth crouched by a building the size of a mountain. It was built of wooden planks that looked like sections of a four-lane highway.

He tried to forget the flight, though he knew it would haunt him for years—the cramped position, the slight kink in his airhose and the large kink in his neck which had caused him such misery, and finally the horror of the landing, when the wheel he clung to had contacted and rolled. Stiff as he was, he'd had to hit the ground ahead of it and leap out of the way.

He moved along the wall, looking for a way in. He would try the doorways as a last resort, for not only were they at the top of steps with seven-foot risers but they were flooded with light.

He stumbled and fell heavily into a dark hollow scooped out at the ground line. It was about four feet deep. He got to his knees, caught a movement in the dim light, and froze. Before him was a black opening through which he could see the bright-yellow stripes of artificial light seeping between enormous floorboards. And in the dim light he was aware of something which crouched beside him in the dark. It was horny and smooth, and at one end two graceful, sensitive whips trembled and twirled.

It was a cockroach, very nearly as long as his leg.

He wet his lips. "After you, friend," he said politely.

As if it had heard him, the creature flirted its antennae and scuttled into the hole. Garth drew a deep breath and followed.

It was black and brilliant, black and brilliant under that floor. Twice he fell into holes, and one of them was wet. Filthy and determined, he explored further and further, until he lost all sense of direction. He didn't know where the entrance hole was and he no longer cared very much. He knew what he was looking for and at last he found it.

Near one wall was a considerable hump on the rough earth floor he walked on. A wide, oval patch of light above showed the presence of a tremendous knot-hole. He climbed toward it.

The wood was soft under his fingers, like balsa. He began tearing out chunks of it, widening the knot-hole. The earth here was about three feet under the hole, so he had to squat and work upward. It was extremely tiring, but he kept at it until he had a hole large enough to put his head through.

Because of the small size of his helmet glass, he had to put his head almost all the way up before he could see anything. And because of the brilliance above, he had to stay there a moment to accustom his eyes to the glare—What he saw made him, for the first time in his life, fully understand the phrase "And when I looked, I thought I was going to faint!"

He dropped back down the hole and lay gasping, with reaction. One of the giantesses was sitting on the floor, propped up by one arm stretched out behind her. And he had busily dug his hole and thrust out his head exactly between her wide-spread thumb and forefinger!

He sat up and looked about him very carefully indeed. He followed the mammoth outline of the girl's shadow, where it crossed the lines of light between the floorboards. And then he lay back patiently to wait until she moved.

He must have dozed, and in the meantime become immune to the thunderous shuffling and subsonic bellowings of the creatures above, for when he opened his eyes again the shadow was gone. He knelt and cautiously put his head up through the hole.

The floor stretched away from him like a pampa. There were eight or nine of the huge women in the room, as far as he could see. Several were in a stage of dress which, under different circumstances, he might have found intriguing.

He pressed up harder. The tanks caught on the edge of the hole. He gritted his teeth and pushed with his legs under the floor and his arms above. He felt the wood yield under his hands. Then the tanks ripped their way through and he was at last in the room.

He backed cautiously up to the baseboard, darting glances in every direction. Making sure that none of the women was looking in his direction, he darted for the only patch of shadow he could see—a loose-hung fishnet that covered a window, serving as sort of a drape. He slid behind it and peered through the mesh. It seemed to be indifferent concealment; yet, from their point of view, he knew he would be hard to locate.

He paused to switch tanks—his air was getting foul—and then took stock.

The women were gathered around a table near the center of the room, rumbling and gesticulating in their strange, slow-motion fashion. None were looking his way. He looked down to the right. A small table stood in the corner and there was another fishnet behind it. Garth moved toward it, passing one leg which was like a redwood tree and, reaching up, twined his hands in the wide mesh of the drape. It sagged alarmingly as his weight came on it. He waited until it was still and then climbed up a few feet. Putting both feet into the mesh he jumped hard to test it. It sagged again, but held.

To the underside of the table seemed the longest thirty feet he had ever determined to travel, but he started up. The fishnet seemed to stretch a foot for every eighteen inches he climbed. He looked down and saw it touch the floor, then begin piling up.

He suddenly remembered the incredible density of the tiny Ffanx invaders, and a great light dawned in his brain.

Excitedly he climbed higher, higher, and at last reached the table top. He swung onto it, teetered for a hair-raising moment on the edge, recovered his balance, and stood on the wooden surface. Sure enough, his footprints showed on the table top as he walked away from the edge.

There was a piece of electrical equipment on the table, which he ignored. He went to the far edge, crouched by the side of the machine, and gazed across to the center table around which the giants were gathered.

His blood froze.

Under a glaring floodlight, in the center of the enormous table, lay a sealed glass cage. Lying in it, devoid of his helmet, lay Bronze's body. The leader, the one who looked so very much like Glory Gehman, was handling the delicate controls of a remote-apparatus which passed a series of rods through the pressure sleeves into the cage. At the end of the rods were clamps, clumps of white material as rough as coconut fibre, tweezers, a swab, and a gleaming scalpel as long as a two-handed sword.

If they're being that particular about atmosphere, he thought, Bronze must be alive!

The flood of joy this thought brought him died a quick death, for it was followed by ... and they're about to vivisect him.

He yielded to a short moment of panic and despair. He rushed back toward the drape as if to slide down it and attack the women by force. He stopped, then got hold of himself.

He looked around him. Suddenly, he straightened and smiled. Then he went into furious action.

"Isn't he pretty!"

The women gathered about the tiny figure. "We shouldn't cut him up until the rest of the girls have a chance to look at him. He's just a doll!" said one.

"You've forgotten that all the Ffanx are just dolls," said the leader coolly. "Do you propose to lead thirty-two hundred women, one by one, past this little devil? You'd have a wave of hysteria I'd as soon not have to handle. Let's keep to ourselves what we have here. We'll learn what we can and file it away."

"Oh, you're so duty-bound," said the blonde petulantly. "Well, go ahead if you must."

They crowded closer. The leader propped her elbows on the table to steady her hands, and carefully manipulated the clamps. One descended over each thigh of the tiny figure and trapped it firmly to the floor of the cage. Two more captured the biceps, and another pair settled over the wrists. Then the scalpel swung up and positioned itself. The leader suddenly stopped.

"Did you leave that thing on?"

In unison they swung toward the corner. One of the women walked over and looked. "No, but the tubes are warm."

"It's a warm night," said another. "Go ahead. Cut."

They gathered about the table again. The blade turned, descended slowly.

"STOP!" roared a voice—a deep, masculine voice.

"A man!" squeaked one of the women. Another quickly drew her tunic together and belted it. A third squeaked "Where? Where? I haven't seen a man in so long I could just—"

"Glory Gehman!" said the voice. "Hally Gehman—short for 'Hallelujah'—remember?"

"Gesell!" gasped the leader.

"The fool," growled the blonde. "I knew a man wouldn't be able to leave us alone. This is his idea of a joke—but he set up the Gateway to play it. No wonder these little devils got through." She raised her voice. "Where are you?"

The blonde snapped her fingers. "It's a broadcast of some sort," she said. "He hasn't answered you once, Glory!" She turned to the corner. "What's my name, Dr. Gesell?"

There was a pause. Somewhere there was a squeaky sound, like the distant chattering of a field creature. "Everybody calls you Butch, towhead," said the voice. "Come over here, tapeworms."

"The recorder!"

"They raced across the room, clustered around the small table.

"I thought you said it was turned off? Look—the tape's moving!" Glory reached out a hand to turn it off.

"Don't turn it off," said the voice. "Now, listen to me. You've got to believe me. I'm Gesell. No matter what you see, no matter what you think, you've got to understand that. Now, hear me out. You'll get your opportunity to test my identity after I'm finished."

"No one but Gesell ever called me Hally," said Glory.

"Shh!" hissed the blonde.

"I'm right here in this room, and you'll see me in a moment. But before you do, Glory, I want to spout some math at you."

"Remember the vibratory interaction theory of matter? It hypothesized that universes interlock. Universe A presents itself for x duration, one cycle, then ceases to exist. Universe B replaces it; C replaces B; D replaces C, each for one micro-milli-sub-n-second of time. At the end of the chain, Universe A presents itself again. The two appearances of Universe A are consecutive in terms of an observer in Universe A. Same with B and C and all the others. Each seems to its observers to be continuous, whereas they are actually recurrent. All that's elementary.

"Here are the formulae for each theoretical universe in a limited series of four inter-recurrent continua . . ."

There followed a series of mathematical gobbledegook which was completely unintelligible to everyone in the room but Glory Gehman. She listened intently, her high-arched brows drawn together in deep thought. She drew out a tablet and stylus from her pocket and began to calculate rapidly as the voice went on.

"Now notice the quantitative shift in the first phase of each cycle. To achieve an overall resonance there has to be a shift. To put it in simple terms, if you drew a hyperbolic curve with a trembling hand, the curve is the overall resonance of the whole series of small cyclic motions. And there's only one way in which that can have a physical effect—in the continuum itself. Each cycle occurs in a slightly altered condition of space-time. That accounts for the super-density of the Ffanx and everything they owned and handled. What was normal to us was rarefied to them. We saw them as dense little androids, and they saw us as rarefied-molecule giants. There must be some point in the cycle where they are rarefied in terms of our condition. But space characteristics are only part of the continuum. The time-rate must alter with it.

"According to my calculations you have been here for something more than seven but less than eight-and-a-half months, and are waiting with considerable patience for the three-year minimum it would take to prepare the cyanide capsule for the Ffanx world.

"It's with mixed feelings that I inform you that the Ffanx war was over twenty-two Earth years ago. Dr. Gilbert Gesell died in a Ffanx raid that closed the Gateway. The Gateway has been opened again momentarily, but something has gone wrong with it—I don't know what. I must tell you too that in terms of Earth standards you cute cuddly creatures are in the neighborhood of seventy-five feet tall.

"So check your figures before you fly off the handle and kill any small dense creature which arrives through a Gateway wearing a breathing helmet. It might be Dr. Gesell's little boy Garth, grown up to be all of seven inches tall, and recording into your tape at its highest speed and playing it back slowly . . ."

"I'm clinging to the fishnet just under the level of the table-top. Treat me gently, sisters. I've come a long way."

There was a concerted lunge for the drape, a concerted reaction of horror away from it. "Ffanx," someone blurted. "Kill it!"

"We have to kill it," said the blonde. "We can't take chances, Glory." Behind her voice was the concentrated horror of the conquest of Earth ... the forcefield pens ... the hollow, piteous presence of the handful of "returned" women. "This could be a new Ffanx trick, a new weapon ..."

"The math is ..."

"The hell with the math!" screamed a girl from the edge of the crowd.

"She's right!"

"She's *right!*"

"Kill it!"

Garth stepped over to the table top and walked toward the tape machine. The circle of women widened instantly. Garth muscled the huge controls, placed his helmet firmly against the microphone, and chattered shrilly as the tape raced through the guides. Then he rewound, stopped the spools, and began the playback:

"I got that, and I must say I expected it. You'll follow your own consciences in the end, but be sure it's your conscience and not your panic that you follow. I want to tell you this, though: Earth is a mess. There's a new dark age back there. It's slipped into a tribal state— polyandrous in some places, feudal in others, matriarchal in many. You three thousand women, and the daughters that many of you will bear, will mean a great deal to Earth."

The chattering ran high.

"Polyandrous?"

"One woman—several husbands."

"Lead me to it! Poly wants an androus!"

"If he's seven inches high here, we'd be seventy-five feet tall there. Oh my!"

Garth's voice cut in. "You'll want to know how you can get back to Earth size, or how to get to Earth when its size corresponds to yours. I can tell you. But I'm not going to. If you can argue about my life, I can bargain with it."

A pause. "Now tell me if you've killed that boy over there." Slyly, Garth added, "Go look at him again. He's six-three, and a hundred and two percent man."

One, two, two more drifted over to the big table, to look with awed eyes at the magnificent miniature.

Glory, as if sensitive to a voice-tone she had noticed, snatched up the mike. "No, he isn't dead. He would have been, but he fired with a blaster just as I put the neo-tourmaline soaker field on him. The blaster threw out all the energy the crystal could absorb."

Garth held up his arms for the mike. When his voice came again, it said, "Glory, get together the best math minds you have here. I want to give you some raw material to work on."

There was a sudden crash of sound. To Garth it was a great thudding bass that struck at his helmet like soft-nosed bullets. To the women it was a shrill siren-alarm.

Glory yelped, "Get the 'copter warm. Asta, Marion, Josephine this time. Jo—check the transistor leads on the direction finder in the plane. It kept losing a stage of amplification this morning." She turned to the microphone. "That's a Gateway. We'll damn soon find out whether the Ffanx war is over or not. I'm going to park you with your friend there. Just pray that these cats will obey orders while I'm gone." She dropped the mike and raced to the big table. "Butch. Put that one in with the other. If you touch either one of them until I get back, so help me I'll pry you loose from your wall eyes. You hear me."

"You'll be sorry for that," snapped the blonde. "When you find out that these lousy Ffanx have been sending out a homing signal for their playmates—they're telepathic, you know—then you can apologize."

"On bended knee," said Glory. "Meantime, A-cup, do as you're told." She ran out.

"Come on. Orders is orders."

Garth watched them come. He took one step backward, then relaxed. He had shot his bolt, and all he could do was to wait. The pudgy one picked him up gingerly, tried to carry him at arm's length, found he was too heavy, and hurried across the floor with him. She set him down gently on the table. One of the women hurried up with a small edition of the cage. Garth stepped in and a gate was sealed. A tube was fitted to it, and Garth heard air hissing in. He was grateful for the increased pressure, his skin had felt raw and distended for hours.

The pudgy one lifted the small cage bodily and set it on top of the larger glass cell in which Bronze lay. A lever was flipped, and Garth dropped ungracefully into the large one.

His first act was to run to Bronze and feel his pulse. It was weak but steady. Garth unbuckled his helmet and pulled it off, then knelt by Bronze.

"Bronze . . ."

No answer.

"Bronze!"

No answer.

"Bronzie boy . . . look at all those women."

"Gug?" Bronze's eyes opened and he blinked owlishly.

Garth chuckled. "Bronze, you were after women. Look, man."

Bronze's gaze got as far as the glass wall, tested its shaky focus, and then penetrated outward. He sat bolt upright. "For me?"

Then he keeled over in a dead faint.

Garth sat and chafed his wrists, laughing weakly. Then, after a while, he went to sleep.

The pudgy one was relieved after a while. Butch waved away her own relief and stayed, elbows on the table, head low, glaring hatred and fear at the men. There was some sort of distant call. All the other women left. But the big blonde still stayed.

Garth had a dream in which he was chasing a girl in a brown cowl. She ran because she feared him, but he chased her because he knew he could show her there was nothing to fear. As he gained on her, he heard Bronze's voice.

"Garth." It was very quiet. Intense, but weak.

Garth sat up abruptly. Something hard and sharp whacked him

in the forehead. There was a gout of blood. He fell back, dazed, then opened his eyes. He saw that Butch had maneuvered the point of the scalpel within a few inches of his forehead as he slept. He could see her looking at him, her face twisted in slow-motion convulsions of laughter. The all but inaudible boom of her voice was a tangible thing threatening the glass.

Garth turned to Bronze. He was lying on his back with one of the U-shaped clamps on his throat. It was pressing just tight enough to pin him down, just tight enough to keep his face scarlet. His breath rasped. "Garth," he whispered.

Garth staggered to his feet. Blood ran into his eyes. There was another deep hoot of laughter from outside. Garth wiped the blood away and staggered toward Bronze. The scalpel whistled down and across his path. He dodged, but lost his footing and fell.

There was a thunderous pounding on the table. Butch was apparently having herself a hell of a time.

Garth looked at the scalpel. It hung limply. He crawled toward Bronze. A tweezer-clamp shot out and caught his ankle. He pulled free of it, leaving four square inches of skin in its serrated jaws. He went on doggedly. He reached Bronze, put a foot on each side of the big man's neck, got a good grip on the U-clamp and pulled it upward. Bronze rolled free, his great lungs pumping. The flat of the scalpel hit Garth between the shoulder-blades and knocked him sprawling next to Bronze.

"How long have we been here?" asked Bronze painfully.

"Day—day and a half. On Earth, that's eight, nine months. Wonder what Viki's doing?"

He looked around, suddenly sat up. Butch was gone.

"Here come the rest of them. We'll know pretty soon."

They stood up and watched the slow, distance-eating march of the giants.

"They're carrying something ... Will you look at those faces, Bronze!"

"They look wild."

"Glory ... See her? The tall cool one."

"I see a tall one," said Bronze, deadpan.

"She's putting something on the big table here. Hey, what is that thing?"

"Looks like a tombstone."

Garth said, "I've heard of making the prisoner dig his own grave, but this—"

The stone was put in the small box and aired. Big hands lifted it and set it on their roof.

"Get out from under."

The stone dropped, teetered. Garth leapt up and steadied it. It settled back on its base.

It was a rough monolith, about three feet tall, cut from soft, snow-white limestone. In it was a chamber with a glass door.

"Will you ever look at that," breathed Bronze.

Garth stared.

Cut into the stone were the words,

THE GATEWAY

OF

GESELL

"I don't get it," said Garth.

Bronze said, "Look in the thing. The little door."

Garth peered, and saw a plastic scroll. He opened the door, took out the scroll and unrolled it. In exquisitely neat script it read:

> *This is your Gateway to all that is human;*
> *to all that sweats, and cries, and tries;*
> *to all hungers, to all puzzlement;*
> *to mistakes compounded,*
> *to mysteries cleared,*
> *to growth, to strength, to complication,*
> *to ultimate simplicity.*
> *Friends, be welcome,*
> *others be warned.*
> *Gesell is your gate*
> *As he was mine.*
> *A closed gate should never be guarded.*

My gate it open, I guard it well.
Gesell knows I love him.
Please tell him I know it too.
Viki (Escaped)

There was a long quiet.

"Escaped," said Garth. "Escaped."

There was a thump over their heads. The airlock box had been placed there. There was a speaker baffle into it. It dropped. Bronze caught it, handed it to Garth.

Garth looked out through the wall and saw Glory, her calm face suffused, her eyes misty.

"Garth Gesell, you've read the scroll. I brought it because I didn't want you to wait; I didn't want you to just hear about it. She fixed your Gateway, Garth, and shoved the stone through so we'd find it. Then, when we were whooping and bawling properly, she let us find her.

"We couldn't have trusted any calculations, any statements. But we examined her and she's Escaped—oh, beyond question. That we could trust. For the one thing the Ffanx would never spend, not even to bait a trap for the biggest game, was a single drop of extradiol, which she carries unmolested. Viki's given us back a world, Garth, just by loving you . . .

"Are you ready to start on the calculations?"

Garth leaned against the wall near the speaker. Standing upright seemed to make his heart labor. "Not until I've seen Viki," he said.

There was a pause. Then Glory's voice again, "Bronze. Put on that helmet."

Unquestioningly, Bronze did. The airlock box thumped above them. Garth sat down and leaned against the wall. His heart would not be quiet.

Bronze was suddenly beside him, helmeted. He clasped Garth's shoulder so hard it hurt, and as suddenly was gone. There was a slight scuffling sound. Garth turned. Bronze, in the lock, was lowering someone into the cage. Then the upper box was taken away.

She stood and looked at him gravely, unafraid. But this time there was a world of difference.

He put out his arms. He, or she, moved. Perhaps both. He pressed her cheek against his, and when he took it away, both were wet. So one of them wept.

Perhaps both.

With her mathematical staff, Glory said, "He was quite right about the shift, you see. He and Viki and Bronze can go back through their own Gateway. But we'll have to open another. We go to a world where we will be only three times the size of the natives. There we build still another Gateway. And that will be Earth, and we'll be home."

"If it's as easy as that," asked the pudgy one, "Why did we have to be so cautious? Why didn't we go straight to that intermediate world and wait there?"

"Because," said Glory Gehman, "the intermediate world is the Ffanx planet. Do you see?"

Earth keeps a solemn festival at the meadows of Hack and Sack, through whose blue arch came first death, and then life.

Never Underestimate

"SHE WAS BRAZEN, of course," said Lucinda, passing the marmalade, "but the brass was beautifully polished. The whole thing made me quite angry, though at the same time I was delighted."

Meticulously Dr. Lefferts closed the newly-arrived *Journal of the Microbiological Institute,* placed it on the copy of *Strength of Materials in Various Radioisotopic Alloys* which lay beside his plate, and carefully removed his pince-nez. "You begin in mid-sequence," he said, picking up a butter knife. "Your thought is a predicate without a stated subject. Finally, your description of your reactions contains parts which appear mutually exclusive." He attacked the marmalade. "Will you elucidate?"

Lucinda laughed good-naturedly. "Of course, darling. Where would you like me to begin?"

"Oh. . . ." Dr. Lefferts made a vague gesture. "Practically anywhere. Anywhere at all. Simply supply more relative data in order that I may extrapolate the entire episode and thereby dispose of it. Otherwise I shall certainly keep returning to it all day long. Lucinda, why do you continually do this to me?"

"Do what, dear?"

"Present me with colorful trivialities in just such amounts as will make me demand to hear you out. I have a trained mind, Lucinda; a fine-honed, logical mind. It must think things through. You know that. Why do you continually *do* this to me?"

"Because," said Lucinda placidly, "if I started at the beginning and went right through to the end, you wouldn't listen."

"I most certainly . . . eh. Perhaps you're right." He laid marmalade onto an English muffin in three parallel bands, and began smoothing them together at right angles to their original lay. "You are right, my dear. That must be rather difficult for you from time to time ... yes?"

"No indeed," said Lucinda, and smiled. "Not as long as I can get your full attention when I want it. And I can."

Dr. Lefferts chewed her statement with his muffin. At last he said, "I admit that in your inimitable—uh—I think one calls it *female* way, you can. At least in regard to small issues. Now do me the kindness to explain to me what stimuli could cause you to"—his voice supplied the punctuation—"feel 'quite angry' and 'delighted' simultaneously."

Lucinda leaned forward to pour fresh coffee into his cooling cup. She was an ample woman, with an almost tailored combination of svelteness and relaxation. Her voice was like sofa-pillows and her eyes like blued steel. "It was on the Boulevard," she said. "I was waiting to cross when this girl drove through a red light under the nose of a policeman. It was like watching a magazine illustration come to life—the bright yellow convertible and the blazing blonde in the bright yellow dress ... darling, I do think you should call this year's bra manufacturers for consultation in your Anti-Gravity Research division. They achieve the most baffling effects ... anyway, there she was and there by the car was the traffic cop, as red-faced and Hibernian a piece of typecasting as you could wish. He came blustering over to her demanding to know begorry—I think he actually did say begorry—was she color-blind now, or did she perhaps not give a care this marnin'?"

"In albinos," said Dr. Lefferts, "color perception is—"

Lucinda raised her smooth voice just sufficiently to override him without a break in continuity. "Now, here was an errant violation of the law, flagrantly committed under the eyes of an enforcement officer. I don't have to tell you what should have happened. What *did* happen was that the girl kept her head turned away from him until his hands were on the car door. In the sun that hair of hers was positively dazzling. When he was close enough—within range, that is—she tossed her hair back and was face to face with him. You could see that great lump of bog-peat turn to putty. And she said to him (and if I'd had a musical notebook with me I could have jotted down her voice in sharps and flats)—she said, 'Why, officer, I did it on purpose just so I could see you up close.' "

Dr. Lefferts made a slight, disgusted sound. "He arrested her."

"He did not," said Lucinda. "He shook a big thick finger at her as if she were a naughty but beloved child, and the push-button blarney that oozed out of him was as easy to see as the wink he gave her. That's what made me mad."

"And well it should." He folded his napkin. "Violations of the law should be immediately pun—"

"The law had little to do with it," Lucinda said warmly. "I was angry because I know what would have happened to you or to me in that same situation. We're just not equipped."

"I begin to see." He put his pince-nez back on and peered at her. "And what was it that delighted you?"

She stretched easily and half-closed her eyes. "The—what you have called the *femaleness* of it. It's good to be a woman, darling, and to watch another woman be female skillfully."

"I quarrel with your use of the term 'skillfully,' " he said, folding his napkin. "Her 'skill' is analogous to an odor of musk or other such exudation in the lower animals."

"It is *not,*" she said flatly. "With the lower animals, bait of that kind means one thing and one thing only, complete and final. With a woman, it means nothing of the kind. Never mind what it *might* mean; consider what it *does* mean. Do you think for a moment that the blonde in the convertible was making herself available to the policeman?"

"She was hypothesizing a situation in which—"

"She was hypothesizing nothing of the kind. She was blatantly and brazenly getting out of paying a traffic fine, and that was absolutely all. And you can carry it one step further; do you think that for one split second the policeman actually believed that she was inviting him? Of course he didn't! And yet that situation is one that has obtained through the ages. Women have always been able to get what they wanted from men by pretending to promise a thing which they know men want but will not or cannot take. Mind you, I'm not talking about situations where this yielding is the main issue.

I'm talking about the infinitely greater number of occasions where yielding has nothing to do with it. Like weaseling out of traffic tickets."

"Or skillfully gaining your husband's reluctant attention over the breakfast table."

Her sudden laughter was like a shower of sparks. "You'd better get down to the Institute," she said. "You'll be late."

He arose, picked up his book and pamphlet, and walked slowly to the door. Lucinda came with him, hooking her arm through his. Suddenly he stopped, and without looking at her, asked quietly, "That policeman was a manipulated, undignified fool, wasn't he?"

"Of course he was, darling, and it made a man of him."

He nodded as if accepting a statistic, and, kissing her, walked out of the house.

Darling, she thought, *dear sweet chrome-plated, fine-drawn, high-polished blueprint . . . I think I've found where you keep your vanity.* She watched him walk with his even, efficient, unhurried stride to the gate. There he paused and looked back.

"This has been going on too long," he called. "I shall alter it."

Lucinda stopped smiling.

"May I come in?"

"Jenny, of course." Lucinda went to the kitchen door and unhooked it. "Come in, come in. My, you're prettier than ever this morning."

"I brought you violets," said Jenny breathlessly. "Just scads of 'em in the woods behind my place. You took your red curtains down. Is that a new apron? My! You had Canadian bacon for breakfast."

She darted in past Lucinda, a small, wiry, vibrant girl with sunlit hair and moonlight eyes. "Can I help with the dishes?"

"Thank you, you doll." Lucinda took down a shallow glass bowl for the violets.

Jenny busily ran hot water into the sink. "I couldn't help seeing," she said. "Your big picture window. . . . Lucinda, you *never* leave the breakfast dishes. I keep telling Bob, someday I'll have the routines you have, everything always so neat, never running out of anything, never in a hurry, never surprised ... anyway, all the way over I could see you just sitting by the table there, and the dishes not done and all ... is everything all right? I mean, don't tell me if I shouldn't ask, but I couldn't help...." Her voice trailed off into an ardent and respectful mumble.

"You're such a sweetheart," Lucinda said mistily. She came over to the sink carrying clean dishtowels and stood holding them, staring out past Jenny's head to the level lawns of the village. "Actually, I did have something on my mind ... something...."

She related the whole conversation over breakfast that morning, from her abrupt and partial mentioning of the anecdote about the blonde and the policeman, to her husband's extraordinary and unequivocal statement about women's power over men: *This has been going on too long. I shall alter it.*

"Is that all?" Jenny asked when she had finished.

"Mm. It's all that was said."

"Oh, I don't think you should worry about that." She crinkled up her eyes, and Lucinda understood that she was putting herself and her young husband in the place of Lucinda and Dr. Lefferts, and trying to empathize a solution. "I think you might have hurt his feelings a little, maybe," Jenny said at length. "I mean, you admitted that you handled him in much the same way as that blonde handled the policeman, and then you said the policeman was a fool."

Lucinda smiled. "Very shrewd. And what's your guess about that parting shot?"

Jenny turned to face her. "You're not teasing me, asking my opinion, Lucinda? I never thought I'd see the day! Not you—you're so wise!"

Lucinda patted her shoulder. "The older I get, the more I feel that among women there is a lowest common denominator of wisdom, and that the chief difference between them is a random scattering of blind spots. No, honey, I'm not teasing you. You may be able to see just where I can't. Now tell me: what do you think he meant by that?"

"'*I shall alter it,*'" Jenny quoted thoughtfully. "Oh, I don't think he meant anything much. You showed him how you could make him do things, and he didn't like it. He's decided not to let you do it any more, but—but...."

"But what?"

"Well, it's like with Bob. When he gets masterful and lays down the law I just agree with him. He forgets about it soon enough. If you agree with men all the time they can't get stubborn about anything."

Lucinda laughed aloud. "There's the wisdom!" she cried. Sobering, she shook her head. "You don't know the doctor the way I do. He's a great man—a truly great one, with a great mind. It's great in a way no other mind has ever been. He's—different. Jenny, I know how people talk, and what a lot of them say. People wonder why I married him, why I've stayed with him all these years. They say he's stuffy and didactic and that he has no sense of humor. Well, to them he may be; but to me he is a continual challenge. The rules-of-thumb that keep most men in line don't apply to him.

"And if he says he can do something, he can. If he says he will do something, he will."

Jenny dried her hands and sat down slowly. "He meant," she said positively, "that he would alter your ability to make him do things. Because the only other thing he could have meant was that he was going to alter the thing that makes it possible for any woman to handle any man. And that just couldn't be. How could he change human nature?"

"How? How? He's the scientist. I'm not. I simply eliminate that 'how' from my thinking. The worrisome thing about it is that he doesn't think in small ways about small issues. I'm afraid that's just what he meant—that he was going to change some factor in humanity that is responsible for this power we have over men."

"Oh ... really," said Jenny. She looked up at Lucinda, moved her hands uneasily. "Lucinda, I know how great the doctor is, and how much you think of him, but—no one man could do such a thing! Not outside of his own home." She grinned fleetingly. "Probably not inside of it, for very long.... I never understood just what sort of a scientist he is. Can you tell me, I mean, aside from any secret projects he might be on? Like Bob, now; Bob's a high-temperature metallurgist. What is the doctor, exactly?"

"That's the right question to ask," Lucinda said, and her voice was shadowed. "Dr. Lefferts is a—well, the closest you could get to it would be to call him a specializing non-specialist. You see, science has reached the point where each branch of it continually branches into specialties, and each specialty has its own crop of experts. Most experts live in the confines of their own work. The doctor was saying just the other day that he'd discovered a fluorine-boron step-reaction in mineralogy that had been known for so long that the mineralogists had forgotten about it—yet it was unknown to metallurgy. Just as I said a moment ago, his mind is great, and—different. His job is to draw together the chemists and the biologists, the pure mathematicians and the practical physicists, the clinical psychologists and the engineers and all the other -ists and -ologies. His speciality is scientific thought as applied to all the sciences. He has no assignments except to survey all the fields and transfer needed information from one to the other. There has never been such a position in the Institute before, nor a man to fill it. And there is no other institute like this one on earth.

"He has entrée into every shop and lab and library in this Institute. He can do anything or get anything done in any of them.

"And when he said 'I shall alter it,' he meant what he said!"

"I never knew that's what he did," breathed Jenny. "I never knew that's what . . . *who* he is."

"That's who he is."

"But what can he change?" Jenny burst out. "What can he change in us, in all men, in all women? What is the power he's talking about, and where does it come from, and what would . . . will . . . happen if it's changed?"

"I don't know," Lucinda said thoughtfully, "I—do—not—know. The blonde in the convertible . . . that sort of thing is just one of the things a woman naturally does, because she is a woman, without thinking of it."

Unexpectedly, Jenny giggled. "You don't plan those things. You just do them. It's nice when it works. A better roast from the butcher. A reminder from one of the men at the bank that a cheque's overdrawn, in time to cover it."

"I know," smiled Lucinda, "I know. It's easy and inaccurate to say that all those men are on the prowl—or all those women either. A few are, but most are not. The willingness of men to do things for women has survived even equal opportunities and equal pay for women. The ability of women to get what they want from men lies completely in their knowledge of that willingness. So the thing my husband wants to alter—*will* alter—lies in that department."

"Lucinda, why don't you just ask him?"

"I shall. But I don't know if I'll get an answer. If he regards it as a security matter, nothing will get it out of him."

"You'll tell me, won't you?"

"Jenny, my sweet, if he tells me nothing, I can't tell you. If he tells me and asks me to keep his confidence, I won't tell you. If he tells me and puts no restrictions on it, I'll tell you everything."

"But—"

"I know, dear. You're thinking that it's a bigger thing than just what it might mean to the two of us. Well, you're right. But down deep I'm confident. I'd pit few women against most men and expect them to win out. But anytime all womankind is against all mankind, the men don't stand a chance. Think hard about it, anyway. At least we should be able to figure out where the attack is coming from."

"At least you admit it's an attack."

"You bet your sweet life it's an attack. There's been a woman behind most thrones all through history. The few times that hasn't been true, it's taken a woman to clean up the mess afterward. We won't give up easily, darling!"

" 'The north wind doth blow, and we shall have snow,' and so on," said Lucinda as she lit the fire. "I'm going to need a new coat."

"Very well," said Dr. Lefferts.

"A fur coat this time."

"Fur coats," pronounced the doctor, "are impractical. Get one with the fur inside. You'll keep warmer with less to carry."

"I want a fur coat with the fur outside, where it shows."

"I understand and at times admire the decorative compulsions," said the doctor, rising from the adjusted cube he used for an easy

chair, "but not when they are unhealthy, uneconomical, and ineffi-
cient. My dear, vanity does not become you."

"A thing that has always fascinated me," said Lucinda in a dan-
gerously quiet voice, "in rabbits, weasels, skunks, pumas, pandas,
and mink, and all other known mammals and marsupials, is their
huge vanity. They *all* wear their fur outside."

He put on his pince-nez to stare at her. "Your logic limits its factors. I fund such sequences remarkable because of the end results
one may obtain. However, I shall not follow this one."

"If you're so preoccupied with efficiency and function," she
snapped, "why do you insist on wearing those pince-nez instead of
getting corneal lenses?"

"Functional living is a pattern which includes all predictable phenomena," he said reasonably. "One of these is habit. I recognize that
I shall continue to like pince-nez as much as I shall continue to dis-
like rice pudding. My functionalism therefore includes these glasses
and excludes that particular comestible. If you had the fur-coat habit,
the possibility of a fur coat would be calculable. Since you have never
had such a coat, we can consider the matter disposed of."

"I think some factors were selected for that sequence," said
Lucinda between her teeth, "but I can't seem to put my finger on the
missing ones."

"I beg your pardon?"

"I said," appended Lucinda distinctly, "that speaking of factors,
I wonder how you're coming with your adjustments of human nature
to eliminate the deadliness of the female."

"Oh, that. I expect results momentarily."

"Why bother?" she said bitterly. "My powers don't seem to be
good enough for a fur coat as it is."

"Oh," he said mildly, "were you using them?"

Because she was Lucinda, she laughed. "No, darling, I wasn't."
She went to him and pressed him back into the big cubicle chair and
sat on the arm. "I was demanding, cynical, and unpleasant. These
things in a woman represent the scorched earth retreat rather than
the looting advance."

"An excellent analogy," he said. "Excellent. It has been a long and bitter war, hasn't it? And now it's coming to an end. It is an extraordinary thing that in our difficult progress toward the elimination of wars, we have until now ignored the greatest and most pernicious conflict of all—the one between the sexes."

"Why so pernicious?" she chuckled. There are times when it's rather fun.

He said solemnly, "There are moments of exhilaration, even of glory, in every great conflict. But such conflicts tear down so much more than they build."

"What's been so damaging about the war between the sexes?"

"Though it has been the women who made men, it has been largely men who have made the world as we know it. However, they have had to do so against a truly terrible obstacle: the emotional climate created by women. Only by becoming an ascetic can a man avoid the oscillations between intoxication and distrust instilled into him by women. And ascetics usually are already insane or rapidly become so."

"I think you're overstating a natural state of affairs."

"I am overstating," he admitted, "for clarity's sake, and off the record. However, this great war is by no means natural. On the contrary, it is a most unnatural state of affairs. You see, *homo sapiens* is, in one small but important respect, an atypical mammal."

"Do tell."

He raised his eyebrows, but continued. "In virtually all species but ours, the female has a rigidly fixed cycle of conjugal acceptability."

"But the human female has a—"

"I am not referring to that lunar cycle, unmentionable everywhere except in blatant magazine advertisements," he said shortly, "but a cycle of desire. Of rut."

"A pretty word." Her eyes began to glitter.

"Mahomet taught that it occurred every eight days, Zoroaster nine days, Socrates and Solomon agreed on ten. Everyone else, as far as I can discover, seems to disagree with these pundits, or to ignore the matter. Actually there are such cycles, but they are subtle at best, and differ in the individual from time to time, with age, physical experience, geography, and even emotional state. These cycles are vestigial; the original, *natural* cycle disappeared early in the history of the species, and has been trembling on the verge ever since. It will be a simple matter to bring it back."

"May I ask how?"

"You may not. It is a security matter."

"May I then ask what effect you expect this development to have?"

"Obvious, isn't it? The source of woman's persistent and effective control over man, the thing that makes him subject to all her intolerances, whims, and bewildering coyness, is the simple fact of her perennial availability. She has no regular and predictable cycle of desire. The lower animals have. During the brief time that a female mouse, a marten, or a mare is approachable, every male of her species in the vicinity will know of it and seek her out; will, in effect, drop everything to answer a basic call. But unless and until that call occurs, the male is free to think of other things. With the human female, on the other hand, the call is mildly present at all times, and the male is *never* completely free to think of other things. It is natural for this drive to be strong. It is unnatural indeed for it to be constant. In this respect Freud was quite correct; nearly every neurosis has a sexual basis. We are a race of neurotics, and the great wonder is that we have retained any of the elements of sanity at all. I shall liberate humanity from this curse. I shall restore the natural alternations of drive and rest. I shall free men to think and women to take their rightful places as thinking individuals beside them, rather than be the forced-draught furnaces of sexual heat they have become."

"Are you telling me," said Lucinda in a small, shocked voice, "that you have found a way to—to neuterize women except for a few hours a month?"

"I am and I have," said Dr. Lefferts. "And incidentally, I must say I am grateful to you for having turned me to this problem." He looked up sharply. "Where are you going, my dear?"

"I've got to th-think," said Lucinda, and ran from the room. If she had stayed there for another fifteen seconds, she knew she would have crushed his skull in with the poker.

"Who-oh, Lucinda? How nice. Come in ... why, what's the matter?"

"Jenny, I've got to talk to you. Is Bob home?"

"No. He's got night duty at the high-temperature lab this week. Whatever is wrong?"

"It's the end of the world," said Lucinda in real anguish. She sank down on the sofa and looked up at the younger woman. "My husband is putting a—a chastity belt on every woman on earth."

"A *what?*"

"A chastity belt." She began to laugh hysterically. "With a time-lock on it."

Jenny sat beside her. "Don't," she said. "Don't laugh like that. You're frightening me."

Lucinda lay back, gasping. "You should be frightened ... Listen to me, Jenny. Listen carefully, because this is the biggest thing that has happened since the deluge." She began to talk.

Five minutes later Jenny asked dazedly, "You mean—if this crazy thing happens, Bob won't ... won't *want* me most of the time?"

"It's you who won't do any wanting. And when you don't, he won't either. ... It isn't that that bothers me so much, Jenny, now that I've had a chance to think about it. I'm worried about the revolution."

"What revolution?"

"Why, this is going to cause the greatest upheaval of all time! Once these cycles become recognized for what they are, there will be fireworks. Look at the way we dress, the way we use cosmetics. Why do we do it? Basically, to appear to be available to men. Practically all perfumes have a musk or musk-like base for that very reason. But how long do you think women will keep up the hypocrisy of lipstick and plunging necklines when men *know* better—*know* that they couldn't possibly be approachable all the time? How many men will let their women appear in public looking as if they were?"

"They'll tie us up in the house the way I do Mitzi-poodle," said Jenny in an awed tone.

"They'll leave us smugly alone with easy minds for three weeks out of four," said Lucinda, "and stand guard over us like bull elks the rest of the time, to keep other men away."

"Lucinda!" Jenny squeaked and covered her face in horror. "What about other women? How can we compete with another woman when she's—she's—and we're not?"

"Especially when men are conditioned the way they are. Women will want to stick to one man, more likely than not. But men—men, building up pressures for weeks on end . . ."

"There'll be harems again," said Jenny.

"This is the absolute, final, bitter end of any power we ever had over the beasts, Jenny—do you see that? All the old tricks—the arch half-promise, the come-on, the manipulations of jealousy—they'll be utterly meaningless! The whole arsenal of womankind is based on her ability to yield or not to yield. And my husband is going to take the choice away from us. He's going to make absolutely certain that at one time we can't yield, and at another time we must!"

"And they'll never have to be nice to us at either time," added Jenny miserably.

"Women," said Lucinda bitterly, "are going to have to work for a living."

"But we do!"

"Oh, you know what I mean, Jenny! The lit-tul wife in the lit-tul home . . . that whole concept is based on women's perpetual availability. We're not going to be able to be homemakers, in that sense, at monthly intervals."

Jenny jumped up. Her face was chalky. "He hasn't stopped any war," she ground out. Lucinda had never seen her like this. "He's started one, and it's a beaut. Lucinda, he's got to be stopped, even if you—we have to. . . ."

"Come on."

They started for Dr. Lefferts' house, striding along like a couple of avenging angels.

"Ah," said Dr. Lefferts, rising politely. "You brought Jenny. Good evening, Jenny."

Lucinda planted herself in front of him and put her hands on her hips. "You listen to me," she growled. "You've got to stop that nonsense about changing women."

"It is not nonsense and I shall do nothing of the kind."

"Dr. Lefferts," said Jenny in a quaking voice, "can you really do this—this awful thing?"

"Of course," said the doctor. "It was quite simple, once the principles were worked out."

"It *was* quite simple? You men you've already—"

Dr. Lefferts looked at his watch. "At two o'clock this afternoon. Seven hours ago."

"I think," said Lucinda quietly, "that you had better tell us just exactly what you did, and what we can expect."

"I told you it is a security matter."

"What has my libido to do with national defense?"

"That," said the doctor, in a tone which referred to *that* as the merest trifle, "is a side issue. I coincided it with a much more serious project."

"What could be more serious than. . . ."

"There's only one thing *that* serious, from a security standpoint," said Lucinda. She turned to the doctor. "I know better than to ask you any direct questions. But if I assume that this horrible thing was done in conjunction with a superbomb test—just a guess, you understand—is there any way for an H-blast to bring about a change in women such as you describe?"

He clasped both hands around one knee and looked up at her in genuine admiration. "Brilliant," he said. "And most skillfully phrased. Speaking hypothetically—hypothetically, you understand," he interjected, waving a warning finger, "a hydrogen bomb has an immense power of diffusion. A jet of energy of that size, at that temperature, for even three or four microseconds, is capable of penetrating the upper reaches of stratosphere. But the effect does not end there. The upward displacement causes great volumes of air to rush in toward the rushing column from all sides. This in turn is carried upward and replaced, a process which continues for a considerable time. One of the results must be the imbalance of any distinct high or low pressure areas within several thousand miles, and for a day or two freak weather developments can be observed. In other words, these primary and secondary effects are capable of diffusing a—ah—substance placed in the bomb throughout the upper atmosphere, where, in a matter of days, it will be diffused throughout the entire envelope."

Lucinda clasped her hands in a slow, controlled way, as if one of them planned to immobilize the other and thereby keep both occupied.

"And is there any substance ... I'm still asking hypothetical questions, you understand—is there anything which could be added to the hydrogen fusion reaction which might bring about these—these new cycles in women?"

"They are not new cycles," said the doctor flatly. "They are as old as the development of warm-blooded animals. The lack of them is, in biological terms, a very recent development in an atypical mammal; so recent and so small that it is subject to adjustment. As to your hypothetical question"—he smiled—"I should judge that such an effect is perfectly possible. Within the extremes of temperature, pressure, and radiation which take place in a fusion reaction, many things are possible. A minute quantity of certain alloys, for example, introduced into the shell of the bomb itself, or perhaps in the structure of a supporting tower or even a nearby temporary shed, might key a number of phenomenal reaction chains. Such a chain might go through several phases and result in certain subtle isotopic alterations in one of the atmosphere's otherwise inert gases, say xenon. And this isotope, acting upon the adrenal cortex and the parathyroid, which are instrumental in controlling certain cycles in the human body, might very readily bring about the effect we are discussing in an atypical species."

Lucinda threw up her hands and turned to Jenny. "Then that's it," she said wearily.

"What's 'it'? What? I don't understand," whimpered Jenny. "What's he done, Lucinda?"

"In his nasty, cold-blooded hypothetical way," said Lucinda, "he has put something in or near an H-bomb which was tested today, which is going to have some effect on the air we breathe, which is going to do what we were discussing at your house."

"Dr. Lefferts," said Jenny piteously. She went to him, stood looking down at him as he sat primly in his big easy chair. "Why—*why?*

Just to annoy us? Just to keep us from having a little, petty influence over you?"

"By no means," said the doctor. "I will admit that I might have turned my ambition to the matter for such reasons. But some concentrated thought brought up a number of extrapolations which are by no means petty."

He rose and stood by the mantel, pince-nez in hand, the perfect picture of the Pedant At Home. "Consider," he said. "*Homo sapiens*, in terms of comparative anatomy, should mature physically at 35 and emotionally between 30 and 40. He should have a life expectancy of between 150 and 200 years. And he unquestionably should be able to live a life uncluttered by such insistent trifles as clothing conventions, unfunctional chivalries, psychic turmoils and dangerous mental and physical escapes into what the psychologists call romances. Women should phase their sexual cycles with those of the seasons, gestate their young longer, and eliminate the unpredictable nature of their psycho-sexual appetites—the very basis of all their insecurity and therefore that of most men. Women will not be chained to these cycles, Jenny, and become breeding machines, if that's what you fear. You will begin to live in and with these cycles as you live with a well-made and serviced automatic machine. You will be liberated from the constant control and direction of your somatic existence as you have been liberated from shifting gears in your car."

"But ... we're not conditioned for such a change!" blazed Lucinda. "And what of the fashion industry ... cosmetics ... the entertainment world ... what's going to become of these and the millions of people employed by them, and the people dependent on all those people, if you do a thing like this?"

"The thing is done. As for these people ..." He paused, "Yes, there will be some disturbance. A considerable one. But in overall historical terms, it will be slight and it will be brief. I like to think that the television serviceman is one who was liberated by the cotton gin and the power loom."

"It's ... hard to think in historical terms just now," said Lucinda. "Jenny, come on."

"Where are you going?"

She faced him, her blued-steel eyes blazing. "Away from you. And I—I think I have a warning to give to the women."

"I wouldn't do that," he said dryly. "They'll find out in time. All you'll succeed in doing is to alert many women to the fact that they will be unattractive to their husbands at times when other women may seem more desirable. Women will not unite with one another, my dear, even to unite against men."

There was a tense pause. Then Jenny quavered, "How long did you say this—this thing will take?"

"I did not say. I would judge between thirty-six and forty-eight hours."

"I've got to get home."

"May I come with you?" asked Lucinda.

Jenny looked at her, her full face, her ample, controlled body. A surprising series of emotions chased themselves across her young face. She said, "I don't think ... I mean ... no, not tonight; I have to—to—goodnight, Lucinda."

When she had gone, the doctor uttered one of his rare chuckles. "She has absorbed perhaps a tenth of this whole concept," he said, "but until she's sure of herself she's not going to let you or any woman near her husband."

"You ... you complacent *pig!*" said Lucinda whitely. She stormed upstairs.

"Hello ... hello—Jenny?"

"Lucinda! I'm—glad you called."

Something cold and tense deep inside Lucinda relaxed. She sat down slowly on the couch, leaned back comfortably with the telephone cradled between her cheek and her wide soft shoulder. "I'm glad you're glad, Jenny darling. It's been six weeks ... how are you?"

"I'm ... all right now. It was pretty awful for a while, not knowing how it would be, waiting for it to happen. And when it did happen, it was hard to get used to. But it hasn't changed things *too* much. How about you?"

"Oh, I'm fine," said Lucinda. She smiled slowly, touched her tongue to her full lower lip. "Jenny, have you told anyone?"

"Not a soul. Not even Bob. I think he's a little bewildered. He thinks I'm being very ... understanding. Lucinda, is it wrong for me to let him think that?"

"It's never wrong for a woman to keep her knowledge to herself if it makes her more attractive," said Lucinda, and smiled again.

"How's Dr. Lefferts?"

"He's bewildered too. I suppose I've been a little ... understanding too." She chuckled.

Over the phone she heard Jenny's answering laughter. "The poor things," she said. "The poor, poor things. Lucinda—"

"Yes, honey?"

"I know how to handle this, now. But I don't really understand it. Do you?"

"Yes, I think I do."

"How can it be, then? How can this change in us affect men that way? I thought *we* would be the ones who would be turned off and on like a neon sign."

"*What?* Now wait a minute, Jenny! You mean you don't realize what's happened?"

"That's just what I said. How could such a change in women do such a thing to the men?"

"Jenny, I think you're wonderful, wonderful, wonderful," breathed Lucinda. "As a matter of fact, I think women are wonderful. I suddenly realized that you haven't the foggiest notion of what's happened, yet you've taken it in stride and used it *exactly* right!"

"Whatever do you mean?"

"Jenny, do you feel any difference in yourself?"

"Why, no. All the difference is in Bob. That's what I—"

"Honey, there *isn't* any difference in you, nor in me, nor in any other woman. For the very first time in his scientific life, the great man made an error in his calculations."

There was a silence for a time, and then the telephone uttered a soft, delighted, long-drawn-out "Oh-h-h-h-h ..."

Lucinda said, "He's sure that in the long run it will have all the benefits he described—the longer life expectancy, the subduing of insecurities, the streamlining of our manners and customs."

310

"You mean that all men from now on will ..."

"I mean that for about twelve days in every two weeks, men can't do anything with us, which is restful. And for forty-eight hours they can't do anything without us, which is"—she laughed—"useful. It would seem that *homo sapiens* is still an atypical mammal."

Jenny's voice was awed. "And I thought we were going to lose the battle of the sexes. Bob brings me little presents every single day, Lucinda!"

"He'd better. Jenny, put down that phone and come over here. I want to hug you. And"—she glanced over at the hall closet, where hung the symbol of her triumph—"I want to show you my new fur coat."

The Sex Opposite

BUDGIE SLID INTO the laboratory without knocking, as usual.

She was flushed and breathless, her eyes bright with speed and eagerness. "Whatcha got, Muley?"

Muhlenberg kicked the morgue door shut before Budgie could get in line with it. "Nothing," he said flatly, "and of all the people I don't want to see—and at the moment that means all the people there are—you head the list. Go away."

Budgie pulled off her gloves and stuffed them into an oversized shoulder-bag, which she hurled across the laboratory onto a work-surface. "Come on, Muley. I saw the meat-wagon outside. I know what it brought, too. That double murder in the park. Al told me."

"Al's jaw is one that needs more tying up than any of the stiffs he taxis around," said Muhlenberg bitterly. "Well, you're not getting near this pair."

She came over to him, stood very close. In spite of his annoyance, he couldn't help noticing how soft and full her lips were just then. *Just then*—and the sudden realization added to the annoyance. He had known for a long time that Budgie could turn on mechanisms that made every one of a man's ductless glands purse up its lips and blow like a trumpet. Every time he felt it he hated himself. "Get away from me," he growled. "It won't work."

"What won't, Muley?" she murmured.

Muhlenberg looked her straight in the eye and said something about his preference for raw liver over Budgie-times-twelve.

The softness went out of her lips, to be replaced by no particular hardness. She simply laughed good-naturedly. "All right, you're immune. I'll try logic."

"Nothing will work," he said. "You will not get in there to see those two, and you'll get no details from me for any of that *couche-con-carne* stew you call a newspaper story."

"Okay," she said surprisingly. She crossed the lab and picked up her handbag. She found a glove and began to pull it on. "Sorry I interrupted you, Muley. I do get the idea. You want to be alone."

His jaw was too slack to enunciate an answer. He watched her go out, watched the door close, watched it open again, heard her say in a very hurt tone, "But I do think you could tell me *why* you won't say anything about this murder."

He scratched his head. "As long as you behave yourself, I guess I do owe you that." He thought for a moment. "It's not your kind of a story. That's about the best way to put it."

"Not my kind of a story? A double murder in Lover's Lane? The maudlin mystery of the mugger, or mayhem in Maytime? No kidding, Muley—you're not serious!"

"Budgie, this one isn't for fun. It's ugly. Very *damn* ugly. And it's serious. It's mysterious for a number of other reasons than the ones you want to siphon into your readers."

"What other reasons?"

"Medically. Biologically. Sociologically."

"My stories got biology. Sociology they got likewise; stodgy truisms about social trends is the way I dish up sex in the public prints, or didn't you know? So—that leaves medical. What's so strange medically about this case?"

"Good night, Budgie."

"Come on, Muley. You can't horrify *me.*"

"That I know. You've trod more primrose pathology in your research than Krafft-Ebing plus eleven comic books. No, Budgie. No more."

"Dr. F.L. Muhlenberg, brilliant young biologist and special medical consultant to the City and State Police, intimated that these aspects of the case—the brutal murder and disfigurement of the embarrassed couple—were superficial compared with the unspeakable facts behind them. 'Medically mysterious,' he was quoted as saying." She twinkled at him. "How's that sound?" She looked at her watch. "And I can make the early editions, too, with a head. Something like DOC SHOCKED SPEECHLESS—and a subhead: Lab Sleuth Suppresses Medical Details of Double Park Killing. Yeah, and your picture."

"If you dare to print anything of the sort," he raged, "I'll—"

"All right, all right," she said conciliatingly. "I won't. I really won't."

"Promise me?"

"I promise, Muley ... *if—*"

"Why should I bargain?" he demanded suddenly. "Get out of here."

He began to close the door. "And something for the editorial page," she said. "Is a doctor within his rights in suppressing information concerning a murderous maniac and his methods?" She closed the door.

Muhlenberg bit his lower lip so hard he all but yelped. He ran to the door and snatched it open. "Wait!"

Budgie was leaning against the doorpost lighting a cigarette. "I *was* waiting," she said reasonably.

"Come in here," he grated. He snatched her arm and whirled her inside, slamming the door.

"You're a brute," she said rubbing her arm and smiling dazzlingly.

"The only way to muzzle you is to tell the whole story. Right?"

"Right. If I get an exclusive when you're ready to break the story."

"There's probably a kicker in that, too," he said morosely. He glared at her. Then, "Sit down," he said.

She did. "I'm all yours."

"Don't change the subject," he said with a ghost of his natural humor. He lit a thoughtful cigarette. "What do you know about this case so far?"

"Too little," she said. "This couple were having a conversation without words in the park when some muggers jumped them and killed them, a little more gruesomely than usual. But instead of being delivered to the city morgue, they were brought straight to you on the orders of the ambulance interne after one quick look."

"How did you know about it?"

"Well, if you must know, I was in the park. There's a shortcut over by the museum, and I was about a hundred yards down the path when I . . ."

Muhlenberg waited as long as tact demanded, and a little longer. Her face was still, her gaze detached. "Go on."

". . . when I heard a scream," she said in the precise tone of voice which she had been using. Then she began to cry.

"Hey," he said. He knelt beside her, put a hand on her shoulder. She shoved it away angrily, and covered her face with a damp towel. When she took it down again she seemed to be laughing. She was doing it so badly that he turned away in very real embarrassment.

"Sorry," she said in a very shaken whisper. "It . . . was that kind of a scream. I've never heard anything like it. It did something to me. It had more agony in it than a single sound should be able to have." She closed her eyes.

"Man or woman?"

She shook her head.

"So," he said matter-of-factly, "what did you do then?"

"Nothing. Nothing at all, for I don't know how long." She slammed a small fist down on the table. "I'm supposed to be a reporter!" she flared. "And there I stand like a dummy, like a wharf rat in concussion-shock!" She wet her lips. "When I came around I was standing by a rock wall with one hand on it." She showed him. "Broke two perfectly good fingernails, I was holding on so tight. I ran toward where I'd heard the sound. Just trampled brush, nothing else. I heard a crowd milling around on the avenue. I went up there. The meat-wagon was there, Al and that young sawbones Regal—Ruggles—"

"Regalio."

"Yeah, him. They'd just put those two bodies into the ambulance. They were covered with blankets. I asked what was up. Regalio waved a finger and said 'Not for school-girls' and gave me a real death-mask grin. He climbed aboard. I grabbed Al and asked him what was what. He said muggers had killed this couple, and it was pretty rugged. Said Regalio had told him to bring them here, even before he made a police report. They were both about as upset as they could get."

"I don't wonder," said Muhlenberg.

"Then I asked if I could ride and they said no and took off. I grabbed a cab when I found one to grab, which was all of fifteen minutes later, and here I am. Here I am," she repeated, "getting a story out of you in the damnedest way yet. You're asking, I'm answering." She got up. "You write the feature, Muley. I'll go on into your icebox and do your work."

He caught her arm. "Nah! No you don't! Like the man said— it's not for school-girls."

"Anything you have in there *can't* be worse than my imagination!" she snapped.

"Sorry. It's what you get for barging in on me before I've had a chance to think something through. You see, this wasn't exactly two people."

"I know!" she said sarcastically. "Siamese twins."

He looked at her distantly. "Yes. 'Taint funny, kiddo."

For once she had nothing to say. She put one hand slowly up to her mouth and apparently forgot it, for there it stayed. "That's what's so ugly about this. Those two were ... torn apart." He closed his eyes. "I can just see it. I wish I couldn't. Those thugs drifting through the park at night, out for anything they could get. They hear something ... fall right over them ... I don't know. Then—"

"All right, all right," she whispered hoarsely. "I can hear you."

"But, damn it," he said angrily, "I've been kicking around this field long enough to know every documented case of such a creature. And I just can't believe that one like this could exist without having been written up in some medical journal somewhere. Even if they were born in Soviet Russia, some translation of a report would've appeared somewhere."

"I know Siamese twins are rare. But surely such a birth wouldn't make international headlines!"

"This one would," he said positively. "For one thing, Siamese twins usually bear more anomalies than just the fact that they are attached. They're frequently fraternal rather than identical twins. More often than not one's born more fully developed than the other. Usually when they're born at all they don't live. But these—"

"What's so special?"

Muhlenberg spread his hands. "They're perfect. They're costally joined by a surprisingly small tissue-organ complex—"

"Wait, professor, 'Costally'—you mean at the chest?"

"That's right. And the link is—was—not major. I can't understand why they were never surgically separated. There may be a reason, of course, but that'll have to wait on the autopsy."

"Why wait?"

"It's all I can do to wait." He grinned suddenly. "You see, you're more of a help than you realize, Budge. I'm dying to get to work on them, but under the circumstances I have to wait until morning. Regalio reported to the police, and I know the coroner isn't going to come around this time of night, not if I could show him quintuplets in a chain like sausages. In addition, I don't have identities, I don't have relatives' releases—you know. So—a superficial examination, a lot of wild guesses, and a chance to sound off to you keep myself from going nuts."

"You're *using* me!"

"That's bad?"

"Yes—when I don't get any fun out of it."

He laughed. "I love those incendiary statements of yours. I'm just not flammable."

She looked at him, up and a little sidewise. "Not at all?"

"Not now."

She considered that. She looked down at her hands, as if they were the problems of Muhlenberg's susceptibility. She turned the hands over. "Sometimes," she said, "I really enjoy it when we share something else besides twitches and moans. Maybe we should be more inhibited."

"Do tell."

She said, "We have nothing in common. I mean, but *nothing*. We're different to the core, to the bone. You hunt out facts and so do I, but we could never share that because we don't use facts for the same thing. You use facts only to find more facts."

"What do you use them for?"

She smiled. "All sorts of things. A good reporter doesn't report

317

just what happens. He reports what he *sees*—in many cases a very different thing. Any way ...”

“Wonder how these biological pressures affected our friends here,” he mused, thumbing over his shoulder at the morgue.

“About the same, I’d judge, with certain important difficulties. But wait—were they men or women, or one of each?”

“I didn’t tell you, did I?” he said with real startlement.

“No,” she said.

He opened his mouth to answer, but could not. The reason came.

It came from downstairs or outside, or perhaps from nowhere or everywhere, or from a place without a name. It was all around them, inside, behind them in time as well as space. It was the echo of their own first cry when they lost the first warmth and found loneliness, early, as everyone must. It was hurt: some the pain of impact, some of fever and delirium, and some the great pressure of beauty too beautiful to bear. And like pain, it could not be remembered. It lasted as long as it was a sound, and perhaps a little longer, and the frozen time after it died was immeasurable.

Muhlenberg became increasingly conscious of an ache in his calves and in the trapezoid muscles of his back. They sent him a gradual and completely intellectualized message of strain, and very consciously he relieved it and sat down. His movement carried Budgie’s arm forward, and he looked down at her hand, which was clamped around his forearm. She moved it away, opening it slowly, and he saw the angry marks of her fingers, and knew they would be bruises in the morning.

She said, “That was the scream. The one I heard. Wasn’t once enough?”

It was only then that he could look far enough out of himself to see her face. It was pasty with shock, and wet, and her lips were pale. He leapt to his feet. “Another one! *Come on!*”

He pulled her up and through the door. “Don’t you understand?” he blazed. “Another one! It can’t be, but somewhere out there it’s happened again—”

She pulled back. "Are you sure it wasn't . . ." She nodded at the closed door of the morgue.

"Don't be ridiculous," he snorted. *"They* couldn't be alive." He hurried her to the stairs.

It was very dark. Muhlenberg's office was in an aging business building which boasted twenty-five-watt bulbs on every other floor. They hurtled through the murk, past the deepest doorways of the law firm, the doll factory, the import-export firm which imported and exported nothing but phone calls, and all the other dim mosaics of enterprise. The building seemed quite deserted, and but for the yellow-orange glow of the landings and the pathetic little bulbs, there were no lights anywhere. And it was as quiet as it was almost dark; quiet as late night; quiet as death.

They burst out onto the old brownstone steps and stopped, afraid to look, wanting to look. There was nothing. Nothing but the street, a lonesome light, a distant horn and, far up at the corner, the distinct clicking of the relays in a traffic-light standard as they changed an ignored string of emeralds to an unnoticed ruby rope.

"Go up to the corner," he said, pointing. "I'll go down the other way. That noise wasn't far away—"

"No," she said. "I'm coming with you."

"Good," he said, so glad he was amazed at himself. They ran north to the corner. There was no one on the street within two blocks in any direction. There were cars, mostly parked, one coming, but none leaving.

"Now what?" she asked.

For a moment he did not answer. She waited patiently while he listened to the small distant noises which made the night so quiet. Then, "Good night, Budge."

"Good—*what?*"

He waved a hand. "You can go home now."

"But what about the—"

"I'm tired," he said. "I'm bewildered. That scream wrung me like a floor-mop and pulled me down too many stairs too fast. There's

319

too much I don't know about this and not enough I can do about it. So go home."

"Aw, Muley . . ."

He sighed. "I know. Your story. Budgie, I faithfully promise you I'll give you an exclusive as soon as I have facts I can trust."

She looked carefully at his face in the dim light and nodded at what she saw there. "All right, Muley. The pressure's off. Call me?"

"I'll call you."

He stood watching her walk away. Quite a gal, he thought. He wondered what had moved her to make that odd remark about inhibitions. They'd certainly never bothered her before. But—perhaps she had something there. Sometimes when you take what is loosely called "everything," you have an odd feeling that you haven't gotten much. He shrugged and ambled back toward the laboratory, pondering morphology, teratology, and a case where *monstra per defectum* could coexist with *monstra per fabricam alienam.*

Then he saw the light.

It flickered out over the street, soft and warm. He stopped and looked up. The light showed in a third-story window. It was orange and yellow, but with it was a flaring blue-white. It was pretty. It was also in his laboratory. No—not the laboratory. The morgue.

Muhlenberg groaned. After that he saved his breath. He needed it badly by the time he got back to the laboratory.

Muhlenberg dove for the heavy morgue door and snatched it open. A great pressure of heat punted a gout of smoke into the lab. He slammed the door, ran to a closet, snatched out a full-length lab smock, spun the faucets in the sink and soaked the smock. From another cabinet he snatched up two glass-globe fire extinguishers. He wrapped the wet cloth twice around his face and let the rest drop over his chest and back. Cradling the extinguishers in one bent forearm, he reached for the side of the door and grabbed the pump-type extinguisher racked there.

Now, suddenly not hurrying, he stepped up on the sill and stood on tiptoe, peering through a fold of the wet cloth. Then he crouched low and peered again. Satisfied, he stood up and carefully pegged the two glass extinguishers, one straight ahead, one to the right and down. Then he disappeared into the smoke, holding the third extinguisher at the ready.

There was a rising moan, and the smoke shook like a solid entity and rushed into the room and away. As it cleared, Muhlenberg, head and shoulders wrapped in sooty linen, found himself leaning against the wall, gasping, with one hand on a knife-switch on the wall. A three-foot exhaust fan in the top sash of one window was making quick work of the smoke.

Racks of chemicals, sterilizers, and glass cabinets full of glittering surgeon's tools lined the left wall. Out on the floor were four massive tables, on each of which was a heavy marble top. The rest of the room was taken up by a chemist's bench, sinks, a partitioned-off darkroom with lightproof curtains, and a massive centrifuge.

On one of the tables was a mass of what looked like burned meat and melted animal fat. It smelled bad—not rotten bad, but acrid and—and *wet,* if a smell can be described that way. Through it was the sharp, stinging odor of corrosive chemicals.

He unwound the ruined smock from his face and threw it into a corner. He walked to the table with the mess on it and stood looking bleakly at it for a time. Suddenly he put out a hand, and with thumb and forefinger pulled out a length of bone.

"What a job," he breathed at length.

He walked around the table, poked at something slumped there and snatched his hand away. He went to the bench and got a pair of forceps, which he used to pick up the lump. It looked like a piece of lava or slag. He turned on a hooded lamp and studied it closely.

"Thermite, by God," he breathed.

He stood quite still for a moment, clenching and unclenching his square jaw. He took a long slow turn around the seared horror on the morgue slab, then carefully picked up the forceps and hurled them furiously into a corner. Then he went out to the lab and picked up the phone. He dialed.

"Emergency," he said. "Hello, Sue. Regalio there? Muhlenberg. Thanks.... Hello, Doc. Are you sitting down? All right. Now get this. I'm fresh out of symmetrical teratomorphs. They're gone...."

Shut up and I'll tell you! I was out in the lab talking to a reporter when I heard the damnedest scream. We ran out and found nothing. I left the reporter outside and came back. I couldn't've been out more'n ten-twelve minutes. But somebody got in here, moved both stiffs onto one slab, incised them from the thorax to the pubis, crammed them full of iron oxide and granulated aluminum—I have lots of that sort of stuff around here—fused 'em with a couple of rolls of magnesium foil and touched 'em off. Made a great big messy thermite bomb out of them. . . . No, dammit, of *course* there's nothing left of them! What would you think eight minutes at seven thousand degrees would do? . . . Oh, dry up, Regalio! I don't know who did it or why, and I'm too tired to think about it. I'll see you tomorrow morning. No—what would be the use of sending anyone down here? This wasn't done to fire the building; whoever did it just wanted to get rid of those bodies, and sure did a job. . . . The coroner? I don't know what I'll tell him. I'm going to get a drink and then I'm going to bed. I just wanted you to know. Don't tell the press. I'll head off that reporter who was here before. We can do without this kind of story. 'Mystery arsonist cremated evidence of double killing in lab of medical consultant.' A block from headquarters, yet. . . . Yeah, and get your driver to keep his trap shut, too. Okay, Regalio. Just wanted to let you know. . . . Well, you're no sorrier'n I am. We'll just have to wait another couple hundred years while something like that gets born again, I guess."

Muhlenberg hung up, sighed, went into the morgue. He turned off the fan and lights, locked the morgue door, washed up at the laboratory sink, and shut the place up for the night.

It was eleven blocks to his apartment—an awkward distance most of the time, for Muhlenberg was not of the fresh-air and deep-breathing fraternity. Eleven blocks was not far enough to justify a cab and not near enough to make walking a negligible detail. At the seventh block he was aware of an overwhelming thirst and a general sensation that somebody had pulled the plug out of his energy barrel. He was drawn as if by a vacuum into Rudy's, a Mexican bar with Yma Sumac and Villa-Lobos on the jukebox.

"Olé, amigo," said Rudy. "Tonight you don' smile."

Muhlenberg crawled wearily onto a stool *"Deme una tequila sour, and skip the cherry,"* he said in his bastard Spanish. "I don't know what I got to smile about." He froze, and his eyes bulged. "Come back here, Rudy."

Rudy put down the lemon he was slicing and came close. "I don't want to point, but who *is* that?"

Rudy glanced at the girl. *"Ay,"* he said rapturously. *"Que chuchin."*

Muhlenberg remembered vaguely that *chuchin* was untranslatable, but that the closest English could manage with it was "cute." He shook his head. "That won't do." He held up his hand. "Don't try to find me a Spanish word for it. There isn't any word for it. Who is she?"

Rudy spread his hands. *"No sé."*

"She by herself?"

"Si."

Muhlenberg put his chin on his hand. "Make my drink. I want to think."

Rudy went, his mahogany cheeks drawn in and still in his version of a smile.

Muhlenberg looked at the girl in the booth again just as her gaze swept past his face to the bartender. "Rudy!" she called softly, "are you making a tequila sour?"

"Si, senorita."

"Make me one too?"

Rudy beamed. He did not turn his head toward Muhlenberg, but his dark eyes slid over toward him, and Muhlenberg knew that he was intensely amused. Muhlenberg's face grew hot, and he felt like an idiot. He had a wild fantasy that his ears had turned forward and snapped shut, and that the cello-and-velvet sound of her voice, captured, was nestling down inside his head like a warm little animal.

He got off the bar stool, fumbled in his pocket for change and went to the jukebox. She was there before him, slipping a coin in, selecting a strange and wonderful recording called *Vene a Mi Casa*, which was a *borracho* version of "C'mon-a My House."

"I was just going to play that!" he said. He glanced at the jukebox. "Do you like Yma Sumac?"

"Oh, yes!"

"Do you like *lots* of Yma Sumac?" She smiled and, seeing it, he bit his tongue. He dropped in a quarter and punched out six sides of Sumac. When he looked up Rudy was standing by the booth with a little tray on which were two tequila sours. His face was utterly impassive and his head was tilted at the precise angle of inquiry as to where he should put Muhlenberg's drink. Muhlenberg met the girl's eyes, and whether she nodded ever so slightly or whether she did it with a single movement of her eyelids, he did not know, but it meant "yes." He slid into the booth opposite her.

Music came. Only some of it was from the records. He sat and listened to it all. Rudy came with a second drink before he said anything, and only then did he realize how much time had passed while he rested there, taking in her face as if it were quite a new painting by a favorite artist. She did nothing to draw his attention or to reject it. She did not stare rapturously into his eyes or avoid them. She did not even appear to be waiting, or expecting anything of him. She was neither remote nor intimate. She was close, and it was good.

He thought, in your most secret dreams you cut a niche for yourself, and it is finished early, and then you wait for someone to come along to fill it—but to fill it exactly, every cut, curve, hollow and plane of it. And people do come along, and one covers up the niche, and another rattles around inside it, and another is so surrounded by fog that for the longest time you don't know if she fits or not; but each of them hits you with a tremendous impact. And then one comes along and slips in so quietly that you don't know when it happened, and fits so well you almost can't feel anything at all. And that is it.

"What are you thinking about?" she asked him.

He told her, immediately and fully. She nodded as if he had been talking about cats or cathedrals or cam-shafts, or anything else beautiful and complex. She said, "That's right. It isn't all there, of course. It isn't even enough. But everything else isn't enough without it."

"What is 'everything else'?"

"You know," she said.

He thought he did. He wasn't sure. He put it aside for later. "Will you come home with me?"

"Oh, yes."

They got up. She stood by the door, her eyes full of him, while he went to the bar with his wallet.

"¿Cuánto le debo?"

Rudy's eyes had a depth he had never noticed before. Perhaps it hadn't been there before. *"Nada,"* said Rudy.

"On the house? *Muchissimo gracias, amigo."* He knew, profoundly, that he shouldn't protest.

They went to his apartment. While he was pouring brandy— brandy because, if it's good brandy, it marries well with tequila— she asked him if he knew of a place called Shank's, down in the warehouse district. He thought he did; he knew he could find it. "I want to meet you there tomorrow night at eight," she said. "I'll be there," he smiled. He turned to put the brandy carafe back, full of wordless pleasure in the knowledge that all day tomorrow he could look forward to being with her again.

He played records. He was part sheer technician, part delighted child when he could demonstrate his sound system. He had a copy of the Confucian "Analects" in a sandalwood box. It was printed on rice-paper and hand-illuminated. He had a Finnish dagger with intricate scrollwork which, piece by piece and as a whole, made many pictures. He had a clock made of four glass discs, the inner two each carrying one hand, and each being rim-driven from the base so it seemed to have no works at all.

She loved all these things. She sat in his biggest chair while he stared out at the blue dark hours and she read aloud to him from "The Crock of Gold" and from Thurber and Shakespeare for laughter, and from Shakespeare and William Morris for a good sadness.

She sang, once.

Finally she said, "It's bedtime. Go and get ready."

He got up and went into the bedroom and undressed. He showered and rubbed himself pink. Back in the bedroom, he could hear the music she had put on the phonograph. It was the second movement of Prokofiev's "Classical" Symphony, where the orchestra is asleep and the high strings tiptoe in. It was the third time she had played it. He sat down to wait until the record was over, and when it was, and she didn't come or speak to him, he went to the living-room door and looked in.

She was gone.

He stood absolutely still and looked around the room. The whole time she had been there she had unostentatiously put everything back after they had looked at it. The amplifier was still on. The phonograph was off, because it shut itself off. The record album of Prokofiev, standing edge-up on the floor by the amplifier, was waiting to receive the record that was still on the turntable.

He stepped into the room and switched off the amplifier. He was suddenly conscious that in doing so he had removed half of what she had left there. He looked down at the record album; then, without touching it, he turned out the lights and went to bed.

You'll see her tomorrow, he thought.

He thought, you didn't so much as touch her hand. If it weren't for your eyes and ears, you'd have no way of knowing her.

A little later something deep within him turned over and sighed luxuriously. Muhlenberg, it said to him, do you realize that not once during that entire evening did you stop and think: this is an Occasion, this is a Great Day? Not once. The whole thing was easy as breathing.

As he fell asleep he remembered he hadn't even asked her her name.

He awoke profoundly rested, and looked with amazement at his alarm clock. It was only eight, and after what he had been through at the lab last night, plus what he had drunk, plus staying up so late, this feeling was a bonus indeed. He dressed quickly and got down to the lab early. The phone was already ringing. He told the coroner to bring Regalio and to come right down.

It was all very easy to explain in terms of effects; the burned morgue room took care of that. They beat causes around for an hour or so without any conclusion. Since Muhlenberg was so close to the Police Department, though not a member of it, they agreed to kill

the story for the time being. If relatives or a carnival owner or somebody came along, that would be different. Meantime, they'd let it
ride. It really wasn't so bad.

They went away, and Muhlenberg called the paper.

Budgie had not come to work or called. Perhaps she was out on
a story, the switchboard suggested.

The day went fast. He got the morgue cleaned up and a lot done
on his research project. He didn't begin to worry until the fourth time
he called the paper—that was about five p.m.—and Budgie still hadn't
come or called. He got her home phone number and called it. No;
she wasn't there. She'd gone out early to work. Try her at the paper.

He went home and bathed and changed, looked up the address
of Shank's and took a cab there. He was much too early. It was barely
seven-fifteen.

Shank's was a corner bar of the old-fashioned type with plate-
glass windows on its corner fronts and flyblown wainscoting behind
them. The booths gave a view of the street corner which did the same
for the booths. Except for the corner blaze of light, the rest of the
place was in darkness, punctuated here and there by the unreal blues
and greens of beer signs in neon script.

Muhlenberg glanced at his watch when he entered, and was appalled.
He knew now that he had been artificially busier and busier as the
day wore on, and that it was only a weak effort to push aside the
thoughts of Budgie and what might have happened to her. His busy-
ness had succeeded in getting him into a spot where he would have
nothing to do but sit and wait, and think his worries through.

He chose a booth on the mutual margins of the cave-like darkness and the pallid light, and ordered a beer.

Somebody—let's be conventional and call him Mr. X—had gone
'way out of his way to destroy two bodies in his morgue. A very
thorough operator. Of course, if Mr. X was really interested in suppressing information about the two pathetic halves of the murdered
monster in the park, he'd only done part of the job. Regalio, Al,
Budgie and Muhlenberg knew about it. Regalio and Al had been all
right when he had seen them this morning, and certainly no attempts

had been made on him. On the other hand, he had been in and around the precinct station and its immediate neighborhood all day, and about the same thing applied to the ambulance staff.

But Budgie . . .

Not only was she vulnerable, she wasn't even likely to be missed for hours by anyone since she was so frequently out on stories. Stories! Why—as a reporter she presented the greatest menace of all to anyone who wanted to hide information!

With that thought came its corollary: Budgie was missing, and if she had been taken care of he, Muhlenberg, was next on the list. Had to be. He was the only one who had been able to take a good long look at the bodies. He was the one who had given the information to the reporter and the one who still had it to give. In other words, if Budgie had been taken care of, he could expect some sort of attack too, and quickly.

He looked around the place with narrowing eyes. This was a rugged section of town. Why was he here?

He had a lurching sense of shock and pain. The girl he'd met last night—that couldn't be a part of this thing. It mustn't be. And yet because of her he found himself here, like a sitting duck.

He suddenly understood his unwillingness to think about the significance of Budgie's disappearance.

"Oh, no," he said aloud.

Should he run?

Should he—and perhaps be wrong? He visualized the girl coming there, waiting for him, perhaps getting in some trouble in this dingy place, just because he'd gotten the wind up over his own fantasies.

He couldn't leave. Not until after eight anyway. What else then? If they got him, who would be next? Regalio, certainly. Then Al. Then the coroner himself.

Warn Regalio. That at least he might do, before it was too late. He jumped up.

There was, of course, someone in the phone booth. A woman. He swore and pulled the door open.

"Budgie!"

He reached in almost hysterically, pulled her out. She spun limply into his arms, and for an awful split second his thoughts were indescribable. Then she moved. She squeezed him, looked up incredulously, squeezed him again. "Muley! Oh, Muley, I'm so glad it's you!"

"Budgie, you lunkhead—where've you been?"

"Oh, I've had the most awful—the most wonderful—"

"Hey, yesterday you cried. Isn't that your quota for the year?"

"Oh, shut up. Muley, Muley, no one could get mixed up more than I've been!"

"Oh," he said reflectively, "I dunno. Come on over here. Sit down. Bartender! Two double whiskey sodas!" Inwardly, he smiled at the difference in a man's attitude toward the world when he has something to protect. "Tell me." He cupped her chin. "First of all, where have you been? You had me scared half to death."

She looked up at him, at each of his eyes in turn. There was a beseeching expression in her whole pose. "You won't laugh at me, Muley?"

"Some of this business is real un-funny."

"Can I *really* talk to you? I never tried." She said, as if there were no change of subject, "You don't know who I am."

"Talk then, so I'll know."

"Well," she began, "it was this morning. When I woke up. It was such a beautiful day! I went down to the corner to get the bus. I said to the man at the newsstand, *'Post?'* and dropped my nickel in his cup, and right in chorus with me was this man …"

"This man," he prompted.

"Yes. Well, he was a young man, about—oh, I don't know how old. Just right, anyway. And the newsdealer didn't know who to give the paper to because he had only one left. We looked at each other, this fellow and I, and laughed out loud. The newsy heard my voice loudest, I guess, or was being chivalrous, and he handed the paper to me. The bus came along then and we got in, and the fellow, the young one, I mean, he was going to take a seat by himself but I said come on—help me read the paper—you helped me buy it."

She paused while the one-eyed bartender brought the drinks.

"We never did look at the paper. We sort of . . . talked. I never met anyone I could talk to like that. Not even you, Muley, even now when I'm trying so. The things that came out . . . as if I'd known him all my—no," she said, shaking her head violently, "not even like that. I don't know. I can't say. It was fine."

"We crossed the bridge and the bus ran alongside the meadow, out there between the park and the fairgrounds. The grass was too green and the sky was too blue and there was something in me that just wanted to explode. But good, I mean, good. I said I was going to play hookey. I didn't say I'd like to, or I felt like it. I said I was going to. And he said let's, as if I'd asked him, and I didn't question that, not one bit. I don't know where he was going or what he was giving up, but we pulled the cord and the bus stopped and we got out and headed cross country."

"What did you do all day?" Muhlenberg asked as she sipped.

"Chased rabbits. Ran. Lay in the sun. Fed ducks. Laughed a lot. Talked. Talked a *whole* lot." Her eyes came back to the present, back to Muhlenberg. "Gosh, I don't know, Muley. I tried to tell myself all about it after he left me. I couldn't. Not so I'd believe it if I listened."

"And all this wound up in a crummy telephone booth?"

She sobered instantly. "I was supposed to meet him here. I couldn't just wait around home. I couldn't stomach the first faint thought of the office. So I just came here.

"I sat down to wait. I don't know why he asked me to meet him in a place like—what on earth is the matter with you?"

"Nothing," choked Muhlenberg. "I was having an original thought called, 'It's a small world.'" He waved her forthcoming questions away. "Don't let me interrupt. You first, then me. There's something weird and wonderful going on here."

"Where was I? Oh. Well, I sat here waiting and feeling happy, and gradually the feeling went away and the gloom began to seep in. Then I thought about you, and the murder in the park, and that fantastic business at your lab last night, and I began to get scared. I didn't know what to do. I was going to run from here, and then I had a reaction, and wondered if I was just scaring myself. Suppose he came and I wasn't here? I couldn't bear that. Then I got scared again and—wondered if he was part of the whole thing, the Siamese-twin murder and all. And I hated myself for even thinking such a thing. I went into a real hassle. At last I squared myself away and figured the only thing to do was to call you up. And you weren't at the lab. And the coroner didn't know where you'd gone and—oh-h-h, *Muley!*"

"It meant that much?"

She nodded.

"Fickle bitch! Minutes after leaving your lover-boy—"

She put her hand over his mouth. "Watch what you say," she said fiercely. "This was no gay escapade, Muley. It was like—like nothing I've ever heard of. He didn't touch me, or act as if he wanted to. He didn't have to; it wasn't called for. The whole thing *was* the whole thing, and not a preliminary to anything else. It was—it was—oh, *damn* this language!"

Muhlenberg thought about the Prokofiev album standing upright by his amplifier. Damn it indeed, he thought. "What was his name?" he asked gently.

"His—" She snapped her head up, turned slowly to him. She whispered, "I never asked him. . . ." and her eyes went quite round.

"I thought not." Why did I say that? he asked himself. I almost know. . . .

He said, suddenly, "Budgie, do you love him?"

Her face showed surprise. "I hadn't thought about it. Maybe I don't know what love is. I thought I knew. But it was less than this." She frowned. "It was more than this, though, some ways."

"Tell me something. When he left you, even after a day like that, did you feel . . . that you'd lost something?"

She thought about it. "Why . . . no. No, I didn't. I was full up to here, and what he gave me he left with me. That's the big difference. No love's like that. Can you beat that? I didn't *lose* anything!"

He nodded. "Neither did I," he said.

"You *what?*"

But he wasn't listening. He was rising slowly, his eyes on the door.

The girl was there. She was dressed differently, she looked trim and balanced. Her face was the same, though, and her incredible eyes. She wore blue jeans, loafers, a heavy, rather loose sweater, and two soft-collar points gleamed against her neck and chin. Her hair hardly longer than his own, but beautiful, beautiful....

He looked down, as he would have looked away from a great light. He saw his watch. It was eight o'clock. And he became aware of Budgie looking fixedly at the figure in the door, her face radiant. "Muley, come on. Come on, Muley. There he is!"

The girl in the doorway saw him then and smiled. She waved and pointed at the corner booth, the one with windows on two streets. Muhlenberg and Budgie went to her.

She sat down as they came to her. "Hello. Sit there. Both of you."

Side by side they sat opposite her. Budgie stared in open admiration. Muhlenberg stared too, and something in the back of his mind began to grow, and grow, and—"No," he said, incredulously.

"Yes," she said, directly to him. "It's true." She looked at Budgie. "She doesn't know yet, does she?"

Muhlenberg shook his head. "I hadn't time to tell her."

"Perhaps you shouldn't," said the girl.

Budgie turned excitedly to Muhlenberg. "You know him!"

Muhlenberg said, with difficulty, "I know ... know—"

The girl laughed aloud. "You're looking for a pronoun."

Budgie said, "Muley, what's he mean? Let me in on it."

"An autopsy would have shown it, wouldn't it?" he demanded.

The girl nodded. "Very readily. That was a close call."

Budgie looked from one to the other. "Will somebody tell me what in blazes this is all about?"

Muhlenberg met the girl's gaze. She nodded. He put an arm around Budgie. "Listen, girl reporter. Our—our friend here's something ... something new and different."

"Not new," said the girl. "We've been around for thousands of years."

"Have you now!" He paused to digest that, while Budgie squirmed and protested, "But—but—but—"

"Shush, you," said Muhlenberg, and squeezed her shoulders gently. "What you spent the afternoon with isn't a man, Budgie, any more than what I spent most of the night with was a woman. Right?"

"Right," the girl said.

"And the Siamese twins weren't Siamese twins, but two of our friend's kind who—who—"

"They were in syzygy." An inexpressible sadness was in the smooth, almost contralto, all but tenor voice.

"In what?" asked Budgie.

Muhlenberg spelled it for her. "In some forms of life," he started to explain, "well, the microscopic animal called paramecium's a good example—reproduction is accomplished by fission. The creature elongates, and so does its nucleus. Then the nucleus breaks in two, and one half goes to each end of the animal. Then the rest of the animal breaks, and presto—two paramecia."

"But you—he—"

"Shaddup," he said. "I'm lecturing. The only trouble with reproduction by fission is that it affords no variation of strains. A single line of paramecium would continue to reproduce that way until, by the law of averages, its dominant traits would all be nonsurvival ones, and bang—no more paramecia. So they have another process to take care of that difficulty. One paramecium rests beside another, and gradually their contracting side walls begin to fuse. The nuclei gravitate toward that point. The side walls then break down, so that the nuclei then have access to one another. The nuclei flow together, mix and mingle, and after a time they separate and half goes into each animal. Then the side walls close the opening, break away from one another, and each animal goes its way.

"That is syzygy. It is in no sense a sexual process, because paramecia have no sex. It has no direct bearing on reproduction either—that can happen with or without syzygy." He turned to their companion. "But I'd never heard of syzygy in the higher forms."

The faintest of smiles. "It's unique with us, on this planet anyway."

"What's the rest of it?" he demanded.

"Our reproduction? We're parthenogenetic females."

"Y-you're a female?" breathed Budgie.

"A term of convenience," said Muhlenberg. "Each individual has both kinds of sex organs. They're self-fertilizing."

"That's a—a what do you call it?—a hermaphrodite," said Budgie. "Excuse me," she said in a small voice.

Muhlenberg and the girl laughed uproariously; and the magic of that creature was that the laughter couldn't hurt. "It's a very different thing," said Muhlenberg. "Hermaphrodites are human. She—our friend there—isn't."

"You're the humanest thing I ever met in my whole life," said Budgie ardently.

The girl reached across the table and touched Budgie's arm. Muhlenberg suspected that that was the very first physical contact either he or Budgie had yet received from the creature, and that it was a rare thing and a great compliment.

"Thank you," the girl said softly. "Thank you very much for saying that." She nodded to Muhlenberg. "Go on."

"Technically—though I know of no case where it has actually been possible—hermaphrodites can have contact with either sex. But parthenogenetic females won't, can't, and wouldn't. They don't need to. Humans cross strains along with the reproductive process. Parthenogenesis separates the two acts completely." He turned to the girl. "Tell me, how often do you reproduce?"

"As often as we wish to."

"And syzygy?"

"As often as we must. Then—we must."

"And that is—"

"It's difficult. It's like the paramecia's, essentially, but it's infinitely more complex. There's cell meeting and interflow, but in tens and then dozens, hundreds, then thousands of millions of cells. The join begins here—" she put her hand at the approximate location of the human heart—"and extends. But you saw it in those whom I burned. You are one of the few human beings who ever have."

"That isn't what I saw," he reminded her gently.

She nodded, and again there was that deep sadness. "That murder was such a stupid, incredible, unexpected thing!"

"Why were they in the park?" he asked, his voice thick with pity. "Why, out there, in the open, where some such human slugs could find them?"

"They took a chance, because it was important to them," she said wearily. She looked up, and her eyes were luminous. "We love the outdoors. We love the earth, the feel and smell of it, what lives from it and in it. Especially then. It was such a deep thicket, such an isolated pocket. It was the merest accident that those—those men found them there. They couldn't move. They were—well, medically you could call it unconscious. Actually, there—there never was a consciousness like the one which comes with syzygy."

"Can you describe it?"

She shook her head slowly, and it was no violation of her complete frankness. "Do you know, you couldn't describe sexuality to me so that I could understand it? I have no—no comparison, no analogies. It—" she looked from one to the other—"it amazes me. In some ways I envy it. I know it is a strife, which we avoid, for we are very gentle. But you have a capacity for enjoying strife, and all the pain, all the misery and poverty and cruelty which you suffer, is the cornerstone of everything you build. And you build more than anyone or anything in the known universe."

Budgie was wide-eyed. "You envy *us*. *You?*"

She smiled. "Don't you think the things you admire me for are rather commonplace among my own kind? It's just that they're rare in humans."

Muhlenberg said slowly, "Just what is your relationship to humanity?"

"It's symbiotic, of course."

"Symbiotic? You live with us, and us with you, like the cellulose-digesting microbes in a termite? Like the yucca moth, which can eat only nectar from the yucca cactus, which can spread its pollen only through the yucca moth?"

She nodded. "It's purely symbiotic. But it isn't easy to explain. We live on that part of humans which makes them different from animals."

"And in turn—"

"We cultivate it in humans."

"I don't understand that," said Budgie flatly.

"Look into your legends. We're mentioned often enough there. Who were the sexless angels? Who is the streamlined fat boy on your Valentine's Day cards? Where does inspiration come from? Who knows three notes of a composer's new symphony, and whistles the next phrase as he walks by the composer's house? And—most important to you two—who really understands that part of love between humans which is not sexual—because we can understand no other kind? Read your history, and you'll see where we've been. And in exchange we get the building—bridges, yes, and aircraft and soon, now, space-ships. But other kinds of building too. Songs and poetry and this new thing, this increasing sense of the oneness of all your species. And now it is fumbling toward a United Nations, and later it will grope for the stars; and where it builds, we thrive."

"Can you name this thing you get from us—this thing that is the difference between men and the rest of the animals?"

"No. But call it a sense of achievement. Where you feel that most, you feed us most. And you feel it most when others of your kind enjoy what you build."

"Why do you keep yourselves hidden?" Budgie suddenly asked. "Why?" She wrung her hands on the edge of the table. "You're so beautiful!"

"We have to hide," the other said gently. "You still kill anything that's . . . different."

Muhlenberg looked at that open, lovely face and felt a sickness, and he could have cried. He said, "Don't you ever kill anything?" and then hung his head, because it sounded like a defense for the murdering part of humanity. Because it was.

"Yes," she said very softly, "we do."

"You can *hate* something?"

"It isn't hate. Anyone who hates, hates himself as well as the object of his hate. There's another emotion called righteous anger. That makes us kill."

"I can't conceive of such a thing."

"What time is it?"

"Almost eight-forty."

She raised herself from her booth and looked out to the corner. It was dark now, and the usual crowd of youths had gathered under the street-lights.

"I made appointments with three more people this evening," she said. "They are murderers. Just watch." Her eyes seemed to blaze.

Under the light, two of the youths were arguing. The crowd, but for a prodding yelp or two, had fallen silent and was beginning to form a ring. Inside the ring, but apart from the two who were arguing, was a third—smaller, heavier and, compared with the sharp-creased, bright-tied arguers, much more poorly dressed, in an Eisenhower jacket with one sleeve tattered up to the elbow.

What happened then happened with frightening speed. One of the arguers smashed the other across the mouth. Spitting blood, the other staggered back, made a lightning move into his coat pocket. The blade looked for all the world like a golden fan as it moved in the cyclic pulsations of the streetlamp. There was a bubbling scream, a deep animal grunt, and two bodies lay tangled and twitching on the sidewalk while blood gouted and seeped and defied the sharpness of creases and the colors of ties.

Far up the block a man shouted and a whistle shrilled. Then the street corner seemed to become a great repulsing pole for humans. People ran outward, rayed outward, until, from above, they must have looked like a great splash in mud, reaching out and out until the growing ring broke and the particles scattered and were gone. And then there were only the bleeding bodies and the third one, the one with the tattered jacket, who hovered and stepped and waited and did not know which way to go. There was the sound of a single pair of running feet, after the others had all run off to silence, and these feet belonged to a man who ran fast and ran closer and breathed heavily through a shrieking police whistle.

The youth in the jacket finally turned and ran away, and the policeman shouted once around his whistle, and then there were two sharp reports and the youth, running hard, threw up his hands and fell without trying to turn his face away, and skidded on it and lay still with one foot turned in and the other turned out.

The girl in the dark sweater and blue jeans turned away from the windows and sank back into her seat, looking levelly into the drawn faces across the table. "Those were the men who killed those two in the park," she said in a low voice, "and that is how we kill."

"A little like us," said Muhlenberg weakly. He found his handkerchief and wiped off his upper lip. "Three of them for two of you."

"Oh, you don't understand," she said, and there was pity in her voice. "It wasn't because they killed those two. It was because they pulled them apart."

Gradually, the meaning of this crept into Muhlenberg's awed mind, and the awe grew with it. For here was a race which separated insemination from the mixing of strains, and apart from them, in clean-lined definition, was a third component, a psychic interflow. Just a touch of it had given him a magic night and Budgie an enchanted day; hours without strife, without mixed motives or misinterpretations.

If a human, with all his grossly efficient combination of functions, could be led to appreciate one light touch to that degree, what must it mean to have that third component, pure and in essence, torn apart in its fullest flow? This was worse than any crime could be to a human; and yet, where humans can claim clear consciences while jailing a man for a year for stealing a pair of shoes, these people repay the cruelest sacrilege of all with a quick clean blow. It was removal, not punishment. Punishment was alien and inconceivable to them.

He slowly raised his face to the calm, candid eyes of the girl. "Why have you shown us all this?"

"You needed me," she said simply.

"But you came up to destroy those bodies so no one would know—"

"And I found you two, each needing what the other had, and blind to it. No, not blind. I remember you said that if you ever could really share something, you could be very close." She laughed. "Remember your niche, the one that's finished early and never exactly filled? I told you at the time that it wouldn't be enough by itself if it *were* filled, and anyone completely without it wouldn't have enough either. And you—" She smiled at Budgie. "You never made any secret about what you wanted. And there the two of you were, each taking what you already had, and ignoring what you needed."

"Headline!" said Budgie, "Common Share Takes Stock."

"Subhead!" grinned Muhlenberg, "Man With A Niche Meets Girl With An Itch."

The girl slid out of the booth. "You'll do," she said.

"Wait! You're not going to leave us! Aren't we ever going to see you again?"

"Not knowingly. You won't remember me, or any of this."

"How can you take away—"

"Shush, Muley. You know she can."

"Yes, I guess she—wait though—wait! You give us all this knowledge just so we'll understand—and then you take it all away again. What good will that do us?"

She turned toward them. It may have been because they were still seated and she was standing, but she seemed to tower over them. In a split second of fugue, he had the feeling that he was looking at a great light on a mountain.

"Why, you poor things—didn't you know? Knowledge and understanding aren't props for one another. Knowledge is a pile of bricks, and understanding is a way of building. Build for me!"

They were in a joint called Shank's. After the triple killing, and the wild scramble to get the story phoned in, they started home.

"Muley," she asked suddenly, "what's syzygy?"

"What on earth made you ask me that?"

"It just popped into my head. What is it?"

"A non-sexual interflow between the nuclei of two animals."

"I never tried that," she said thoughtfully.

"Well, don't until we're married," he said. They began to hold hands while they walked.

Baby Is Three

I FINALLY GOT in to see this Stern. He wasn't an old man at all. He looked up from his desk, flicked his eyes over me once, and picked up a pencil. "Sit over there, Sonny."

I stood where I was until he looked up again. Then I said, "Look, if a midget walks in here, what do you say—sit over there, Shorty?"

He put the pencil down again and stood up. He smiled. His smile was as quick and sharp as his eyes. "I was wrong," he said, "but how am I supposed to know you don't want to be called Sonny?"

That was better, but I was still mad. "I'm fifteen and I don't have to like it. Don't rub my nose in it."

He smiled again and said okay, and I went and sat down.

"What's your name?"

"Gerard."

"First or last?"

"Both," I said.

"Is that the truth?"

I said, "No. And don't ask me where I live either."

He put down his pencil. "We're not going to get very far this way."

"That's up to you. What are you worried about? I got feelings of hostility? Well, sure I have. I got lots more things than that wrong with me or I wouldn't be here. Are you going to let that stop you?"

"Well, no, but—"

"So what else is bothering you? How you're going to get paid?" I took out a thousand-dollar bill and laid it on the desk. "That's so you won't have to bill me. *You* keep track of it. Tell me when it's used up and I'll give you more. So you don't need my address. Wait," I said, when he reached toward the money. "Let it lay there. I want to be sure you and I are going to get along."

He folded his hands. "I don't do business this way, Son—I mean, Gerard."

"Gerry," I told him. "You do, if you do business with me."

"You make things difficult, don't you? Where did you get a thousand dollars?"

"I won a contest. Twenty-five words or less about how much fun it is to do my daintier underthings with Sudso." I leaned forward. "This time it's the truth."

"All right," he said.

I was surprised. I think he knew it, but he didn't say anything more. Just waited for me to go ahead.

"Before we start—*if* we start," I said, "I got to know something. The things I say to you—what comes out while you're working on me—is that just between us, like a priest or a lawyer?"

"Absolutely," he said.

"No matter what?"

"No matter what."

I watched him when he said it. I believed him.

"Pick up your money," I said. "You're on."

He didn't do it. He said, "As you remarked a minute ago, that is up to me. You can't buy these treatments like a candy bar. We have to work together. If either one of us can't do that, it's useless. You can't walk in on the first psychotherapist you find in the phone book and make any demand that occurs to you just because you can pay for it."

I said tiredly, "I didn't get you out of the phone book and I'm not just guessing that you can help me. I winnowed through a dozen or more head-shrinkers before I decided on you."

"Thanks," he said, and it looked as if he was going to laugh at me, which I never like. "Winnowed, did you say? Just how?"

"Things you hear, things you read. You know. I'm not saying, so just file that with my street address."

He looked at me for a long time. It was the first time he'd used those eyes on me for anything but a flash glance. Then he picked up the bill.

"What do I do first?" I demanded.

"What do you mean?"

"How do we start?"

"We started when you walked in here."

So then I had to laugh. "All right, you got me. All I had was an opening. I didn't know where you would go from there, so I couldn't be there ahead of you."

"That's very interesting," Stern said. "Do you usually figure everything out in advance?"

"Always."

"How often are you right?"

"All the time. Except—but I don't have to tell you about no exceptions."

He really grinned this time. "I see. One of my patients has been talking."

"One of your ex-patients. Your patients don't talk."

"I ask them not to. That applies to you, too. What did you hear?"

"That you know from what people say and do what they're about to say and do, and that sometimes you let'm do it and sometimes you don't. How did you learn to do that?"

He thought a minute. "I guess I was born with an eye for details, and then let myself make enough mistakes with enough people until I learned not to make too many more. How did you learn to do it?"

I said, "You answer that and I won't have to come back here."

"You really don't know?"

"I wish I did. Look, this isn't getting us anywhere, is it?"

He shrugged. "Depends on where you want to go." He paused, and I got the eyes full strength again. "Which thumbnail description of psychiatry do you believe at the moment?"

"I don't get you."

Stern slid open a desk drawer and took out a blackened pipe. He smelled it, turned it over while looking at me. "Psychiatry attacks the onion of the self, removing layer after layer until it gets down to the little sliver of unsullied ego. Or: psychiatry drills like an oil well, down and sidewise and down again, through all the muck and rock, until it strikes a layer that yields. Or: psychiatry grabs a handful of sexual motivations and throws them on the pinball-machine of your life, so they bounce on down against episodes. Want more?"

I had to laugh. "That last one was pretty good."

"That last one was pretty bad. They are all bad. They all try to simplify something which is complex by its very nature. The only thumbnail you'll get from me is this: no one knows what's really wrong with you but you; no one can find a cure for it but you; no one but you can identify it as a cure; and once you find it, no one but you can do anything about it."

"What are *you* here for?"

"To listen."

"I don't have to pay somebody no day's wage every hour just to listen."

"True. But you're convinced that I listen selectively."

"Am I?" I wondered about it. "I guess I am. Well, don't you?"

"No, but you'll never believe that."

I laughed. He asked me what that was for. I said, "You're not calling me Sonny."

"Not you." He shook his head slowly. He was watching me while he did it, so his eyes slid in their sockets as his head moved. "What is it you want to know about yourself, that made you worried I might tell people?"

"I want to find out why I killed somebody," I said right away.

It didn't faze him a bit. "Lie down over there."

I got up. "On that couch?"

He nodded.

As I stretched out self-consciously, I said, "I feel like I'm in some damn cartoon."

"What cartoon?"

"Guy's built like a bunch of grapes," I said, looking at the ceiling. It was pale gray.

"What's the caption."

" 'I got trunks full of 'em.' "

"Very good," he said quietly.

I looked at him carefully. I knew then he was the kind of guy who laughs way down deep when he laughs at all.

He said, "I'll use that in a book of case histories some time. But it won't include yours. What made you throw that in?" When I didn't answer, he got up and moved to a chair behind me where I couldn't see him. "You can quit testing, Sonny. I'm good enough for your purposes."

I clenched my jaw so hard, my back teeth hurt. Then I relaxed. I relaxed all over. It was wonderful. "All right," I said. "I'm sorry." He didn't say anything, but I had that feeling again that he was laughing. Not at me, though.

"How old are you?" he asked me suddenly.

"Uh—fifteen."

"Uh—fifteen," he repeated. "What does the 'uh' mean?"

"Nothing. I'm fifteen."

"When I asked your age, you hesitated because some other number popped up. You discarded that and substituted 'fifteen.'"

"The hell I did! I *am* fifteen!"

"I didn't say you weren't." His voice came patiently. "Now what was the other number?"

I got mad again. "There wasn't any other number! What do you want to go pryin' my grunts apart for, trying to plant this and that and make it mean what you think it ought to mean?"

He was silent.

"I'm fifteen," I said defiantly, and then, "I don't like being only fifteen. You know that. I'm not trying to insist I'm fifteen."

He just waited, still not saying anything.

I felt defeated. "The number was eight."

"So you're eight. And your name?"

"Gerry." I got up on one elbow, twisting my neck around so I could see him. He had his pipe apart and was sighting through the stem at the desk lamp. "Gerry, without no 'uh!'"

"All right," he said mildly, making me feel real foolish.

I leaned back and closed my eyes.

Eight, I thought. Eight.

"It's cold in here," I complained.

Eight. Eight, plate, state, hate. I ate from the plate of the state and I hate. I didn't like any of that and I snapped my eyes open. The ceiling was still gray. It was all right. Stern was somewhere behind me with his pipe, and he was all right. I took two deep breaths, three, and then let my eyes close. Eight. Eight years old. Eight, hate. Years, fears. Old, cold. *Damn* it! I twisted and twitched on the couch, trying to find a way to keep the cold out. I ate from the plate of the—

I grunted and with my mind I took all the eights and all the rhymes and everything they stood for, and made it all black. But it wouldn't stay black. I had to put something there, so I made a great big luminous figure eight and just let it hang there. But it turned on its side and inside the loops it began to shimmer. It was like one of those movie shots through binoculars. I was going to have to look through whether I liked it or not.

Suddenly I quit fighting it and let it wash over me. The binoculars came close, closer, and then I was there.

Eight. Eight years old, cold. Cold as a bitch in the ditch. The ditch was by a railroad. Last year's weeds were scratchy straw. The ground was red, and when it wasn't slippery, clingy mud, it was frozen hard like a flowerpot. It was hard like that now, dusted with hoar-frost, cold as the winter light that pushed up over the hills. At night the lights were warm, and they were all in other people's houses. In the daytime the sun was in somebody else's house too, for all the good it did me.

I was dying in that ditch. Last night it was as good a place as any to sleep, and this morning it was as good a place as any to die. Just as well. Eight years old, the sick-sweet taste of porkfat and wet bread from somebody's garbage, the thrill of terror when you're stealing a gunnysack and you hear a footstep.

And I heard a footstep.

I'd been curled up on my side. I whipped over on my stomach because sometimes they kick your belly. I covered my head with my arms and that was as far as I could get.

After a while I rolled my eyes up and looked without moving. There was a big shoe there. There was an ankle in the shoe, and another shoe close by. I lay there waiting to get tromped. Not that I cared much any more, but it was such a damn shame. All these months on my own, and they'd never caught up with me, never even come close, and now this. It was such a shame I started to cry.

The shoe took me under the armpit, but it was not a kick. It rolled me over. I was so stiff from the cold, I went over like a plank. I just kept my arms over my face and head and lay there with my eyes closed. For some reason I stopped crying. I think people only cry when there's a chance of getting help from somewhere.

When nothing happened, I opened my eyes and shifted my forearms a little so I could see up. There was a man standing over me and he was a mile high. He had on faded dungarees and an old Eisenhower jacket with deep sweat-stains under the arms. His face was shaggy, like the guys who can't grow what you could call a beard, but still don't shave.

He said, "Get up."

I looked down at his shoe, but he wasn't going to kick me. I pushed up a little and almost fell down again, except he put his big hand where my back would hit it. I lay against it for a second because I had to, and then got up to where I had one knee on the ground.

"Come on," he said. "Let's go."

I swear I felt my bones creak, but I made it. I brought a round white stone up with me as I stood. I hefted the stone. I had to look at it to see if I was really holding it, my fingers were that cold. I told him, "Stay away from me or I'll bust you in the teeth with this rock."

His hand came out and down so fast, I never saw the way he got one finger between my palm and the rock, and flicked it out of my grasp. I started to cuss at him, but he just turned his back and walked up the embankment toward the tracks. He put his chin on his shoulder and said, "Come on, will you?"

He didn't chase me, so I didn't run. He didn't talk to me, so I didn't argue. He didn't hit me, so I didn't get mad. I went along after him. He waited for me. He put out his hand to me and I spit at it. So he went on, up to the tracks, out of my sight. I clawed my way up. The blood was beginning to move in my hands and feet and they felt like four point-down porcupines. When I got up to the roadbed, the man was standing there waiting for me.

The track was level just there, but as I turned my head to look along it, it seemed to be a hill that was steeper and steeper and turned over above me. And next thing you know, I was lying flat on my back looking up at the cold sky.

The man came over and sat down on the rail near me. He didn't try to touch me. I gasped for breath a couple of times, and suddenly felt I'd be all right if I could sleep for a minute—just a little minute. I closed my eyes. The man stuck his finger in my ribs, hard. It hurt.

"Don't sleep," he said.

I looked at him.

He said, "You're frozen stiff and weak with hunger. I want to take you home and get you warmed up and fed. But it's a long haul up that way, and you won't make it by yourself. If I carry you, will that be the same to you as if you walked it?"

"What are you going to do when you get me home?"

"I told you."

"All right," I said.

He picked me up and carried me down the track. If he'd said anything else in the world, I'd of laid right down where I was until I froze to death. Anyway, what did he want to ask me for, one way or the other? I couldn't of done anything.

I stopped thinking about it and dozed off.

I woke up once when he turned off the right of way. He dove into the woods. There was no path, but he seemed to know where he was going. The next time I woke from a crackling noise. He was carrying me over a frozen pond and the ice was giving under his feet. He didn't hurry. I looked down and saw the white cracks raying out under his feet, and it didn't seem to matter a bit. I bleared off again.

He put me down at last. We were there. "There" was inside a room. It was very warm. He put me on my feet and I snapped out of it in a hurry. The first thing I looked for was the door. I saw it and jumped over there and put my back against the wall beside it, in case I wanted to leave. Then I looked around.

It was a big room. One wall was rough rock and the rest was logs with stuff shoved between them. There was a big fire going in the rock wall, not in a fireplace, exactly; it was a sort of hollow place.

There was an old auto battery on a shelf opposite, with two yellowing electric light bulbs dangling by wires from it. There was a table, some boxes and a couple of three-legged stools. The air had a haze of smoke and such a wonderful, heartbreaking, candy-and-crackling smell of food that a little hose squirted inside my mouth.

The man said, "What have I got here, Baby?"

And the room was full of kids. Well, three of them, but somehow they seemed to be more than three kids. There was a girl about my age—eight, I mean—with blue paint on the side of her face. She had an easel and a palette with lots of paints and a fistful of brushes, but she wasn't using the brushes. She was smearing the paint on with her hands. Then there was a little Negro girl about five with great big eyes who stood gaping at me. And in a wooden crate, set up on two sawhorses to make a kind of bassinet, was a baby. I guess about three or four months old. It did what babies do, drooling some, making small bubbles, waving its hands around very aimless, and kicking.

When the man spoke, the girl at the easel looked at me and then at the baby. The baby just kicked and drooled.

The girl said, "His name's Gerry. He's mad."

"What's he mad at?" the man asked. He was looking at the baby.

"Everything," said the girl. "Everything and everybody."

"Where'd he come from?"

I said, "Hey, what is this?" but nobody paid any attention. The man kept asking questions at the baby and the girl kept answering. Craziest thing I ever saw.

"He ran away from a state school," the girl said. "They fed him enough, but no one bleshed with him."

That's what she said—"bleshed."

I opened the door then and cold air hooted in. "You louse," I said to the man, "you're from the school."

"Close the door, Janie," said the man. The girl at the easel didn't move, but the door banged shut behind me. I tried to open it and it wouldn't move. I let out a howl, yanking at it.

"I think you ought to stand in the corner," said the man. "Stand him in the corner, Janie."

Janie looked at me. One of the three-legged stools sailed across to me. It hung in midair and turned on its side. It nudged me with its flat seat. I jumped back and it came after me. I dodged to the side, and that was the corner. The stool came on. I tried to bat it down and just hurt my hand. I ducked and it went lower than I did. I put one hand on it and tried to vault over it, but it just fell and so did I. I got up again and stood in the corner, trembling. The stool turned right side up and sank to the floor in front of me.

The man said, "Thank you, Janie." He turned to me. "Stand there and be quiet, you. I'll get to you later. You shouldn'ta kicked up all that fuss." And then, to the baby, he said, "He got anything we need?"

And again it was the little girl who answered. She said, "Sure. He's the one."

"Well," said the man. "What do you know!" He came over. "Gerry, you can live here. I don't come from the school. I'll never turn you in."

"Yeah, huh?"

"He hates you," said Janie.

"What am I supposed to do about that?" he wanted to know.

Janie turned her head to look into the bassinet. "Feed him." The man nodded and began fiddling around the fire.

Meanwhile, the little Negro girl had been standing in the one spot with her big eyes right out on her cheekbones, looking at me. Janie went back to her painting, and the baby just lay there same as always, so I stared right back at the little Negro girl. I snapped, "What the devil are you gawking at?"

She grinned at me. "Gerry ho-ho," she said, and disappeared. I mean she really disappeared, went out like a light, leaving her clothes where she had been. Her little dress billowed in the air and fell in a heap where she had been, and that was that. She was gone.

"Gerry hee-hee," I heard. I looked up, and there she was, stark naked, wedged in a space where a little outcropping on the rock wall stuck out just below the ceiling. The second I saw her she disappeared again.

"Gerry ho-ho," she said. Now she was on top of the row of boxes they used as storage shelves, over on the other side of the room.

"Gerry hee-hee!" Now she was under the table. "Gerry ho-ho!" This time she was right in the corner with me, crowding me.

I yelped and tried to get out of the way and bumped the stool. I was afraid of it, so I shrank back again and the little girl was gone.

The man glanced over his shoulder from where he was working at the fire. "Cut it out, you kids," he said.

There was a silence, and then the girl came slowly out from the bottom row of shelves. She walked across to her dress and put it on.

"How did you do that?" I wanted to know.

Janie said, "It's easy. She's really twins."

"Oh," I said. Then another girl, exactly the same, came from somewhere in the shadows and stood beside the first. They were identical. They stood side by side and stared at me. This time I let them stare.

"That's Bonnie and Beanie," said the painter. "This is Baby and that—" she indicated the man—"that's Lone. And I'm Janie."

I couldn't think of what to say, so I said, "Yeah."

Lone said, "Water, Janie." He held up a pot. I heard water trickling, but didn't see anything. "That's enough," he said, and hung the pot on a crane. He picked up a cracked china plate and brought it over to me. It was full of stew with great big lumps of meat in it, and thick gravy and dumplings and carrots. "Here, Gerry. Sit down."

I looked at the stool. "On that?"

"Sure."

"Not me," I said. I took the plate and hunkered down against the wall.

"Hey," he said after a time. "Take it easy. We've all had chow. No one's going to snatch it away from you. Slow down!"

I ate even faster than before. I was almost finished when I threw it all up. Then for some reason my head hit the edge of the stool. I dropped the plate and spoon and slumped there. I felt real bad.

Lone came over and looked at me. "Sorry, kid," he said. "Clean up, will you, Janie?"

Right in front of my eyes, the mess on the floor disappeared. I didn't care about that or anything else just then. I felt the man's hand on the side of my neck. Then he tousled my hair.

"Beanie, get him a blanket. Let's all go to sleep. He ought to rest a while."

I felt the blanket go around me, and I think I was asleep before he put me down.

I don't know how much later it was when I woke up. I didn't know where I was and that scared me. I raised my head and saw the dull glow of the embers in the fireplace. Lone was stretched out on it in his clothes. Janie's easel stood in the reddish blackness like some great preying insect. I saw the baby's head pop up out of the bassinet, but I couldn't tell whether he was looking straight at me or away. Janie was lying on the floor near the door and the twins were on the old table. Nothing moved except the baby's head, bobbing a little.

I got to my feet and looked around the room. Just a room, only the one door. I tiptoed toward it. When I passed Janie, she opened her eyes.

"What's the matter?" she whispered.

"None of your business," I told her. I went to the door as if I didn't care, but I watched her. She didn't do anything. The door was as solid tight closed as when I'd tried it before.

I went back to Janie. She just looked up at me. She wasn't scared. I told her, "I got to go to the john."

"Oh," she said. "Why'n't you say so?"

Suddenly I grunted and grabbed my guts. The feeling I had I can't begin to talk about. I acted as if it was a pain, but it wasn't. It was like nothing else that ever happened to me before.

"Okay," Janie said. "Go back to bed."

"But I got to—"

"You got to what?"

"Nothing." It was true. I didn't have to go no place.

"Next time tell me right away. I don't mind."

I didn't say anything. I went back to my blanket.

"That's all?" said Stern. I lay on the couch and looked up at the gray ceiling. He asked, "How old are you?"

"Fifteen," I said dreamily. He waited until, for me, the gray ceiling acquired walls and a floor, a rug and lamps and a desk and a chair with Stern in it. I sat up and held my head a second, and then I looked at him. He was fooling with his pipe and looking at me. "What did you do to me?"

"I told you. I don't do anything here. You do it."

"You hypnotized me."

"I did not." His voice was quiet, but he really meant it.

"What was all that, then? It was . . . it was like it was happening for real all over again."

"Feel anything?"

"Everything." I shuddered. "*Every* damn thing. What was it?"

"Anyone doing it feels better afterward. You can go over it all again now any time you want to, and every time you do, the hurt in it will be less. You'll see."

It was the first thing to amaze me in years. I chewed on it and then asked, "If I did it by myself, how come it never happened before?"

"It needs someone to listen."

"Listen? Was I talking?"

"A blue streak."

"Everything that happened?"

"How can I know? I wasn't there. You were."

"You don't believe it happened, do you? Those disappearing kids and the footstool and all?"

He shrugged. "I'm not in the business of believing or not believing. Was it real to you?"

"Oh, hell, yes!"

"Well, then, that's all that matters. Is that where you live, with those people?"

I bit off a fingernail that had been bothering me. "Not for a long time. Not since Baby was three." I looked at him. "You remind me of Lone."

"Why?"

"I don't know. No, you don't," I added suddenly. "I don't know what made me say that." I lay down abruptly.

The ceiling was gray and the lamps were dim. I heard the pipestem click against his teeth. I lay there for a long time.

"Nothing happens," I told him.

"What did you expect to happen?"

"Like before."

"There's something there that wants out. Just let it come."

It was as if there was a revolving drum in my head, and on it were photographed the places and things and people I was after. And it was as if the drum was spinning very fast, so fast I couldn't tell one picture from another. I made it stop, and it stopped at a blank segment. I spun it again, and stopped it again.

"Nothing happens," I said.

"Baby is three," he repeated.

"Oh," I said. "That." I closed my eyes.

That might be it. Might, sight, night, light. I might have the sight of a light in the night. Maybe the baby. Maybe the sight of the baby at night because of the light . . .

There was night after night when I lay on that blanket, and a lot of nights I didn't. Something was going on all the time in Lone's house. Sometimes I slept in the daytime. I guess the only time everybody slept at once was when someone was sick, like me the first time I arrived there. It was always sort of dark in the room, the same night and day, the fire going, the two old bulbs *hanging* yellow by their wires from the battery. When they got too dim, Janie fixed the battery and they got bright again.

Janie did everything that needed doing, whatever no one else felt like doing. Everybody else did things, too. Lone was out a lot. Sometimes he used the twins to help him, but you never missed them, because they'd be here and gone and back again *bing!* like that. And Baby, he just stayed in his bassinet.

I did things myself. I cut wood for the fire and I put up more shelves, and then I'd go swimming with Janie and the twins sometimes. And I talked to Lone. I didn't do a thing that the others couldn't do, but they all did things I couldn't do. I was mad, mad all the time about that. But I wouldn't of known what to do with myself if I wasn't mad all the time about something or other. It didn't keep us from bleshing. Bleshing, that was Janie's word. She said Baby told

353

it to her. She said it meant everyone all together being something, even if they all did different things. Two arms, two legs, one body, one head, all working together, although a head can't walk and arms can't think. Lone said maybe it was a mixture of "blending" and "meshing," but I don't think he believed that himself. It was a lot more than that.

Baby talked all the time. He was like a broadcasting station that runs twenty-four hours a day, and you can get what it's sending any time you tune in, but it'll keep sending whether you tune in or not. When I say he talked, I don't mean exactly that. He semaphored mostly. You'd think those wandering, vague movements of his hands and arms and legs and head were meaningless, but they weren't. It was semaphore, only instead of a symbol for a sound, or such like, the movements were whole thoughts.

I mean spread the left hand and shake the right high up, and thump with the left heel, and it means, "Anyone who thinks a starling is a pest just don't know anything about how a starling thinks" or something like that.

Lone couldn't read the stuff and neither could I. The twins could, but they didn't give a damn. Janie used to watch him all the time. He always knew what you meant if you wanted to ask him something, and he'd tell Janie and she'd say what it was. Part of it, anyway. Nobody could get it all, not even Janie. Lone once told me that all babies know that semaphore. But when nobody receives it, they quit doing it and pretty soon they forget. They *almost* forget. There's always some left. That's why certain gestures are funny the world over, and certain others make you mad. But like everything else Lone said, I don't know whether he believed it or not.

All I know is Janie would sit there and paint her pictures and watch Baby, and sometimes she'd bust out laughing, and sometimes she'd get the twins and make them watch and they'd laugh, too, or they'd wait till he was finished what he was saying and then they'd creep off to a corner and whisper to each other about it. Baby never grew any. Janie did, and the twins, and so did I, but not Baby. He just lay there.

Janie kept his stomach full and cleaned him up every two or three days. He didn't cry and he didn't make any trouble. No one ever went near him.

Janie showed every picture she painted to Baby, before she cleaned the boards and painted new ones. She had to clean them because she only had three of them. It was a good thing, too, because I'd hate to think what that place would of been like if she'd kept them all; she did four or five a day. Lone and the twins were kept hopping getting turpentine for her. She could shift the paints back into the little pots on her easel without any trouble, just by looking at the pictures one color at a time, but turps was something else again. She told me that Baby remembered all her pictures and that's why she didn't have to keep them. They were all pictures of machines and gear-trains and mechanical linkages and what looked like electric circuits and things like that. I never thought too much about them.

I went out with Lone to get some turpentine and a couple of picnic hams, one time. We went through the woods to the railroad track and down a couple of miles to where we could see the glow of a town. Then the woods again, and some alleys, and a back street.

Lone was like always, walking along, thinking, thinking.

We came to a hardware store and he went up and looked at the lock and came back to where I was waiting, shaking his head. Then we found a general store. Lone grunted and we went and stood in the shadows by the door. I looked in.

All of a sudden, Beanie was in there, naked like she always was when she traveled like that. She came and opened the door from the inside. We went in and Lone closed it and locked it.

"Get along home, Beanie," he said, "before you catch your death."

She grinned at me and said, "Ho-ho," and disappeared.

We found a pair of fine hams and a two-gallon can of turpentine. I took a bright yellow ballpoint pen and Lone cuffed me and made me put it back.

"We only take what we need," he told me.

After we left, Beanie came back and locked the door and went home again. I only went with Lone a few times, when he had more to get than he could carry easily.

I was there about three years. That's all I can remember about it. Lone was there or he was out, and you could hardly tell the difference. The twins were with each other most of the time. I got to like Janie a lot, but we never talked much. Baby talked all the time, only I don't know what about.

We were all busy and we bleshed.

I sat up on the couch suddenly.

Stern said, "What's the matter?"

"Nothing's the matter. This isn't getting me any place."

"You said that when you'd barely started. Do you think you've accomplished anything since then?"

"Oh, yeah, but—"

"Then how can you be sure you're right this time?" When I didn't say anything, he asked me, "Didn't you like this last stretch?"

I said angrily, "I didn't like or not like. It didn't mean nothing. It was just—just talk."

"So what was the difference between this last session and what happened before?"

"My gosh, plenty! The first one, I felt everything. It was all really happening to me. But this time—nothing."

"Why do you suppose that was?"

"I don't know. You tell me."

"Suppose," he said thoughtfully, "that there was some episode so unpleasant to you that you wouldn't dare relive it."

"Unpleasant? You think freezing to death isn't unpleasant?"

"There are all kinds of unpleasantness. Sometimes the very thing you're looking for—the thing that'll clear up your trouble—is so revolting to you that you won't go near it. Or you try to hide it. Wait," he said suddenly, "maybe 'revolting' and 'unpleasant' are inaccurate words to use. It might be something very desirable to you. It's just that you don't want to get straightened out."

"I *want* to get straightened out."

He waited as if he had to clear something up in his mind, and then said, "There's something in that 'Baby is three' phrase that bounces you away. Why is that?"

356

"Damn if I know."

"Who said it?"

"I dunno ... uh ..."

He grinned. "Uh?"

I grinned back at him. "I said it."

"Okay. When?"

I quit grinning. He leaned forward, then got up.

"What's the matter?" I asked.

"I didn't think anyone could be that mad." I didn't say anything. He went over to his desk. "You don't want to go on any more, do you?"

"No."

"Suppose I told you you want to quit because you're right on the very edge of finding out what you want to know?"

"Why don't you tell me and see what I do?"

He just shook his head. "I'm not telling you anything. Go on, leave if you want to. I'll give you back your change."

"How many people quit just when they're on top of the answer?"

"Quite a few."

"Well, I ain't going to." I lay down.

He didn't laugh and he didn't say, "Good," and he didn't make any fuss about it. He just picked up his phone and said, "Cancel everything for this afternoon," and went back to his chair, up there out of my sight.

It was very quiet in there. He had the place soundproofed.

I said, "Why do you suppose Lone let me live there so long when I couldn't do any of the things that the other kids could?"

"Maybe you could."

"Oh, no," I said positively. "I used to try. I was strong for a kid my age and I knew how to keep my mouth shut, but aside from those two things I don't think I was any different from any kid. I don't think I'm any different right now, except for what difference there might be from living with Lone and his bunch."

"Has this anything to do with 'Baby is three'?"

I looked up at the gray ceiling. "Baby is three. Baby is three. I went up to a big house with a winding drive that ran under a sort of theater-marquee thing. Baby is three. Baby . . ."

"How old are you?"

"Thirty-three," I said, and the next thing you know I was up off that couch like it was hot, and heading for the door.

"Don't be foolish," Stern said. "Want me to waste a whole afternoon?"

"What's that to me? I'm paying for it."

"All right, it's up to you."

I went back. "I don't like any part of this," I said.

"Good. We're getting warm then."

"What made me say 'Thirty-three'? I ain't thirty-three. I'm fifteen. And another thing. . . ."

"Yes?"

"It's about that 'Baby is three.' It's me saying it, all right. But when I think about it—it's not my voice."

"Like thirty-three's not your age?"

"Yeah," I whispered.

"Gerry," he said warmly, "there's nothing to be afraid of."

I realized I was breathing too hard. I pulled myself together. I said, "I don't like remembering saying things in somebody else's voice."

"Look," he told me. "This head-shrinking business, as you called it a while back, isn't what most people think. When I go with you into the world of your mind—or when you go yourself, for that matter—what we find isn't so very different from the so-called real world. It seems so at first, because the patient comes out with all sorts of fantasies and irrationalities and weird experiences. But everyone lives in that kind of world. When one of the ancients coined the phrase 'truth is stranger than fiction,' he was talking about that.

"Everywhere we go, everything we do, we're surrounded by symbols, by things so familiar we don't ever look at them or don't see them if we do look. If anyone ever could report to you exactly what he saw and thought while walking ten feet down the street, you'd get the most twisted, clouded, partial picture you ever ran across. And nobody ever looks at what's around him with any kind of

attention until he gets into a place like this. The fact that he's looking at past events doesn't matter; what counts is that he's seeing
clearer than he ever could before, just because, for once, he's trying.

"Now—about this 'thirty-three' business. I don't think a man
could get a nastier shock than to find he has someone else's memories. The ego is too important to let slide that way. But consider: all
your thinking is done in code and you have the key to only about a
tenth of it. So you run into a stretch of code which is abhorrent to
you. Can't you see that the only way you'll find the key to it is to
stop avoiding it?"

"You mean I'd started to remember with . . . with somebody else's
mind?"

"It looked like that to you for a while, which means something.
Let's try to find out what."

"All right." I felt sick. I felt tired. And I suddenly realized that
being sick and being tired was a way of trying to get out of it.

"Baby is three," he said.

Baby is maybe. Me, three, thirty-three, me you Kew you.

"Kew!" I yelled. Stern didn't say anything. "Look I don't know
why, but I think I know how to get to this, and this isn't the way.
Do you mind if I try something else?"

"You're the doctor," he said.

I had to laugh. Then I closed my eyes.

There, through the edges of the hedges, the ledges and wedges of
windows were shouldering up to the sky. The lawns were sprayed-
on green, neat and clean, and all the flowers looked as if they were
afraid to let their petals break and be untidy.

I walked up the drive in my shoes. I'd had to wear shoes and my
feet couldn't breathe. I didn't want to go to the house, but I had to.

I went up the steps between the big white columns and looked
at the door. I wished I could see through it, but it was too white and
thick. There was a window the shape of a fan over it, too high up,
though, and a window on each side of it, but they were all crudded
up with colored glass. I hit on the door with my hand and left dirt
on it.

Nothing happened, so I hit it again. It got snatched open and a tall, thin colored woman stood there. "What you want?"

I said I had to see Miss Kew.

"Well, Miss Kew don't want to see the likes of you," she said. She talked too loud. "You got a dirty face."

I started to get mad then. I was already pretty sore about having to come here, walking around near people in the daytime and all. I said, "My face ain't got nothin' to with it. Where's Miss Kew? Go on, find her for me."

She gasped. "You can't speak to me like that!"

I said, "I didn't want to speak to you like any way. Let me in." I started wishing for Janie. Janie could of moved her. But I had to handle it by myself. I wasn't doing so hot, either. She slammed the door before I could so much as curse at her.

So I started kicking on the door. For that, shoes are great. After a while, she snatched the door open again so sudden I almost went on my can. She had a broom with her. She screamed at me, "You get away from here, you trash, or I'll call the police!" She pushed me and I fell.

I got up off the porch floor and went for her. She stepped back and whupped me one with the broom as I went past, but anyhow I was inside now. The woman was making little shrieking noises and coming for me. I took the broom away from her and then somebody said, "Miriam!" in a voice like a grown goose.

I froze and the woman went into hysterics. "Oh, Miss Kew, look out! He'll kill us all. Get the police. Get the—"

"Miriam!" came the honk, and Miriam dried up.

There at the top of the stairs was this prune-faced woman with a dress on that had lace on it. She looked a lot older than she was, maybe because she held her mouth so tight. I guess she was about thirty-three—*thirty-three*. She had mean eyes and a small nose.

I asked, "Are you Miss Kew?"

"I am. What is the meaning of this invasion?"

"I got to talk to you, Miss Kew."

"Don't say, 'got to.' Stand up straight and speak out."

The maid said, "I'll get the police."

Miss Kew turned on her. "There's time enough for that, Miriam. Now, you dirty little boy, what do you want?"

"I got to speak to you by yourself," I told her.

"Don't you let him do it, Miss Kew," cried the maid.

"Be quiet, Miriam. Little boy, I told you not to say 'got to.' You may say whatever you have to say in front of Miriam."

"Like hell." They both gasped. I said, "Lone told me not to."

"Miss Kew, are you goin' to let him—"

"Be quiet, Miriam! Young man, will you keep a civil—" Then her eyes popped up real round. *"Who* did you say ..."

"Lone said so."

"Lone." She stood there on the stairs looking at her hands. Then she said, "Miriam, that will be all." And you wouldn't know it was the same woman, the way she said it.

The maid opened her mouth, but Miss Kew stuck out a finger that might as well of had a riflesight on the end of it. The maid beat it.

"Hey," I said, "here's your broom." I was just going to throw it, but Miss Kew got to me and took it out of my hand.

"In there," she said.

She made me go ahead of her into a room as big as our swimming hole. It had books all over and leather on top of the tables, with gold flowers drawn into the corners.

She pointed to a chair. "Sit there. No, wait a moment." She went to the fireplace and got a newspaper out of a box and brought it over and unfolded it on the seat of the chair. "Now sit down."

I sat on the paper and she dragged up another chair, but didn't put no paper on it.

"What is it? Where is Lone?"

"He died," I said.

She pulled in her breath and went white. She stared at me until her eyes started to water.

"You sick?" I asked her. "Go ahead, throw up. It'll make you feel better."

"Dead? Lone is dead?"

"Yeah. There was a flash flood last week and when he went out the next night in that big wind, he walked under a old oak tree that got gulled under by the flood. The tree come down on him."

"*Came* down on him," she whispered. "Oh, no . . . it's not true."

"It's true all right. We planted him this morning. We couldn't keep him around no more. He was beginning to st—"

"Stop!" She covered her face with her hands.

"What's the matter?"

"I'll be all right in a moment," she said in a low voice. She went and stood in front of the fireplace with her back to me. I took off one of my shoes while I was waiting for her to come back. But instead she talked from where she was. "Are you Lone's little boy?"

"Yeah. He told me to come to you."

"Oh, my dear child!" She came running back and I thought for a second she was going to pick me up or something, but she stopped short and wrinkled up her nose a little bit. "Wh-what's your name?"

"Gerry," I told her.

"Well, Gerry, how would you like to live with me in this nice big house and—and have new clean clothes—and everything?"

"Well, that's the whole idea. Lone told me to come to you. He said you got more dough than you know what to do with, and he said you owed him a favor."

"A favor?" That seemed to bother her.

"Well," I tried to tell her, "he said he done something for you once and you said some day you'd pay him back for it if you ever could. This is it."

"What did he tell you about that?" She'd got her honk back by then.

"Not a damn thing."

"Please don't use that word," she said, with her eyes closed. Then she opened them and nodded her head. "I promised and I'll do it. You can live here from now on. If-if you want to."

"That's got nothin' to do with it. Lone *told* me to."

"You'll be happy here," she said. She gave me an up-and-down. "I'll see to that."

"Okay. Shall I go get the other kids?"

"*Other* kids—children?"

"Yeah. This ain't for just me. For all of us—the whole gang."

"Don't say 'ain't.'" She leaned back in her chair, took out a silly little handkerchief and dabbed her lips with it, looking at me the whole time. "Now tell me about these—these other children."

"Well, there's Janie, she's eleven like me. And Bonnie and Beanie are eight, they're twins, and Baby. Baby is three."

"Baby is three," she said.

I screamed. Stern was kneeling beside the couch in a flash, holding his palms against my cheeks to hold my head still; I'd been whipping it back and forth.

"Good boy," he said. "You found it. You haven't found out *what* it is, but now you know *where* it is."

"But for sure," I said hoarsely. "Got water?"

He poured me some water out of a thermos flask. It was so cold it hurt. I lay back and rested, like I'd climbed a cliff. I said, "I can't take anything like that again."

"You want to call it quits for today?"

"What about you?"

"I'll go on as long as you want me to."

I thought about it. "I'd like to go on, but I don't want no thumping around. Not for a while yet."

"If you want another of those inaccurate analogies," Stern said, "psychiatry is like a road map. There are always a lot of different ways to get from one place to another place."

"I'll go around by the long way," I told him. "The eight-lane highway. Not that track over the hill. My clutch is slipping. Where do I turn off?"

He chuckled. I liked the sound of it. "Just past that gravel driveway."

"I been there. There's a bridge washed out."

"You've been on this whole road before," he told me. "Start at the other side of the bridge."

"I never thought of that. I figured I had to do the whole thing, every inch."

"Maybe you won't have to, maybe you will, but the bridge will be easy to cross when you've covered everything else. Maybe there's nothing of value on the bridge and maybe there is, but you can't get near it till you've looked everywhere else."

"Let's go." I was real eager, somehow.

"Mind a suggestion?"

"No."

"Just talk," he said. "Don't try to get too far into what you're saying. That first stretch, when you were eight—you really lived it. The second one, all about the kids, you just talked about. Then, the visit when you were eleven, you felt that. Now just talk again."

"All right."

He waited, then said quietly, "In the library. You told her about the kids."

I told her about . . . and then she said . . . and something happened, and I screamed. She comforted me and I cussed at her.

But we're not thinking about that now. We're going on.

In the library. The leather, the table, and whether I'm able to do with Miss Kew what Lone said.

What Lone said was, "There's a woman lives up on the top of the hill in the Heights section, name of Kew. She'll have to take care of you. You got to get her to do that. Do everything she tells you, only stay together. Don't you ever let any one of you get away from the others, hear? Aside from that, just you keep Miss Kew happy and she'll keep you happy. Now you do what I say." That's what Lone said. Between every word there was a link like steel cable, and the whole thing made something that couldn't be broken. Not by me it couldn't.

Miss Kew said, "Where are your sisters and the baby?"

"I'll bring 'em."

"Is it near here?"

"Near enough." She didn't say anything to that, so I got up. "I'll be back soon."

"Wait," she said. "I—really, I haven't had time to think. I mean—I've got to get things ready, you know."

I said, "You don't need to think and you are ready. So long."

From the door I heard her saying, louder and louder as I walked away, "Young man, if you're to live in this house, you'll learn to be a good deal better mannered—" and a lot more of the same.

I yelled back at her, "Okay, *okay!*" and went out.

The sun was warm and the sky was good, and pretty soon I got back to Lone's house. The fire was out and Baby stunk. Janie had knocked over her easel and was sitting on the floor by the door with her head in her hands. Bonnie and Beanie were on a stool with their arms around each other, pulled up together as close as they could get, as if was cold in there, although it wasn't.

I hit Janie in the arm to snap her out of it. She raised her head. She had gray eyes—or maybe it was more a kind of green—but now they had a funny look about them, like water in a glass that had some milk left in the bottom of it.

I said, "What's the matter around here?"

"What's the matter with what?" she wanted to know.

"All of yez," I said.

She said, "We don't give a damn, that's all."

"Well, all right," I said, "but we got to do what Lone said. Come on."

"No." I looked at the twins. They turned their backs on me. Janie said, "They're hungry."

"Well, why not give 'em something?"

She just shrugged. I sat down. What did Lone have to go get himself squashed for?

"We can't blesh no more," said Janie. It seemed to explain everything.

"Look," I said, "I've got to be Lone now."

Janie thought about that, and Baby kicked his feet. Janie looked at him. "You can't," she said.

"I know where to get the heavy food and the turpentine," I said. "I can find that springy moss to stuff in the logs, and cut wood, and all."

But I couldn't call Bonnie and Beanie from miles away to unlock doors. I couldn't just say a word to Janie and make her get water and blow up the fire and fix the battery. I couldn't make us blesh.

We all stayed like that for a long time. Then I heard the bassinet creak. I looked up. Janie was staring into it.

"All right," she said. "Let's go."

"Who says so?"

"Baby."

"Who's running things now?" I said, mad. "Me or Baby?"

"Baby," Janie said.

I got up and went over to bust her one in the mouth, and then I stopped. If Baby could make them do what Lone wanted, then it would get done. If I started pushing them all around, it wouldn't. So I didn't say anything. Janie got up and walked out the door. The twins watched her go. Then Bonnie disappeared. Beanie picked up Bonnie's clothes and walked out. I got Baby out of the bassinet and draped him over my shoulders.

It was better when we were all outside. It was getting late in the day and the air was warm. The twins flitted in and out of the trees like a couple of flying squirrels, and Janie and I walked along like we were going swimming or something. Baby started to kick, and Janie looked at him a while and got him fed, and he was quiet again.

When we came close to town, I wanted to get everybody close together, but I was afraid to say anything. Baby must of said it instead. The twins came back to us and Janie gave them their clothes and they walked ahead of us, good as you please. I don't know how Baby did it. They sure hated to travel that way.

We didn't have no trouble except one guy we met on the street near Miss Kew's place. He stopped in his tracks and gaped at us, and Janie looked at him and made his hat go so far down over his eyes that he like to pull his neck apart getting it back up again.

What do you know, when we got to the house somebody had washed off all the dirt I'd put on the door. I had one hand on Baby's arm and one on his ankle and him draped over my neck, so I kicked the door and left some more dirt.

"There's a woman here name of Miriam," I told Janie. "She says anything, tell her to go to hell."

The door opened and there was Miriam. She took one look and

366

jumped back six feet. We all trailed inside. Miriam got her wind and screamed, "Miss Kew! Miss Kew!"

"Go to hell," said Janie, and looked at me. I didn't know what to do. It was the first time Janie ever did anything I told her to.

Miss Kew came down the stairs. She was wearing a different dress, but it was just as stupid and had just as much lace. She opened her mouth and nothing came out, so she just left it open until something happened. Finally she said, "Dear gentle Lord preserve us!"

The twins lined up and gawked at her. Miriam sidled over to the wall and sort of slid along it, keeping away from us, until she could get to the door and close it. She said, "Miss Kew, if those are the children you said were going to live here, I quit."

Janie said, "Go to hell."

Just then, Bonnie squatted down on the rug. Miriam squawked and jumped at her. She grabbed hold of Bonnie's arm and went to snatch her up. Bonnie disappeared, leaving Miriam with one small dress and damnedest expression on her face. Beanie grinned enough to split her head in two and started to wave like mad. I looked where she was waving, and there was Bonnie, naked as a jaybird, up on the banister at the top of the stairs.

Miss Kew turned around and saw her and sat down plump on the steps. Miriam went down, too, like she'd been slugged. Beanie picked up Bonnie's dress and walked up the steps past Miss Kew and handed it over. Bonnie put it on. Miss Kew sort of lolled around and looked up. Bonnie and Beanie came back down the stairs hand in hand to where I was. Then they lined up and gaped at Miss Kew.

"What's the matter with her?" Janie asked me.

"She gets sick every once in a while."

"Let's go back home."

"No," I told her.

Miss Kew grabbed the banister and pulled herself up. She stood there hanging on to it for a while with her eyes closed. All of a sudden she stiffened herself. She looked about four inches taller. She came marching over to us.

"Gerard," she honked.

I think she was going to say something different. But she sort of checked herself and pointed. "What in heaven's name is *that?*" And she aimed her finger at me.

I didn't get it right away, so I turned around to look behind me. "What?"

"That! That!"

"Oh!" I said. "That's Baby."

I slung him down off my back and held him up for her to look at. She made a sort of moaning noise and jumped over and took him away from me. She held him out in front of her and moaned again and called him a poor little thing, and ran and put him down on a long bench thing with cushions under the colored-glass window. She bent over him and put her knuckle in her mouth and bit on it and moaned some more. Then she turned to me.

"How long has he been like this?"

I looked at Jane and she looked at me. I said, "He's always been like he is."

She made a sort of cough and ran to where Miriam was lying flaked on the floor. She slapped Miriam's face a couple of times back and forth. Miriam sat up and looked us over. She closed her eyes and shivered and sort of climbed up Miss Kew hand over hand until she was on her feet.

"Pull yourself together," said Miss Kew between her teeth. "Get a basin with some hot water and soap. Washcloth. Towels. Hurry!" She gave Miriam a big push. Miriam staggered and grabbed at the wall, and then ran out.

Miss Kew went back to Baby and hung over him, titch-titching with her lips all tight.

"Don't mess with him," I said. "There's nothin' wrong with him. We're hungry."

She gave me a look like I'd punched her. "Don't speak to me!"

"Look," I said, "we don't like this any more'n you do. If Lone hadn't told us to, we wouldn't never have come. We were doing all right where we were."

"Don't say 'wouldn't never,'" said Miss Kew. She looked at all

of us, one by one. Then she took that silly little hunk of handkerchief and pushed it against her mouth.

"See?" I said to Janie. "All the time gettin' sick."

"Ho-ho," said Bonnie.

Miss Kew gave her a long look. "Gerard," she said in a choked sort
of voice, "I understood you to say that these children were your sisters."

"Well?"

She looked at me as if I was real stupid. "We don't have little colored girls for sisters, Gerard."

Janie said, *"We* do."

Miss Kew walked up and back, real fast. "We have a great deal
to do," she said, talking to herself.

Miriam came in with a big oval pan and towels and stuff on her
arm. She put it down on the bench thing and Miss Kew stuck the
back of her hand in the water, then picked up Baby and dunked him
right in it. Baby started to kick.

I stepped forward and said, "Wait a minute. Hold on now. What
do you think you're doing?"

Janie said, "Shut up, Gerry. He says it's all right."

"All right? She'll drown him."

"No, she won't. Just shut up."

Working up a froth with the soap, Miss Kew smeared it on Baby
and turned him over a couple of times and scrubbed at his head and
like to smothered him in a big white towel. Miriam stood gawking
while Miss Kew lashed up a dishcloth around him so it come out
pants. When she was done, you wouldn't of known it was the same
baby. And by the time Miss Kew finished with the job, she seemed
to have a better hold on herself. She was breathing hard and her
mouth was even tighter. She held out the baby to Miriam.

"Take this poor thing," she said, "and put him—"

But Miriam backed away. "I'm sorry, Miss Kew, but I am leaving here and I don't care."

Miss Kew got her honk out. "You can't leave me in a predicament
like this! These children need help. Can't you see that for yourself?"

Miriam looked me and Janie over. She was trembling. "You ain't safe, Miss Kew. They ain't just dirty. They're crazy!"

"They're victims of neglect, and probably no worse than you or I would be if we'd been neglected. And don't say 'ain't.' Gerard!"

"What?"

"Don't say—oh, dear, we have so much to do. Gerard, if you and your—these other children are going to live here, you shall have to make a great many changes. You cannot live under this roof and behave as you have so far. Do you understand that?"

"Oh, sure. Lone said we was to do whatever you say and keep you happy."

"Will you do whatever I say?"

"That's what I just said, isn't it?"

"Gerard, you shall have to learn not to speak to me in that tone. Now, young man, if I told you to do what Miriam says, too, would you do it?"

I said to Jane, "What about that?"

"I'll ask Baby." Janie looked at Baby and Baby wobbled his hands and drooled some. She said, "It's okay."

Miss Kew said, "Gerard, I asked you a question."

"Keep your pants on," I said. "I got find out, don't I? Yes, if that's what you want, we'll listen to Miriam, too."

Miss Kew turned to Miriam. "You hear that, Miriam?"

Miriam looked at Miss Kew and at us and shook her head. Then she held out her hands a bit to Bonnie and Beanie.

They went right to her. Each one took hold of a hand. They looked up at her and grinned. They were probably planning some sort of hellishness, but I guess they looked sort of cute. Miriam's mouth twitched and I thought for a second she was going to look human. She said, "All right, Miss Kew."

Miss Kew walked over and handed her the baby and she started upstairs with him. Miss Kew herded us along after Miriam. We all went upstairs.

They went to work on us then and for three years they never stopped.

"That was hell," I said to Stern.

"They had their work cut out."

"Yeah, I s'pose they did. So did we. Look, we were going to do exactly what Lone said. Nothing on earth could of stopped us from doing it. We were tied and bound to doing every last little thing Miss Kew said to do. But she and Miriam never seemed to understand that. I guess they felt they had to push every inch of the way. All they had to do was make us understand what they wanted, and we'd of done it. That's okay when it's something like telling me not to climb into bed with Janie.

"Miss Kew raised holy hell over that. You'd of thought I'd robbed the Crown Jewels, the way she acted. But when it's something like, 'You must behave like little ladies and gentlemen,' it just doesn't mean a thing. And two out of three orders she gave us were like that. 'Ah-ah!' she'd say. 'Language, language!' For the longest time I didn't dig that at all. I finally asked her what the hell she meant, and then she finally come out with it. But you see what I mean."

"I certainly do," Stern said. "Did it get easier as time went on?"

"We only had real trouble twice, once about the twins and once about Baby. That one was real bad."

"What happened?"

"About the twins? Well, when we'd been there about a week or so we began to notice something that sort of stunk. Janie and me, I mean. We began to notice that we almost never got to see Bonnie and Beanie. It was like that house was two houses, one part for Miss Kew and Janie and me, and the other part for Miriam and the twins. I guess we'd have noticed it sooner if things hadn't been such a hassle at first, getting into new clothes and making us sleep all the time at night, and all that. But here was the thing: We'd all get turned out in the side yard to play, and then along comes lunch, and the twins got herded off to eat with Miriam while we ate with Miss Kew. So Janie said, 'Why don't the twins eat with us?'

" 'Miriam's taking care of them, dear,' Miss Kew says.

"Janie looked at her with those eyes. 'I know that. Let 'em eat here and I'll take of 'em.'

"Miss Kew's mouth got all tight again and she said, 'They're little colored girls, Jane. Now eat your lunch.'

"But that didn't explain anything to Jane or me, either. I said, 'I want 'em to eat with us. Lone said we should stay together.'

" 'But you *are* together,' she says. 'We all live in the same house. We all eat the same food. Now let us not discuss the matter.'

"I looked at Janie and she looked at me, and she said, 'So why can't we all do this livin' and eatin' right here?'

"Miss Kew put her fork down and looked hard. 'I have explained it to you and I have said that there will be no further discussion.'

"Well, I thought that was real nowhere. So I just rocked back my head and bellowed, 'Bonnie! Beanie!' And *bing,* there they were.

"So all hell broke loose. Miss Kew ordered them out and they wouldn't go, and Miriam come steaming in with their clothes, and she couldn't catch them, and Miss Kew got to honking at them and finally at me. She said this was too much. Well, maybe she had had a hard week, but so had we. So Miss Kew ordered us to leave.

"I went and got Baby and started out, and along came Janie and the twins. Miss Kew waited till we were out the door and next thing you know she ran out after us. She passed us and got in front of me and made me stop. So we all stopped.

" 'Is this how you follow Lone's wishes?' she asked.

"I told her yes. She said she understood Lone wanted us to stay with her. And I said, 'Yeah, but he wanted us to stay together more.'

"She said come back in, we'd have a talk. Jane asked Baby and Baby said okay, so we went back. We had a compromise. We didn't eat in the dining room no more. There was a side porch, a sort of verandah thing with glass windows, with a door to the dining room and a door to the kitchen, and we all ate out there after that. Miss Kew ate by herself.

"But something funny happened because of that whole cockeyed hassle."

"What was that?" Stern asked me.

I laughed. "Miriam. She looked and sounded like always, but she started slipping us cookies between meals. You know, it took me years to figure out what all that was about. I mean it. From what I've learned about people, there seems to be two armies fightin' about race. One's fightin' to keep 'em apart, and one's fightin' to get 'em together. But I don't see why both sides are so *worried* about it! Why don't they just forget it?"

"They can't. You see, Gerry, it's necessary for people to believe they are superior in some fashion. You and Lone and the kids—you were a pretty tight unit. Didn't you feel you were a little better than all of the rest of the world?"

"Better? How could we be better?"

"Different, then."

"Well, I suppose so, but we didn't think about it. Different, yes. Better, no."

"You're a unique case," Stern said. "Now go on and tell me about the other trouble you had. About Baby."

"Baby. Yeah. Well, that was a couple of months after we moved to Miss Kew's. Things were already getting real smooth, even then. We'd learned all the 'yes, ma'am, no, ma'am' routines by then and she'd got us catching up with school—regular periods morning and afternoon, five days a week. Jane had long ago quit taking care of Baby, and the twins walked to wherever they went. That was funny. They could pop from one place to another right in front of Miss Kew's eyes and she wouldn't believe what she saw. She was too upset about them suddenly showing up bare. They quit doing it and she was happy about it. She was happy about a lot of things. It had been years since she'd seen anybody—years. She'd even had the meters put outside the house so no one would ever have to come in. But with us there, she began to liven up. She quit wearing those old-lady dresses and began to look halfway human. She ate with us sometimes, even.

"But one fine day I woke up feeling real weird. It was like somebody had stolen something from me when I was asleep, only I didn't know what. I crawled out of my window and along the ledge into Janie's room, which I wasn't supposed to do. She was in bed. I went and woke her up. I can still see her eyes, the way they opened a little slit, still asleep, and then popped up wide. I didn't have to tell her something was wrong. She knew, and she knew what it was.

" 'Baby's gone!' she said.

"We didn't care then who woke up. We pounded out of her room and down the hall and into the little room at the end where Baby slept. You wouldn't believe it. The fancy crib he had, and the white chest of drawers, and all that mess of rattles and so on, they were gone, and there was just a writing desk there. I mean it was as if Baby had never been there at all.

"We didn't say anything. We just spun around and busted into Miss Kew's bedroom. I'd never been in there but once and Jane only a few times. But forbidden or not, this was different. Miss Kew was in bed, with her hair braided. She was wide awake before we could get across the room. She pushed herself back and up until she was sitting against the headboard. She gave the two of us the cold eye.

" 'What is the meaning of this?' she wanted to know.

" 'Where's Baby?' I yelled at her.

" 'Gerard,' she says, 'there is no need to shout.'

"Jane was a real quiet kid, but she said, 'You better tell us where he is, Miss Kew,' and it would of scared you to look at her when she said it.

"So all of a sudden Miss Kew took off the stone face and held out her hands to us. 'Children,' she said, 'I'm sorry. I really am sorry. But I've just done what is best. I've sent Baby away. He's gone to live with some children like him. We could never make him really happy here. You know that.'

"Jane said, 'He never told us he wasn't happy.'

"Miss Kew brought out a hollow kind of laugh. 'As if he could talk, the poor little thing!'

" 'You better get him back here,' I said. 'You don't know what you're fooling with. I told you we wasn't ever to break up.'

"She was getting mad, but she held on to herself. 'I'll try explain it to you, dear,' she said. 'You and Jane here and even the twins are all normal, healthy children and you'll grow up to be fine men and women. But poor Baby's—different. He's not going to grow very much more, and he'll never walk and play like other children.'

" 'That doesn't matter,' Jane said. 'You had no call to send him away.'

"And I said, 'Yeah. You better bring him back, but quick.'

"Then she started to jump salty. 'Among the many things I have taught you is, I am sure, not to dictate to your elders. Now, then, you run along and get dressed for breakfast, and we'll say no more about this.'

"I told her, nice as I could, 'Miss Kew, you're going to wish you brought him back right now. But you're going to bring him back soon. Or else.'

"So then she got up out of her bed and ran us out of the room."

I was quiet a while, and Stern asked, "What happened?"

"Oh," I said, "she brought him back." I laughed suddenly. "I guess it's funny now, when you come to think of it. Nearly three months of us getting bossed around, and her ruling the roost, and then all of a sudden we lay down the law. We'd tried our best to be good according to her ideas, but, by God, that time she went too far. She got the treatment from the second she slammed her door on us. She had a big china pot under her bed, and it rose up in the air and smashed through her dresser mirror. Then one of the drawers in the dresser slid open and a glove come out of it and smacked her face.

"She went to jump back on the bed and a whole section of plaster fell off the ceiling onto the bed. The water turned on in her little bathroom and the plug went in, and just about the time it began to overflow, all her clothes fell of their hooks. She went to run out of the room, but the door was stuck, and when she yanked on the handle it opened real quick and she spread out on the floor. The door slammed shut again and more plaster come down on her. Then we went back in and stood looking at her. She was crying. I hadn't known till then that she could.

" 'You going to get Baby back here?' I asked her.

"She just lay there and cried. After a while she looked up at us. It was real pathetic. We helped her up and got her to a chair. She just looked at us for a while, and at the mirror, and at the busted ceiling, and then she whispered, 'What happened? What happened?'

" 'You took Baby away,' I said. 'That's what.'

"So she jumped up and said real low, real scared, but real strong: 'Something struck the house. An airplane. Perhaps there was an earthquake. We'll talk about Baby after breakfast.'

"I said, 'Give her more, Janie.'

"A big gob of water hit her on the face and chest and made her nightgown stick to her, which was the kind of thing that upset her most. Her braids stood straight up in the air, more and more, till they dragged her standing straight up. She opened her mouth to yell and the powder puff off the dresser rammed into it. She clawed it out.

" 'What are you doing? What are you doing?' she says, crying again.

"Janie just looked at her, and put her hands behind her, real smug. 'We haven't done anything,' she said.

"And I said, 'Not yet we haven't. You going to get Baby back?'

"And she screamed at us, 'Stop it! Stop it! Stop talking about that mongoloid idiot! It's no good to anyone, not even itself! How could I ever make believe it's mine?'

"I said, 'Get rats, Janie.'

"There was a scuttling sound along the baseboard. Miss Kew covered her face with her hands and sank down on the chair. 'Not rats,' she said. 'There are no rats here.' Then something squeaked and she went all to pieces. Did you ever see anyone really go to pieces?"

"Yes," Stern said.

"I was about as mad as I could get," I said, "but that was almost too much for me. Still, she shouldn't have sent Baby away. It took a couple of hours for her to get straightened out enough so she could use the phone, but we had Baby back before lunch time." I laughed.

"What's funny?"

"She never seemed able to rightly remember what had happened to her. About three weeks later I heard her talking to Miriam about it. She said it was the house settling suddenly. She said it was a good thing she'd sent Baby out for that medical checkup—the poor little thing might have been hurt. She really believed it, I think."

"She probably did. That's fairly common. We don't believe anything we don't want to believe."

"How much of this do you believe?" I asked him suddenly.

"I told you before—it doesn't matter. I don't want to believe or disbelieve it."

"You haven't asked me how much of it I believe."

"I don't have to. You'll make up your own mind about that."

"Are you a *good* psychotherapist?"

"I think so," he said. "Whom did you kill?"

The question caught me absolutely off guard. "Miss Kew," I said. Then I started to cuss and swear. "I didn't mean to tell you that."

"Don't worry about it," he said. "What did you do it for?"

"That's what I came here to find out."

"You must have really hated her."

I started to cry. Fifteen years old and crying like that!

He gave me time to get it all out. The first part of it came out in noises, grunts and squeaks that hurt my throat. Much more than you'd think came out when my nose started to run. And finally—words.

"Do you know where I came from? The earliest thing I can remember is a punch in the mouth. I can still see it coming, a fist as big as my head. Because I was crying. I been afraid to cry ever since. I was crying because I was hungry. Cold, maybe. Both. After that, big dormitories, and whoever could steal the most got the most. Get the hell kicked out of you if you're bad, get a big reward if you're good. Big reward: they let you alone. Try to live like that. Try to live so the biggest, most wonderful thing in the whole damn world is just to have 'em let you alone!

"So a spell with Lone and kids. Something wonderful: you belong. It never happened before. Two yellow bulbs and a fireplace and they light up the world. It's all there is and all there ever has to be.

"Then the big change: clean clothes, cooked food, five hours a day school; Columbus and King Arthur and a 1925 book on Civics that explains about septic tanks. Over it all a great big square-cut lump of ice, and you watch it melting and the corners curve, and you know it's because of you, Miss Kew ... hell, she had too much control over herself ever to slobber over us, but it was there, that feeling. Lone took care of us because it was part of the way he lived. Miss Kew took care of us, and none of it was the way she lived. It was something she wanted to do.

"She had a weird idea of 'right' and a wrong idea of 'wrong,' but she stuck to them, tried to make her ideas do us good. When she couldn't understand, she figured it was her own failure . . . and there was an almighty lot she didn't understand and never could. What went right was our success. What went wrong was her mistake. That last year, that was . . . oh, good."

"So?"

"So I killed her. Listen," I said. I felt like I had to talk fast. I wasn't short of time, but I had to get rid of it. "I'll tell you all I know about it. The one day before I killed her. I woke up in the morning and the sheets crackly clean under me, the sunlight coming in through white curtains and bright red-and-blue drapes. There's a closet full of my clothes—mine, you see; I never had anything that was really mine before—and downstairs Miriam clinking around with breakfast and the twins laughing. Laughing with *her*, mind you, not just with each other like they always did before.

"In the next room, Janie moving around, singing, and when I see her, I know her face will shine inside and out. I get up. There's *hot* hot water and the toothpaste bites my tongue. The clothes fit me and I go downstairs and they're all there and I'm glad to see them and they're glad to see me, and we no sooner get set around the table when Miss Kew comes down and everyone calls out to her at once.

"And the morning goes by like that, school with a recess, there in the big long living room. The twins with the ends of their tongues stuck out, drawing the alphabet instead of writing it, and then Janie, when it's time, painting a picture, a real picture of a cow with trees and a yellow fence that goes off into the distance. Here I am lost between the two parts of a quadratic equation, and Miss Kew bending close to help me, and I smell the sachet she has on her clothes. I hold up my head to smell it better, and far away I hear the shuffle and klunk of filled pots going on the stove back in the kitchen.

"And the afternoon goes by like that, more school and some study and boiling out into the yard, laughing. The twins chasing each other, running on their two feet to get where they want to go; Jane dappling the leaves in her picture, trying to get it just the way Miss Kew says it ought to be. And Baby, he's got a big play-pen. He don't move around much any more, he just watches and dribbles some, and gets packed full of food and kept as clean as a new sheet of tinfoil.

"And supper, and the evening, and Miss Kew reading to us, changing her voice every time someone else talks in the story, reading fast and whispery when it embarrasses her, but reading every word all the same.

"And I had to go and kill her. And that's all."

"You haven't said why," Stern said.

"What are you—stupid?" I yelled.

Stern didn't say anything. I turned on my belly on the couch and propped up my chin in my hands and looked at him. You never could tell what was going on with him, but I got the idea that he was puzzled.

"I said why," I told him.

"Not to me."

I suddenly understood that I was asking too much of him. I said slowly, "We all woke up at the same time. We all did what somebody else wanted. We lived through a day someone else's way, thinking someone else's thoughts, saying other people's words. Jane painted someone else's pictures. Baby didn't talk to anyone, and we were all happy with it. Now do you see?"

"Not yet."

"God!" I said. I thought for a while. "We didn't blesh."

"Blesh? Oh. But you didn't after Lone died, either."

"That was different. That was like a car running out of gas, but the car's there—there's nothing wrong with it. It's just waiting. But after Miss Kew got done with us, the car was taken all to pieces, see?"

It was his turn to think a while. Finally he said, "The mind makes us do funny things. Some of them seem completely reasonless, wrong, insane. But the cornerstone of the work we're doing is this: there's a chain of solid, unassailable logic in the things we do. Dig deep enough and you find cause and effect as clearly in this field as you do in any other. I said *logic,* mind; I didn't say 'correctness' or 'rightness' or 'justice' or anything of the sort. Logic and truth are two very different things, but they often look the same to the mind that's performing the logic.

"When that mind is submerged, working at cross-purposes with the surface mind, then you're all confused. Now in your case, I can see the thing you're pointing at—that in order to preserve or to rebuild that peculiar bond between you kids, you had to get rid of Miss Kew. But I don't see the logic. I don't see that regaining that 'bleshing' was worth destroying this new-found security which you admit was enjoyable."

I said, desperately, "Maybe it wasn't worth destroying it."

Stern leaned forward and pointed his pipe at me. "It *was* because it made you do what you did. After the fact, maybe things look different. But when you were moved to do it, the important thing was to destroy Miss Kew and regain this thing you'd had before. I don't see why and neither do you."

"How are we going to find out?"

"Well, let's get right to the most unpleasant part, if you're up to it."

I lay down. "I'm ready."

"All right. Tell me everything that happened just before you killed her."

I fumbled through that last day, trying to taste the food, hear the voices. A thing came and went and came again: it was the crisp feeling of the sheets. I thrust it away because it was at the beginning of that day, but it came back again, and I realized it was at the end, instead.

I said, "What I just told you, all that about the children doing things other people's way instead of their own, and Baby not talking, and everyone happy about it, and finally that I had to kill Miss Kew. It took a long time to get to that, and a long time to start doing it. I guess I lay in bed and thought for four hours before I got up again. It was dark and quiet. I went out of the room and down the hall and into Miss Kew's bedroom and killed her."

380

"How?"

"That's all there is!" I shouted, as loud as I could. Then I quieted down. "It was awful dark ... it still is. I don't know. I don't want to know. She did love us. I know she did. But I had to kill her."

"All right, all right," Stern said. "I guess there's no need to get too gruesome about this. You're—"

"What?"

"You're quite strong for your age, aren't you, Gerard?"

"I guess so. Strong enough, anyway."

"Yes," he said.

"I still don't see that logic you were talking about." I began to hammer on the couch with my fist, hard, once for each word: "Why— did—I—have—to—go—and—do—that?"

"Cut that out," he said. "You'll hurt yourself."

"I ought to get hurt," I said.

"Ah?" said Stern.

I got up and went to the desk and got some water. "What am I going to do?"

"Tell me what you did after you killed her, right up until the time you came here."

"Not much," I said. "It was only last night. I went back to my room, sort of numb. I put all my clothes on except my shoes. I carried them. I went out. Walked a long time, trying to think, went to the post office when it opened. Miss Kew used to let me go for the mail sometimes. Found this check waiting for me for the contest. Cashed it at the bank, opened an account, took eleven hundred bucks. Got the idea of getting some help from a psychiatrist, spent most of the day looking for one, came here. That's all."

"Didn't you have any trouble cashing the check?"

"I never have any trouble making people do what I want them to do."

He gave a surprised grunt.

"I know what you're thinking—I couldn't make Miss Kew do what I wanted."

"That's part of it," he admitted.

"If I had of done that," I told him, "she wouldn't of been Miss

Kew any more. Now the banker—all I made him do was be a banker."

I looked at him and suddenly realized why he fooled with that pipe all the time. It was so he could look down at it and you wouldn't be able to see his eyes.

"You killed her," he said—and I knew he was changing the subject—"and destroyed something that was valuable to you. It must have been less valuable to you than the chance to rebuild this thing you used to have with the other kids. And you're not sure of the value of that." He looked up. "Does that describe your main trouble?"

"Just about."

"You know the single thing that makes people kill?" When I didn't answer, he said, "Survival. To save the self or something which identifies with the self. And in this case that doesn't apply, because your setup with Miss Kew had far more survival value for you, singly and as a group, than the other.

"So maybe I just didn't have a good enough reason to kill her."

"You had, because you did it. We just haven't located it yet. I mean we have the reason, but we don't know why it was important enough. The answer is somewhere in you."

"Where?"

He got up and walked some. "We have a pretty consecutive life-story here. There's fantasy mixed with the fact, of course, and there are areas in which we have no detailed information, but we have a beginning and a middle and an end. Now, I can't say for sure, but the answer may be in that bridge you refused to cross a while back. Remember?"

I remembered, all right. I said, "Why that? Why can't we try something else?"

He quietly pointed out, "Because you just said it. Why are you shying away from it?"

"Don't go making big ones out of little ones," I said. Sometimes the guy annoyed me. "That bothers me. I don't know why, but it does."

"Something's lying hidden in there, and you're bothering *it* so it's fighting back. Anything that fights to stay concealed is very possibly the thing we're after. Your trouble is concealed, isn't it?"

"Well, yes," I said, and I felt that sickness and faintness again, and again I pushed it away. Suddenly I wasn't going to be stopped any more. "Let's go get it." I lay down.

He let me watch the ceiling and listen to silence for a while, and then he said, "You're in the library. You've just met Miss Kew. She's talking to you; you're telling her about the children."

I lay very still. Nothing happened. Yes, it did; I got tense inside, all over, from the bones out, more and more. When it got as bad as it could, still nothing happened.

I heard him get up and cross the room to the desk. He fumbled there for a while; things clicked and hummed. Suddenly I heard my own voice:

"Well, there's Jane, she's eleven like me. And Bonnie and Beanie are eight, they're twins, and Baby. Baby is three."

And the sound of my own scream—

And nothingness.

Sputtering up out of the darkness, I came flailing out with my fists. Strong hands caught my wrists. They didn't check my arms; they just grabbed and rode. I opened my eyes. I was soaking wet. The thermos lay on its side on the rug. Stern was crouched beside me, holding my wrists. I quit struggling.

"What happened?"

He let me go and stood back watchfully. "Lord," he said, "what a charge!"

I held my head and moaned. He threw me a hand-towel and I used it. "What hit me?"

"I've had you on tape the whole time," he explained. "When you wouldn't get into that recollection, I tried to nudge you into it by using your own voice as you recounted it before. It works wonders sometimes."

"It worked wonders this time," I growled. "I think I blew a fuse."

"In effect, you did. You were on the trembling verge of going into the thing you don't want to remember, and you let yourself go unconscious rather than do it."

"What are you so pleased about?"

"Last-ditch defense," he said tersely. "We've got it now. Just one more try."

"Now hold on. The last-ditch defense is that I drop dead."

"You won't. You've contained this episode in your subconscious mind for a long time and it hasn't hurt you."

"Hasn't it?"

"Not in terms of killing you."

"How do you know it won't when we drag it out?"

"You'll see."

I looked up at him sideways. Somehow he struck me as knowing what he was doing.

"You know a lot more about yourself now than you did at the time," he explained softly. "You can apply insight. You can evaluate it as it comes up. Maybe not completely, but enough to protect yourself. Don't worry. Trust me. I can stop it if it gets too bad. Now just relax. Look at the ceiling. Be aware of your toes. Don't look at your toes. Look straight up. Your toes, your big toes. Don't move your toes, but feel them. Count outward from your big toes, one count for each toe. One, two, three. Feel that third toe. Feel the toe, feel it, feel it go limp, go limp, go limp. The toe next to it on both sides gets limp. So limp because your toes are limp, all of your toes are limp—"

"What are you doing?" I shouted at him.

He said in the same silky voice, "You trust me and so do your toes trust me. They're all limp because you trust me. You—"

"You're trying to hypnotize me. I'm not going to let you do that."

"You're going to hypnotize yourself. You do everything yourself. I just point the way. I point your toes to the path. Just point your toes. No one can make you go anywhere you don't want to go, but you want to go where your toes are pointed where your toes are limp where your . . ."

On and on and on. And where was the dangling gold ornament, the light in the eyes, the mystic passes? He wasn't even sitting where I could see him. Where was the talk about how sleepy I was supposed to be? Well, he knew I wasn't sleepy and didn't want to be sleepy. I just wanted to be toes. I just wanted to be limp, just a limp toe. No brains in a toe, a toe to go, go, go eleven times, eleven, I'm eleven ...

I split in two, and it was all right, the part that watched the part that went back to the library, and Miss Kew leaning toward me, but not too near, me with the newspaper crackling under me on the library chair, me with one shoe off and my limp toes dangling ... and I felt a mild surprise at this. For this was hypnosis, but I was quite conscious, quite altogether there on the couch with Stern droning away at me, quite able to roll over and sit up and talk to him and walk out if I wanted to, but I just didn't want to. Oh, if this was what hypnosis was like, I was all for it. I'd work at this. This was all right.

There on the table I'm able to see that the gold will unfold on the leather, and whether I'm able to stay by the table with you, with Miss Kew, with Miss Kew ...

"... and Bonnie and Beanie are eight, they're twins, and Baby. Baby is three."

"Baby is three," she said,

There was a pressure, a stretching apart, and a ... a breakage. And with a tearing agony and a burst of triumph that drowned the pain, it was done.

And this is what was inside. All in one flash, but all this.

Baby is three? My baby would be three if there were a baby, which there never was ...

Lone, I'm open to you. Open, is this open enough?

His irises like wheels. I'm sure they spin, but I never catch them at it. The probe that passes invisibly from his brain, through his eyes, into mine. Does he know what it means to me? Does he care? He doesn't care, he doesn't know; he empties me and I fill as he directs me to; he drinks and waits and drinks again and never looks at the cup.

When I saw him first, I was dancing in the wind, in the wood, in the wild, and I spun about and he stood there in the leafy shadows, watching me. I hated him for it. It was not my wood, not my gold-spangled fern-tangled glen. But it was my dancing that he took, freezing it forever by being there. I hated him for it, hated the way he looked, the way he stood, ankle-deep in the kind wet ferns, looking like a tree with roots for feet and clothes the color of earth. As I stopped he moved, and then he was just a man, a great ape-shouldered, dirty animal of a man, and all my hate was fear suddenly and I was just as frozen.

He knew what he had done and he didn't care. Dancing . . . never to dance again, because never would I know the woods were free of eyes, free of tall, uncaring, dirty animal men. Summer days with the clothes choking me, winter nights with the precious decencies round and about me like a shroud, and never to dance again, never to remember dancing without remembering the shock of knowing he had seen me. How I hated him! Oh, how I hated him!

To dance alone where no one knew, that was the single thing I hid to myself when I was known as Miss Kew, that Victorian, older than her years, later than her time; correct and starched, lace and linen and lonely. Now indeed I would be all they said, through and through, forever and ever, because he had robbed me of the one thing I dared to keep secret.

He came out into the sun and walked to me, holding his great head a little on one side. I stood where I was, frozen inwardly and outwardly and altogether by the core of anger and the layer of fear. My arm was still out, my waist still bent from my dance, and when he stopped, I breathed again because by then I had to.

He said, "You read books?"

I couldn't bear to have him near me, but I couldn't move. He put out his hard hand and touched my jaw, turned my head up until I had to look into his face. I cringed away from him, but my face would not leave his hand, though he was not holding it, just lifting it. "You got to read some books for me. I got no time to find them."

I asked him, "Who are you?"

"Lone," he said. "You going to read books for me?"

"No. Let me go, let me go!"

He laughed at me. He wasn't holding me.

"What books?" I cried.

He thumped my face, not very hard. It made me look up a bit more. He dropped his hand away. His eyes, the irises were going to spin ...

"Open up in there," he said. "Open way up and let me see."

There were books in my head, and he was looking at the titles ... he was not looking at the titles, for he couldn't read. He was looking at what I knew of the books. I suddenly felt terribly useless, because I had only a fraction of what he wanted.

"What's that?" he barked.

I knew what he meant. He'd gotten it from inside my head. I didn't know it was in there, even, but he found it.

"Telekinesis," I said.

"How is it done?"

"Nobody knows if it can be done. Moving physical objects with the mind!"

"It can be done," he said. "This one?"

"Teleportation. That's the same thing—well, almost. Moving your own body with mind power."

"Yeah, yeah, I see it," he said gruffly.

"Molecular interpenetration. Telepathy and clairvoyance. I don't know anything about them. I think they're silly."

"Read about 'em. It don't matter if you understand or not. What's this?"

It was there in my brain, on my lips. *"Gestalt."*

"What's that?"

"Group. Like a cure for a lot of diseases with one kind of treatment. Like a lot of thoughts expressed in one phrase. The whole is greater than the sum of the parts."

"Read about that, too. Read a whole lot about that. That's the *most* you got to read about. That's important."

He turned away, and when his eyes came away from mine it was like something breaking, so that I staggered and fell to one knee. He went off into the woods without looking back. I got my things and ran home. There was anger, and it struck me like a storm. There was fear, and it struck me like a wind. I knew I would read the books, I knew I would come back, I knew I would never dance again.

So I read the books and I came back. Sometimes it was every day for three or four days, and sometimes, because I couldn't find a certain book, I might not come back for ten. He was always there in the little glen, waiting, standing in the shadows, and he took what he wanted of the books and nothing of me. He never mentioned the next meeting. If he came there every day to wait for me, or if he only came when I did, I have no way of knowing.

He made me read books that contained nothing for me, books on evolution, on social and cultural organization, on mythology, and ever so much on symbiosis. What I had with him were not conversations; sometimes nothing audible would pass between us but his grunt of surprise or small, short hum of interest.

He tore the books out of me the way he would tear berries from a bush, all at once; he smelled of sweat and earth and the green juices his heavy body crushed when he moved through the wood.

If he learned anything from the books, it made no difference in him.

There came a day when he sat by me and puzzled something out.

He said, "What book has something like this?" Then he waited for a long time, thinking. "The way a termite can't digest wood, you know, and microbes in the termite's belly can, and what the termite eats is what the microbe leaves behind. What's that?"

"Symbiosis," I remembered. I remembered the words. Lone tore the content from the words and threw the words away. "Two kinds of life depending upon one another for existence."

"Yeah. Well, is there a book about four-five kinds doing that?"

"I don't know."

Then he asked, "What about this? You got a radio station, you got four-five receivers, each receiver is fixed up to make something different happen, like one digs and one flies and one makes noise, but each one takes orders from the one place. And each one has its own power and its own thing to do, but they are all apart. Now: is there life like that, instead of radio?"

"Where each organism is a part of the whole, but separated? I don't think so . . . unless you mean social organizations, like a team, or perhaps a gang of men working, all taking orders from the same boss."

388

"No," he said immediately, "not like that. Like one single ani-mal." He made a gesture with his cupped hand which I understood.

I asked, "You mean a *gestalt* life-form? It's fantastic."

"No book has about that, huh?"

"None I ever heard of."

"I got to know about that," he said heavily. "There is such a thing. I want to know if it ever happened before."

"I can't see how anything of the sort could exist."

"It does. A part that fetches, a part that figures, a part that finds out, and a part that talks."

"Talks? Only humans talk."

"I know," he said, and got up and went away.

I looked and looked for such a book, but found nothing remotely like it. I came back and told him so. He was still a very long time, looking off to the blue-on-blue line of the hilly horizon. Then he drove those about-to-spin irises at me and searched.

"You learn, but you don't think," he said, and looked again at the hills.

"This all happens with humans," he said eventually. "It happens piece by piece right under folks' noses, and they don't see it. You got mind-readers. You got people can move things with their mind. You got people can move themselves with their mind. You got people can figure anything out if you just think to ask them. What you ain't got is the one kind of person who can pull 'em all together, like a brain pulls together the parts that press and pull and feel heat and walk and think and all the other things.

"I'm one," he finished suddenly. Then he sat still for so long, I thought he had forgotten me.

"Lone," I said, "what do you do here in the woods?"

"I wait," he said. "I ain't finished yet." He looked at my eyes and snorted in irritation. "I don't mean 'finished' like you're thinking. I mean I ain't—completed yet. You know about a worm when it's cut, growin' whole again? Well, forget about the cut. Suppose it just grew that way, for the first time, see? I'm getting parts. I ain't fin-ished. I want a book about that kind of animal that is me when I'm finished."

"I don't know of such a book. Can you tell me more? Maybe if you could, I'd think of the right book or a place to find it."

He broke a stick between his huge hands, put the two pieces side by side and broke them together with one strong twist.

"All I know is I got to do what I'm doing like a bird's got to nest when it's time. And I know that when I'm done I won't be anything to brag about. I'll be like a body stronger and faster than anything there ever was, without the right kind of head on it. But maybe that's because I'm one of the first. That picture you had, the caveman . . ."

"Neanderthal."

"Yeah. Come to think of it, he was no great shakes. An early try at something new. That's what I'm going to be. But maybe the right kind of head'll come along after I'm all organized. Then it'll be something."

He grunted with satisfaction and went away.

I tried, for days I tried, but I couldn't find what he wanted. I found a magazine which stated that the next important evolutionary step in man would be a psychic rather than a physical direction, but it said nothing about a—shall I call it a *gestalt* organism? There was something about slime molds, but they seem to be more a hive activity of amoebae than even a symbiosis.

To my own unscientific, personally uninterested mind, there was nothing like what he wanted except possibly a band marching together, everyone playing different kinds of instruments with different techniques and different notes, to make a single thing move along together. But he hadn't meant anything like that.

So I went back to him in the cool of an early fall evening, and he took what little I had in my eyes, and turned from me angrily with a gross word I shall not permit myself to remember.

"You can't find it," he told me. "Don't come back."

He got up and went to a tattered birch and leaned against it, looking out and down into the wind-tossed crackling shadows. I think he had forgotten me already. I know he leaped like a frightened animal when I spoke to him from so near. He must have been completely immersed in whatever strange thoughts he was having, for I'm sure he didn't hear me coming.

I said, "Lone, don't blame me for not finding it. I tried."

He controlled his startlement and brought those eyes down to me. "Blame? Who's blamin' anybody?"

"I failed you," I told him, "and you're angry."

He looked at me so long I became uncomfortable.

"I don't know what you're talkin' about," he said.

I wouldn't let him turn away from me. He would have. He would have left me forever with not another thought; he didn't *care!* It wasn't cruelty or thoughtlessness as I have been taught to know those things. He was as uncaring as a cat is of the bursting of a tulip bud.

I took him by the upper arms and shook him, it was like trying to shake the front of my house. "You *can* know!" I screamed at him. "You know what I read. You must know what I think."

He shook his head.

"I'm a person, a woman," I raved at him. "You've used me and used me and you've given me nothing. You've made me break a lifetime of habits—reading until all hours, coming to you in the rain and on Sunday—you don't talk to me, you don't look at me, you don't know anything about me and you don't care. You put some sort of a spell on me that I couldn't break. And when you're finished, you say, 'Don't come back.'"

"Do I have to give something back because I took something?"

"People do."

He gave that short, interested hum. "What do you want me to give you? I ain't got anything."

I moved away from him. I felt . . . I don't know what I felt. After a time I said, "I don't know."

He shrugged and turned. I fairly leaped at him, dragging him back. "I want you to—"

"Well, damn it, what?"

I couldn't look at him; I could hardly speak. "I don't know. There's something, but I don't know what it is. It's something that—I couldn't say if I knew it." When he began to shake his head, I took his arms again. "You've read the books out of me; can't you read the . . . the *me* out of me?"

"I ain't never tried." He held my face up, and stepped close. "Here," he said.

His eyes projected their strange probe at me and I screamed. I tried to twist away. I hadn't wanted this, I was sure I hadn't. I struggled terribly. I think he lifted me right off the ground with his big hands. He held me until he was finished, and then let me drop. I huddled to the ground, sobbing. He sat down beside me. He didn't try to touch me. He didn't try to go away. I quieted at last and crouched there, waiting.

He said, "I ain't going to do much of that no more."

I sat up and tucked my skirt close around me and laid my cheek on my updrawn knees so I could see his face. "What happened?"

He cursed. "Damn mishmash inside you. Thirty-three years old—what you want to live like that for?"

"I live very comfortably," I said with some pique.

"Yeah," he said. "All by yourself for ten years now 'cept for someone to do your work. Nobody else."

"Men are animals, and women . . ."

"You really hate women. They all know something you don't."

"I don't want to know. I'm quite happy the way I am."

"Hell you are."

I said nothing to that. I despise that kind of language.

"Two things you want from me. Neither makes no sense." He looked at me with the first real expression I have ever seen in his face: a profound wonderment. "You want to know all about me, where I came from, how I got to be what I am."

"Yes, I do want that. What's the other thing I want that you know and I don't?"

"I was born some place and growed like a weed somehow," he said, ignoring me. "Folks who didn't give even enough of a damn to try the orphanage routine. I lived with some other folks for a while, tried school, didn't like it. Too small a town for them special schools for my kind, retarded, y'know. So I just ran loose, sort of in training to be the village idiot. I'da made it if I'd stayed there, but I took to the woods instead."

"Why?"

He wondered why, and finally said, "I guess because the way people lived didn't make no sense to me. I saw enough up and down, back and forth, to know that they live a lot of different ways, but none of 'em was for me. Out here I can grow like I want."

"How is that?" I asked over one of those vast differences that built and receded between him and me so constantly.

"What I wanted to get from your books."

"You never told me."

For the second time he said, "You learn, but you don't think. There's a kind of—well, *person.* It's all made of separate parts, but it's all one person. It has like hands, it has like legs, it has like a talking mouth, and it has like a brain. That's me, a brain for that person. Damn feeble, too, but the best I know of."

"You're mad."

"No, I ain't," he said, unoffended and completely certain. "I already got the part that's like hands. I can move 'em anywhere and they do what I want, though they're too young yet to do much good. I got the part that talks. That one's real good."

"I don't think you talk very well at all," I said. I cannot stand incorrect English.

He was surprised. "I'm not talking about me! She's back yonder with the others."

"She?"

"The one that talks. Now I need one that thinks, one that can take anything and add it to anything else and come up with a right answer. And once they're all together, and all the parts get used together often enough, I'll be that new kind of thing I told you about. See? Only—I wish it had a better head on it than me."

My own head was swimming. "What made you start doing this?"

He considered me gravely. "What made you start growing hair in your armpits?" he asked me. "You don't figure a thing like that. It just happens."

"What is that . . . that thing you do when you look in my eyes?"

"You want a name for it? I ain't got one. I don't know how I do it. I know I can get anyone I want to do anything. Like you're going to forget about me."

I said in a choked voice, "I don't want to forget about you."

"You will." I didn't know then whether he meant I'd forget, or I'd *want* to forget. "You'll hate me, and then after a long time you'll be grateful. Maybe you'll be able to do something for me some time. You'll be that grateful that you'll be glad to do it. But you'll forget, all right, everything but a sort of . . . feeling. And my name, maybe."

I don't know what moved me to ask him, but I did, forlornly. "And no one will ever know about you and me?"

"Can't," he said. "Unless . . . well, unless it was the head of the animal, like me, or a better one." He heaved himself up.

"Oh, wait, wait!" I cried. He mustn't go yet, he mustn't. He was a tall, dirty beast of a man, yet he had enthralled me in some dreadful way. "You haven't given me the other . . . whatever it was."

"Oh," he said, "Yeah, that."

He moved like a flash. There was a pressure, a stretching apart, and a . . . a breakage. And with a tearing agony and a burst of triumph that drowned the pain, it was done.

I came up out of it, through two distinct levels:

I am eleven, breathless from shock from a transferred agony of that incredible entrance into the ego of another. And:

I am fifteen, lying on the couch while Stern drones on, ". . . quietly, quietly limp, your ankles and legs as limp as your toes, your belly goes soft, the back of your neck is as limp as your belly, it's quiet and easy and all gone soft and limper than limp . . ."

I sat up and swung my legs to the floor. "Okay," I said.

Stern looked a little annoyed. "This is going to work," he said, "but it can only work if you cooperate. Just lie—"

"It did work," I said.

"What?"

"The whole thing. A to Z." I snapped my fingers. "Like that."

He looked at me piercingly. "What do you mean?"

"It was right there, where you said. In the library. When I was eleven. When she said, 'Baby is three.' It knocked loose something that had been boiling around in her for three years, and it all came blasting out. I got it, full force; just a kid, no warning, no defenses. It had such a—a pain in it, like I never knew could be."

"Go on," said Stern.

"That's really all. I mean that's not what was in it; it's what it did to me. What it was, a sort of hunk of her own self. A whole lot of things that happened over about four months, every bit of it. She knew Lone."

"You mean a whole *series* of episodes?"

"That's it."

"You got a series all at once? In a split second?"

"That's right. Look, for that split second I *was* her, don't you see? I was her, everything she'd ever done, everything she'd ever thought and heard and felt. Everything, everything, all in the right order if I wanted to bring it out like that. Any part of it if I wanted it by itself. If I'm going to tell you about what I had for lunch, to I have to tell you everything else I've ever done since I was born? No. I tell you I *was* her, and then and forever after I can remember anything she could remember up to that point. In just that one flash."

"A *gestalt,*" he murmured.

"Aha!" I said, and thought about that. I thought about a whole lot of things. I put them aside for a moment and said, "Why didn't I know all this before?"

"You had a powerful block against recalling it."

I got up excitedly. "I don't see why. I don't see that at all."

"Just natural revulsion," he guessed. "How about this? You had a distaste for assuming a female ego, even for a second."

"You told me yourself, right at the beginning, that I didn't have that kind of a problem."

"Well, how does this sound to you? You say you felt pain in that episode. So—you wouldn't go back into it for fear of re-experiencing the pain."

"Let me think, let me think. Yeah, yeah, that's part of it—that thing of going into someone's mind. She opened up to me because I reminded her of Lone. I went in. I wasn't ready; I'd never done it before, except maybe a little, against resistance. I went all the way in and it was too much; it frightened me away from trying it for years. And there it lay, wrapped up, locked away. But as I grew older, the power to do that with my mind got stronger and stronger, and still I was afraid to use it. And the more I grew, the more I felt, down deep, that Miss Kew had to killed before she killed the . . . what I am. My God!" I shouted. "Do you know what I am?"

"No," he said. "Like to tell me about it?"

"I'd like to," I said. "Oh, yes, I'd like that."

He had that professional open-minded expression on his face, not believing or disbelieving, just taking it all in. I had to tell him, and I suddenly realized that I didn't have enough words. I knew the things, but not the names for them.

Lone took the meanings and threw the words away.

Further back: *"You read books. Read books for me."*

The look of his eyes. That—"opening up" thing.

I went over to Stern. He looked up at me. I bent close. First he was startled, then he controlled it, then he came even closer to me.

"My God," he murmured. "I didn't look at those eyes before. I could have sworn those irises spun like wheels . . ."

Stern read books. He'd read more books than I ever imagined had been written. I slipped in there, looking for what I wanted.

I can't say exactly what it was like. It was like walking in a tunnel, and in this tunnel, all over the roof and walls, wooden arms stuck out at you, like the thing at the carnival, the merry-go-round, the thing you snatch brass rings from. There's a brass ring on the end of each of these arms, and you can take any one of them you want to.

Now imagine you make up your mind which rings you want, and the arms hold only those. Now picture yourself with a thousand hands to grab the rings off with. Now just suppose the tunnel is a zillion miles long, and you can go from one end of it to the other, grabbing rings, in just the time it takes you to blink once. Well, it was like that, only easier.

It was easier for me to do than it had been for Lone.

Straightening up, I got away from Stern. He looked sick and frightened.

"It's all right," I said.

"What did you do to me?"

"I needed some words. Come on, come on. Get professional."

I had to admire him. He put his pipe in his pocket and gouged the tips of his fingers hard against his forehead and cheeks. Then he sat up and he was okay again.

"I know," I said. "That's how Miss Kew felt when Lone did it to her."

"What *are* you?"

"I'll tell you. I'm the central ganglion of a complex organism which is composed of Baby, a computer; Bonnie and Beanie, teleports; Jane, telekineticist; and myself, telepath and central control. There isn't a single thing about any of us that hasn't been documented: the teleportation of the Yogi, the telekinetics of some gamblers, the idiot savant mathematicians, and most of all, the so-called poltergeist, the moving about of household goods through the instrumentation of a young girl. Only in this case every one of my parts delivers at peak performance.

"Lone organized it, or it formed around him; it doesn't matter which. I replaced Lone, but I was too underdeveloped when he died, and on top of that I got an occlusion from that blast from Miss Kew. To that extent you were right when you said the blast made me subconsciously afraid to discover what was in it. But there was another good reason for my not being able to get in under that 'Baby is three' barrier.

"We ran into the problem of what it was I valued more than the security Miss Kew gave us. Can't you see now what it was? My *gestalt* organism was at the point of death from that security. I figured she had to be killed or it—*I*—would be. Oh, the parts would live on: two little colored girls with a speech impediment, one introspective girl with an artistic bent, one mongoloid idiot, and me—ninety per cent short-circuited potentials and ten per cent juvenile delinquent." I laughed. "Sure, she had to be killed. It was self-preservation for the *gestalt.*"

Stern bobbled around with his mouth and finally got out: "I don't—"

"You don't need to," I laughed. "This is wonderful. You're fine, hey, fine. Now I want to tell you this, because you can appreciate a fine point in your specialty. You talk about occlusions! I couldn't get past the 'Baby is three' thing because in it lay the clues to what I really am. I couldn't find that out because I was afraid to remember that I had failed in the thing I had to do to save the *gestalt.* Ain't that purty?"

"Failed? Failed how?"

"Look. I came to love Miss Kew, and I'd never loved anything before. Yet I had reason to kill her. She *had* to be killed; I *couldn't* kill her. What does a human mind do when presented with imperative, mutually exclusive alternatives?"

"It—it might simply quit. As you phrased it earlier, it might blow a fuse, retreat, refuse to function in that area."

"Well, I didn't do that. What else?"

"It might slip into a delusion that it had already taken one of the courses of action."

I nodded happily. "I didn't kill her. I decided I must; I got up, got dressed—and the next thing I knew I was outside, wandering, very confused. I got my money—and I understand now, with super-empathy, how I can win *anyone's* prize contest—and I went looking for a head-shrinker. I found a good one."

"Thanks," he said dazedly. He looked at me with a strangeness in his eyes. "And now that you know, what's solved? What are you going to do?"

"Go back home," I said happily. "Reactivate the superorganism, exercise it secretly in ways that won't make Miss Kew unhappy, and we'll stay with her as long as we know it pleases her. And we'll please her. She'll be happy in ways she's never dreamed about until now. She rates it, bless her strait-laced, hungry heart."

"And she can't kill your—*gestalt* organism?"

"Not a chance. Not now."

"How do you know it isn't dead already?"

"How?" I echoed. "How does your head know your arm works?"

He wet his lips. "You're going home to make a spinster happy. And after that?"

I shrugged. "After that?" I mocked. "Did the Peking man look at Homo Sap walking erect and say, 'What will he do after that?' We'll live, that's all, like a man, like a tree, like anything else that lives. We'll feed and grow and experiment and breed. We'll defend ourselves." I spread my hands. "We'll just do what comes naturally."

"But what can you do?"

"What can an electric motor do? It depends on where we apply ourselves."

Stern was very pale. "But you're the only such organism ..."

"Are we? I don't know. I don't think so. I've told you parts have been around for ages—the telepaths, the *poltergeists*. What was lacking was the ones to organize, to be heads to the scattered bodies. Lone was one, I'm one; there must be more. We'll find out as we mature."

"You—aren't mature yet?"

"Lord, no!" I laughed. "We're an infant. We're the equivalent of about a three-year-old-child. So you see, there it is again, and this time I'm not afraid of it; Baby is three." I looked at my hands. "Baby is three," I said again, because the realization tasted good. "And when this particular group-baby is five, it might want to be a fireman. At eight, maybe a cowboy or maybe an FBI man. And when it grows up, maybe it'll build a city, or perhaps it'll be President."

"Oh, God!" he said. "God!"

I looked down at him. "You're afraid," I said. "You're afraid of *Homo Gestalt.*"

He made a wonderful effort and smiled. "That's bastard terminology."

"We're a bastard breed," I said. I pointed. "Sit over there."

He crossed the quiet room and sat at the desk. I leaned close to him and he went to sleep with his eyes open. I straightened up and looked around the room. Then I got the thermos flask and filled it and put it on the desk. I fixed the corner of the rug and put a clean towel at the head of the couch. I went to the side of the desk and opened it and looked at the tape recorder.

Like reaching out a hand, I got Beanie. She stood by the desk, wide-eyed.

"Look here," I told her. "Look good, now. What I want to do is erase all this tape. Go ask Baby how."

She blinked at me and sort of shook herself, and then leaned over the recorder. She was there—and gone—and back, just like that. She pushed past me and turned two knobs, moved a pointer until it clicked twice. The tape raced backward past the head swiftly, whining.

"All right," I said, "beat it."

She vanished.

I got my jacket and went to the door. Stern was still sitting at the desk, staring.

"A *good* head-shrinker," I murmured. I felt fine.

Outside I waited, then turned and went back in again.

Stern looked up at me. "Sit over there, Sonny."

"Gee," I said. "Sorry, sir. I got in the wrong office."

"That's all right," he said.

I went out and closed the door. All the way down to the store to buy Miss Kew some flowers, I was grinning about he'd account for the loss of an afternoon and the gain of a thousand bucks.

Story Notes

by Paul Williams

"Shadow, Shadow on the Wall": first published in *Imagination,* February 1951. Apparently written April or May 1950. There is little information available regarding the exact dates of composition of many of the stories in this volume or the sequence in which they were written. In a letter to his mother dated March 21, 1950, Sturgeon fretted: *Aside from my TV show and a short I wrote last weekend, I haven't written an original line since last May.* "Last May" was when Theodore Sturgeon began working at Time Inc., writing direct mail copy for *Fortune* magazine. The Time Inc. job lasted until late in 1951. Sturgeon wrote "The Hurkle Is a Happy Beast" for *The Magazine of Fantasy & Science Fiction* in late April 1949. (The "TV show" he refers to was a speculative project that never came to fruition).

On June 19, 1950 TS wrote to J. Francis McComas, one of the editors who'd bought "The Hurkle": *Here's IT STAYED, the fantasy of which I spoke to you.* This story—presumably rejected by F&SF, who didn't publish their second Sturgeon story until November 1953—is clearly "Shadow, Shadow on the Wall" *("He stayed, he did," said Bobby. "He stayed!").* "Shadow" could not have been the "short I wrote last weekend," since TS says he wrote it in 28 days (see below), so if we believe Sturgeon wrote no stories between May 1949 and March 1950, "Shadow" must have been written in April or May 1950.

Theodore Sturgeon told interviewer Paul Sammon in 1977 [in response to a question about his writing habits]: *Another time when I wrote a story I had a bad writer's block. I was working for Time Inc., and felt I really wanted to write something. But I'd come home from work and try to write and find that I couldn't. So I finally decided to turn the coin over, and create a situation where I would not be trying hard to write, but trying hard not to write. This is what I did: I decided I would double-space the typewriter and write to the bottom of the page. One page every day. And if I stopped in the middle of the word, with a hyphen, I would not write another word on another page. This created a situation where I'd get to the bottom of my page and say, "This is crazy! At least let me finish this sentence!" But I wouldn't let myself do it. So in twenty-eight days I wrote a story that ran twenty-eight pages, and it came out beautifully. I've become one of the world's great experts at breaking writer's blocks. In almost any case, I can break anyone's block.* In another 1977 interview, with D. Scott Apel, TS described the same incident and specifically identifies the 28-day story as "Shadow, Shadow on the Wall." He added, jokingly: *That technique was so successful that I never used it again.*

Sturgeon's introduction to "Shadow, Shadow on the Wall" in his 1984 collection *Alien Cargo: Good old wicked stepmother; this isn't the first, and certainly not the last of them to supply us with entertainment. Somebody once made a short film of this; the little boy was just great, the rest misunderstood, so it was never seen. There's one line in here I'm really proud of: the fury of the woman who, having banished the child to the bedroom, finds him happy as a little clam.* "Don't you know you're being punished?" *she shouts. Very heavy, that. Nobody can punish you if you can achieve the mindset that says whatever they're doing to you isn't punishment.*

TS's own childhood experiences with a seemingly sadistic stepparent are recounted in his 1965 memoir *Argyll* (published posthumously).

"The Stars Are the Styx": first published in the first issue of *Galaxy Science Fiction*, October 1950. Probably written in summer 1950. It is noteworthy that Theodore Sturgeon contributed stories to the debut issues of both of the magazines that would transform the character of science fiction in the 1950s and beyond: *The Magazine of Fantasy & Science Fiction* and *Galaxy,* monthly short story magazines that immediately established themselves as the equals of John

W. Campbell's *Astounding Science-Fiction* in terms of reader popularity and of editorial influence on how authors wrote and what they
wrote about and what they considered "science fiction" to be. In
both cases, the editors were eager to have a Sturgeon story in their
debut issues not only because of his popularity with the genre's readers but because in different ways the editors of both magazines saw
the Sturgeon name as symbolic of the type of science fiction they
hoped and intended to offer in their ambitious new publications.
And indeed, this turned out to be true. Theodore Sturgeon, already
beloved by science fiction readers and other sf writers for the stories
he wrote for *Astounding* and its sister magazine *Unknown* in 1939-
1947, was in many ways the prototypical science fiction (and fantasy) short story writer of the 1950s (the decade in which he would
do his very best work).

"The Stars Are the Styx" was adapted (apparently with scripts
by Sturgeon) as a radio drama twice, for "Tales of Tomorrow" (aired
Jan. 29, 1953) and for "X Minus One" (aired July 27, 1956). (Sturgeon, whose Star Trek scripts are favorites among aficionados, did
his first paying television writing in September 1951 when he adapted
Robert Heinlein's short story "Ordeal in Space" for CBS Stage 14.)

In 1979 Dell Books published a collection of stories by TS called
The Stars Are the Styx, with a cover by Rowena Morrell depicting
Sturgeon as Charon. In his introduction to the title story, TS wrote:

*I've written elsewhere about the strange way things that I write
about seem to happen about fifteen years later. It's a small thing, but
in writing this in 1950 I had no idea in the world that in fifteen years
couples would be dancing separately, each more or less doing their
own thing. In '65 they began doing just that. Nor did I dream that
this, of all the stories I was writing at the time, would one day be
the title story of a collection like this.*

When the narrator in "Stars" asks Judson for a *simple statement*
because complicated matters are not important, *he is echoing a cod-
ification articulated by other Sturgeon characters in "Quietly" and
"What Dead Men Tell" (see Story Notes in Volume V.). And when
he guesses people are attracted to Jud because he gives them the feeling he* can be reached . . . touched . . . affected. . . We like feeling that

we have an effect on someone, *it seems likely that the author is examining the happy and mysterious response of strangers when they meet Theodore Sturgeon.*

The line *"Modesty is not so simple a virtue as honesty,"* one of the old books says turns up in an essay by Sturgeon called "The Naked I" (the manuscript is in the Sturgeon papers; date and place of publication uncertain), which begins:

Modesty is not so simple a virtue as honesty.

I wish I'd said that. Matter of fact, I did and I do and most probably I will, because it's one of those thoughts you can take home and chew over and find the flavor increasing. The man I got it from, however, is one Bernard Rudofsky, in a long out-of-print book called Are Clothes Modern?—*which in itself is another such thought.*

I am naked. I am naked now as I sit here writing this. I wear clothes as seldom as possible because I am more comfortable that way. I wear clothes a) when I must and b) when I want to, and at no other time.

Amongst the Sturgeon papers are several notes in which TS attempts to plot a sequel to "The Stars Are the Styx." For example:

Charon decides to go Out. When he gets there he finds that in the first place none of the Outbounders are wanted; second, that the great synapse is equally unwanted and useless to a really hidebound Earth. He goes back to Curbstone and finds ancient papers which describe the whole scheme as a riddance for neurotics and potential rebels.

Lucy Menger in her 1981 book *Theodore Sturgeon* points out that: "The idea that misfits can contribute to society is central to 'The Stars Are the Styx.' In this story, Sturgeon capsulizes his thoughts on misfits when his narrator muses: 'When you come right down to it, misfits are that way either because they lack something or because they have something *extra*.' "

Editor's blurb from the first page of the original magazine appearance: ON CURBSTONE, GOING OUT MEANT A 6,000 YEAR DATE!

"Rule of Three": first published in *Galaxy Science Fiction*, January 1951. Written October 1950. Among the papers belonging to Sturgeon's estate is a letter on *Time* letterhead dated Oct. 11. The year must be 1950 (because TS wasn't writing for Horace Gold's *Galaxy* in Oct. '49 and didn't sell him a story in fall '51). There is no salutation; the person he's writing to could be either his estranged wife Mary Mair or the young woman who would become his third wife the following year, Marion McGahan. The letter is signed and not a carbon, so presumably was not delivered (anyway, it was still among Sturgeon's papers when he died three decades later). The letter is relevant here because I am certain the story TS has just shown to Horace and is planning to rewrite all day tomorrow is "Rule of Three." (See notes on "Make Room for Me" for info about "the other one.") So here is the entire text of a note written by TS in the midst of working on "Rule of Three" (which I regard as one of his major works and arguably as important a message-in-a-bottle-from-outer-space as we humans may ever receive):

I haven't seen you in <u>so</u> long . . . [ellipses in original] *I was half out of my mind with exhaustion when I spoke to you the other night—about 4 hours sleep in 48. I can't take too much of that, but I had to.*

Horace liked the story but wants a rewrite. He's right, damn him. He's also very impressed with the other one I told you about—the one I wrote with someone else—particularly since it has a new year's eve sequence and is ideal for his December issue. So I've got to rewrite that one too. The way I hope to handle it is this: Tomorrow I'll stay home and work all day, finishing the 9000-worder. (Tonight, by the way, I'm lecturing at CCNY.) Friday evening I've got a dianetic emergency to handle—his third session, which I think will straighten him out. Saturday I'll work on the 13,000-word one. After that I hope to be able to see you, if I can't snatch a couple of hours between times.

Hold tight, darling, and be careful of the door.

(The letter is signed, *Love, Ted.*)

Sturgeon's 1979 introduction to "Rule of Three": *My preoccupation for some time has been with the nature of marriage, and whether or not we haven't gotten ourselves off on the wrong foot. Divorce statistics would seem to indicate that there is nothing more*

destructive of marriage than monogamy. "Let me not to the mar-
riage of true minds admit impediment," wrote Elizabeth Barrett (a
monogamist if there ever was one), but she had a point there.
Although the person who wrote "Rule of Three" clearly regarded
the desirability of monogamy as axiomatic, the astute reader—another
term for postgame quarterbacking—might find in it the seeds of later
ideation. One tends to work out one's own convictions in writing
fiction—especially in science fiction—and to test them against pos-
sibilities, however untimely or unformed or wishful or improbable.
Anyway, in this story (1951) one may find what is possibly the first
suggestion in science fiction that love may not after all be confined
to gender or to monogamy. Here are the seeds of later work like
More Than Human, *and the growing concept that perhaps, after*
all, the greatest advance we can make is to accept what we are, and
then to grok, to blesh, to meld, to join. Real science fiction talk, that,
ain't it?

In his 1953 magazine article "Why So Much Syzygy?" TS wrote:
What I have been trying to do all these years is investigate this mat-
ter of love, sexual and asexual... To do this I've had to look at the
individual components... In "Rule of Three" and "Synthesis"
["Make Room for Me"] *I had (in reverse order) a quasi-sexual rela-*
tionship among three people, and one among six so it could break
down into three couples and be normal. In "The Stars Are the Styx"
I set up several (four, as I remember) different kinds of love moti-
vations for mutual comparisons.

Magazine blurb: OF COURSE YOU'D BE HOST TO GUESTS
FROM OUTER SPACE; IT'S COMMON COURTESY. BUT BEING
A HOST CAN HAVE A PARTICULARLY NASTY MEANING!

"Make Room for Me": first published in *Fantastic Adventures*, May
1951. Originally written in 1946 in collaboration with Rita Dragonette. Apparently rewritten—see Oct. 11, 1950 letter quoted in
"Rule of Three" note—in October 1950. Regarding that letter,
"Make Room for Me" does indeed include a New Year's Eve sequence
and is therefore surely the "other" story referred to. This letter is
the only place I know of where Sturgeon acknowledges that the story

was co-written *(the one I wrote with someone else)*. In 1976 I interviewed Rita Dragonette; she told me that she and Ted wrote "Make Room for Me" together early in 1946 when the two of them, who had been friends in high school in Philadelphia, were living together in New York City. She said they completed a version then, but. . . "I never saw it again until Phil Klass came to me and said, 'Look at this,' and there it was in print. Under Sturgeon's name. And he thought he could make it all right by giving me a check. . ." Dragonette's contribution to the story was not mentioned when the story was included in the collection *Sturgeon in Orbit* in 1964.

The three characters in the story—which must have been called "Synthesis" at one time, judging from Sturgeon's mention of it under that name in his 1953 article—are caricatures of Rita (Vaughn), Ted (Dran Hamilton) and their high school pal Manny Staub (Manuel). Rita (a published poet under the name Ree Dragonette) told me that she and Manny and Ted had "talked about these things in high school—the trinity, the three of us, about the need to coalesce, to be re-embodied. . . Some of the conversations [in the story] were verbatim."

In a 1978 interview with Larry Duncan, TS said, *I think that the greatest piece of music that I know of is Bach's* Passacaglia and Fugue in C Minor. In 1975, he told Paul Williams: *I have one or two real long-term friends. A man called Manny Staub has been my close friend ever since high school ... he left high school to join the Marines, and was decorated for bravery in action, in China, long before World War Two. He was blown off his bicycle by a bomb one time.* [In high school] *we went to movies together, we used to walk all over Philadelphia, we made all the museums and we went to concerts ... I think we had a rather profound effect on one another.*

In his 1964 introduction to this story (chiefly about the magazine editor who published it in 1951), Sturgeon said: *Howard Browne bought this one, because, he said, he liked it. He must have found it a refuge from what he was doing at the time, for it is a strange and filmy kind of effort, whereas Howard was writing ... a series of hard-heel detective novels...*

"Special Aptitude": first published under the title "Last Laugh" in *Other Worlds,* March 1951.

Theodore Sturgeon to Paul Williams, December 1975: *I became a cadet in the Penn State Nautical School when I was seventeen... It was a terrible experience. The fourth class, which is the youngest, were absolutely brutalized and enslaved by the others.... The fourth class had to line up, put on their dungarees upside down and backwards, stand at attention... They would come along and they would fill your mouth with rock salt; or they'd say, "take a seat." "Take a seat" meant, go into a half-squat, with your arms stretched out in front of you, and stay that way till you collapse. It was absolutely brutal, the indignities, they'd open your mail and read it aloud in the mess hall.* Sturgeon recalled with horror that the officers *watched these shit sessions and did nothing to stop it.*

Editor's blurb from the first page of the original magazine appearance: THERE WAS NOTHING SO TERRIBLE AS THE GABBLERS. HUMAN EARS COULD NOT WITHSTAND THEIR HORRID UPROAR—AND DEATH TO ALL COMERS GLARED FROM THEIR EYES.

"The Traveling Crag": first published in *Fantastic Adventures,* July 1951.

Sturgeon's introduction to this story in *Alien Cargo* (1984): *For years I have felt that this is one of the worst stories I ever wrote. A lot of people have said they think otherwise, so here it is.*

TS had worked as a literary agent himself for other science fiction writers, including William Tenn and A. Bertram Chandler, throughout 1946.

The line from Weiss's second story that Naome reads to Cris—*Jets blasting, Bat Durston came screeching down through the atmosphere of Bbllzznaj*—is an inside joke. H. L. Gold used this line in an ad for *Galaxy* that ran in the first issue of that magazine, October 1950. Under the heading "You'll Never See It in *Galaxy!*" are parallel columns, one a science fiction story that begins "Jets blasting, Bat Durston came screeching down" etc. and the other a pulp western story that begins, "Hoofs drumming, Bat Durston came galloping down through the narrow pass..." Gold's point was that *Galaxy* (unlike some of its competitors) was not going to publish routine genre fiction transplanted to a science-fictional setting.

Lucy Menger (in *Theodore Sturgeon,* 1981): "In 'The Traveling Crag' and 'Rule of Three' Sturgeon seems to have been haunted by a vision of what man could be and tormented by the difference between this vision and the actuality around him. Aliens in 'TTC' express this anguish concisely: 'There are few races in cosmic history with a higher potential than yours or with a more miserable expression of it.'"

"Excalibur and the Atom": first published in *Fantastic Adventures,* August 1951.

Interesting that TS, in the course of this story, indicates his awareness of T. H. White's *The Sword in the Stone* (1938) and C. S. Lewis's *That Hideous Strength* (1945).

This story has never appeared in a Sturgeon collection or any other book before.

Magazine blurb: THEY SAY A PRIVATE EYE CAN HANDLE ANYTHING FROM A BOTTLE TO A BLONDE. BUT WHEN MERLIN CAME IN WITH A SWORD, THINGS BEGAN TO POP!

"The Incubi of Parallel X": first published in *Planet Stories,* September 1951.

Sturgeon's introduction to this story in *Sturgeon in Orbit* (1964): *THE INCUBI OF PARALLEL X is the most horrible title to appear over my byline, and I'm sure Malcolm Reiss, the editor, will forgive me for saying so. It was a typical* Planet Stories *title, and I've been sitting here trying to remember some of the parody titles George O. Smith used to dream up, I can, too, but I can't share them with you, not even in these liberated days...*

"Never Underestimate": first published in *Worlds of If,* March 1952. Probably written autumn 1951, as Sturgeon's pregnant wife Marion was successfully persuading him to leave his Time Inc. job and move to the country and devote more of his time to his writing.

This story has never appeared in a Sturgeon collection before.

The first page of this story may be considered a playful discussion of the logic behind Sturgeon's distinctive manner of hooking his readers with the opening lines of his stories.

In 1972 TS told interviewer David Hartwell *I used to write a lot of very funny stuff* and cited "Never Underestimate" as an example.

There are notable thematic links between "Never Underestimate" and "The Martian and the Moron" (1948) and Sturgeon's 1960 novel *Venus Plus X*.

"The Sex Opposite": Another thematic precursor to *Venus Plus X*. First published in *Fantastic Stories*, Fall 1952. In the Sturgeon papers is a letter from Howard Browne dated Jan. 21, 1952, addressed to TS at 862 Union Street in Brooklyn: "Enclosed is our check No. 11492 in the amount of $170.00. This represents payment in full of all magazine rights to your story "The Sex Opposite," which will appear in a forthcoming issue of our new FANTASTIC." This tells us the story was written before Ted and Marion moved out of New York City, possibly as late as December 1951.

In 1976 Marion Sturgeon told me she first met Ted at a party and again on his birthday in 1950: "He was working for Time Inc. then. Then we began to get together; his marriage was already breaking up. Then we moved to Brooklyn, to Union Street. I worked in the Brooklyn Public Library. And that's when we used to go to Rudy's Restaurant, which is in one of his stories ["The Sex Opposite"], a Mexican restaurant in midtown Manhattan."

About the move to Congers in Rockland County, Marion said, "I'd had the idea of living in the country with a writer, that was one of my little dreams. And so I wanted Ted very much to stop working at Time Inc. It didn't fit in at all with what I'd imagined."

In a chapter on Sturgeon in his 1956 book of criticism *In Search of Wonder*, Damon Knight wrote: "He writes about people first and other marvels second. More and more, the plots of his short stories are mere contrivances to let his characters expound themselves. 'It Wasn't Syzygy,' 'The Sex Opposite' and 'A Way of Thinking' are such stories: the people stand out from their background like Rubens figures that have strayed onto a Mondrian canvas: graphic evidence that Sturgeon, like Bradbury, long ago went as far as he could within the limitations of this field without breaking them."

I think what I have been trying to do all these years is to investigate this matter of love, sexual and asexual. I investigate it by writing about it because I don't know what the hell I think until I tell somebody about it. And I work so assiduously at it because of a conviction that if one could understand it completely, one would have the key to cooperation itself: to creative inspiration: to self-sacrifice and that rare but real anomaly, altruism: in short, to the marvelous orchestration which enables us to keep ahead of our own destructiveness.

...Why so much syzygy? [in TS's stories]—*well, it's pretty obvious why a clear-cut method of non-reproductive exchange should be so useful in such an overall investigation. It's beautifully open to comparison and analog. It handles all sorts of attachments felt by any sensitive person which could not conceivably be sexually based.*

—TS, in "Why So Much Syzygy?" (1953)

Editor's blurb from the first page of the original magazine appearance:

SOMEONE ONCE SAID THAT THEODORE STURGEON HAS ONLY ONE REAL STORY TO TELL, BUT THAT HE TELLS IT SO WELL EDITORS WILL GO ON BUYING IT FOREVER. DON'T YOU BELIEVE IT! THE BASIS FOR SUCH A REMARK COMES FROM THE AUTHOR'S VARIATIONS ON A SINGLE THEME: SOMEWHERE IN THE UNIVERSE ARE ALIEN BEINGS THAT CAN HELP MAN TO GAIN HIS RIGHTFUL HERITAGE.

IF ALL THIS SOUNDS TOO ESOTERIC, DON'T LET US MIS-LEAD YOU. THE SEX OPPOSITE OPENS WITH THE MURDER OF TWO LOVERS IN A NIGHT-SHROUDED PARK AND ENDS WITH A TRIPLE SLAYING ON A STREET CORNER. AND OUT OF IT COMES THE TENDER STORY OF A YOUNG COUPLE WHO MIGHT NEVER HAVE FOUND LOVE HAD NOT DEATH POINTED OUT THE WAY...

"Baby Is Three": first published in *Galaxy Science Fiction,* October 1952. Written circa May 1952 in the author's new home in Congers, New York with his wife Marion and their new baby Robin. The appearance of this story in Galaxy created a stir of enthusiasm in the science fiction community, and a book editor asked Sturgeon to expand "Baby Is Three" into a novel. This he did by writing two long stories about the events preceding and following those described in "Baby Is Three." This novel, *More Than Human,* is Sturgeon's best-known work. It was published in autumn 1953, and won the International Fantasy Award in 1954. SF critic and novelist James Blish described *More Than Human* as "one of the very few authentic masterpieces science fiction can boast."

The text of "Baby Is Three" in this volume is that of the original *Galaxy* story, not the revised version that makes up the middle section of *More Than Human.* The magazine story and novel section differ significantly in their last pages; in the novel, Miss Kew is in fact dead.

On June 25, 1952, TS sent the following note to his friend Judith Merril on a postcard: *It's okay I wrote one and migod it's <u>fine</u>. Sold it + everything and I think maybe if I do more and like doing it as much I won't have to worry about who I'm: I'll find out.*

From Sturgeon's 1978 introduction to *Theodore Sturgeon's More Than Human, The Graphic Story Version* (Byron Preiss Visual Publications): *Some time in the spring of 1952, living in a little stone house in the woods in Rockland County, New York, I sat down and knocked out yet another story because by that time I knew how to knock out stories. As I recall, I hadn't a clear idea in my head as to what it was going to be about, except that I had recently read a novel by Pearl Buck called* Pavilion of Women, *in which there was a minor character, a Chinese monk, who took care of a ragged passel of kids in a cave somewhere in the wilderness. The image would not scrape off, and I knew I was going into something similar somehow. It took about eight days and I sent it off to Horace Gold at* Galaxy *magazine. He bought it and I paid some rent and bought some furnace oil and hamburger and paper towels and the like for my wives and children, and got to work on something else.*

Next thing you know it was October, and the story, called "Baby Is Three," was in print, and to my immense and total astonishment began pulling rave mail from all over. Truly, I had an "I didn't know it was loaded" feeling about the whole thing—not that I felt it was a bad job, but I really had no idea it would hit that hard. Anthology requests began to come in almost immediately here and from England, France, and Latin America. The mail was just lovely.

A year or so later, a book publisher asked me for a novel. The only thing I wanted to write about at that length was something about where the people in "Baby Is Three" came from, and something more about where they went to. I went to New York and had lunch with some people and we worked out a deal whereby if I wrote 30,000 words of events before "Baby," and thirty more after, but wrote them in such a way that each could stand as a separate novelette, then they would undertake to sell them to high-paying slick-paper magazines before book publication. (That way, I suspect, they could salve their consciences about the miniscule advance they were willing to pay.) I chuntered around with ideas for a few months, then suddenly sat down and wrote the first part, "The Fabulous Idiot," and the third part, "Morality," in about three weeks.

I lugged the two stories in to New York and found that, as is often the practice with publishers, all the people I had dealt with had been fired, transferred, or kicked upstairs, and their replacements didn't know anything about any handshake agreement to sell the stories to magazines first. They just wrapped up the whole thing and published it as a book.

TS, in his liner notes to a 1977 Caedmon LP called "Baby Is Three [abridged] from *More Than Human* read by the author," talks about *Pavilion of Women* as above and goes on: *That was the springboard; there is no accounting for the myriad variables which went into the rest of it; why, for example, I structured it from the appearance of young Gerry in a psychiatrist's office instead of any of the many other ways in which it might have been done. It went very quickly—two weeks or so, if I remember correctly, and all first draft.*

Also in the Caedmon notes he says: *The heart and soul of* More Than Human *is, clearly, the second part, "Baby Is Three." It appeared in* Galaxy, *a science fiction magazine under the editorial guidance of Horace L. Gold. Its explosive acceptance astonished and puzzled me almost as much as did the later reception of the book, and its inclusion in the* [Science Fiction] Hall of Fame, *chosen by successive ballots by my peers in the Science Fiction Writers of America, is a matter of great gratification to me.* In his introduction to the 1973 book *The Science Fiction Hall of Fame, Volume Two,* editor Ben Bova says that when the members of SFWA were asked to select the ten best science fiction stories of all time out of a list of 76 they had previously nominated, "Baby Is Three" was fifth in total votes. Overall, Theodore Sturgeon was the author receiving the second largest number of votes, after Robert Heinlein.

Stern, the psychotherapist in "Baby Is Three," *is the shrink that I have always wanted, but have never been able to find,* Theodore Sturgeon told Paul Williams in a taped interview February 29, 1976. *He's the same shrink as Dr. Outerbridge* [In TS's 1961 novel *Some of Your Blood*], *same guy, operates the same way. His operative technique is basically basic Dianetics; and the only reason I ever got away with that is I never said so out loud, because it has such a violent image against it, and we've got this appalling willingness to throw the baby out with the bathwater. Dianetics worked—not "worked" but* works—*absolutely magically. But because Hubbard turned into a megalomaniac, and a classic kook, which he is (and I don't care if Process comes and shoots me for that, that's the truth), you cannot, absolutely cannot put down the value of basic Dianetics, as laid out in the first third of the original book, which has been drastically rewritten since then. . .* (L. Ron Hubbard, the science fiction writer, synthesized—not invented, as TS points out elsewhere in the interview—Dianetics, later known as Scientology, in 1950. John W. Campbell and Theodore Sturgeon were early practitioners.)

As that 1976 interview continued, TS talked about some of his experiences as an auditor (Dianetics therapist) in the two years before he wrote "Baby Is Three": *There's a funny little laugh and you just know that someone's discharged.* By the end of 1951, TS said, *I departed from Dianetics. I had audited 102 hours and been audited myself six hours, and I really began to feel the imbalance.*

In his introduction to the Graphic Story Version, Sturgeon mentions that as of 1978 *More Than Human* had been optioned by film companies eleven separate times (and never filmed). He says, *The weirdest of these involves one of the greatest directors of all time (I won't tell you his name) and me, who wrote a screenplay and two complete revisions in only twenty-eight days, when all of a sudden the company blew apart.* (The director/co-writer was Orson Welles.)

Editor's blurb from the first page of the original magazine appearance: GERARD'S PROBLEM WOULD DISMAY ANY PSYCHOTHERAPIST. HE KNEW HIS NAME WITHOUT KNOWING HIS IDENTITY; WHAT HE DID, BUT NOT WHAT HE WAS. WORSE YET, HE DIDN'T KNOW HOW MANY OF HIM THERE WERE!

Corrections and addenda:

Some intriguing comments by TS on "Hurricane Trio" (Vol. IV) have come to light. In a letter to Anthony Boucher at the *Magazine of Fantasy & Science Fiction* in May 1956 accompanying a submission ("And Now the News"), Sturgeon wrote:

If you really feel this yarn is not close enough to conventional science fiction, I can ... put the story in the near future and therefore in the s-f matrix. I did this kind of job only once before, adding a space ship to "Hurricane Trio" to get it into Galaxy; *it was a slick before that, rejected all over... Eleanor Stierham: "The woman doesn't exist who would take such a risk." Bull's balls! HT was a true story and I was there!*

Appendix

Two Autobiographical Essays

"Author, Author"
by Theodore Sturgeon
from *Fanscient,* Spring 1950

THEY SAY I make puns, which I deny; it's only that typos creep in and I have an aural word sense. I'll demonstrate that later; it means that what I read and what I write, I hear.

I was born on Staten Island, which is populated mostly by the dead and people from Brooklyn. This birth occurred 2/26/18, according to the records. I went four years to a veddy social Staten Island private school, two weeks to a public school, thence to Philadelphia where I was two weeks in the fifth grade and got shoved into the sixth. This one I completed, and then went to a boarding school in Pennsylvania where in a year I learned how to smoke, drink, gamble, swear and swim. After six weeks in the eighth grade in summer school, I was dumped into an enormous education factory in Philadelphia at the age of twelve. I weighed 95 pounds and was utterly bewildered, but anyway I was a high school student. I was a high school student for six solid years. I never took a subject I didn't flunk at one time or another. Like someone named Robin English, I was released. That was in '36.

I don't seem to be able to recall the process of living my life in a particularly consecutive order. Things happened at various times. I put in six months as a cadet on a training ship. She had been with Dewey at Manila. She was 135 feet at the waterline and had 160' masts. She had steel sides and a wooden bottom, and a loosefooted rig because her sails were so near the deck that booms would have swept off the deck housing. We tacked her by taking in all sail and dragging it across the deck by hand while we turned her with the engines. She was painted all white and burned coal. I didn't like her much. There were 173 people aboard. After that I cut loose and went to sea on my own account—coastwise freighters, then tankers.

I worked in a glass factory once, taking silver off mirrors with fuming acid. Drove a tractor-trailer truck between Philadelphia and Albany. Worked in an oil refinery, hoeing grass between tanks in a storage farm. Had a job once with a crew who came north by train and brought Model A Fords all the way back to Greensboro. Pulled rope with a circus—the Al G. Barnes show in Canada. Ran a luxury resort in Jamaica. It was wonderful. We had 17 servants, and except for weekends we had them mostly to ourselves. During the war I operated 17 quarters and barracks, three messhalls and a food warehouse for the Army, which qualified me to run the specialized lubrication disbursement, from which I naturally began to operate heavy equipment. For that I got flown to Puerto Rico to run bulldozer and power shovel for the Navy. I loved it, though ten hours a day, seven days a week for nearly three years makes you sort of lose track of things. But if you know anyone with an inferiority complex you can cure him by perching him in the saddle of a Caterpillar D-8 for a few months. When the day arrives that behind all that Diesel and racket, you suddenly are aware that your nerve-endings are up there on the blind side of your blade, you gain something that you'll never lose. It does to you what marriage does, in that respect. It doesn't matter whether you ever pull another steering clutch. It's a thing that's built.

Meant to mention that I had a rugged bout with acute rheumatic fever when I was 15. It left me with a 16% enlargement. My heart used to push out between my ribs when it beat, which for a while it did reluctantly. It got better year after year until now only a specialist can detect that slight squish in the beat if I lie in a certain position after heavy exercise. But it kept me out of the Army during the war. Cardiac cripple. They wouldn't let me man a typewriter, let alone an armchair. But 70 hours a week under that sun was fine. Yours not to reason why....

I played guitar with a square-dance orchestra once, in the Poconos. They had a 35-foot diving platform at that resort. I used to do 2½ somersaults off it. Once someone put an overflow board in the dam during the night and the lake rose 18 inches and I didn't know it. I hit the water face first and flattened my eyeballs. Couldn't see a thing for a whole day.

I lived in Brooklyn for a while with an Englishman who was writing confessions. He prided himself on being a word-rate writer who didn't give a damn for art. I did, at the time. But I meant no insult at all when I said casually that he was a hack. He got no end insulted. So to settle the argument we looked it up in his dictionary, which was an English publication. In it I found one of the most pathetic lines I have ever read. It said, "HACK, n. A literary drudge; as one who compiles dictionaries."

I shipped out one time with a guy named Kelley. He's around in some of my copy. He was one of the most amazing people I have ever met. He's in Atlanta now, I think, but he was like one of those creatures JWC's always trying to goad us into writing about, which thinks as well as a man, but not like a man. I was sitting in a honky-tonk in Port Arthur, Texas, one night. There was a girl called Bernice who had taken quite a shine to Kelley and they'd been pretty thick at the south end of our trips. Bernice had just gotten wind of the fact that Kelley was sporting a girl down the street at Pete's Place, and she didn't like it at all. So when Kelley walked in, Bernice reached behind her and pulled an electric fan off the shelf and threw it at his head with the same motion. It was a big electric fan and it didn't have any guard on it. Kelley ducked it, seeming to move much more slowly than he actually did. He didn't move his feet, but sort of bent his head aside and turned his shoulders and let the fan go by. It hit the wall and chewed up the partition. Nobody said anything. Now anyone else in the world who believed in do-as-you-would-be-done-by would have thrown the fan back at the girl. Not Kelley. He walked over and picked her up over his head and threw her at the fan. She slid on out the door and down the stairs. Kelley went out after her, taking his time, stepped around her where she lay halfway down the flight, and went on back to Pete's Place.

I was profoundly impressed—not by what he'd done, but by the way he thought. I've used that kind of reversal in plot treatments many times. It's one thing to turn front to back. It's something else again, just as logical but much more rare, to make a mirror image.

I'd rather be writer than a human being. Wrote a story for WEIRD once and put a lot into it. It was real good catharsis and it did me good. A few days after it was published I got a letter from South Africa. There was a girl in the story who died, and this letter contained a poem which was an epitaph for her. As poetry it was so-so. But I had to reread it a half-dozen times to find out why it struck me as vaguely familiar. Then I got it. It was composed entirely of lines picked up here and there through the story, with only an occasional slight alteration to fit the form.

Thoughts are cloud-shapes, formless, without size or any particular hue. But code them—make words of them—and they take on some fraction of what they mean to you. Recode those words into typescript; they're read, printed, proofed, distributed. Suppose, then, another mind half a world away decodes that type into words and those words into thoughts and from that multiple fractionation finds it in him not only to create, but to re-create some of the particular pulse-pound and gland-squirt that went into it . . . that makes me humble. I'm ashamed of that story. I wish I'd polished it until it was worth having that effect on someone. You can kid around about the writing racket from now till then, but you can't get away from the fact that if writing can do a thing like that, a writer undertakes a truly awesome responsibility.

I said at the start that my puns and perhaps a suspicion of what's called a style have their source in the fact that I hear what I read. I hear what I write, and I don't think it hurts what comes out. There are times when the mood of narration dictates a more conscious approach to the words that you use and their order. It's easy to prove that the treatment's unseen, but it yields an incredible smoothness of flow to your work.

There probably wouldn't be one reader in a hundred thousand who would realize that the above paragraph is written most laboriously in anapestic feet; that is, there are two unaccented syllables followed by a strong accent, but with most of the sentences beginning and ending in the middle of the foot so that the thing doesn't get sing-song. This happens to be my prime kick in writing. It's a thing you don't dare do very often; but when you apply it lightly and briefly, you find yourself woven into your copy with a completeness that can't be approached in any other way that I know of. But be careful; the trick's more dangerous than opium. There are a zillion different kinds of feet you can use. The largest charge of it I ever put into a story was in one of my WEIRD TALES, or proving grounds, yarns, when I used a monster that changed its meter every time it changed its mood. That went on for three thousand words. Have fun, chillun.

Men behind *Fantastic Adventures*
Theodore Sturgeon
from *Fantastic Adventures,* August 1951

I don't know who's going to find out more about Ted Sturgeon by what follows—you or I. In any case, I appreciate this opportunity to sound off. There is no one who doesn't dote on capital "I"—if not as a subject, then at least as a theme.

I was born overseas, on February 26, 1918, which makes me older than I ought to be according to the way I act. Place: Staten Island, which is Richmond County and the forgotten borough of New York City, on which, to this very day, you can milk a cow and get lost in the woods. My mother is the end-product of years and years of high-church Anglican functionaries; my great grandfather was Bishop of Quebec, my maternal uncle, the Archbishop of the West Indies, and there are a baker's dozen of ministers in my immediate family. My father is a businessman from a clan which settled in this country in 1640.

I went to school for my first four years in a veddy social private school on Staten Island, then went to Philadelphia where I was advanced half a year in a public school there. I finished the last half of the fifth grade and the first half of the sixth fairly honestly, and then went to a boarding school in Gettysburg, where in a year I learned how to smoke, swim, gamble, and cuss. Then I finished the last half of the eighth grade in summer school and was deposited, trembling, bewildered, underweight and aged twelve, in an enormous education factory called Overbrook High School. Its 4700 students were processed on three shifts, and the organization of classes and subjects was a direct carry-over from the grade schools which I had not attended. Everybody knew what to do about everything, except for me, and I was no end astonished. I remained astonished for six years.

I managed to flunk every single subject I ever took at one time or another, without exception. I had a sole interest—apparatus gymnastics. I was going to finish school and get an athletic scholarship to Temple, and would do p.g. work in physical education at

Springfield, and then I would go down to Sarasota and work out with Barnum and Bailey until I got to be a high-horizontal performer. It made like a blueprint. I went out for the gym team and gained sixty pounds in the first year. I became captain and manager and got my Temple scholarship and an honorary membership in the Philadelphia Turngemeinde and fourth place in the East Coast Championships in the AAU for horizontal bar. They all said I was a natural for the City Championship.

Then along came acute rheumatic fever, a 16 per cent heart enlargement, and the information from a specialist that there wouldn't be any more gymnastics for Sturgeon—not in the last season or ever.

I suppose I took it as hard as anyone might who had spent a third of his lifetime with a single aim which was suddenly to be denied. I went into a major flat spin. I finished school and won a scholarship in the Pennsylvania State Nautical School and lied to the medical examiners and spent six months being a cay-det on a ship which had been with Dewey at Manila. She had steel sides and a wooden bottom. We tacked her by taking in all sail and turning her with the engines and putting the sails out on the other side. She was painted white and burned coal, and most of the seamanship we learned was with holystone and soojy-rag. I quit after six months and got a job as a bonafide sailor on a coastwise freighter for fifty-five bucks a month.

I went to sea for almost three years. One day I worked out a way to cheat the express company out of a few thousand clams but, lacking the moral character to pull the job, I wrote it into a story instead. It sold on sight, and I was so delighted to have my name in print that I quit my job, went ashore, and became a professional. They paid me five dollars for it. I sold the same outfit—a newspaper syndicate—one and sometimes two stories a week at the same price for about four months. That was my sole income, but I made it. Ever make a vegetable stew out of six cents worth of soup greens?

Then somebody brought me Vol. I No. I of *Unknown,* and I realized that this magazine and I had places to go. I sold my first magazine story there, and when I had about filled its inventory, branched out to its sister magazine *Astounding Science Fiction.* Since then I have sold to practically every magazine in the field. My current effort is neither my first nor my last for *Fantastic Adventures*.

In 1940, after a half dozen sales, I figured I was ready to be a pillar of society, and I got married. In mid-'41 I went to Jamaica in the West Indies to run a luxury resort hotel. In December, this country found itself at war, and in February I was working as Assistant Chief Steward at the U.S. Army air base there. Late that year I was flown to Puerto Rico to run bulldozers and power shovels in a rock quarry at a Naval base. In '43 the bases all closed down and, having been rejected for the third time by the service, I settled down to write again. Nothing happened.

I have two daughters; one was born in the first year of my marriage, and the second in '43, in Puerto Rico. Came the end of current resources, and I made a quick ten-day trip to the States to fire my agent, see some editors, and get a much-needed slant on markets. My ten-day trip extended to eight months and wound up in a divorce—and Flat Spin Number Two, which went on for about three years.

Now, I'm employed by Time Inc., and I'm the entire advertising-promotion department of all four editions of *Time* International. Where to from here, I can't say. Wherever it is, I'm sure it'll be interesting.

So much for the highlights. Now a word about what this has meant to me and my work.

I'm a blond blue-eyed Aryan Protestant with a profound distaste for the privileges extended to anyone for these accidents. I have experienced a sense of worship—lying under the stars in the Yucatan Channel—watching a rainbow by moonlight—watching a certain sunset in the Gulf of Mexico—in many diverse places, but never in a church, and I have seen some beauties.

I think that no one can achieve the stature of a man unless he has been unjustly hurt.

I think that the only important things are basic things; that basic things are always simple things; and that therefore complicated things may be exciting, or frightening, or amusing, or instructive; but if they're complex, by definition they're not important.

I believe in marriage, and see it as a sharing of everything capable of being shared, the stature of the marriage depending upon the number of things shared. But I also believe that where sharing is not possible, privacy is imperative.

I believe that the most constructive force in human thought is laughter *with*, and that the most destructive one is laughter *at*.

And I most sincerely believe that I am a member of humanity; that humanity's mistakes and stupidities are mine and have their weight on my conscience, and that by the same token humanity's achievements are mine; that therefore I deserve the privileges and am bound by the duties of this extraordinary species.